Desolate Sands

Conrad Jones

Conrad Jones

Cover Image by Darrell Bate

Darrell Bate

https://www.flickr.com/photos/29452563@N08/

Copyright © 2014 Conrad Jones

All rights reserved.

ISBN-13: 978-1495297304
ISBN-10: 1495297306:

Prologue

As the sun melted into the sea at the horizon, the sky around the dazzling orb turned red, with hues of orange and streaks of yellow. The sea became almost colourless and the tips of white horses reflected the dying rays like diamonds twinkling on the waves. The North Star was climbing and Venus was shining brightly where the sky began to merge from blue to black. It was a vista that no camera could give justice to; that magical time when day turned to night. Sunset here was his special place. The jibes and taunts couldn't reach him here. Here, he was at one with the Iron Men, cold and emotionless, almost indestructible; almost.

The artist who built the iron men had called it 'Another Place' but it wasn't; it was his place, his desolate place. He first visited the statues out of curiosity, but as soon as he saw the figures on the sand, his heart broke as he wandered from one to the next, laying his hands on each one as if to say hello. They accepted him without question or reason. He didn't have to impress to belong. This was the reason he did what he did. He hadn't realised for a long time that there was a point to it. At first it was just something that he had to do, but then when he first saw them, his purpose became crystal clear. Suddenly all the blood and all the screams had a purpose. It was like a bolt of lightning striking him. Lights came on in the dark places of his mind and he realised what it was all for. It was for them.

Seagulls circled and soared above and the familiar smell of the sea filled his senses. The birds dive-bombed the litter on the sand dunes, the squawking and the flapping of their wings would reach a frenzied pitch as nightfall closed in. Then they would fly home to roost. As the sun sank lower, the iron men were in different stages of submergence. Some were completely gone, others were waist deep; only the statues nearest the dunes were left untouched by the advancing waves, but he knew it was simply a matter of time before they were engulfed by the sea once again. His heart ached as he watched them suffer the relentless tide overwhelming them. Day after day, tide after tide they endured their watery burial. The men nearest the dunes were virtually consumed by the sand. He wasn't sure which was worse, engulfed by the waves or buried by the shifting sands. Although they were many, each was desperately alone. Their cold iron companions gave them no comfort. They were many, yet tragically alone. They were frozen in time, staring out to sea for eternity and their plight tortured him. Their loneliness drove him insane. Or was he insane before he saw them? He couldn't remember a time when he was sane. What he did know was that his soul was like theirs; made from iron and hollow inside. He felt no empathy or sympathy. The screams of the dying excited him; their begging made him prolong their agony, not bring it to a speedy ending. His victims were the flotsam of life. They were nothing and nobody, not missed by anyone and so it was apt that they suffered in the sand as the iron men did. He had to find others for them, others who were lost and alone. He could help them bring solace to each other. He looked across the beach and scanned the miles of dunes. The last of the sightseers and dog walkers had gone. It was time to act, time to create. The girl would be awake soon and when she did, she would panic. They always did; especially when he made the final alteration to their bodies. It was painful for them, but they lived longer so that they had time to appreciate what he was creating. They had more time to endure their inevitable, unavoidable death. He had listened to them and heard them suffer. When death came, it was a blessing. It was time to cut and stitch before he had to dig again.

Chapter 1

Richard Tibbs sipped his tea. It was flavourless and the plastic cup barely warmed his flaky wrinkled fingers. Blue veins threaded the back of his pink hands making peaks and troughs beneath the liver spots. He was younger than he looked and they were still strong. He looked at his upturned left hand for a nail to nibble, but they were bitten to the quick and engrained with dirt and sand. Despite being desperately nervous, the nails were unappetising so he decided to leave them alone for now. If the detectives didn't appear soon, he planned to leave so that he could have a cigarette. He felt uncomfortable as if he was being watched. The two-way mirror always made him feel paranoid.

"Nervous are we, Tibbs?" The interview room door opened and Anne Jones walked in. "I'm DI Jones. My friends call me Annie but you can call me DI Jones." She smiled revealing slightly oversized front teeth, white but naturally so. The braver members of her team affectionately called her 'Bugsy' but not to her face. When she was riled, she had a stare that Medusa would have been proud of. "You look worried, what's the problem?"

"Have you been watching me through the mirror?"

"Of course we have," she replied coldly. "I want some idea of who I'm talking to. Why are you so nervous?"

"You bloody lot," Tibbs muttered and slurped the tepid liquid. His thin lips quivered as he watched another detective squeeze his huge frame through the door. Tibbs' watery eyes darted around the room. Annie thought that he looked older than his file indicated that he was. "This place makes me nervous. Every time I come here, you lot stitch me up."

"Maybe you should make a point not to be here at all," Annie advised, sarcastically. Beneath his scruffy exterior, his frame looked strong for his age. His loose fitting clothes disguised wide shoulders and a narrow waist. "There are two types of people here, good guys and scumbags. If you're not in the first group, it is best to stay away."

"Oh, I do try to stay away, believe me I do, but you lot hound me regardless." He winked sarcastically.

"Really?" Annie flicked through a thick brown folder and raised her eyebrows, "Two shoplifting convictions, two charges of assault and you were charged with the sexual assault of a minor, and let's not forget that you were found in possession of fifty indecent images. Exactly which of those crimes were you stitched up on?"

"I was found not guilty of the sexual assault charges," Tibbs' oversized ears flushed purple as he spoke. Long grey whiskers sprouted from them and mingled with his sideburns. Dark red blood vessels in his cheeks looked ready to burst. "That was all a mistake; I wouldn't touch those young ones that way. The images on my computer weren't random kids. I'm not one of them kiddie fiddlers and I resent you implying that I am one, when you don't know the full story."

"You were released with no further action, Tibbs." Annie sat down and smiled thinly. Placing the file on the desk between them, she smoothed the grey material of her trousers and crossed her legs. Her black hair was cut short around her face giving her an elfin look, boyish but attractive. "That is not the same as a not guilty verdict and if the information in this file is correct, some of the images on your computer were borderline at best, so you can resent the fact if you like but you resemble the fact more. Now what do you want to talk to me about?"

"If you're going to grill me again, then you can bugger off," Tibbs began to tremble. "Smug cow. You think you're so special don't you with your posh suit and your shiny shoes. I've come here to help you out so I don't have to say anything to you. If you want to patronise me, then I'll just go now!"

"Calm down, Tibbs. I'm DS Stirling," the male officer said in a harsh scouse accent. His close cropped hair and broken nose gave the look of an aging pugilist. "The DI just needs you to know that at this point in proceedings, we're viewing anything you say as suspect. You're on the sex offenders register."

"I came here voluntarily."

"Yes," Annie said. "Why?"

Tibbs eyed the big detective through weary blue eyes. The whites were crisscrossed with red. Years of whisky and wine had rotted him from the inside out. "Get this straight, Posh, I never harmed those girls," he pointed a shaking finger at Annie. "You don't understand what happened."

"Do you think my suit is posh, Sergeant?" She asked sarcastically. She didn't like Tibbs but if he had information then it would be foolish not to listen to him. She decided to change track and try to diffuse the situation.

"Primani at a guess?"

"Bang on."

"I think DC Cooper is wearing the same one today."

"Well, I bought mine first." Annie shrugged and pretended not to be concerned about her, suit but the corners of her mouth turned downwards giving her true feelings away. "You can't buy anything from there without four other people turning up for work wearing the same thing."

"Pile it high and sell it cheap," Stirling went along with her ploy. "Do you know the place?"

"What is it called?" Tibbs relaxed a little.

"Primark."

"It's a new one on me," Tibbs commented. "The city centre has changed so much recently. I hardly recognise the place nowadays. You can't stop change."

"Change is for the better though," Annie said. "The city centre looks so contemporary now."

"Anyway," Stirling shrugged and sat back in his chair. The bolts which held it to the floor restricted its movement. The tiny interview room wasn't designed for men of his size. "Enough of this chitchat. What can we do for you?" He folded his arms across his chest stretching the seams of his leather jacket to the limit. "Make it quick, Mr Tibbs."

"Like I said, I have some information."

"About what?"

"I'm not sure exactly, but it's important."

"You're not sure what your information is about?" Annie repeated.

"Well, I know what it's about, obviously, but I'm not sure what category it slots into."

"Tell us what it is and we'll sort that out."

"I need assurances first."

"About what?"

"I had two police officers at my door last week." Tibbs

scratched an itch beneath his arm revealing a rent in the material. Annie imagined a colony of lice nesting in there. She watched him with her alert brown eyes, analysing every inch of him. His matted grey hair was thick with grease. Large flecks of scalp clung to the roots refusing to leave their host. She didn't think that a shower would dent the grime. He would need to be wheeled through a car wash, slowly. "Second time this month."

"We know that, it's in your file," Annie said, irritably. "That's what happens when you're on the register."

"Its harassment," Tibbs waived his finger again. "They have no right knocking on my door every time something happens. I didn't touch those girls. Not the way they said that I did, anyway."

"They have every right. That's what we do," Annie sighed. "We have a list of bad guys and when something happens, we go and talk to them. You're one of them. Now if you're here to make a complaint, then you're wasting your time and ours." Something flickered in the scruffy man's eyes. Annie wasn't sure if it was anger or hatred or something else. He looked wounded by her remarks. Genuinely offended. She had seen fake innocence and manufactured pride a thousand times but Tibbs was different. His eyes looked at the floor and then at the two detectives as if he was debating something in his mind. He looked troubled indeed. "Is that why you're here? To make a complaint about harassment?"

"No." Tibbs looked unwilling to explain. His hands trembled as he stared at the table.

"What do you want, Tibbs?" Annie pushed. "Our time is valuable."

"I want to get you lot off my back. I want to show that I'm a good man really, by helping you," he swallowed nervously and licked his thin lips, "I've got information. Valuable information, but I want assurances first." His eyes narrowed, looking from one to the other.

"Assurances about what?" Stirling asked suspiciously. "We're not here to make deals, Tibbs."

"Then I'm not saying anything."

"In which case, you can spend the night in the cells for wasting police time." Stirling sat forward intimidating him.

"Won't be the first time I've seen someone locked up for nothing, Detective," Tibbs shrugged. Stirling tutted audibly. "I've seen the inside of more cells than you have, trust me. What I have to tell you is important but it could also get me killed."

Annie studied his face. His record said that he was a tired old offender, a liar, a thief and a sex offender. Normally she wouldn't give credence to a word he said but his eyes were telling the truth. "Okay, Tibbs." Annie tilted her head as she spoke. "Whatever you tell us, is in confidence for now."

"And no tape recording?"

"No tapes."

"And you'll have a word with uniform to leave off me?"

"Don't push your luck, Tibbs," Stirling growled. Annie shot him a glance and he backed off. He looked confused. Annie Jones had seen something that he hadn't but then that's why she was the boss.

"You're on the sex offenders list and there's nothing we can do about that." Annie smiled thinly. "No tape recording and providing you're not involved in anything illegal that you tell us about, we'll keep our source hushed up." Annie put out her hand and she quivered in disgust as he shook it with a grimy hand. Annie was surprised by the strength in his grip. "Be warned that if you're involved in anything, then all bets are off." Tibbs nodded silently. "This had better be good."

"I know that you're looking for Lacey Taylor." Tibbs slurped his brew noisily. His eyes didn't move from Annie's. There was intelligence behind his stare. "I saw it on the telly. She's been missing for a while now hasn't she?"

Annie looked at Stirling and raised her eyebrows. "Over a week but it's hardly been kept a secret. Everyone in the city knows that she's missing. She's a high profile community activist."

"Is that what you call her?" Tibbs scoffed. A globule of spittle hit the desk and he wiped it away with the back of his hand. He wiped his mouth before speaking. "Nosy busybody, more like," he laughed dryly. "She is a first class pain in the arse for some people." He winked knowingly. "I could name a few people who won't shed any tears about her disappearance." A sly smile showed crooked yellow teeth with more gaps in them than a council fence. "Certain members of the community that she championed wanted her to retire early, shall we say?"

"Listen to me, Tibbs." Annie leaned forward and put her elbows on the table. She sensed that Tibbs knew something. Something important. "If you know something about the disappearance of Lacey Taylor, then spit it out."

"Can I have a hot cup of tea?"

"No."

"Cigarette?"

"I'm losing my patience." Annie glared at him.

"You're a hard woman." Tibbs smiled and sighed. "I think I know who took her."

"You think that you do?"

"Yes."

"I'm listening," Annie tried to keep her voice calm. They had been waiting for a break in that case. The investigation into her disappearance had no leads to follow and their interviews had hit a wall of silence. "What have you heard?"

"Heard?" Tibbs frowned dramatically. "Nothing. I haven't heard anything. Nobody is saying anything and that's why this information is so valuable." He winked again.

Annie breathed in deeply and remained quiet. Men like Tibbs liked it when they were in control of an interview. It was usually the other way around. The shoe was on the other very smelly foot today. She waited. Sometimes, silence prompted them to speak. Tibbs coughed, his lungs sounded flooded with phlegm. Annie grimaced as he cleared his throat to speak.

"I haven't heard anything, but I've seen something." His yellow smile appeared again but was met with icy stares. The detectives didn't look impressed, yet. "Something that I think is very important."

"Get on with it," Stirling snapped. "Personally, I think you're full of crap."

"Do you?" Tibbs reached into his pocket. "Take a look at this." He dropped a plastic bag onto the desk. "I think this belongs to your missing lady." The bag was a white nondescript carrier bag. Tibbs tipped out the contents. "I haven't touched it," he grinned. "I didn't want to damage any forensic evidence. There could be prints on it."

Annie picked up a decorative dog collar with her pen and looked at it. "Pink leather, Cilla written in diamante studs and Lacey

Taylor's name and address on the tag." She looked open mouthed at Stirling. Granules of sand dropped onto the table top. "This is her dog's collar. Get it to forensics immediately."

Stirling picked up the collar with the bag and walked to the door. "Can you get this to the lab please," he said to the uniformed officer who was outside. "Mark it as a priority in the Lacey Taylor case."

"Guv."

Tibbs waited until the big detective returned to his seat. He had their attention and that's what he wanted. "She went missing with her dog, didn't she?" Tibbs grinned from ear to ear. "As soon as I saw it I knew it was her dog's collar."

"Where did you get this?"

"I found it in a litter bin."

"Where?"

"Crosby Beach."

"The dog?"

"She wasn't attached to it I'm afraid."

"You can remember exactly which bin?"

"I might be able to."

"Might?"

"Well, things are a bit tight at the moment." Tibbs shrugged. "I know you pay informers. Would there be a reward or anything?"

"We might be able to sort something out," Annie said irritably. "I'll ask you again. Can you remember exactly which bin?"

"Probably," he grinned, "and there's something else."

"What?"

"This is where I need assurances."

"Go on."

"I saw the men who put it in the bin and I saw the van which they drove away in." He smiled slyly and tapped his nose. "I think that I recognise one of them. He's a real bad lad."

"His name?" Annie snapped.

"Until you can guarantee me protection and a reward," Tibbs sat back and shook his head stubbornly, "his name has slipped my mind."

"Okay, we'll park the name for now." Annie called his bluff. "We won't be making any arrests until we know if you're telling us the truth or not."

"What?" Tibbs said shocked.

"Get up," Stirling growled. "You can wait in the cells until we're ready to go and have a look at exactly where you say you found this."

"In the cells?" Tibbs spluttered. Spittle flew from his thin lips. "What for?"

"Withholding information, wasting police time," Annie shrugged, "that'll do for a start."

Chapter 2

The drive from Liverpool city centre took them along the coast road heading north. The docks were busy as usual; a five mile rainbow of coloured containers stacked ten high dominated the river bank. For the following half hour of the drive, the city turned to suburbs and then the vista changed to agricultural land and golf courses. They took a left through Crosby village towards the beaches and reached the coastal reserve ten minutes later. The approach road took them through overhanging trees, annuals, deciduous and evergreens. The trees thickened and the boughs formed a canopy, making it dark and gloomy until they reached the sand. The smell of the sea drifted into the vehicle through the vents, mingling with the scent of pine.

Annie pulled off the tarmac into a sandy car park, which serviced the dunes, the beach and the nature reserves. It was a school day and raining heavily. Only the diehard dog walkers and bird watchers braved the coast on a day like this. Uniformed officers were taping off the paths which ran through the sharp grasses. To the left, the paths ran to the wooded areas of the nature reserves. The trees thickened the further inland you walked. On the right they threaded their way through the dunes and around a huge boating lake to the beach. She shivered as a powerful gust of wind shook the Volvo. The anticipation of leaving the car made her subconsciously cold inside. The rain fell almost horizontally and the wipers struggled to keep up with the downpour.

"The van was parked here?" she asked Tibbs' reflection in the rear view mirror.

"Over there in the corner." He pointed towards the trees.

"The back doors were right next to the path."

"Were there any other vehicles?" Stirling turned around to look at him.

"One or two, but I couldn't tell you what they were."

Annie rolled her eyes skyward. "So you saw a white transit size van but you can't remember what make?"

"I might be able to." Tibbs winked in the mirror. "You know if I was a real informer, on the payroll so to speak, then my memory might be sharper."

"Don't fuck me around, Tibbs." Annie twisted in her seat. "I've told you that we'll sort something out but right now, your information is going to get us nowhere. I need results to give to my governor before he'll authorise a penny."

"Well, I suppose I'll have to trust you then won't I." Tibbs shrugged. "Although it goes against the grain after how you lot have treated me over the years."

"Can we cut the sob story and get to the facts, please," Annie snapped. Her eyes said all that Tibbs needed to know. She was at her limit.

"It was a Mercedes."

"Big or small?" Stirling asked. "Sprinter or Vito?"

"Now then," Tibbs toyed. "Let me think. It was the smaller type, the Vito. Did I say it was white?"

Annie opened a tourist map of the area and spread it over the steering wheel and the dashboard. It showed the paths, ponds, bird watching hides and picnic areas. It wasn't to scale but it had far more detail of the paths than an Ordinance Survey map. "You're sure the bin is on this path?"

"Positive. I've walked it a hundred times."

Annie followed the path with her finger and when she saw where it led to, she realised immediately that Tibbs was telling the truth. She felt anger bubbling inside her, but decided to hold her tongue for the moment. She would confront him later, once she had the information that she needed. "How far down is the bin?"

"A hundred yards, no more than that."

"You're sure?"

"Positive."

"On the left or the right?"

"The right."

"What were you doing here, Tibbs?"

"I come here often for a walk." He flushed red and looked out of the window. His eyes gave something away; an untruth. The glass was beginning to steam up and visibility was further hindered by rivulets of rain trickling down. "It clears my mind coming here. Gets me out of the city and doesn't cost a fortune in petrol."

"Shut up and get out." Annie sighed as she opened the door. "You make me sick, you lying bastard." Rain hit her immediately and the wind tugged violently at her trench coat. She grabbed the collars with her right hand to keep the weather out, but the wind blew through the material as if it wasn't there. A uniformed officer was struggling to keep the crime scene tape from blowing away. "Get out now, Tibbs," she shouted angrily.

"I didn't sign up for this," he grumbled as he reluctantly opened the door. The wind made the map flap against the windscreen. "It's bloody freezing." Dark clouds raced across the sky releasing tons of rainwater before they headed inland. He looked at Stirling for moral support. "What's she being so arsey about?"

"I'm not sure, Tibbs, but I would think it has something to do with something she's seen marked on the map at the end of that path," Stirling growled. "You must think that we were born yesterday. Get out!"

"I don't know what her problem is," Tibbs grumbled as he climbed out. "Bloody cheek of it." His protestations went unheard. "I am an innocent man." He whistled the riff to the tune but the look from the big detective cut his rendition short. "I thought Liverpool was famous for a sense of humour," he mumbled.

"What did you say?"

"Nothing."

"Right, Tibbs," Annie shouted over the wind. "Take us to the spot." She leaned into the wind as they trudged across the sand. A uniformed sergeant approached. His ruddy face was craggy and water dripped from his nose. "Anything, Sergeant?"

"The council last emptied the litter bins on Monday." He looked at Tibbs and frowned. "Your informer said he found the dog collar yesterday?"

"That's what he said," Annie nodded. She understood the look of distaste on his face as he recognised Tibbs. "So they haven't been emptied?"

"No, Guv." He pointed to the trees. "We've taken the contents of every litter bin from here up to the housing estate on the far side of the nature reserve, eight in total."

"Good work," Annie said taking hold of his arm by the elbow. She led him out of earshot of Tibbs. "I know he's a scumbag, but that dog collar belonged to Lacey Taylor. Now I'm assuming the worst here, but I think she's pushing up the daffodils in there somewhere and he's the only solid lead we've had since she went missing."

"I understand, Guv." The sergeant smiled thinly. "Most of my informers come from the slime beneath the city too. She's been gone a while, it doesn't look good, does it?"

"Not good at all."

"We'll get the bins to forensics as soon as we're sure we've got them all. Do you think we should widen the search?"

"Yes, I do," she grimaced. "Sorry. I know it's a nightmare in this weather but we need to take them all. Have your men empty every bin within the reserve but tell forensics to focus on the ones from this path first, okay?"

"Guv."

"The K-9 team is here," Stirling shouted. A dark blue van pulled to a halt near the tree line. The dog handlers waved hello through the window. "They've allocated us two cadaver dogs. I'll send them along the path first?"

Annie nodded in agreement, waved her hand to the dog handlers and walked back to Tibbs. "Okay." She pointed her finger at his chest. "You walk me right through everything you did and saw yesterday. If I think you're pissing me around or leaving something out, I'll nick you for breaching your bail conditions. Do you understand me?"

"What do you mean breaching my conditions?"

"Don't push me, Tibbs." Annie shook her head. "We both know where that path leads to don't we?"

"I don't know what you're on about. I've never been all the way down there." Tibbs nodded, meekly. Breaching his bail by any description could earn him a three year spell behind bars. "I parked over there near the hotdog van." Annie noted with surprise that the trader had chosen to persevere despite the weather. "He's here every day regardless of how severe the weather is," Tibbs said reading her mind.

The trader looked on cheerfully as the police cordoned off the reserve. His tea, coffee and hotdog sales would double with the influx of uniformed customers. Business was business. She turned to Stirling. "Has anyone spoken to him yet?" She looked towards the happy trader.

"Not yet, Guv." He looked over. "I wanted to talk to him myself first."

"Good, do that."

"I could murder a cup of tea," Tibbs grinned. "It would warm me up."

"Shut up," Annie snapped again. Tibbs looked like a slapped child, unsure of why he'd been hit. "You parked up and then what?"

"I bought a hotdog and a nice cup of tea," Tibbs emphasised the words sulkily, "and then I walked across the car park and down the path there."

"Show me exactly where." Annie waited for him to move before following. Her face was darker than the clouds. They stepped onto the sandy path and headed for the trees. The canopy of leaves offered some relief from the driving rain but the wind whistled between the boughs, finding them easily. It seemed to search for the gaps in their clothing seeking out their flesh. No matter how tightly she pulled her coat fastened, icy drafts sneaked through. Uniformed officers nodded silent hellos as they past. They carried black bin bags which were tagged and sealed in clear plastic liners. They eyed Tibbs with suspicion and revulsion. "Looks like you've got a lot of fans," Annie commented, sarcastically.

"They've got me all wrong," Tibbs moaned. His bottom lip drooped sulkily. "I sat here for a while on that bench. I like to watch the ducks on the pond." He pointed to a wooden bench positioned next to a kidney shaped pond. Reeds grew around the edges and mallards meandered across the water heading for shelter; chevron shaped ripples spread behind them. "I was finishing my tea when I saw them dumping the collar in that bin."

"So they came from further up the reserve?"

"No." Tibbs shook his head. "That's why I thought it was odd. They came from the car park the same way we came. There are bins all around the car park so I wondered why they walked up here. The guy stuffed the collar under the other rubbish. If he had just thrown something in then it wouldn't have seemed out of the ordinary. That's why I looked. I don't normally go rummaging through bins."

Annie looked down the path towards the car park. "So you didn't pass them on the way here?"

"No."

"And they didn't follow you down the path?"

"No."

"How can you be sure that they weren't behind you?"

"I just am." Tibbs blushed and his eyes darted to the floor.

"You're lying to me." Annie scowled.

"I'm not."

"It's no more than seventy yards from where you said the van was parked, to that bin."

"About that."

"So it took you, what, a minute to reach here?"

"I walked slowly, just ambling."

"So we'll call it a minute and a half tops," Annie pushed. "How many times did you look behind you in ninety seconds?"

"A few." He coughed nervously. "I get nervous, you know, in case someone recognises me from the papers. I've been beaten up three times, no thanks to you lot."

"How many times did you look behind you?"

"I don't know for God's sake!"

"Guess."

"What?"

"Have a guess. Humour me."

"I don't remember." He looked away. Annie was afraid that he would clam up completely.

"I think you should get us some tea," she turned to Stirling. He frowned. She winked at her colleague and looked at Tibbs. "Do you want some tea and a hotdog like you had yesterday?"

"Yes," Tibbs nodded defiantly. "Extra onions and mustard and three sugars in my tea."

"I'll have a coffee," Annie said, thoughtfully, "and ask the trader if he can remember Tibbs from yesterday." She winked again. "I don't understand why he's helping us out here. He's got his own agenda but I don't know what it is yet." Stirling appeared to get the message. He grinned and walked back towards the car park. "Sit down, Tibbs." She gestured to the bench.

"It's soaked," he whinged but her demeanour dared him to challenge her. He pulled his coat beneath his behind and slumped onto the bench, folding his arms grumpily. "I'm trying to help you out here and you're treating me like a criminal."

Annie ignored him and walked back to the bin. Tibbs was right in the fact that there were at least two bins closer to the car park. She wandered off the path into the trees looking for footprints. Twigs and rotting foliage covered the sand but she ascertained that if anyone had walked beneath the trees, there would be evidence somewhere. It didn't add up. Neither did what he had told them so far. Yet he had walked into the police station and handed in a crucial link to a missing person. What was he playing at? Usually when that happened, someone was trying to deflect guilt. She walked back onto the path when she saw Stirling returning. He had a cardboard carry tray with three polystyrene cups and a grease stained brown paper bag balanced on top.

"How do you know they were in the white van if you were walking the other way?" she asked Tibbs, as the refreshments were handed out. The greasy hotdog looked like it had artery hardening nutritional value. "You can't see the car park from here so how did you know which vehicle they were in?"

Tibbs opened his mouth to speak and then stopped. He took the lid from his tea and blew on it thoughtfully. Annie knew that he was composing his next set of lies. "I must have seen them when I went to the bin to see what they'd thrown away. I think so anyway, my memory is not too sharp."

"No you didn't," Annie frowned. "I've stood next to the bin and you can't see the vehicles on the car park from there. There's a bend in the path which obscures it from view."

"Maybe I walked down the path a bit to make sure they had gone." He slurped his tea nervously. "My memory's a bit cloudy on that bit."

"Bullshit." Annie smiled sourly. She looked at her partner. "What did our friendly hotdog man have to say?"

"Funny but he doesn't remember anyone fitting your description buying a hotdog with extra mustard and onions," Stirling raised his eyebrows as he spoke. Tibbs seemed to shrink into himself. "However he did say that you're a regular here and he does remember you buying six quid worth of sweets and chocolate and a cup of tea." Stirling shook his head in disgust. "The only bit of your tale which is true is that you bought tea; the rest is bullshit."

"So you bought the sweets," Annie surmised. "Then you walked through the reserve to the school at the end of the path, handed out the sweets, had a peep at the kids for a while then walked back. That's how you saw them near the bin isn't it? You were coming from the other direction."

"School?" Tibbs croaked.

"Don't wind me up, Tibbs."

He looked at his feet and slurped his tea. "I wasn't doing any harm."

"You're in serious breach of you bail conditions, sunshine."

"I know. That's why I bent the truth a little bit." Tibbs stared into his tea. His hands trembled. "I wanted to help you without dropping myself in the crap. I didn't want to get into trouble but I did see them dumping that collar, honestly."

"You don't know the meaning of honesty."

"I couldn't ignore it," Tibbs insisted. "They dumped the collar and I knew it was evidence that something terrible has happened to Lacey. I had to come in and tell you."

She listened to his argument and thought that despite her personal feelings, she needed him to talk. "Where did you see them first?" Annie asked calmly.

"Over there on the far side of the pond." Tibbs indicated to a path fifty yards further on. "They were coming through the trees so I watched them."

"Go on."

"I thought they might be a couple of queers until I recognised one of them," he shrugged. "Then I saw one of them dump the collar in the bin. I walked on and saw them get into the van. Once they'd gone, I went back to see what they had thrown away."

"And you recognised one of them?"

"Well," he paused, "sort of."

"What do you mean, sort of?"

"He looks like a member of a family, which is well known in town for all the wrong reasons."

"Looks like?"

"He had a very strong family resemblance," Tibbs slurped again. "You know what I mean. He has to be related."

"To who?"

"I want guaranteed immunity from prosecution and total anonymity," Tibbs said stubbornly. "I'm too old to go to jail especially as a nonce. You lot have made sure that I'll be a target for the rest of my days and if this certain family gets wind of me talking to you, I'm fish food."

"I can't guarantee anything," Annie warned. "Until we know what we're dealing with here."

"Then I can't remember."

"I want the name of the man you recognise," Annie demanded.

"I can't remember," Tibbs sulked. "It's slipped my mind."

"You're in big trouble, Tibbs," Stirling said angrily. "Get up and show me exactly where you first saw them." He gestured with his head. "I'll tell uniform to extend the cordon up to that path, Guv. Then I'll have him locked up for breach of bail until his memory improves."

"Good. I'll go and tell the K-9 unit to start up there." Annie walked back towards the car park and pondered what to do with Tibbs. If he really did have a name, she wasn't sure if they could prove anything on the strength of his word alone, especially if it was purely on the back of a family resemblance. They needed his testimony but he was an unreliable witness, breaking his bail conditions. As she neared the edge of the trees, the rain seemed to intensify. Her head was bombarded by heavy drips from the branches above. The smell of pine trees scented the sea air. Despite the weather, it was a peaceful place.

The dogs were barking as she approached and their handlers looked perplexed. "Has your witness given us anything useful, Guv?"

"A fucking headache, Sergeant," she answered the uniformed officer and grimaced. "There's a primary school down that path and I'm certain that's why he was here."

"We picked him up last year near a playground. He had touched a couple of little girls, sisters. I wanted to lock Tibbs up and throw away the key," he said. "There's no stopping an offender like him. If they're determined to mingle with kids, then they will find a way."

"Well, until we can string them up from a gibbet, we're stuck with it," she sighed. "I need the K-9 unit up the path just beyond the first pond. It would be great, if they can start there please."

"Guv!" One of the handlers called.

"Hey," she replied, confused, "can you take the dogs up this path please?"

"No need, Guv." The handler pushed his peaked hat up from his forehead. Water poured from the brim. "We've got a hit here."

"What do you mean?" Annie asked confused.

"The dogs were only out of the van for a minute when they indicated a hit. He's sat down on the spot there." He pointed to where one of the dogs was sat down wagging his tail excitedly. "They've indicated something dead, just inside the trees over here."

"Are they sure?" Annie asked instantly regretting it.

"Dobson has never been wrong yet, Guv." The handler smiled proudly patting his Spaniel. Sand clung to his brown fur making him look like he had beige boots on. "If he says there's a body here then I'll bet my house that he's right."

"I know he's the best there is, sorry," Annie frowned as she thought about the situation. "Let's get the recovery team on it straight away."

"I think we're going to need more than one team, Guv," the second handler said. He was ten yards further into the trees. The gathering turned to look at him. "Sally has found another one here."

Chapter 3

Annie Jones sipped a cup of coffee and watched the CSI teams through the windscreen. Officers clad in white boiler suits and blue plastic overshoes worked painstakingly beneath the trees, protected from the elements by two gazebo style tents. The white canvas structures were ten yards apart, identical in appearance, yet all the activity was focused beneath just one of them. Annie was thinking that it was a bleak place to be buried, when the passenger door opened and a gust of wind whistled in from the sea.

"Kathy Brooks wants us, Guv." Stirling's gruff voice disturbed her thoughts. "She's got that look on her face again." He commented sarcastically. "You know the one," he smiled.

"The 'I know something that you don't' look?" Annie raised her eyebrows. "That means that she's got something good."

Annie opened her door and cursed when she spilt her coffee over her black boots. She tipped the rest onto the sand and dropped the plastic cup into a nearby bin. Stinging grains of sand threatened to blind her as the wind gusted around her. Having short hair was a bonus in the wind, but her ears were numbed in seconds. Stirling pretended not to notice her mishap and they wandered towards the trees in silence. As they neared the first tent, the familiar smell of human decay reached them. Annie took a tub of Vick's from her pocket, smeared a blob onto her top lip and handed it to her partner. The powerful vapour rub masked the sickly sweet smell of the dead temporarily but only just. Two CSI officers ducked out of the tent to allow them access.

"Guv." They acknowledged her rank as they passed.

Annie waved a hello and stepped inside. "Kathy," she greeted. "What have we got?"

"I haven't got a clue," Kathy frowned. "Certainly not what I was looking for, that's for sure." She gestured to the well excavated trench before them. "This is macabre indeed. I have never seen anything like this before."

"You always say that," Annie joked but her smile disappeared as she digested the scene. "What the hell?" her voice trailed away and her jaw dropped open. "Is that Lacey Taylor?"

"She's been buried standing up." Kathy ignored Annie's question. "We've exposed the body to the shoulders so far and there is no obvious cause of death jumping out at me."

"What is sticking out of her face?"

"We found tubes which were inserted into her nostrils."

"Tubes?"

"As we skimmed the surface, I initially thought they were drinking straws in the sand," she explained, "but when we tried to remove them we realised that they went much deeper than a drinking straw and that they were attached to something below the surface."

"Something being the body?"

"Exactly."

"What is the significance of the tubes?"

"The sand is so embedded into the flesh that it's difficult to be sure exactly what I'm dealing with here, but these tubes had a purpose." She raised her finger to reinforce the point, "On further inspection I could see that they were fluoroplastic tubes."

"What like a medical tube?"

"Exactly."

"Your thoughts?" Annie frowned.

"Well, it's used to probe, infuse, as catheters or for oxygen supply," she paused.

"I'm not sure that I follow."

"They are used primarily to vent or feed." She looked at Annie and watched the colour drain from her face, "I can only assume they were used for their primary function."

"Venting, feeding?"

"Both I think."

"To keep her alive?"

"I can't see any other reason for them at the moment."

"Someone buried her and kept her alive in the sand after the burial?"

"Abhorrent isn't it?" Kathy grimaced.

"What is around her eyes?" Annie asked quietly. The face was encrusted with salt and sand making it difficult to distinguish the facial features. "And the lips look the same."

"The eyelids have been sewn together," Kathy shook her head in disbelief. "So have the lips. The tubes appear to have been glued into the nostrils and then taped to the forehead so that they would protrude from the sand."

"She looks like a big prawn," Stirling thought aloud.

"Jim!" Annie snapped.

"Just an observation," he mumbled. "The bastard buried her

alive and fed her through a tube?" Stirling was incredulous.

"See here," Kathy pointed the end of the tubes. "The tape has deteriorated but the tips of the tubes are coloured, red and black. I'm guessing one for feeding, one for breathing."

"Jesus Christ," Stirling muttered. "Is it Lacey Taylor?"

"I don't think that it is, Sergeant," Kathy took a deep breath. "I can't be one hundred percent certain until I get her back to the lab, but I'm ninety-five percent sure that it isn't."

"Run it by me." Annie couldn't take her eyes from the corpse. "Why do you think that?"

"I've found earrings, which are out of character for your missing person." She pointed to a specimen packet. "Would you agree?"

"Yes," Annie agreed looking at the thick gold hoops. "Her daughter told us that she wasn't wearing any jewellery. In any case they're too flamboyant for Lacey." A sick feeling gripped her. "Anything else?"

"Even though our victim was kept alive," Kathy shrugged, "she couldn't have survived more than a couple of days after burial, a week at the most. The lack of oxygen in the sand would slow down decomposition but even with that in mind, the flesh is too far gone for it to fit the timescale of when your missing woman disappeared. Some of the flesh is putrefied in patches," Kathy said almost disappointedly. "This poor soul has been here for a couple of months at least."

"I can't imagine what she was thinking when she was...." Annie thought out loud.

"Best not to try." Kathy shook her head. "Like I said, I've never seen anything like it before." They stood and stared at the head and shoulders of the victim. Annie agreed that she looked almost prawn-like with the tubing running vertically from her nostrils, above her matted hair but she didn't voice it.

"What about the second site?" Stirling broke the uncomfortable silence.

"Oh that one is far less traumatic to explain." Kathy smiled thinly. "Dead seagull. We've disposed of it in the 'not relevant' bin."

"We need to get the K-9 unit back." Annie looked at Stirling as she tried to compose herself. "This is a nightmare, but we need to remember that we're almost certain that Lacey Taylor is buried here somewhere. We can't lose sight of that. We're going to need two investigations running in tandem, unless we can establish if they're connected."

"Can I give you some advice?" Kathy frowned, thoughtfully.

"What's on your mind?"

"I need a day to extract our victim and get some preliminary results back at the lab," she bit her top lip. "I could really do with all your resources focused on that until I've finished completely; I wouldn't want another find diluting my efforts here."

Annie thought for a second as they held a glance. They had worked together many times and Annie read between the lines. Her reasoning was rational and well thought out. "We'll hold the dogs off until first light tomorrow morning?"

"Perfect, thanks," Kathy said flatly as she turned back to the grim task of recovering the victim. "I need to press on."

Annie ducked beneath the canvas and headed onto the car park. Stirling followed with a confused expression. Annie's face was dark in thought so he waited for her to speak. She looked over at the burger van on the far side of the car park. A huddle of CSI officers were munching a variety of breakfast buns and guzzling hot tea while they had the chance. The aromas of bacon, sausage and black pudding mingled with the salty air. Seagulls soared in circles high above them waiting for the crusts to be thrown. One of the officers called over. "Do you want anything, Guv?"

"Normally my mouth would be watering at the smell of bacon but right now I don't think I could stomach anything," she replied, flatly. She waved the offer away.

"I've lost my appetite too." Stirling wiped his nose with his sleeve but the smell of death refused to move. "Order me a bacon and sausage buttie, brown sauce," he called back. He caught Annie rolling her eyes skyward. "What?"

"I thought you'd lost your appetite?"

"I have," he shrugged, "normally I'd have two."

"Of course you would, sorry." She tried a smile which didn't quite work.

"I think we're going to be very busy, Guv," he frowned, "what do you think?"

"This is going to blow up in our faces," Annie muttered. "Let's get uniform to scour the woods around the pond where Tibbs first spotted our suspects. If there are footprints or disturbed ground, then I want them found before the weather washes them away completely."

"Okay, Guv," Stirling nodded. "What are you thinking?" His huge shoulders shrugged again and he dug his spade-like hands deep into his leather jacket. Raindrops dripped from his broken nose. "Why aren't we bringing the dogs in yet?"

"You heard what Kathy said." Annie stamped her boots on the compacted sand to keep her feet warm. "I agree with her."

"I'm not sure that I follow."

"You saw the state of that victim."

"Someone took a lot of time on her."

"The thought that went into it is sickening." Annie shivered. "There's no way that was his first victim. He's built up to that."

"Kathy thinks that there are more victims buried here, doesn't she?"

"Yes, she does." Annie took out her mobile.

"I agree with her. I want every available detective drafted into MIT today. I'll call the governor, you organise uniform backup."

"I'm on it, Guv."

"Go and eat your sandwich first," Annie added, as an afterthought, "once this kicks off, we'll be lucky if we get a proper meal for a while."

Chapter 4

Janice Nixon sheltered in the doorway of an abandoned newsagent on Sheil St. The windows on the entire block were boarded up with corrugated iron sheets. Over the years, they had been plastered in layers of fly posters advertising concerts, albums and exhibitions. The once bright posters were now peeling and faded. The entire area screamed to be demolished but the city's property developers had taken a massive hit in the recession. The promised rebuilding of the inner city had ground to a halt, leaving acres of rundown Victorian slums half occupied. It was bedsit land gone tragically wrong. Students lived in close proximity to the long-term unemployed, the unemployable, drug addicts and street walkers. You can smell the abject poverty in the air. Every city has their crumbling embarrassing areas, but the Kensington area of Liverpool is down there with the country's worst.

It hadn't stopped raining for three nights consecutively, narrowing down her customer base. Most of the punters available were in cars. Passing foot trade was down to the bare minimum. The winter nights had pros and cons for the street girls. They could start as soon as it went dark and begin earning money earlier in the day, which was a pro, but the rain and the cold were the cons. She'd worked the streets long enough to know what clothing worked. Her leather miniskirt and knee length boots attracted the most punters but some nights her exposed thighs were numbed by the cold. Ten minutes in a nice warm car was sometimes a blessed relief, no matter how depraved the punter's request was or how badly they stank.

"Alright, Janet?" A pretty black face appeared around the corner. Her tartan miniskirt did little to hide her modesty. She had a wiggle to her walk befitting of the catwalk. "Fucking freezing again, innit?"

"Hey, Tasha, when you can get my name right, you can stand in my doorway," she said sourly. "My name is Janice, this is my pitch and you need to fuck off somewhere else. It's dead enough tonight without you poaching my punters."

"Take a chill pill," Tasha moaned. She was much younger and had a fragility about her. She thought that she was streetwise but her tough veneer was nothing more than a glass front. Janice could see through it and it was breakable. She was new and she thought that she was bulletproof. They all did in the beginning. "I was bored down standing down there. There's not many girls out tonight. I just came for a chat, innit? Have you got a spare smoke?"

"You walked past the only two shops in the area which are still open, to get here?" Janice laughed. "They both sell smokes so why haven't you got any?"

"I've just come out. I'm skint, innit?" A van slowed and neared the kerb. Both woman instantly smiled and pouted. The driver looked like a weirdo to Janice but then most of them did. "Fuck off, Tasha, I'm warning you!" She muttered behind her best sultry grin. The driver didn't seem to be impressed and he picked up speed, tyres sloshing spray across the pavement. Fifty yards on, the brake lights illuminated and the vehicle slowed. "Probably another time waster but you're not helping. Punters get nervous when there's more than one of us here. You need to get back down the road so that I can earn some money."

"You need to chill out," Tasha said patronisingly. "I don't know if you've noticed, girl, I'm black." She twirled around and wiggled her hips with her arms in the air. "Some like white chocolate and some like it dark. Not many like both, girl. You know what I mean?" A wide smile softened her tired features. "We could be a team."

"You're away with the fairies," Janice laughed. It was hard not to like Tasha. She had a carefree way about her. Youth gave her the ability to hope. Janice had lost all hope years ago. "You don't take this shit seriously enough."

"Why would I?"

"Because you should," Janice said, reaching into her fake Gucci handbag. She took out her Lamberts and offered one. "How long have you been out here?"

"Six months," Tasha quipped taking the cigarette. "It's just until I can find a proper job and get myself a place of my own, so that I can go back to university, you know."

"Oh, I know, alright." Janice lit both of their smokes. "I said the same thing eight years ago. Not the university bit, of course," she frowned. "I'm thick as pig shit." They both laughed loudly. Janice took another deep drag, "I had ambitions too but they never came to anything," she said, with a sad smile. "Eight years, God knows how many doses of the clap and good hidings I've had. I'm still out here. It's no place for an intelligent young girl like you. You should get out now before it's too late."

"You ever tried to give it up?"

"Every day since I started," Janice inhaled deeply as she spoke. "I was aiming to save enough to go travelling but it never happened. I always wanted to inter-railing you know. London, Paris, Rome and Venice; Venice was the one place that I really wanted to see. You know the canals and the gondolas."

"Romantic, yes?" Tasha laughed.

"Like the Cornetto advert," Janice said.

"You silly cow!"

"Oh well, they were my dreams back then."

"There's still time," Tasha cooed.

"For you maybe," Janice shrugged. "I'll just take one day at a time."

"We could work this spot together, keep each other company and keep an eye out for each other." Tasha fluttered her eyelashes and tilted her head. "You could teach me the ropes. You're an old pro!"

"Fuck off," Janice laughed. "Cheeky bitch."

"Serious though, we could team up?"

"I've struggled enough out here without having to babysit you." As she spoke, Janice watched the transit slow down again before it came to a complete stop. The driver made a tight u-turn and pulled into the opposite kerb. "Looks like white van man has changed his mind." The headlights dazzled them, impeding their view of the driver. Janice could make out a black beanie hat and dark glasses. "Sunglasses in the dark," she scoffed, "how not to look like a kerb crawler in one easy lesson, idiot."

The van edged closer, almost level with them and white exhaust fumes drifted into the cold damp air. Yellow hazard lights blinked, warning passing traffic that the vehicle was stationary. The wipers flicked back and to silently. The driver stared across the road at them. He didn't smile. He didn't indicate that he was interested in their services. He just stared.

"I'm not walking over there." Janice shuddered as she returned the driver's stare. She could almost feel his eyes boring into her through his lenses. "That's trouble, if ever I saw it."

"Well, I can't afford to be picky," Tasha sighed. She flicked her cigarette into a puddle. "If you're sure that you're going to pass?"

"Go for it, if you want to," Janice shrugged. The hairs on the back of her neck bristled. "Just be careful."

"Always am." Tasha held up clenched fists. She turned and jogged across the road, narrowly avoiding being flattened by a Fiat. A horn blared loudly making Janice jump. The noise broke the hypnotic effect of his stare. Janice watched as Tasha raised her middle finger to the driver of the Fiat and then ran around the far side of the van. A few words were exchanged and then Tasha was in the passenger seat within seconds. The driver removed his shades and Janice took a sharp breath. His eyes bulged unnaturally from his face. They were prominent from the sockets to an unusual level. She could clearly see the whites of his eyes directly above and below the iris. He reminded her of a footballer she had seen recently on the television, but she couldn't place his name. He turned and stared at Janice and she shivered involuntarily. He looked at her like she was something from a freak show. A thin smile crossed his lips. He seemed to enjoy the look of shock on her face.

Tasha leaned over and waved as the van pulled away, a worried expression on her face. The driver gave Janice a last look as the vehicle moved off. He looked her up and down, as if sizing up how tall she was and then put his glasses back on. A cold shudder ran down her spine and she felt her legs tremble. She watched transfixed as the van's brake lights faded into the distance and then disappeared as it turned off the main road. The persistent rain turned into a deluge and she had a terrible sinking feeling in her guts.

Chapter 5

The Major Investigation Team gathered on the fifth floor of Merseyside's police headquarters, situated on the banks of the River Mersey. Built in an era when public unrest was one of the considerations given to an architect, the concrete fortress looked conspicuously out of place against the backdrop of the stunning historical buildings at the water's edge and the aesthetically designed shopping complexes behind it. That morning, the hardcore of forty detectives who made up the team had been boosted to sixty members by an influx of seconded officers. The urgency of the case was reflected in the quality of detectives which had been loaned. A bank of ten high definition screens displayed images relating to the scene. Annie could feel the tension in the room. It was like the moments before a thunder storm breaks.

"You can see from the crime scene photographs that we are dealing with an organised killer." Annie looked at the faces in the room. The gathering could have been a cross section from the United Nations. The borough's diversity policy had worked. "Forensics can't give us an identification of the victim yet, fingerprints are out of the question and dental records useless."

Confused glances were exchanged between the team but no one wanted to stop Annie mid flow. The newer members of the team didn't want to attract unwanted attention to themselves by asking an obvious question. "I know that you're all wondering why we have no prints or dental evidence," she grimaced. "At least I hope you're wondering why we can't recover any prints or dental imprints, or you shouldn't be here." She smiled.

A ripple of laughter spread through the room. "Why can't we

lift any prints, Guv?" Stirling asked with fake enthusiasm, "for those of you who don't know me, I'm DS Jim Stirling." There had been no time for formal introductions. He smiled at the gathering although to most, his smile was more frightening than his frown.

"Thanks for asking that question, Sergeant," Annie smiled briefly. "You need to know everything, so if you have a question, no matter how obvious, ask it. Are we clear?"

"Guv," the gathering mumbled. She clicked a series of postmortem images onto a bank of digital screens. The smiles in the room disappeared. "The killer removed her teeth before he sewed her lips closed with twine."

"Fishing twine?" A female detective asked. All eyes turned to her. "DC Mason, from the Matrix Unit," she looked around and introduced herself.

"We're assuming that at the moment."

"Do you want me to check it out, Guv?" Mason asked keenly. She had olive skin and dark brown eyes contributed by her father's Lebanese genes. "My dad was a keen angler and he would only use one brand. Fishermen are creatures of habit. If we can identify the brand, we can narrow down the retailers."

"Put it on your list." Annie nodded making a mental note that Mason was a sharp cookie.

"What about the fingerprints, Guv?" A voice from the back of the room asked. "Why can't forensics lift them?"

"The killer super glued her hands to her thighs, and her legs were glued together," Annie said, as she clicked another series of images to demonstrate the point. "Kathy Brooks is trying to salvage something from the resin used but it appears that it was so strong, it dissolved the skin on her fingertips."

"Was she sexually assaulted?"

"It's too early to tell for sure, but bruising to the inner thighs would indicate that she was."

"Do we know what the cause of death is, Guv?"

"She choked," Annie grimaced. "The killer sewed her eyes closed and then cemented tubes into her nostrils before she was buried standing upright in the sand. The post postmortem shows traces of blood, mucus and a mixture of saline and electrolyte solution in her lungs and her stomach. Kathy thinks that she was being fed with saline and electrolytes from the surface via a tube in her nose but her throat swelled blocking the oesophagus and the fluid found its way into her respiratory system."

"Oh my God!" murmurs rippled amongst the crowd.

"How long was she alive down there, Guv?"

"It's impossible to say, but Kathy estimates that it could have been a week or more." The impact of the gruesome nature of the victim's death stunned the detectives into silence. "We're looking for a very sick killer."

"This is a complicated MO," Stirling spoke. "We're absolutely positive that the killer has worked up to this."

"There's no doubt about it," Annie agreed. "We need to scour all historical cases where anything remotely close to this has occurred. I want the search for similarities thrown country wide. This killer has developed his style over years not months. He also has knowledge of remote sites in the locality so we're going to narrow the search down to men who were born here or have lived here for a length of time."

"What about the victim, Guv?" DC Mason asked. She clicked her teeth with the nib of a ballpoint.

"That's why you're here from the Matrix unit, Detective." Annie raised her eyebrows. She addressed the rest of the group. "As you all know, Matrix works undercover on the city's streets. Their help in identifying the victim will be invaluable." She smiled at Mason. "We're going to have to wait for a possible hit in the DNA banks but while we do, your unit is best placed to find us a missing girl who fits our victim's description. I want you to use all your contacts to find us a possible name." A computer enhanced photograph appeared. "We have no missing person reports of anyone who fits her age or description, so we have to assume she hasn't been missed by anyone. This is what we think she looked like."

"A working girl?"

"Possibly," Annie nodded. "Vice are talking to their regulars to see if there's been any assaults, attempted abductions, or anything out of the ordinary lately. They'll be feeding back to us with any information."

"Has anybody else thought that it might be something to do with the iron men?" The room fell silent and all eyes fell onto a detective named Lewis. He shifted uncomfortably and blushed. "It might be way off but when I saw that the victim had been buried standing with her arms glued to her sides, the first thing I thought of was the statues on the beach nearby."

Glances were exchanged and the general consensus seemed to be that it was a possibility. "I hadn't considered it, Lewis but you are making a valid connection there. Let's find out who worked on the construction of the statues, contractors, labourers and the like. You may have a point."

"Could be much simpler than that; it could be just personal, Guv," another strange face offered an alternative theory. "The killer obviously wanted the victim to suffer by prolonging her death."

"Maybe, but it's not my first choice of motive," Annie shook her head. "A crime of passion may well display excessive violence but this has the hallmarks of a well thought out and well executed pattern killer."

"Are you suggesting we have a serial?"

"Not yet and neither will anyone in this room. Understand?" Annie made sure that everyone understood her meaning before she moved on. "This is what we think she looked like before she was mutilated and put in the sand. We have a digital impression of what she may have looked like."

"We've printed copies off and they're piled on the desk over there." Stirling pointed to the far side of the room. "Take a handful when you're out and about. Someone knows her and they know that she's missing. We need a starting point for this and we need it quickly."

"I'm holding a press conference at two o'clock and this image will be in the evening editions of the Echo and on Granada Reports, so the telephones will be red hot by teatime." Annie raised a finger as she spoke. "The details of this murder will not be released in any depth." She looked at as many pairs of eyes as she could in a pause. "Let me be very clear. As far as the press are concerned, we have found a woman aged between eighteen and thirty with shoulder length brown hair and brown eyes. She's below average height, five two." She paused for effect. "Nothing more will be released and that's the way it stays. Are we clear?"

"Guv." The room replied in unison.

"Where does Lacey Taylor fit into this?"

"I'm glad you asked me that," Annie nodded. "The answer is categorically that she doesn't. The K-9 units are searching the tree line at the reserve this morning and until we find Lacey, she is not to be mentioned in the same sentence as our victim."

"I'm handling the Lacey Taylor search," Stirling explained, "we're going to keep the investigations separate for now but you all need to know what we have on her disappearance." He gestured to Annie and she changed the images with the remote. "This is Richard Tibbs, convicted sex offender and this is the dog collar, which he witnessed being dumped in a litter bin a hundred metres from where we found our victim. He says that he saw two men leaving the scene in a white Mercedes Vito and he also claims to recognise one of the men. He came in to divulge that information, although he's since changed his mind on that."

"How come?" A Chinese detective asked. Stirling recognised him as an experienced Drugs Squad officer.

"We know that he purchased sweets from the burger van here." He pointed to an aerial shot of the beach. "Then he walked through the nature reserve to this housing estate, where funnily enough, there's a primary school." Shaking heads and muttered derogatory words were exchanged as the detectives clicked onto the reason why Tibbs was there. "He was demanding anonymity and immunity for breaking his bail conditions but once we were aware of his breach, we couldn't agree to his terms."

"So he's conveniently forgotten who he saw?"

"Basically, yes," Stirling nodded. "The fact is that we know this dog collar belonged to Lacey Taylor. She's been missing now for nine days without any communication to her family or friends and no activity on her mobile or bank account. It doesn't look good for her."

"We are assuming the worst," Annie added. "Given that Tibbs saw the collar being dumped and the fact that there was a van in the vicinity, we think Lacey is in the woods somewhere." The gathering seemed to agree with their theory. It was difficult not to in

Annie's opinion. "Okay, you know which teams you have been assigned to. We recap today's findings at twenty-two hundred hours." She looked at their facial expressions to gauge the reaction to the thought of an extended shift. There wasn't a hint of dissension. "Let's get on with it."

Chapter 6

"Take a left here, innit?" Tasha pointed to an alleyway as she spoke. "Pull in anywhere down there. It's quiet and safe and I need the money upfront, okay?"

The driver indicated and steered the van down the alleyway between two rows of derelict terraced houses, which backed onto each other. It was wide enough to fit a bin wagon through but too narrow for two vehicles to pass. The ground was littered with soggy fast food wrappers, a rotten double mattress and a rolled up carpet. Tall weeds had sprouted at the base of the walls, which sheltered the backyards. Shards of broken glass were cemented on top of the walls, anti-intrusion technology at its best in the 1960's. The van smelled of disinfectant and a musky aftershave that she couldn't identify. He hadn't said a word since she agreed the price and climbed into the van. Some of them were like that while others didn't shut up even when she was servicing them.

"You don't say much do you?" He ignored her. His silence was unnerving. "You know one of my regulars talks about his pigeons continuously until he's finished, which I found strange at first, but it takes all sorts doesn't it?"

He looked out of the window oblivious to her chattering. Some punters were kind and gentle, others brutally rough and ice cold. This one was different again. There was something creepy about his silence and his eyes were scarily abnormal.

"Here is fine," she said wanting to get the job and get out as quickly as possible. The van slowed to a stop and he pulled the handbrake on. The engine idled and the wipers squeaked back and forth, struggling to clear the incessant rain from the glass. The driver sat still, staring out of the window, his face expressionless. "There's no need to be nervous," she said trying to coax a reaction, "I won't bite you, unless you want me to, of course." She smiled and then rolled her eyes when no response came. He took a deep breath and sighed. His hands remained on the steering wheel as he turned to look at her. She felt anxious beneath his gaze. "Do you always wear sunglasses at night?" she joked. "If you're trying to look suspicious then you're doing a good job of it."

He took his shades off and looked at her. His bulbous eyes threatened to pop out of his face. "I wear them because my eyes protrude," he grinned. "They make people, uncomfortable, should we say."

"I can see why," she said too quickly. She instantly regretted saying it. The protrusion made his gaze feel like a piercing glare. He had a haunted expression as if his thoughts were somewhere else whilst his eyes drilled into her soul. They were unblinking eyes.

"Shut up and get on with it," he said flatly. His accent wasn't local. His voice was smooth and tinged with an accent from the Middle East maybe, she thought. He removed his hat revealing neatly trimmed black hair. His appearance was foreign, his skin olive. Apart from his eyes, he was handsome.

"You should leave that hat off," she commented. "It makes you look ten years younger."

"I removed it because it's warm in here," he said staring through her. "Not to impress you."

"Sorry I spoke."

"Do you have any children?"

"What?"

"Children?" he tilted his head as if analyzing her thoughts. "Do you have any children?"

"No," she replied confused, "not that it's any business of

yours."

"It is my business," he corrected her. "Too many children are left alone while their mothers prostitute themselves. Now I don't have to worry about it. Get on with it."

"Erm, there's no need to be an obnoxious asshole and there's the little matter of the money first," Tasha tried to speak in an assertive tone but the crack in her voice said she was nervous. "Twenty-five with, or thirty without, just like we agreed."

He reached into his breast pocket with his right hand and removed three ten pound notes. Handing the notes to her, he undid his anorak and stared at her. It was a look which most couldn't return without looking away. Tasha hesitated as she put the money into her bra, thinking seriously about not finishing their transaction and bolting instead, but she needed the money. She needed it badly. First thing on the list was meth and second was a half bottle of vodka to help through the nightshift. Her nerves were jangling as she slid across the passenger seat and reached for his belt buckle. She could see her reflection in the window and the image was disconcerting. There were dark circles beneath her once dazzling eyes. She knew that the drugs were aging her rapidly but it wouldn't be like that forever. Once she re-enrolled in university, she would get clean.

She fumbled with the buckle. The rolls of fat hanging over his belt obstructed her. When it came free she breathed a sigh of relief and flicked the button open before tugging the zip down. "Slide your pants over your hips so I can get to it," she said impatiently, "I haven't got all night." He smiled for the first time and she noticed how crooked his teeth were. She should have felt more relaxed but she didn't, she felt a bolt of fear shoot through her. His smile was more of sneer. There was evil behind it. She could sense menace. The thought of what she had to do made her feel nauseous but she'd learned to take her mind to another place while she performed. It had been that way as far back as she could remember. Her stepfather had stolen her childhood years, sneaking into her room whenever her mother went to the bingo. He had taken every opportunity possible to undress her, bathe her and abuse her. She was an only child, which meant that he could focus all his twisted attention on her. When she was twelve, she had her first period and suddenly the abuse stopped. He died of lung cancer a year later and she watched his disintegration from a strange perspective. Part of her wanted him to suffer indefinitely but somewhere inside she pitied him. The grief she felt when he died ran unexplainably deep. She could never forgive him but she couldn't forget the times that he was kind either. Eventually she stopped looking for explanations within and she kept the skill of disassociating herself from her body and turned it to good use on the streets. Stepping into the role of a working girl was an easy transition.

"Let the dog see the rabbit," she sighed as she bent towards his groin.

His left hand grabbed a fistful of hair on the back of her head. At first she thought he liked it rough but when he twisted it painfully and pushed her face closer to his own, she realised he meant to harm her. Adrenalin rushed into her veins and she lashed out. She pushed her hands against his thigh trying to pull free but he was strong. Her fingers dug into his legs and her feet kicked at the door. She thrashed about violently trying to break free but he held her in a vice-like grip. A scream rose in her throat but before she could let it out, she heard the crackling noise of electricity. Red hot pain shot through her neck. Her teeth cracked together painfully as her muscles went into spasm and she could smell burning flesh. Although white lightning flashed in her brain, she knew that it was her flesh that she could smell. His smile widened as she twitched and bucked into unconsciousness.

Chapter 7

"Why are we splitting the dog teams up?" Sergeant Atherton asked irritably. The wind from the sea was still bitterly cold and his temper was wearing thin. "They work better as a unit. We can cover more area that way."

"When you have one area to search?"

"Well, yes."

"This time, we don't have just one area to search," Stirling said slowly. "We need two areas searched at the same time," Stirling shrugged. "It's not fucking rocket science, is it?"

"Funny guy," Atherton whined.

"I'm not trying to be funny."

"It wouldn't be so bad if we knew why we are searching two areas."

"Because we need two areas searching. That's all you need to know for now."

"What's all the secrecy about?"

"I can't say anything just yet but we have two possible dump sites to cover. We can't let the press get hold of it yet." Stirling shrugged and studied the area beneath the trees with his eyes. "You have swept the entire path on both sides?"

"Both sides are clear." CSI officers were combing the area to the left of the path while the dog unit searched the opposite side. "At least the rain has stopped, although anything on the sand will already be useless."

"We wouldn't split up the dogs. Is Bugsy interfering again?" Atherton muttered. "My hounds would be proud of those teeth."

"If I was you," Stirling pointed his finger, "I'd shut my mouth and get on with the job."

"You would, Stirling," the dog handler snapped. "You're so far up her arse that you could clean her teeth from the inside."

"She's the best DI that I've worked under," Stirling snarled, "and your only problem is that she wears a skirt. What's up? Does it dent your ego taking orders from a woman?"

"No," Atherton replied nervously. Stirling was a big man with a formidable reputation. "My problem is being told how to do my job by a pen-pushing bint that hasn't got a clue about working with cadaver dogs."

"Oh and your unit is shit hot, is it?"

"We're the best there is."

"Kathy Brooks and the CSI team wasted three hours uncovering a rotting shite-hawk because your dog indicated a body. A very expensive seagull!" Stirling stepped into his personal space. "It hasn't been mentioned to the Super because Annie asked Kathy to leave it out of her report, so before you go shooting your big mouth and running her down, I'd have a think about it."

"I didn't realise," Atherton stuttered.

"No you didn't, did you," Stirling said angrily. "But while budgets are being slashed, I'd be very careful who to criticise, especially when you've unnecessarily added a few grand to the investigation."

"It's been a long week. I'm just tired," Atherton blushed. "Sorry."

"Bollocks," Stirling lowered his voice. Some of the officers nearby had noticed their exchange. He smiled to put them at ease. "If

I hear you calling the DI, 'Bugsy', again, we're going to be rolling around in the sand." Stirling turned the insult back on him. "Do you understand me?"

"Perfectly," Atherton replied hoarsely. He straightened himself up and walked away embarrassed. "I'll go and check on the progress."

"You do that."

"Sarge," a voice called from behind him. He turned and trudged up the sandy path to where the CSI officer stood. The sun was shining weakly though the tree canopy but it was low in the sky and had no warmth in it. "Can you take a look at this?" the white clad figure asked.

"What have you got?"

"The sand is too wet to hold any footprints but look here." He pointed excitedly as he spoke. Stirling scanned the elephant grass, which was interspersed with reeds at the edge of the kidney shaped pond. A hundred metres across the water, he could see the bench where Tibbs had sat while Annie grilled him. "See there in the mud. There are two sets of footprints, which look like they were made by training shoes to me. The imprint looks pretty sharp. I could lift them."

"I think you're right," Stirling agreed. "We'll need casts of them please." He noticed that the reeds were snapped in places. "It looks to me like someone put something into the water."

"How deep do you think it is?"

"Waist high, no more than that."

"I'll get the waders out of the van and sweep the shallows."

"Okay." Stirling grimaced as he looked at the dark pond.

"The DI is going to love this. If there's anything in there, I hope it's near the edge or we'll need the dive team too."

"This area is clear," Atherton called from the trees. "Unless you've got any objections, I suggest we join the other dog units near the dunes?"

"We were told that the men who dumped the dog collar walked from this path around the pound to the car park," Stirling recounted. "The dogs have searched all the way to the road?"

"There and back again," Atherton raised his eyebrows. "Bearing in mind where your information came from, I'm hardly surprised that you've come up with nothing. Tibbs is a lying kiddie-fiddler. I'm amazed a detective with your years of service would listen to a word he said."

"Well we did and until we call the area clear, we finish the job," Stirling sounded unconvincing. "If you've finished the woods, let's get all the dog units concentrated near the dunes."

"Good idea," Atherton rolled his eyes. He looked like he was about to add another cutting remark when the radio crackled.

"Guv," a voice came through the static.

"Go ahead," Atherton answered.

"We could do with a hand over here." There was concern in the voice.

"What's up?"

"Sally has sat down on three so far and I'm not more than two hundred metres from the car park." Atherton looked at Stirling with his mouth open. He wasn't sure whether to be worried or not.

"She had better not be sitting on bloody seagulls again," he said flatly. "I'm bringing Dobson over now." Atherton shrugged and half smiled. "They can't all be shite-hawks, although part of me hopes that they are."

"Definitely not, Guv," the voice crackled again. "CSI team have found tubes in the sand just below the surface. "It looks like we've got three more prawns."

Atherton blushed at the final comment. "Sorry. I call him empty-head because he doesn't think before he speaks."

"Prawns?" Stirling asked incredulously. "It's one thing calling the victims prawns and another doing it over the comms. Have a word with him will you? There could be half a dozen nerds listening to us on scanners."

"I will do," Atherton jogged off as he spoke. "Are you coming?"

"I'll wait until the pond has been searched," Stirling shouted after him. "The DI is questioning Tibbs but when she's finished, she'll be in charge down there so don't let her hear empty-head calling the victims prawns." Atherton nodded and jogged on, a wry grin on his face. Stirling had a good idea where empty-head had heard the derogatory term first. Dark humour was common at the crime scenes he had worked on. He replayed images of the past in his mind as he walked along the edge of the pond. Recovering bodies from water was never pleasant. The longer the victim was submerged, the more advanced the decay became. He recalled a case when a lifeboat crew attempted to extract a body from the Mersey Estuary. It was so rotten that the arms were pulled off during the struggle. Lacey Taylor had been missing for weeks. If she was in the pond, her body would be bloated and would float to the surface unless it was weighted.

"We're going to start over here, Guv," a voice disturbed his thoughts. Stirling looked back as saw two CSI officers clad in green rubber waders, which reached to just below the armpits. "We'll take the casts when we've searched the water."

"Okay," Stirling waved. "There's nothing in the sand here to indicate that anyone ventured far from the path. If they had carried a dead body then they wouldn't want to carry it any further than absolutely necessary, especially if it was weighted."

"I wouldn't want to dump a body too close to the edge though, Guv."

"I'm guessing it was dark," Stirling thought out loud. "They carried the body from the car park. All the way up that path, around the pond and along here to this side. I would have deemed this the furthest point away from where most people walk, wouldn't you?"

"I suppose so." The CSI shrugged as he squelched into the water. Thick black mud sucked at his limbs and he had to wrench his feet free to move forward. He probed the pond bed with a white pole, searching for anything that didn't belong there. "It's very shallow here. I'll try further out and you check that side," he said to his colleague. "Go easy with your pole."

"Said the choirboy to the priest," Stirling laughed.

"The old ones are the best."

"Unless you're a Catholic, and then it's offensive."

"Are you a catholic?"

"No."

"Shut up then."

"When you've finished your stand up routine, I've found something."

"What is it?" Stirling peered over the reeds but he couldn't see anything. He edged along the bank to a better vantage spot. The CSI probed the water feeling out the shape beneath the water. His colleague approached him from the right. His movement created chevron shaped ripples on the surface. "I'm pretty sure that we've got a body, Sarge. I'm waist deep but I think we can lift it between us."

"Hey," Stirling shouted to the officers nearby, "come and give us a lift here."

"Guv." Four white clad men jogged to the pond.

The officers in waders bent double and strained to move the dead weight from the muddy water. The sandy gunk on the bed seemed to suck the object down, refusing to release it. No matter how hard they tried, it wouldn't budge. "It's not going to shift, Guv," one of them panted. His face was ruddy with exertion. "It feels like a tarpaulin. I can feel a chain wrapped around it so I think it's weighted."

"It looks like we're going to get our feet wet," Stirling laughed dryly as he slipped his coat off. He hung it on a tree and then trudged into the reeds. Icy water ran into his shoes, seeping between his toes. His feet were instantly numbed by the cold. The other officers followed his example, without question. "Two of you at each end, I'll grab the middle." He waited until they had a grip and then nodded, "on three. One, two, lift."

A blue plastic tarpaulin broke free of the surface. A thick rusty chain was wrapped around it; wire mesh encased the entirety, keeping the contents from spilling out. Pondweed and sludge clung to the blue material. The sulphur-like smell of rotting vegetation and decaying pond life filled the air, followed by the cloying stench of decomposition. "Let's move it to the bank there. We don't want to trample on those prints." They moved as a unit until they were clear of the pond and gently laid the bundle on the ground. Stirling parted the plastic at one end of the roll and looked at the others. They exchanged glances. "Well, I didn't expect that." Stirling shook his head and grimaced as the stench of rotting flesh hit him. "Unless Lacey Taylor had hairy toes, big feet and hadn't shaved her legs for a year or two, this isn't her."

The CSI officer at the opposite end fumbled with the mesh to find an opening. He recoiled as he peered inside. "Jesus," he gasped. The blood drained from his face and he put his hand over his mouth. "The head's been removed, Guv."

"Brilliant," Stirling muttered. He took off his shoes to pour the water out, instantly regretting it as his socks became encrusted with sand. "Get him to the lab, pronto. We need to know who he is and we need to know quickly."

"Guv."

"I want the rest of the pond dragged," he added as he banged his sandy socks against a tree. He struggled into his coat and some of the warmth returned. "It looks to me that Lacey Taylor was involved in more than running youth centres."

Chapter 8

"Interview with Richard Tibbs, twenty-second of November, twenty-fourteen," Annie Jones prepped the tape. "Officers present, DI Anne Jones and DC Steven Lewis. Time is nine hundred hours." She sat back in her chair and looked at Tibbs with a stony glare. "This is a one off opportunity to help you to help yourself," she paused. "You are withholding vital information regarding the identity of a suspect in a possible murder investigation. If you want to get out of here anytime soon, then you need to start cooperating."

"You gave me your word that there would be no tapes," Tibbs croaked. He looked tired and ten years older than the last time she sat in the interview room with him. A sleepless night in the cells hadn't agreed with him. He looked hopeless. Not for the first time in his life, he felt defeated. "I came here to help and we had a deal."

"That was before you lied to me and it became obvious that you'd breached your bail conditions," Annie snapped. "Now all assurances are null and void unless you start cooperating. You went to a primary school with sweets."

"It's not what you think."

"It never is. Start talking or you're on your way to Walton."

Tibbs hesitated before he spoke. Walton wasn't somewhere that a sex offender wanted to be, unless they had a death wish. "I'll tell you what I saw, as long as you understand that I won't testify."

"I can't promise anything."

"Then I'm not saying anything. It's that simple. I cannot testify."

"You're a nonce, Tibbs," Lewis snapped. "You're on the sex

offender's register and you went to a primary school with sweets. The judge will lock you up without blinking."

"They won't."

"They will and don't kid yourself, Tibbs."

"It's all so unfair," Tibbs sighed. He smiled sadly. "You don't have a clue about me."

"I know enough."

"You look at the register and you can't see past it." Tibbs shook his head. His eyes were sunken and weary. "I thought detectives were supposed to delve into all the evidence before they come to a conclusion. Innocent until proven guilty doesn't really exist does it?"

"It does and we do investigate thoroughly," Annie said vehemently. "There is enough in your file to tell me that you should have been locked up the last time you were in court, but the judge was a do-gooding arsehole and gave you a second chance."

"There is nothing in my file prior to two years ago is there?"

"No."

"I've had a bad time that's all."

"Rubbish," Annie said. "No sooner are you back on the street when you find a primary school within access of a remote location where you can park your car and stroll through a nature reserve without arousing suspicion. You're a danger to the public."

"It's not like that," Tibbs sighed. His gaze drifted to the light on the ceiling. A mesh cage protected it to stop suspects from turning the bulb into a weapon. He'd seen hundreds of them; hundreds of cells, hundreds of interview rooms. "It is not like you think."

"That's exactly how it is."

"I know how it looks," Tibbs said, resigned to the overwhelming facts stacked against him. "But it isn't what you think."

"We've interviewed the children and the teachers at the school. They recognise your picture." Annie studied his face for his reaction. "You were arrested for loitering near a playground last month. Do you recall it?"

"Of course I do," Tibbs said angrily. "I'm not an idiot. I know what you think of me, but I'm not stupid and you don't know all the facts. I will never forget it."

"Good," Annie countered, "then you'll be able to explain to the judge why less than a month later you bought chocolates and approached a primary school. You can't help yourself can you?"

"No," Tibbs looked at the ceiling as he spoke. "My life would be normal if I could. You don't understand. Nobody does."

"I do," Annie frowned as she spoke. "I understand that you need to be behind bars and unless you cooperate, that's exactly where you will be."

"You lot have got me all wrong," Tibbs squeezed his nose between his finger and thumb. A tear ran free and a sob choked him. "You always had me wrong." Annie was surprised to see his eyes fill up with tears, although there was neither empathy nor sympathy for him. "I wouldn't harm those kids. You're right that I can't stay away from them but I wouldn't harm them." Hot tears ran down his cheeks. He wiped them away with the back of his hand and sniffled loudly.

"Save it for the judge, Tibbs," Annie said coldly. "You're

crying because you were caught red handed. You don't give a shit about how much you ruin the lives of the children and their families."

"I know I've ruined lives but not the way you think. I do care," Tibbs said quietly. "That's my problem. I care very much." He looked at the brackets, which fastened the table to the floor and his mind went back to a better time. "We're not that different me and you."

"Now you are tripping."

"Did you know that I was a police officer of sorts once?"

Annie laughed and looked at her colleague. "Of course you were."

"It's true," a tear escaped his eye as he spoke. "I remember it was such a normal time when people didn't spit at me in the street, not the good ones anyway."

"Is this another fairytale?" Annie said sourly. "I think it would be mentioned in your file somewhere. I'm losing my patience with this, Tibbs."

"Hey you're not far off the mark there." Tibbs looked back at the floor. His expression was full of melancholy. "It seems like a fairytale now." He gazed into space, his thoughts far away from the tiny interrogation room. The scuffed walls and stale air were replaced with blue skies and the smell of cut grass. "I was a Redcap for nine years."

"A what?" Annie frowned. The nickname rang a bell but she couldn't grasp it.

"An RMP," Tibbs nodded slowly. "Royal Military Police. My last posting was Basra during Desert Storm."

"Bollocks," she slapped the desk with her palm. "I've read your file." She opened it and his picture looked back at her.

"Of course you have."

"There's no mention of any military service." She stabbed the pages with her index finger.

"There won't be," he said. "I was given a different name after Iraq."

"Why?" Annie snapped.

"I was put into witness protection."

"What," she hissed. "This is ridiculous!"

"I had to testify against some of our own men. They're very dangerous men." He stared into her eyes. Annie couldn't see any deception in his. "That's all that I can say."

"What was your real name?" She still wasn't sure.

"Nigel Dunn," he answered calmly, "Captain Nigel Dunn."

Annie looked incredulous. "Go and check this," she ordered her DC. Lewis seemed shocked by the claim.

"Guv," he said standing up. He flashed Tibbs a disbelieving glance as he left the room. "I'll follow the trail of bullshit to Lala Land. He's lying through his teeth."

"It's true," Tibbs shrugged. "When I came back from Iraq, they whisked me into protection and I couldn't cope."

"Why did they put you into the program?"

"I can't tell you, but I will say that some very senior personnel were involved."

"Go on."

"I was the key witness," Tibbs said. "Once I had testified, I still wasn't safe. They couldn't allow me back into normal service. They pensioned me off and eventually, I was joined by my family."

"You had a family?"

"I had a wife and a beautiful daughter." His lips quivered as he spoke. A deep breath seemed to calm him before he carried on. "We were moved from pillar to post to keep my identity secret, but it meant that my wife couldn't contact her family. She couldn't cope. She had a breakdown and it all fell to pieces."

"What were their names?" Annie didn't believe a word of it. She pushed her hair back from her face and smoothed her trousers irritably. She didn't want to believe him but something about his demeanour had her rattled; the hairs on the back of her neck prickled.

"Mary." He smiled at her memory. "Mary was my wife. Our daughter was Nicola."

"I don't believe you."

"Your detective will come back and verify it."

"Where are they now?"

"Mary died." Tibbs looked straight into her eyes. "She killed herself with an overdose two years after I was discharged. Her family blamed me and they were right, it was my fault. If I hadn't testified then none of it would have happened. Mary would be alive and I would have my family with me. I should have refused to testify."

"Testified against who?"

"I can't tell you."

"If you're bullshitting me," Annie left the sentence hanging.

"You can check it."

"We are."

"Good," Tibbs said calmly. "I'm sick of people looking at me as if I'm slime."

"Where is your daughter?"

"After the suicide, she was taken into care and then adopted by her aunt," his voice broke. "I was drunk all the time. I couldn't deal with leaving the army and I fell apart when Mary killed herself. As I said, Nicola was adopted by her aunt, who despised me. When I tried to find her, the family took an injunction out on me. I couldn't compromise my new identity and the family made it impossible for me to see her."

"Go on," Annie was intrigued.

"Nicola grew up in Woolton Village; she married and had two daughters of her own, Rosie and Rebecca Milton."

Annie grabbed the file and flipped through it. The surname rang alarm bells in her head. She looked at Tibbs open mouthed. "The two girls you were charged with assaulting in the park?" she shook her head. "Their surname was Milton."

"Yes," he grimaced. "I shouldn't have gone near them but I couldn't help myself. I didn't assault them. I hugged them. They didn't know me, I was drunk and it was blown out of all proportion."

"Oh my God, why didn't you tell them who you were?" Annie was still to be convinced but if he was telling the truth, it was a tragedy.

"I couldn't do that. They're too young to understand."

"Is that why there was no further action?" Annie saw the pieces slot into place. "It explains why the judge let you walk."

"My solicitor declared my real identity to the courts at the last minute, but it had to be handled that way to keep my identity secret."

"Well, I'll be buggered." She muttered beneath her breath. "What about the rest of your sheet?"

"I'm a drunken idiot, nothing more than that."

"The assault charges?"

""I followed Nicola's first husband to a pub one night," he shrugged. "He met another woman. He was cheating on my daughter."

"So you hit him?"

"I was drunk."

"He didn't know who you were?"

"Obviously," Tibbs smiled. "I didn't say anything in court that time. I just took the slap on the wrist."

"The shoplifting?"

"Whisky," he blushed. "I was broke and needed a drink. I hold my hands up to that and before you ask, the images of children on my computer were my grandchildren. I downloaded them from Facebook. I trawled the close family's pages and copied the images of them. Obviously some of them were holiday photos and your colleagues thought the worst; can't say that I blame them to be honest."

"For God's sake, Tibbs." Annie frowned. She wanted to feel guilty for the way she'd acted towards him but she felt angry instead. "Why didn't you identify yourself when you came in?"

"If I do that," he said shaking his head, "They'll stop my pension and as you can see, I'm not fit for the work place. I'm trapped inside Richard Tibbs, suspected child molester and honorary member of the sex offenders list."

"Does Nicola know that you're her father?"

"No." He shrugged. "Her aunt told her that I was dead. It's better that she believes that. Look at me. I'm an aging drunk with nothing to offer her. I didn't know what to say to her, so I watched her from a distance. I watched my family grow up and I couldn't even speak to them."

"And the primary school at Crosby?" Annie grabbed the file again. "What were you doing taking sweets to the kids there?"

"That's where my granddaughters go to school now, but their surname has changed," Tibbs nodded. "Nicola was divorced from their father and they took her new husband's surname, Williams."

"So you bought sweets for your grandchildren."

"Yes."

"This is why you were so adamant that we can't use your statement?"

"Yes."

Annie sat back and sighed. She couldn't believe that she had misread him. As she mulled over the facts, it all made sense. "Okay, if this all checks out, then you have my word that we won't reveal our source." Annie splayed her fingers on the table and sat forward. "I still need that name though."

Tibbs bit his top lip and paused, "one of them was the double of John Ryder. I actually thought it was him at first."

"I can see why you were anxious about naming that family." Annie raised her eyebrows. "What made you so sure that it wasn't him?"

"I saw John Ryder on the front page of the Echo once. He had a tattoo below his ear." Tibbs touched his neck instinctively. "The man I saw was younger and didn't have the tattoo."

The interview room door opened and the young detective appeared. He looked sheepish. "I've checked with the MOD. They wouldn't tell me much but they have a Richard Tibbs on the payroll. They confirmed that he was Captain Dunn. If we want any more information, we need a court order. His story checks out, Guv."

"Could you make sure that Mr Tibbs is fed and watered before you release him," Annie stood up. "I may need you to do a line-up at some point. We won't use your evidence but it would help us if we know we have the right man."

"No problem," Tibbs nodded and smiled thinly.

"What did I miss?" Lewis asked confused.

"A lifetime," Tibbs smiled.

"So it's Mr Tibbs now then, Guv?" Lewis frowned. "Are we just going to swallow this bullshit?"

"I'll fill you in on the way back to Crosby Beach," Annie said taking a last look at Tibbs. Annie had an uneasy feeling in her gullet. She sensed that there was a storm brewing over Richard Tibbs but she didn't know why. She put it down to instinct. "You take care of yourself."

"You too, Detective."

Chapter 9

Tasha James woke up with the urge to vomit. Her throat was so dry that she couldn't swallow. Her memory of where she had been was cloudy at first but the stinging pain in her neck reminded her that she had been knocked out by a punter with a stun gun. Although her mind was numbed from the electric shock, she was aware that she was in danger. She had to allow her senses to return fully before she tried to move. The vision of the punter's bulging eyes was emblazoned on her mind. There was evil behind them. His voice had no emotion; he was an automaton, ice cold and malevolent. She listened intently and tried to work out where she was, reluctant to move an inch in case it attracted another belt from the stun gun. Her limbs felt strange. Her fingers and toes tingled, yet they felt alien. She desperately wanted to move but she daren't. There wasn't a sound to be heard; nothing that she could use to pinpoint her location; no car engines, voices or music. Just silence. She waited for long minutes resisting the urge to sit up, open her eyes, scream and run as fast as her legs would carry her. The older girls had warned her that if a punter turns psycho, compliancy could save her life. Although she was terrified, she knew that the next few minutes of her life could make the difference between life and death. Moving could provoke another attack. She had to remain still until she was in control of her faculties and had a better idea of how bad her situation was.

Mentally she checked over herself. Apart from the burning sensation caused by the Taser, there were no obvious signs of serious injuries. There was no pain. She didn't feel bruised or wet. If the man with the scary eyes had stunned her in order to rape her, then she didn't think it had happened yet. Her underwear was intact although she could feel cool air on her legs and stomach so he must have removed her outer clothing. She wasn't outdoors. She was sure of that, but she didn't think that she was still in the van. It might have been better to have woken up dumped in an alleyway rather than this. At least all she would have to worry about was the rain soaking her. She was indoors somewhere. The air that she breathed was room temperature. There was no breeze on her flesh and no birds tweeting or dogs barking. It would have been bad enough to be roughed up, but this was much worse. Being attacked by a punter was an occupational hazard but it was usually quick and brutal. A planned abduction was rare, even for a working girl and they rarely ended well. This was an orchestrated kidnapping and of that there was no denying. Every inch of her body trembled with fear.

She listened once more for any giveaway sound. It was essential that she picked up any clue as to how dire her situation was. There was nothing but silence. She opened her eyes. Just a squint at first. She kept her head still and moved her eyes left to right. There was no bogeyman stood over her, no monster waiting to bite deep into her throat. The man with the bulging eyes wasn't there. She could see wooden joists above her and a single low wattage bulb hung uncovered from an ancient flex. The dim light couldn't penetrate into the corners of the room. The darkness was pushed back a few yards at the most. She couldn't tell if there was someone lurking in the dark shadows, waiting and watching. He could be sat there with a razor, bulging eyes staring at her, waiting for her to wake up. This could be a game of cat and mouse, stunning her and then waiting until she awoke before hurting her again and then what? Would he keep her locked up for years like the women she had seen on the news? Sex slaves kept alive to abuse at will. Some of them had actually given birth to children and brought them up in captivity. Was that what he planned to do? Keep her as a pet? Was death a better option? She couldn't decide. Would he rape her and then dump her in the river or bury her in a shallow grave? Debating whether death was the preferable option to a life of slavery and abuse wasn't helping her to remain calm. The more she thought about her options, the more her heart raced. She felt that it might burst through her chest. Her mother's face drifted into her mind, kind and caring. How disappointed she would be to see her now, selling her body to buy crack and vodka, putting her life in danger; her only daughter susceptible to assault and abuse on a daily basis. She would be sick with fear if she knew the half of it.

Tasha took a deep calming breath and then opened her eyes fully. She waited long seconds for an attack to come.

Nothing.

The rafters above supported dusty floorboards. She thought that she was below ground, in a cellar maybe. The walls were plastered smoothly and painted magnolia, the floor concrete. As her eyes became accustomed to the gloom, she noticed a trolley to her left against the wall. Stainless steel instruments glinted on a canvas roll, scalpels, hooked needles, bone saws, metacarpal saws, forceps, scissors and syringes. Tasha was twelve months into a nurses' course when she began to struggle with the fees and her rent. She had spent a week on a theatre placement. The instruments were familiar to her. So were the procedures that they were designed for; slicing, cutting, peeling, amputating and stitching; destruction and reconstruction. Surgery was a gift to the sick under controlled conditions with the correct drugs administered, but in a dark dank cellar it was nothing but a nightmare even to the most twisted mind.

This wasn't a hospital. Whatever the man with the bulging eyes had planned for her, it appeared to involve surgery. She sat up quickly and looked around in a panic. The muscles in her chest threatened to crush the breath from her lungs. She swung her legs off the table and squeezed her thigh muscles between fingers and thumb to encourage blood flow. Her eyes settled on the scalpels, glinting, sharp and threatening and ready to slice. They were almost magnetic in drawing her eyes to them. Their evil glint fuelled the burning fear that she felt. She looked away to gather her composure. Her clothes were folded neatly in a pile on a hardback chair which was pushed against the wall to her left. She was grateful that her underwear had not been removed as she wrestled her limbs into her garments. Escaping and putting as much distance as possible between herself and this place was her only thought. Whoever her attacker was, he had underestimated her. Leaving her untied with weapons to hand was a huge mistake. She struggled into her boots and then ran to the trolley. Tasha picked up a scalpel and the largest pair of scissors that she could find and then stumbled to end of the room to find the door. If her attacker tried to stop her, she would cut him to ribbons before he could overcome her again. She would escape or die trying.

Although the light was poor, all that she could see were smooth plastered walls and a concrete floor. She cursed and ran back to the table, turning to face each corner of the room, one at a time. Smooth plastered walls and a concrete floor. Although it was ridiculous, Tasha dashed to the trolley and pulled it violently away from the wall, desperately hoping that it was hiding a small door.

Nothing.

She kicked the chair over.

Nothing.

The table was made from stainless steel and despite its weight, she flipped it over.

Nothing.

She walked around the room at least four times before she had to accept that there was no door.

Chapter 10

"I don't know what to think about Tibbs, Guv," Stirling said, hunching his shoulders against the sea breeze. What little warmth the sun had offered was waning as it plummeted towards the horizon once again. The sea appeared to be dark green with hues of grey, as it advanced across the wide sandy beach towards the dunes. Foamy white rolls crashed onto the shoreline, creeping forward before slowly retreating beneath the next wave. The statues stood stoically as the tide engulfed them. It was a fascinating yet disturbing image. One hundred iron men in various stages of burial or submergence, or in some cases, both. "I had him down as a pervert, yet he's some kind of war hero. It's unbelievable how wrong we could be."

"Not really," Annie offered. "Given the facts that we had, what else were we to think? If it walks like a duck and sounds like a duck, then you can bet that it is a duck. Tibbs walked like a duck."

"I suppose so, but maybe we should have dug deeper into his past before we dived in."

"How could we?" Annie protested. Stirling was right but she was trying to offset her guilt by blaming their workload. "He was on the register and we discovered that he had approached a school. What else could we do?"

"I guess you're right, but I can't help but think we should have looked deeper first off."

"If we had time to do that every time we sat down with an informer, then great, but we don't. And if we had done an extended background check, we would have hit a brick wall at the MOD. We don't have time to delve any deeper."

"I think we should make time."

"You think too much."

"I don't know about that." Stirling laughed gruffly. "You said that I should think things through more carefully."

"Did I?"

"You did."

"That was a different set of circumstances."

"Was it?"

"It was."

"Fair enough, Guv," he laughed. "I'm struggling to think straight on this one, Guv."

"You and me both, Sergeant," she muttered, as she looked across the car park to the dunes. Three K-9 units were tracking in a grid pattern, followed closely by CSI officers. Yellow tape billowed in the wind and a dozen uniformed officers ferried tools and evidence to and from the search site. There were four more gazebos erected since the last time she had seen the site, a dead body beneath each. More uniformed officers scurried towards the dunes with poles and canvas to erect another. "How many bodies do we have now?"

"Six more hits so far." Stirling shivered, his expression grim. "We've got a headless body in the pond and seven women tortured and buried alive and we don't know if any of the bodies are Lacey Taylor yet. We need another fifty detectives to put a dent in this, Guv."

"It's not as complicated as it seems." Annie allowed herself a half smile. It was easy to feel overwhelmed by some cases but she knew how to see the woods behind the trees. "We're looking for one serial killer," she said convincingly. "The victim in the pond is a separate entity. I'm sure of it."

"And Lacey Taylor?"

"She's there somewhere."

"I agree," Stirling said. "The body in the pond looks gang related, whereas this lot here, Jesus only knows what is going on. We have one very sick individual on our hands."

"There's no doubt about that; we could really do with a break on the identities of the victims before we can get a grip on either investigation properly."

"Kathy called five minutes before you got here," Stirling sounded hopeful. "She's working on our pond guy immediately before she gets back to the," he hesitated mid sentence, "back to the others, Guv." He corrected himself before he let slip.

"Okay, let's leave the recovery teams to do their stuff and get back to the station. We can come back when the victims are uncovered. Until then, I want to hear every snippet of information as it comes in. When this gets going, our feet won't touch the ground."

"Have you seen the press arriving, Guv?" Stirling asked as he watched yet another van reaching the cordon before being turned away. A growing number of telescopic lenses were gathered waiting for the merest glimpse of a dead body.

"They can smell blood." Annie sighed. "The more bodies that we find, the more interested they will be."

Chapter 11

"He's greying and his bone mass is thinning. From his teeth, I would say that he was in his forties," Kathy Brooks said as she washed blood from her latex gloves. The smell of disinfectant mingled with rotting flesh was eye-watering and it was difficult to control the gag reflex. "He was about six feet tall, white European with dark hair and a managerial job." She held up a dead hand. "His palms were soft, unhardened by manual labour. The nails on his left hand are well manicured, which isn't cheap to maintain. The fingernails on the right were ripped out before he died." She pointed to his wrists and ankles. "He was bound with plastic zip-ties, hands and feet and tortured. "His torso is badly bruised and he sustained four cracked ribs, bruised kidneys and a ruptured testicle. He was subjected to a sustained beating over an extended period of time. Obviously the head was removed before the body was dumped."

"So he was either tortured as a punishment or interrogated," Annie grimaced. "Nothing there to give us a name?" she asked Stirling.

"His prints are being run now, Guv," he checked his watch as he spoke. "We'll have an answer in the next half an hour."

"If he's in the system" Annie said doubtfully. "Look at him. He has no tattoos, no scars on his hands or body. He doesn't look like our average gang related torture victim."

"He could be higher up the food chain."

"If he is, then he'll be reported missing," Annie agreed. "Have we got people checking with missing persons outside the county?"

"Yes, Guv." Stirling checked his mobile as he spoke. "They're aware of what's going on. Smithy is crosschecking all missing males that fit this description. I've told him to contact me as soon as anything comes in."

"Good. Do you know what killed him?" Annie turned back to Kathy.

"The cause of death is exsanguination," Kathy added. "I think that he was still alive when they began to cut off his head."

"That's enough to ruin your day," Stirling mumbled. "Poor bastard."

"Save the sympathy until we know who he is," Annie grinned. "I thought you were going to look deeper into things in the future."

"I am," Stirling shrugged. "Even if he's a scrotum, you've got to have a twinge of sympathy for him."

"This was a punishment killing," Annie sounded sure.

"If it was, we have to assume that he has a connection to Lacey Taylor and the prawns are nothing to do with this," Stirling said.

"Prawns?" Annie repeated shocked. She raised her eyebrows. She looked at the dead women in various states of decay. They all had antenna like tubes glued to their faces. "Will you stop calling them prawns. That's out of order."

"Sorry, Guv," he blushed. "It's what we've been calling the victims. You know with the tubes and such like."

"I know where it came from; who said it first?" Annie was half amused and half annoyed.

"Actually it was me," Kathy shrugged. "We don't have a name for them yet so I made one up for now. Sorry, but I was thinking aloud and someone must have picked up on it."

"I'm surprised at you, Kathy," Annie said briskly. "If the press gets hold of that, I'll be toast. Anyhow, what have you got on our other victims?" She understood the mirth in the prawn tag but she couldn't endorse it by using the term. Kathy walked to the next trolley.

"We've extracted three victims so far." Kathy pulled back a spotlight. "They're all the same as the first woman. The teeth were removed, lips and eyelids stitched closed and the arms and hands fastened to the body with adhesive and fishing twine. The legs and feet are glued together too. The tubing was glued into the nostrils of all the victims before they were buried upright in the sand."

"Can you give us a description of all the victims and I need a chronology of when you estimate their burial took place. If we're to have any chance of identifying them, we need to know when they went missing."

Kathy pointed to the victim's arm. "She's about the same age as the first, homemade tattoos on her arms and shoulders. I'll get pictures of them over to you. These look like track marks to me. She was an addict but the tattoos will help you."

"Which brings us back to the working girl theory," Annie nodded. "That's why no one has noticed them disappearing."

"We've put pressure on vice to speak to all the active street walkers to see if we can identify anyone who has fallen off the radar recently." Stirling frowned. "I'll chase up the DI over there and see what he's got for us, but I'm sure that if they had anything, they'd have given it to us by now."

"I know that you'll have your hands full, Kathy," Annie said smiling. "But I need every detail sent over as you get it. You have whatever authority you need to get me the results back as soon as you can. If you need more technicians, you have my go ahead."

"And the costs?"

"Not an issue."

"I'll draft in the labs from Cheshire and Cumbria," Kathy turned away and peeled off her gloves. She took out her mobile and held it up. "With their people on board, I can get everything to you in forty-eight hours."

"I need it today, Kathy."

"Impossible," she shook her head. "You'll have postmortem results by tomorrow but the tox-screens and DNA will take time. I'm sorry, but I'm a scientist not a magician."

"I know," Annie muttered. "Although if you have got any tricks up your sleeve, now's the time to use them."

"Leave it with me. We'll be as quick as we can."

Annie nodded and turned to walk out of the lab. She glanced back at the body on the trolley and couldn't help but agree that there was indeed a resemblance to a giant prawn.

Chapter 12

John Ryder was angry, very angry. He had spent ten years climbing to the top of the organised crime ladder without being prosecuted for so much as a parking ticket. The other crime families dubbed him as 'Teflon John' because nothing stuck to him. It hadn't been an accident either; his success was due to a razor sharp intellect and a ruthless intolerance of mistakes. Business was good and he had only a few enemies. His problems were much closer to home.

He sipped an expensive Merlot from a crystal wine glass as he struggled to keep his temper from boiling over. His laptop screen showed the female DI of the city's Major Investigation Team holding a press conference and in front of him, a copy of the evening edition of the Echo lay folded on a marble coffee table. Both the newspaper and the detective carried the news of a decapitated male found near Crosby Beach. He shifted uncomfortably on a brown leather captain's chair while he listened to his stepson making one excuse after another. He ran his hand over his closely cropped hair, salt and pepper patches had crept backwards from above the ears. The spread of grey had quickened in the last few years aging him, yet his pale green eyes and chiselled jaw ensured that he could still turn a woman's head when he walked into a room. He was wide at the shoulder and narrow at the hip and his dress sense was second to none, unlike his wayward stepson who looked like an extra from a cheap sportswear catalogue.

"Charlie Keegan had it coming to him. He was a twat," Brendon Ryder moaned. "It's his fault that bitch got onto us in the first place. He was lining his pockets with government grants and when he was investigated my name was thrown into the hat. I couldn't have that kind of exposure from the law. Lacey Taylor actually called my mobile and told me that she was going to have me arrested."

"She did," Bren's sidekick piped up. He was dressed in almost identical sportswear to Brendon. "She actually called his mobile. What a fucking cheek."

"Shut up, Gary," Bren snapped.

"I'm just backing you up mate," Gary said offended. "You know like you said to."

"Shut up."

"Both of you shut up! What exactly did she find out from Keegan?" John asked impatiently.

"We were shifting some gear through some of the girls at the youth clubs in Toxteth," Bren bragged. "We were clearing a grand a week and we never went near the place. There was no way she could have bubbled me."

"A grand a week?" John rolled his eyes. "You've brought the police down on yourself for a measly grand a week?"

"Oh, it's on just 'myself' is it?" Bren felt the distance John had put between them and it rankled. "It's not just me the police are sniffing around though is it?"

"No it isn't," John replied angrily. "Thanks to you, we'll all have a microscope shoved up our arse!"

"If Keegan hadn't been robbing from the council, none of this would have happened. He was your contact, not mine."

"That's the only reason that I'm listening to a word you say. I should have dealt with him earlier." John relented slightly. "If he turned on us, then that's unforgivable."

"Exactly what I thought all along," Bren said encouraged.

"Exactly what we thought all along, John," Gary repeated. "It was unforgivable."

"All we did was what you would have done, but you weren't here," Brendon said excitedly.

"He's right," Gary agreed enthusiastically. "You weren't here."

"Gary!" John snapped

"What?"

"Shut your face!" John turned to his stepson. "No you didn't do what I would have done. You fucked things up. That's what you did."

"We were rushed into acting."

"It was a rush," Gary agreed. "We said at the time that it was a rush."

John shot him a withering glance which silenced him. "So you thought that killing him and dumping his body into a pond which is three feet deep was the best way of handling it?" John asked sarcastically. He sipped the rich red and savoured the fruity flavour on his tongue. Under different circumstances, he might have enjoyed it. "You've got the brains of a breeze-block and that's pushing it to the limit."

"It was supposed to be temporary," Bren said. He opened the top button of his Ralph Lauren polo shirt. His stepfather frightened him. Although he had brought him up from the age of six, he didn't love or respect him. He never had. John Ryder had tolerated him all his life because he married his mother. Bren was the price he had to pay to love his mother. Although he had tried to make the great John

Ryder proud, he had failed at every turn. "Matrix were all over me like a rash. I knew that if they lifted Keegan, he would turn us in. I had to get rid of him. I was going to move his body as soon as the pressure was off. They only found him because of the other murders there!"

"That's true," Gary mumbled. "They never would have found him if it wasn't for the other murders, John."

"You're a fucking retard and so is your friend." John snapped.

"Thanks, Dad," Bren retorted sarcastically.

"Where is Lacey Taylor?" John ignored the slight. "Please don't tell me that she's in the pond too?"

"Of course not," Bren said.

"That would be silly," Gary added.

"You're really not helping," Bren turned to his friend. "Shut up."

"Where is she?"

"I did a real number on her." Bren sniggered, his immaturity and lack of intelligence plain for all in the room to see. "She was cocky at first until I started on the dog. Then she told me everything that she had on us." His chest inflated proudly although nobody else seemed to be impressed. The other men in the room were older, wiser and infinitely more battle-hardened than the crowing Ryder junior. "When I started to cut Keegan's head off, she crapped in her pants and screamed like a baby but I made sure she couldn't say anything to the police. She can't talk now, I made sure of that."

John Ryder had an expression of disgust on his face. He shook his head slowly and rubbed his eyes. "I don't need the sordid details, Brendon. I asked you where she was."

"I buried her."

"By yourself?"

"Yes."

"So nobody but you knows where she is?"

"Nobody."

"Who dumped Keegan in the pond?"

"We did."

"Who is 'we'?"

"Gary and I," Bren smiled nervously. His face turned crimson and his lips twitched. "We hired a van and dumped him and the dog. Didn't we, Gary?" His partner in crime was an overweight man with a head shaped like a pumpkin. He shuffled uncomfortably, scratched at a colony of puss filled pimples on the back of his neck and looked down at his oversized Reeboks.

"Were you involved in selling the gear too, Gary?" John glared at the fat youth.

"It was just a bit of crack, John," Gary muttered. "We never touched your stuff."

"You were dealing behind my back."

"Sorry, John," Gary's bottom lip quivered.

"Are you?"

"Yes, I am."

"I think you're sorry because you got caught." John pointed

his finger at both of them. "If this idiot hadn't dumped a dead body in a puddle where everyone could see it, then you'd still be skimming a grand a week from me."

"We just needed a bit of extra cash, John," Gary explained nervously.

"What for?" John snapped. "A new tracksuit, or to put a boom-box and a chrome exhaust on your Clio?"

"I sold the Clio, John."

"What?"

"I sold the Clio last week," Gary said oblivious to his employer's mood. "I bought a Focus turbo. I got a great deal on it."

"Shut up!" John shouted. He looked at a gorilla in a Calvin Klein suit. "Shut that stupid fucker up before I shut him up for good." The gorilla walked across the marble tiles and towered above Gary. He didn't say anything to him; he didn't need to. His sheer bulk looming over him had frightened him into silence. Gary stared at his trainers and tucked his sweaty hands into his tracksuit pockets.

"I'll ask you again," John turned to his stepson. "Where is she?"

"What is your problem?" Bren whined. "You don't give me credit for anything I do. You were banging my mum and sunning yourself by the pool in Spain while it was all going Pete Tong here!" His stepfather's face darkened with anger. Nobody raised their voice to John Ryder. He knew that he was stepping over the mark.

"Don't you ever talk about your mother like that again."

"Sorry."

"In front of my men?" John said almost in a whisper. His

eyes narrowed. "You dare to disrespect your mother in front of my men?"

"I said I'm sorry."

"You will be," John nodded. "I can't believe the mess you've made, retard."

"I had no choice but to sort them out. Did I, Geoff?"

All eyes turned to a slightly built man who was looking out of the window, his back turned to the gathering. Geoff looked out over the river. The ferries were crossing at the middle point of the river and the passengers of both waved to each other like long lost friends and a huge cruise ship sat regally as its cargo of tourists disembarked onto the Pierhead. "I told you to leave well alone until John got back off holiday." Geoff turned to face them. His tanned features were creased by five decades of crime and his grey Armani suit hung open over a crisp white shirt. A gold chain shimmered where a tie might sit. The stylish look was in keeping with the other older men, who looked on anxiously. Bren and Gary looked scruffy amongst them. "In fact, we all told you to leave Keegan and the woman alone, but you ignored our advice. Gary was warned too."

"It wasn't you lot that the police were following, was it?" Bren protested. "That bitch was going to go to the police with what she knew about Keegan and that would have led back to us."

"All the more reason to lie low, you fool," Geoff growled. His dark eyes burrowed into him. "Now it's just a matter of time before they come knocking on our door."

"You still haven't answered my question," John interrupted. "Where is Lacey Taylor?"

Gary and Bren swapped nervous glances but neither spoke. Bren sighed and stood up. "I buried her myself. She's further down the beach. A lot further down."

"At Crosby?" John snapped, his eyes widening. "Right near Keegan's body? Under the noses of the police sniffer dogs?"

"About a mile into the dunes," Bren muttered. "It was dark and pissing down with rain. She was heavy but she's far enough away for them not to find her."

"So she's buried a stone's throw away from where the police are searching?"

"A stone's throw?" Bren snapped. "She's a mile away at least!"

"In an area where the police have dogs searching?" John had a look of disdain on his face. "You retard."

"Don't call me that. They won't look that far away," Bren said defiantly. "It was just unlucky that they found a dead body near the pond."

"Bullshit!" John shouted. "My source at Canning Place tells me that they went there to search on the back of a tip-off."

"What tip-off?" Bren protested.

"You tell me, you retard," John snapped and pointed his finger at Bren. "What could possibly have alerted the MIT to search there?"

"I don't know."

"You made a mistake," his father said calmly. "What was it?"

"I don't know," Bren looked at Gary for help but he was still enthralled by his training shoes desperately trying to avoid making eye contact with John Ryder. "Can you think of anything, Gary?"

"No," he muttered. His voice trembled. "We even went back in the daylight to make sure we hadn't left anything behind."

"And?"

"Nothing."

"So you went back and checked that nothing was obviously amiss?"

"Yes."

"Then what tipped the police off?"

"Nothing, John honestly," Gary rambled. "I must have dropped the dog's collar cause we found that near the pond but we made it right and dumped it, didn't we, Bren. So it can't have been that."

"Oh, for fuck's sake," Bren whispered. "I told you to shut your mouth."

"You found what dog's collar?" John's eyes narrowed. The tension in the room was palpable.

"The bitch had a dog," Bren muttered. "We must have dropped the collar when we carried her through the dunes."

"And you recovered it the next day?"

"Yes. Gary picked it up in the dunes then we went back to the pond. We checked that Keegan's body was weighted properly. It was. There was no sign of anything untoward."

"Where did you dump the collar?"

"In a litter bin," Gary announced proudly. The looks he received from the others silenced him quickly. "I made sure it was underneath all the crap, honestly."

"Please tell me that you didn't dump it in a bin near the pond." John Ryder stood up angrily. He walked over to where Gary stood. "Look me in the eyes and tell me that you didn't dump it near to the pond."

"I didn't know, Dad," Bren stuttered. "I didn't know he'd dumped it there until we were ten miles down the road."

"Did it have a tag on it?"

"What?"

"Was it engraved with her name and address?"

"I don't know," Gary mumbled. "There was some writing on it but I can't read."

"Did you go back when you realised what he had done?" John turned to his stepson.

"Yes."

"And?"

"It was gone."

John Ryder slapped Bren hard with an open hand. His face darkened where the blow struck, a bruise formed immediately. "You bloody idiot. That's how the police were tipped off. Someone found the collar and took it to the police."

"I didn't know until it was too late." Bren whimpered. "It was him. He fucked it up. Like I said, we were miles down the road when I asked him what he had done with it. We went straight back."

"This is a mess." John Ryder shook his head. "Your mother will crucify me if you end up in clink. They will connect the collar with Taylor and they may have a witness to connect you to the collar."

"Wait a minute. Let's calm down. The only evidence which puts them at the scene is the collar," Geoff spoke clearly. "We have to assume that whoever took it to the police can place them at the scene. Find them and there's no credible evidence to link them to the murder of Keegan, apart from each other."

"Assuming that they don't find Lacey Taylor," John added.

"Of course. The only other person who can put Bren at the scene is Gary," Geoff pointed to him. He gestured with his head and two of the onlookers moved towards him. One stood behind him the other stood at his side. "Gary is the only witness."

"I won't say anything, John!" Gary panicked. "I swear to God that I won't say anything. Bren is my mate."

"Have you talked to anybody about this?"

"No!"

"You haven't told anyone else about any of this?"

"No, honestly." Gary protested. "I wouldn't say anything!"

"Sorry, Gary but we don't do mistakes." John shook his head. "You've left me with no choice."

"I promise, John!" His plea was cut short by a thick forearm which encircled his throat from behind. The pressure on his larynx was unbearable and it was all he could do to gasp before his windpipe was crushed. He felt himself lifted from the floor and his head was jerked sharply to the left. His feet danced in the air for a second. There was a brief flash of red hot pain at the base of his skull as he felt his neck snap and then there was nothing.

"Get rid of him," Geoff ordered. The limp body was carried from the room into a wide hallway while arrangements for its disposal were made. "Now then, Bren, you need to remember everything that you can about Crosby Beach. We need to find out who saw you there and you will tell me the exact spot where Lacey Taylor is buried. Understand?"

Brendon Ryder nodded as he watched his best friend being dragged across a blue Wilton carpet and his legs began to tremble. He knew that the only reason he was alive was because his stepfather saw fit to let him live, but there was no guarantee that he would maintain that point of view for the foreseeable future.

Chapter 13

"Hello, Janice, thanks for coming to talk to us. I'm Detective Inspector Annie Jones," she said, holding out her right hand. Janice shook her hand feebly, uncomfortable at being in close proximity of the law, especially another female. It never bothered her that the male officers knew that she was a brass but it mattered when they were female. "The Vice Squad is helping us to look for missing women and they said that one of your friends hasn't been seen for a few days," Annie said, noting that they were in the same interview room where Richard Tibbs had sat. "There's no need to be nervous. We just need you to tell us what you told Vice today."

"Is Tasha in danger?"

"Yes, she is," Annie nodded. "Do you know her surname?"

"No," Janice blushed. "It's not something we do out there, swap names, I mean."

"I understand. We've found the bodies of several women buried on Crosby Beach and we think they may be working girls."

"Like Tasha?"

"Exactly like Tasha."

"Oh God," Janice sighed. "Is she one of them?"

"No," Stirling answered. "All the bodies that we have found have been there too long, but that doesn't mean that she's not in trouble."

"You said Tasha went missing the night before last." Annie checked the statement. "Tuesday night, right?"

"Right," Janice nodded. "I haven't seen her since and neither have the other girls. We knocked on her flat too. She wasn't in. She never goes anywhere, so I knew that she had been taken."

"Vice forced the door of her flat an hour ago," Stirling said solemnly. "There's no sign of her."

"What can you tell us about that night?" Annie asked.

"I knew he wasn't right," Janice said quietly. "I should never have let her go with him."

"With who?"

"The bloke I told the coppers about." Janice looked from Annie to Stirling for their reaction. "The bloke with the bug eyes, in the white van."

"Tell me about him."

"When I first saw him, he had sunglasses on and a black beanie hat," Janice recalled. "He took the glasses off and those eyes!"

"You said they bulged," Annie asked confused.

"Yes. Almost like a cartoon."

"And he was white?"

"Yes." She thought about it. "Maybe olive skinned."

"About thirty, you said?"

"I'm guessing, but yes."

"You've never seen him before?"

"No," Janice shivered inside. "I would remember those eyes."

"You said the van was a Ford Transit?" Stirling asked.

"Yes. A white one."

"They're all white aren't they?" Annie grinned.

"Don't think they make any other colour," Janice chuckled.

"And the detective from vice said that you can remember something about the number plate?"

"Yes," Janice blushed. "STD. Has a special meaning to us girls." Annie and Stirling exchanged glances and smiled. "I can't remember it all. I'm thick as pig shit, but I remember that much." Janice looked sad for a moment. "I told her that just before she got into that van."

"What?"

"I told her that I was thick as pig shit."

"You liked her?"

"She was okay."

"We'll find her if she's out there."

"I hope so," Janice smiled. "She wants to go back to nursing college."

Annie didn't think that she would but there was always hope while there wasn't a body. "Can you think of any other girls who have disappeared in the last twelve months?"

"How long have you got?" Janice rolled her eyes skyward. "Girls come and go every week." She shrugged and held out her hands. "One minute they're there and the next, they're gone. Some of them turn up and some don't."

"It's a transient workforce," Stirling commented.

"A what?"

"Never mind," Stirling muttered.

"I told you I'm thick as pig shit."

"We don't think you're thick, Janice," Stirling said guiltily.

Janice eyed him but felt unsure about the sincerity in his voice. "Look, most of the girls on the game are junkies. They need money but the job isn't for everyone. Some girls can handle it, others can't."

"How do you mean?" Annie asked.

"Well, there was a mate of mine, Alice," Janice began. "I didn't see her for three months and then I bumped into her in a hotel near Chester. I was working a private gig, you know, a hotel visit and there she was sitting in the restaurant with some guy old enough to be her father. She had a wedding ring on. I would have said hello but I didn't want to drop her in it, you know."

"Could have been embarrassing," Annie agreed.

"Very," Janice joked. "Who is your friend? Oh, we were on the game together in Liverpool!"

"Not a good start to a new marriage."

"No."

"A happy ending for her though, eh?"

"Not really," Janice looked at her hands, a faraway look on her face.

"Why don't you think so?"

"She is still going to bed with someone she doesn't love and isn't attracted to for money, no matter how you dress it up." A narrow smile crossed her lips. "She's still on the game and she knows it."

"But if you had time to think about it properly," Stirling pushed the issue. "Do you think you could remember the names of any girls who simply vanished and no one heard from again?"

"Maybe."

"We need you to try."

"Okay, I'll have a think."

"Anything else that you can remember about that van, anything at all?" Stirling asked.

"There was a wheel trim missing." Janice's eyes closed as if she was picturing the scene. She smiled widely and looked at Annie. "I think that they only make wheel trims in sets of three."

"You're right," Annie laughed. "There's always one missing."

"I hope that I can help you find Tasha."

"Good. What you have told us helps," Annie coached. "Which trim was missing?"

"Rear driver's side."

Annie stood up from the table and smiled. "I'm going to send someone down here with descriptions of the women that we've found. I want you to have a good look at them and see if they ring any bells, okay?"

"Okay," Janice nodded. "Will it take long?"

"Shouldn't do why?"

"I'm broke," Janice shrugged her shoulders and looked at the table. "I need to get to work."

"Janice," Annie frowned, "there's a psycho out there taking women off the streets. Give it a miss for a while until we catch him."

"I can't afford to," Janice said quietly. "I don't claim benefits. Grafting is the only income that I have."

"It's dangerous," Stirling said concerned.

"It's always dangerous, Sergeant," Janice smiled. She was flattered by his concern. He was her type, big and mean. "Thanks for your concern but I need to go to work."

"Not today," Annie said as she opened the door. "We'll make sure that you get enough to cover your earnings for the next few days. We need you to look at the e-fits okay?"

"Oh, okay." Janice smiled widely. "Thank you!"

"Thank you for coming in," Stirling said. "I know how hard it is for you to talk to us." Their eyes met and lingered for a second. Something registered. In a different time and another place, there could have been something between them. "You've been very helpful. Wait here."

Chapter 14

Tasha looked around the cellar and tried to remain calm. Her grip on the sharp implements which she held in her hands was so tight that her knuckles were white. The floor was made of concrete. There were no trapdoors or hatches. Although the walls were plastered, behind it they were solid brick, no plasterboard or stud walling. She didn't know much about construction but the only way to enter the room was from above. Tasha strained her neck to follow the rafters from one end of the room to the other. Sure enough, in the far right corner, the rafters were cut. There were dark hinges screwed onto the floorboards above. The hatch above was her only way out but it was also her abductor's way in. It was too high for her to reach, even if she stood on the trolley and there was no handle to pull it down. The only way to open it was from above.

She sank to her knees and tried to calm herself. Her breathing was fast and shallow. It was cool but perspiration formed on her back regardless, making her feel clammy and uncomfortable. There was no sound from above; no television or radio, footsteps or voices. She thought about screaming for help but she had to assume that whoever lived in the building above knew that she was in the cellar. They had either carried out, or were party to her arrest. Passers-by wouldn't hear her. She was sure of that. Her captor would have gagged her and tied her up if there was any chance of her attracting attention by screaming. It was probably a remote location. All she could achieve by screaming was alerting her kidnapper that she was conscious. She had choices to make. Wait for him to return and submit or fight, or she could use the blades on her veins and end it herself.

A tiny red light caught her eye. It was to the right of the hatch. He was watching her on camera, or maybe it was to record whatever he did to women in the basement with his surgical tools, probably both. Either way it sent ice cold fear racing through her veins, chilling her to the bone. The urge to pee was becoming more urgent than the urge to vomit. The urge to scream was overwhelmingly at the top of the urge list but peeing was accelerating fast and ready to overtake on the inside rail. She squeezed her thighs together and tried to force it from her mind. Screaming was useless. She needed to maintain her strength for the fight with her attacker. It was inevitable that he would come back and when he did, she would use every ounce of energy that she had left to escape. He would have to kill her to hurt her. Tasha had decided that compliance wasn't an option this time. This wasn't her stepfather with his twisted version of affection and sickening sexual fantasies. Nor was it an inebriated punter acting out his urges to rape and abuse; she could switch off for them but not this. She couldn't hide in the dark recesses of her mind while a lunatic played doctors with a scalpel. Whatever he had planned, she wasn't playing. While she still had breath in her lungs, she would fight. She had been an athlete at school. Her genes were from Jamaica, gifting her with lean powerful limbs. She wasn't as fit as she had been but she could summon enough strength to plunge a pair of scissors deep into her attacker's eye socket or to slash his jugular vein with the scalpel. The nightmare she would suffer if she failed would add strength to her struggle. She felt comfort from the weapons that she held and they gave her hope. Slim fragile hope, but hope in any guise was welcome. Although empowered by sharp steel, she still needed to pee. The thought of wetting herself during the imminent battle made up her mind. She had to satisfy the burning urge.

Tasha shuffled into the corner beneath the camera. She pulled her thong down her thighs and sighed as she released the offending liquid. The splashing noise sounded deafening against the silence and the warm aroma of urine drifted to her. She was nearly finished when she heard a noise above. Despite the pressure from her bladder, the jet of urine stopped in a millisecond as she clenched tight. She listened intently. Footsteps. Not directly above but definitely in the building above. They were tentative footsteps. Someone above was nervous, unsure and listening as intently as she was.

"Hello," a man's voice called. It was a cautious call; searching and unsure if there was anybody there. It was the type of call people on the television made when a mad axe-man was hiding nearby. The type of 'hello' that the caller didn't want an answer to. "Hello." She heard it again, closer this time. He was uncertain and hesitant, yet he was searching. Tasha wanted to scream out for help but fear gripped her. "Hello."

There was no reply, no second set of footsteps heading towards the first. There was almost an echo, not quite but almost as if the rooms above were spacious but not cavernous. If she could hear him then he would be able to hear her.

"Hello," the voice grew louder. "Is anybody there?" The footsteps were at the far end of the room. "Mister Weston, are you there?"

Tasha realised that whoever he was, he was looking for the occupier, her kidnapper. She pulled up her underwear and screamed at the top of her voice.

Chapter 15

The MIT office was only half full but it was a hive of activity nonetheless. The investigation was picking up momentum as leads turned up names, and names turned into results which could be explored, verified or discounted. The press had been informed that a number of bodies had been recovered from the area around Crosby Beach. One of the local journals broke the news with the headline, 'Butcher of Crosby Beach Slaughters Five', which began an international media frenzy that gained momentum by the hour. When two more bodies were discovered, the attention intensified. Crowds of reporters gathered at the entrance roads to the beaches, held back by uniformed officers. Some of the more enterprising hacks hired rowing boats and motor cruisers to take pictures of the forensic operation from the sea. Detective Superintendent Alec Ramsay had been appointed as the senior detective. He had been a week into a joint taskforce meeting of Interpol with his foreign counterparts in London when the case broke and now, he was struggling to keep up with the details. Annie had relayed what they knew but the scale of the investigation meant that it was an uncontrollable beast which needed to be reined in quickly. Alec ran his fingers through his greying sandy hair and studied the detectives in the room. They were the cream of the division, handpicked from every department to work on the case. Happy with the quality of the team, he listened as another briefing began.

"Charlie Keegan was forty years old," Stirling talked excitedly to the remnants of the team who were in the office. The majority were out and about chasing information across the city. "We have circulated his record; you should all have a copy to hand." Stirling looked around as nodding heads confirmed that copies had been distributed. "He fronted a property development company, New

Generation Holdings. They specialise in buying up property and land, which local governments can't afford to keep on, parks, schools, libraries, community centres and the like."

"They fund projects such as youth clubs in the more deprived areas of the city, which looks good on paper, but what they're actually doing is snapping up real estate," Annie added.

"Vulture capitalists," Alec joked. A ripple of laughter spread through the crowd. "Is it a legitimate operation?"

"That is where Keegan gets interesting, Guv," Annie carried on. "Over the last six months, there've been a number of allegations about bribes being taken, especially over property grants in the more affluent areas like Woolton and Mossley Hill."

"The real estate value of a school with playing fields in those areas would run into the millions." Alec shrugged. His wrinkles deepened as a wry smile crossed his lips. "You could build ten, five bedroom houses on a decent sized plot like a library; fifty on a school playing field. Who owns the company?"

"Keegan was a director," Stirling explained, "we're checking Companies House for the other directors' names but so far, all we have are a number of shell companies registered in Russia."

"There were a number of high profile campaigns, which ran to stop the sale of public land." Annie flicked images from protests onto the screens. "A Facebook campaign reached a million likes and a petition with a hundred thousand signatures was handed into the Town Hall last month. Have a guess who led the campaigns."

"Lacey Taylor," Alec answered. "She was all over the television trying to stop the sale of that special school in Woolton."

"Correct," Annie said as the images changed again. "So we have Keegan, tortured and decapitated and Lacey Taylor is missing.

She ran the campaigns against Keegan's acquisitions and now we have to assume they're both dead."

"And your informant, Richard Tibbs?" Alec prompted.

"He saw two men walking near the pond where we found Keegan and he saw one of them stuff the dog collar into a litter bin, here." Stirling pointed to a photo of the area. "The collar belongs to Lacey Taylor's dog. Her family has verified that much. Tibbs told us that one of the men bears a strong family resemblance to John Ryder."

"Could he actually be a relative?" Alec asked.

"Ryder doesn't have any kids." Annie smiled.

"Sounds like there's a 'but' coming."

"But he is married to his brother's widow, Laura Ryder and she has a son, Brendon. John Ryder is stepfather to his brother's son."

"Keeping it in the family?" Alec grunted.

"The brother, James, died in suspicious circumstances when Brendon was a toddler." Stirling pointed to the crime scene images. "His body was washed up near the airport. From the time of death and the internal injuries found on the victim, it was deemed that he jumped from Runcorn Bridge the day before he was found."

"What's the mystery?" Alec opened his top button and slipped off his grey suit jacket. The back of his shirt was un-ironed. Since his wife died, only the front was ironed properly. The backs were skimmed over at best. "Was foul play considered?"

"He was wealthy, healthy and had no enemies." Annie raised her eyebrows and smiled. "The Ryder brothers inherited a substantial property portfolio when their parents died in ninety-nine. Laura inherited James's share when he 'jumped' from the bridge."

"The postmortem showed bruising to the upper arms, consistent with being restrained and lifted and there were traces of an adhesive residue on his top lip," Stirling explained, "but the suicide note was deemed as genuine and he'd been to see his GP the week prior complaining of anxiety and insomnia. The coroner ruled it as suicide."

"And then John marries her and gets the lot." Alec frowned and deep lines creased his forehead. "Can we link the Ryders to New Generation Holdings?"

"We're looking into it," Annie nodded. "If there's a link, we'll find it, not that that would give us grounds for arrest but we could question them."

"I'm not prepared to wait." Alec rubbed the dimple on his chin. "Bring the stepson in," Alec ordered. "Put him in a line-up and see if Tibbs can identify him."

"He won't agree to a line-up, Guv." Annie shook her head. "We've got nothing on him and if John Ryder gets a sniff of what we're doing, he'll have him out of the country in a second. He has property all over the place."

"Maybe you're right. A drawn out extradition battle will make us look incompetent. Okay, if we can't put him in a line-up, find him for an informal chat," Alec suggested, "and make sure Tibbs gets to see his picture in the office somewhere. If he recognises him then at least we know we're on the right track."

"You know that we can't use his evidence?"

"Yes but if we shake their tree, something might fall out." Alec pointed to Stirling. "Send Jim. He's got the tact of a wrecking ball. If anyone can provoke a response, it'll be him."

"Thanks, Guv. I'll take that as a compliment."

"You're welcome, but it wasn't meant as a compliment."

"I'll get on it now, Guv," Stirling said smiling. Although they had nothing to hold Brendon Ryder on, he was itching to make an arrest and question him. The DS had given a green light and that was all he needed. He picked up his leather jacket and tapped a DC on the shoulder. They headed for the lifts with a purpose. "I'll arrange for uniform to pick up Tibbs on the way, Guv."

Alec knew that he was treading on thin ice but he had to give his detectives as much rope as he could without hanging them. "Okay, Inspector," he turned back to Annie and clapped his hands together. "What have we got on the prawns?"

"Guv!" she chided. Another ripple spread through the room. "Am I the only one not calling them prawns?"

"Until we've got some names," Alec shrugged. "What have we got?"

"Seven victims in various stages of decay." Annie flicked a series of images onto the screens. "Kathy is estimating that the oldest body was buried two years ago, possibly longer. The most recent is this one here, which we found first near the car park. She'd been there over a month but not much more than that."

"All buried alive?"

"Yes."

"We have no identities yet?"

"No but we have three, who match names and descriptions on the missing persons' lists. We're crosschecking DNA where we can. I'm hoping that we'll have names later today."

"What about this missing girl?"

"Tasha James." Annie brought up another image. "She was last seen getting into a van. We have traffic looking for a white Ford van with STD on the number plate." She looked towards DC Mason, who was taking a call. She nodded and gave a thumbs-up signal. "They think it's registered to a hire company in Huyton. They're coming back with a name any minute now."

"We've got an address, Guv," Mason grinned. She scribbled the number down. "One, six, three Breck Road. The van's registered to a Mark Weston. He's got no priors."

Alec and Annie exchanged worried glances. It was an exciting breakthrough. Having no priors didn't mean much when dealing with a serial. They couldn't take any chances. "Take armed backup and see what Mr Weston has to say for himself," Alec said concerned. "Find Tasha Jenkins and take her home."

"Get a uniformed unit from the area to cruise by and see if the van is there," Annie ordered. "Put a unit on the rear of the house too. Tell them we'll be fifteen minutes and I want to know what we're dealing with before we get there, okay?"

"Guv."

"I'll call in as soon as we have anything," she said to Alec as she walked away. "My team with me. Let's go."

Chapter 16

Francis Grant nearly jumped out of his skin when the screaming started. Although it was muffled, it was definitely close by, in the house; probably below him. It was high pitched, ear-splitting, desperate screaming. Someone was terrified and screaming for help at the very top of their vocal range. He froze as he tried to pinpoint where it was coming from. The screams seemed to grow louder and more desperate. He took one step into the living room and listened again. It was coming from beneath him. The room had high ceilings and ornate plaster coving as did all houses from that era. A bare light bulb hung from a fancy ceiling rose, which deserved a chandelier. He searched the wall for the switch but couldn't find it; his fingers stroked bare plaster. His imagination pictured barbed wire and broken glass and razorblades waiting to puncture his fingertips. His mind played tricks on him while fear grabbed him from within.

On the occasions he'd been before, he'd never noticed details like that but now he wished that he had. He peered behind a dark panelled door but saw nothing but shadows. The heavy curtains were closed. It smelled of damp, dust and mothballs but there was something else too, something rotten. The place gave him the creeps. The owners wanted the building put on the market and he could see why. The string of recent tenants had neglected the house. It was a decaying hovel and its value was depreciating rapidly as the area became less desirable. He was the junior estate agent and always pulled the crappy jobs. This one wasn't just crap, it was frightening. He glanced over his shoulder at the hallway. Although it was dark there too, it seemed preferable to stepping into the living room. His brain told him to go back out of the front door, telephone the police and hand in his notice, but the girl's screams mesmerised him. How could he walk out without helping? It should have been easy enough to do. Francis was the first to shout at the television when a character was heading for the darkness where the deranged killer was hiding with a drill or a chainsaw. 'Why would they do that? I would run and call the police.' But here he was, faced with an empty hovel and a woman screaming in the cellar. His instincts said run as fast as you can, but he just couldn't leave without at least trying to help. He took a sharp breath, reached around the door and fumbled for the light switch. His fingers touched a brass plate, its coldness felt soothing against his sweaty palm. He slid his index finger across the metal until it reached the rocker but he hesitated when the screaming stopped. He paused, held his breath and waited for a sound. Maybe he had imagined it.

"Please help me," she screamed again. He could hear her words clearly. This was the real deal and the woman was distraught.

"Where are you?" he called back.

"I'm in the cellar."

"Are you hurt?"

"Yes," she shouted. Her voice was garbled. "He hit me with a Taser. Please get me out of here."

"I'll call the police." Francis reached for his mobile and dialled nine, nine, nine. His phone displayed that there was no signal. "Shit, shit," he hissed. "How did you get down there?"

"I don't know. Please hurry up!"

"Are there any stairs?"

"No," she shouted.

"No stairs," he whispered. "How the hell do I get down there then?" He felt for the switch again. He reached the rocker and his fingers scrambled to press it. "Come on, switch on for God's sake," he muttered. The bulb flickered into life and cast a dull light around the room. The darkness receded but not far enough to make him feel comfortable.

"There's a hatch in the corner above where I am," she shouted. "Get me out before he comes back please."

He looked towards where her voice emanated from. A beige three-seater occupied the centre of the room. The seat cushions were stained dark where it was most worn; the stuffing flattened unevenly. To the left, a matching armchair was pushed back against the wall. The arms had been blackened over decades by an army of sweaty hands and a dark black stain had spread from the seat down to the floor as if a tacky fluid had been spilled and allowed to dry. It could have been blood, but then it could have been blackcurrant cordial too. Whatever it was, it was years old. It seemed to belong to the room. Filth and grime, stains and odours were all in keeping with the decor. They belonged there. There were no pictures or paintings, photographs or mirrors on the walls. They were bare and cold looking. Dark scuff marks gathered on the plaster around the armchair and Francis couldn't help but liken them to claw marks. Maybe the girl had been dragged into the cellar kicking and screaming for her life. Maybe she wasn't the first. Looking at the number of scratches and their positions, there had been many. A shiver ran down his spine as he envisaged them, naked and bleeding, bloody, battered and bruised as a demon sucked them down into the depths. Razor sharp teeth cut through flesh and bones, muscle and intestines splattering the walls with visceral matter. He saw their nails splitting and breaking as they clawed at the walls, desperate to escape what awaited them in the cellar. His imagination taunted him with images from his worst nightmares and her screams fuelled his imagination further. He couldn't move from the spot.

"Please hurry up," she screamed more urgently this time. "Please!"

"I'm coming," Francis mumbled. He looked at his mobile again, as if by some magic, it might have picked up a signal. No signal. He was reluctant to step further into the room. It was as if an invisible rope was clipped to his belt, stopping him from going any further. He swallowed hard, his throat dry and his senses ultra-aware. The hairs on the back of his neck prickled like tiny spines, each one sending its own message to his brain, run, run, run; their message as urgent as the girl's yet far more malevolent. His feet felt encased in concrete; his brain numbed by fear. He was acutely aware that the woman was in danger yet he couldn't do anything to help her. The same malignant evil that she felt threatened him too. It blocked the receptors in his limbs, forbidding him to move forward. Although he couldn't understand the terror that gripped him, he couldn't deny its existence. He took one last glance at his mobile. No signal.

"Can you see the hatch?" She shouted. "Oh God, please hurry up. Please hurry!"

Her voice was so desperate, so scared that he felt sickened by her fear. Despite his empathy, he couldn't move. "I can't see the hatch," he lied. From the position of her voice, he guessed the hatch was beneath the armchair. It would explain its odd position in the room. "I'm going to phone the police but I'll have to go outside. I won't be a minute."

"No, no, no!" the voice screamed. It was bloodcurdling to hear. "Don't leave me!" Her voice reached a new crescendo. Her words were thick with phlegm. "Please don't leave me down here!"

"Oh, Jesus," he whispered to himself. Her screaming became an incoherent babble. "Pull yourself together, Francis." He took a hesitant step into the room. Then another. Behind the door was an open fireplace with a slate mantelpiece. The grate was empty; the tiles covered in soot. It hadn't warmed this place for many years. Francis doubted that even if the fire did roar again, the heat would be sucked out of the building, along with the light and the oxygen and the hope.

That's what was missing from this place, light and hope; replaced by fear and malevolence.

"Please help me!"

He stepped in further. Six inches, no more and looked around again. A second armchair sat adjacent to the fireplace and a threadbare rug covered the hearth.

"Oh, God help me, please help me," her desperation increased. He could feel it in her voice; sense it in the air. The very atmosphere was tainted with desolation. His chest felt tight and he struggled to get oxygen into his lungs. The room was empty except for the three-piece suite.

"Don't leave me down here, please!"

He took a deep breath and walked across the room, each step almost painful. It felt as if the floor would open up and swallow him, or a giant mantrap would snap shut and sever his foot at the ankle. Fear gripped him like a giant icy hand. The anticipation of something dreadful about to happen was suffocating. "I'm coming," he rasped, his voice restricted. "I'm coming," he tried harder. "Hang on!"

"Please hurry!"

He reached the armchair and dragged it away from the wall. The castors beneath squeaked against the bare floorboards, scoring the wood as he pulled.

"I can hear you," she shouted. "I'm down here right underneath you!"

Sure enough, there was a hatch cut into the floorboards. Francis ran his fingers around the edge. Cool air from the cellar touched his skin. He pulled his hand back as if shocked by electricity or white hot metal. The evil beneath was tangible. He could almost taste the decay, smell the decomposition and hear the voices of the dead. He felt their anguish and hopelessness, yet his limbs failed him. He couldn't run from the despondency no matter how powerful the desire to leave.

"Let me out," her voice rocked him back to reality. "For God's sake get me out of here, please!"

"I'm trying," Francis lied again. "Stay calm!" He studied the hatch and his heart quickened. A heavy bolt fastened it and a thick padlock held the bolt locked. There was no way to move it without the key to the padlock. "Shit, shit, shit," he shouted. He wiped perspiration from his brow.

"What are you waiting for? Hurry up, please!"

"I can't."

"What do you mean? Help me!"

"I can't," he shouted louder.

"Please get me out," her voice was laced with panic. "He has scalpels down here. He's going to hurt me, please!"

"Jesus!" Who has scalpels in the cellar? His mind raced. Who has scalpels anywhere, for God's sake?

"Get me out. Why can't you just get me out?"

"It's locked," he shouted. "I'll have to go and call the police!"

"No, please don't leave me!"

"I'll be two minutes," he felt sickened leaving her there. He could feel her fear through the floor. "I promise that I won't be long."

"No!"

"I'll find a signal outside and call the police," he shouted. "Hang on there."

"Oh, God please don't leave me here," she wailed. The sound was heartbreaking. "Please don't let him hurt me, please!"

"I'll be quick," he shouted. "I'll call them and come back until they arrive."

"Promise me!"

"I promise."

Francis turned away from the hatch. As he did, fifty thousand volts entered his body via the skin on his neck. His teeth felt as if they were on fire, as electricity arced between them like tiny bolts of lightning. He saw evil bulging eyes staring at him. Despite the malice in them, they seemed to be smiling. The smell of his flesh cooking was the last thing his senses registered before they shut down completely.

Chapter 17

Richard Tibbs knew that he was being followed. He had served long enough in the military to spot surveillance from a mile away. It was decades since his service days but some things never fade. His body was weakened by age and rotted by alcohol, but he could function when he needed to. Adrenalin flooded into his veins. It made him feel alert and alive. He switched lanes and the tail followed suit. They cut up the vehicle behind them and Tibbs heard the horn blaring loudly three times. Headlights flashed and the driver shook a fist. As the tail closed the gap, Tibbs switched lanes again and took a left turn into a cul-de-sac. He pulled up onto the kerb and waited for the vehicle to follow. The rear view mirror remained empty. He thought that he might be being paranoid.

He waited another minute and then put the Volvo in first gear, ambling to the end of the close before turning around and heading back towards the main carriageway. The Jeep was stationary in a bus stop, waiting for him to emerge; so much for paranoia. Tibbs wasn't sure if they were being purposely obvious or if they were just stupid. He turned left onto the main road and pulled into the traffic. At the next set of lights, he made a u-turn on the dual carriageway, cut across two lanes of rush hour traffic and pulled into the drive-thru lane of McDonald's. The Cherokee Jeep made the same manoeuvre and pulled into a parking bay near the exit. The driver left the engine running and pretended to read a newspaper. His passenger was making a call on his mobile. This convinced Tibbs that his hunch was a fact. They were tailing him and there was no doubt about it.

He moved forward one car length and waited for his turn at the speaker box. There were several scenarios to consider. Number one was the police may be following him because a sex offence had been committed locally and he was a suspect because he was on the register. It was plausible but unlikely. If he was a suspect, then they would have stopped him and questioned him without wasting time to see where he was going.

"Welcome to McDonald's Hunts Cross," a metallic voice greeted him. "May I take your order please?"

"I'll have a coffee please." Tibbs glanced at the Jeep. The driver stared over the top of the newspaper watching him intently. Both men in the vehicle were suited but they weren't the police. The worst detectives on the force would do a better job of following him without being spotted. They were amateurs.

"What type?"

"What," Tibbs asked confused.

"What type of coffee?"

"What do you have?"

"Americano, expresso, latte, mocha and cappuccino."

"Oh," Tibbs realised his mistake. "Latte please."

"Large?"

"What?"

"Is that a large Latte?"

"Yes, yes, whatever."

"Would you like any food with that, apple pie or chocolate do-nut?"

"Oh for God's sake!" Tibbs snapped. "Just the coffee!"

"Thank you for using the drive-thru, please pay at the first window."

Tibbs pushed the Volvo into first gear and trundled to the first window where a pretty teenager greeted him with a sour expression. She had headphones on and was obviously taking the next order from a customer with better manners than he had displayed. She slapped his change into his palm without offering any further directions to the next window. He hardly noticed her offence, he focused on the men in the Cherokee and tried to fathom who they were. Another possibility was that they were reporters from the local press. They could have been tipped off by someone at the police station that he was a witness in the Crosby Beach murders. After all, it was his evidence that had prompted the police to search the area. The discovery of dead women was all over the news. Unfortunately, the lack of details, victims' names and grieving relatives had left a news black-hole. There was a total void of information, which forced reporters to speculate and interview anyone remotely connected to the area. When situations like this arose, reporters often paid well for the names of anyone linked to the investigation. It wasn't a huge leap of belief that a junior officer had tipped off the press with his name. It was possible but again unlikely. Reporters rarely travelled in twos and the men looked more like enforcers than paparazzi.

"One large Latte," another voice chirped as a purple cup was shoved towards his face. "Any sugar?"

"Do you get paid more for every question you ask?" Tibbs snapped. His pulse quickened as he thought about the final scenario. He pulled away slowly and slipped the coffee into a holder on the dashboard.

"Arsehole," he heard the presenter mumble. On another occasion he would have been offended. This time around, he didn't have time to be offended. His initial concern when he went to the police with his information had been identifying one of the men as being a relation to John Ryder. He had mulled it over a thousand times. His apprehension had been derived from his experience throughout life. If you expect the worse possible outcome to happen, then double its impact and you won't be disappointed when you're up to your neck in shit.

The men in the Jeep were gangsters connected to John Ryder. They had to be. Tibbs had no choice. Now he was convinced that they were enforcers and that they were following him, he had no options. During his tour of Iraq, he had been followed many times. He had been trained to identify a tail and then to respond aggressively. A tail would wait until the target reached an unpopulated area and then strike. He couldn't allow that to happen. He was unarmed and he couldn't fight the men. If he went home, they would follow him. If he tried to outrun them, they would catch him. His experience and training kicked in and he did the only thing that he could do. One thing was certain, they wouldn't expect it.

Tibbs revved the engine and steered the Volvo at the Jeep. The tyres squealed as the vehicle hurtled towards his target. He noted the expression of surprised panic on the faces of the men in the Cherokee and it made him smile. A moment before impact, he took his hands from the wheel so that his arms wouldn't break; he closed his eyes and waited for the brutal collision to come.

Chapter 18

Francis Grant woke up with a start. Cold water filled his mouth and nostrils. He choked and tried to wipe his face but his arms were fixed behind his back. The shock of the cold water took his breath away. He tried to kick out and stand up but his ankles were bound too. At first he was confused. What had happened? His mind blocked the memories as long as it could to protect him but as his senses returned, the images came back like an icicle slicing through his brain. Cold stabbing fear penetrated his consciousness.

"Wake up!" A hard slap accompanied the demand. "Wake up!" Louder this time. Francis opened his eyes and recoiled when he saw the face before him. The man had prominent staring eyes, which were odd. Francis remembered his Auntie Jo, who had Graves disease. Her eyes bulged like his. It was a problem created by a diseased thyroid gland, or at least that's what he thought his mother had told him. He loved Auntie Jo but her eyes forced him to stare at her, which provoked several sly digs to the back of his head from his mother. It seemed so long ago. He was sitting awkwardly in the armchair near the fireplace. The smell of cinders lingered.

"What's your name?" Another hard slap. The stinging pain mingled with a burning sensation beneath his chin where the Taser hit him.

"Francis." Francis tasted blood in his mouth. The inside of his cheek had split against a tooth. He wanted to spit but he daren't. "Francis Grant."

"What are you doing here, Francis Grant?" The unblinking eyes seemed to look inside his head for the answer. Lying seemed pointless as he had done nothing wrong; nothing, except discovering that a woman was being held captive in the cellar.

"Burnells sent me," Francis stuttered. "They sent you four letters to arrange access but they didn't receive any reply. They sent me here to gain access."

"Burnells?"

"The letting agency," Francis nodded. "The owners want to sell the property but we couldn't get hold of you. They sent me to measure up."

"What did the girl say to you?" The man's voice was calm but laced with suspicion.

"Nothing," Francis mumbled. It had gone quiet in the cellar. He wondered what had happened to her. Had he slit her throat or gagged her, or knocked her out with the stun gun? The poor woman had been terrified and he had done nothing but dither and pee his pants. He hadn't peed his pants but he may as well have. It would have been more useful if he had run out of the house. At least he could have phoned the police and he wouldn't be trussed up like a prized pig.

"Nothing?" A thin smile crossed his lips. "You expect me to believe that she said nothing to you?" He forced his thumb into Francis's right nostril and drilled it upwards deep and hard. The nail scratched the fragile tissue of the sinuses as the digit threatened to penetrate inside his skull. "Nothing?" He forced it harder.

"Stop, stop!" Francis babbled. The man withdrew the offending thumb and smiled. "Please don't hurt me." His eyes watered with the pain.

"Do you know how far I've got my thumb before?" He pointed to the second knuckle of his thumb. "All the way. You can feel the back of the eye if you twist your hand around."

"She was screaming for help," Francis gasped. "She asked for help and said that she was in the cellar, that's it."

"Shame."

"What do you mean?"

"It's a shame."

"What is?"

"That you let yourself in."

"I knocked. Honestly." It seemed important to make that point no matter how irrelevant it was.

"Flat tyre." The man shook his head. He appeared to be talking to himself. "A flat tyre delayed me by half an hour. The drugs wear off, the girl wakes up and you walk in. Shame."

"I haven't seen anything," his voice trembled. Francis didn't like where this was going. "I'll walk away and say that I couldn't get in. I promise that I won't say a word."

"Really?"

"Really."

"You could walk away and never tell a soul that you heard a young woman screaming for her life in the cellar of house that you service?" His voice was rich with sarcasm and disbelief. "I wish I could believe you."

"You can," Francis tried to sound convincing. He knew how futile it was. Who could walk away and never say anything? He had to offer a believable option. His mind worked faster than it ever had before. "Look, you get the woman out of here and leave me tied up."

"Why would I do that?"

"Because it would take me hours to break free or attract attention," Francis tried his best to sell the idea. "The office won't look for me until after seven at best. To be honest, they're so clueless it could be tomorrow before they realise that I'm missing. You would have plenty of time to get away and hide her."

"You're clever, Francis but you're missing a very important point," the man smiled. It was serpent like. "Only you know that you have been here."

"No, no, you're forgetting my office," Francis stuttered. "They'll report me missing."

"Will they?" he stopped to think. "You said that they were clueless."

"They sent me here."

"Maybe they did but did you actually arrive?" he smiled again. "No one knows except me, you and the girl. She won't say anything and I won't so that just leaves you."

"I called them to say that I had to use the keys to gain entry."

"Why would you do that?"

"Company policy," Francis insisted. "If we can't make contact with the tenant and use the keys, we have to inform the office to cover us."

"You know one of the things that I like about this house," he grinned again, the bulbous eyes unblinking. "I have never been able to get a signal here. It's a black spot, absolute peace and quiet. Shall we look at your phone and see who you have called?"

"I used my work phone."

"Not this one?" He held up the mobile phone.

"No," Francis shook as he lied. "I leave the work phone in the car."

"Do you?"

"Yes."

"Shame."

"It's true."

"Liar."

"Why don't you escape while you can," Francis tried hard not to cry. "Leave me here and get away."

"I think I'll stay."

"Then let me go, please," Francis said hoarsely. "I'll go straight to the airport and get on a plane. I've got some money. I won't come back for weeks. You'll have plenty of time to hide your tracks."

"You would do all that?"

"Yes," Francis said with quivering lips. His eyes filled with tears. "I want to live. I'll do anything you want."

"I'm afraid we have a quandary there," he whispered. "You see, I need you to be quiet, which means that you have to die."

"I will say nothing," Francis sobbed. "I promise."

"I believe that you mean that right now but once you're safe, you'll call the police."

"I won't. I don't know that woman and I don't care what happens to her."

"Maybe you don't but it will nag at you," he gloated. "The

screams of a woman stay in your mind and they eat away at you. Some feel sympathy, some feel guilt and some feel something completely different. You will feel guilty and eventually you will talk."

"I won't."

"I can't take that chance."

"Please."

"You may want to live at this moment but I think that you will want to die soon. In fact, you'll beg for death to take you; they always do. I've heard so many of them." He was going to say something else but a piercing scream interrupted him. It was the woman in the cellar. There were no words, just a long high pitched wail. Francis did what seemed the natural thing to do under the circumstances. He screamed too.

Chapter 19

Richard Tibbs pretended to be unconscious. His head drooped, his chin rested on his chest and a string of saliva dribbled onto his jacket. A crowd of people had gathered around the crash, trying their best to help. Tibbs kept his doors locked so that nobody could get inside. Despite being surrounded by the crowd he had generated, he wasn't safe. He could hear do-gooders knocking on the window, asking if he was okay. Playing dead was the best thing to do for now. The sound of sirens came quickly and he welcomed the arrival of the first police car. He heard assertive voices giving instructions to move back. The police officers were taking control of the situation. A sharp rapping on the window prompted him to pretend to regain his faculties.

"Can you hear me, Sir?" a gruff voice accompanied the knocking.

"Yes," Tibbs said pretending to be groggy. He needed to assess the scene quickly. The men from the Cherokee were talking to one police officer, while a second was next to his driver's door. One of the men had a nose bleed and they both looked shocked and very angry. More shocked than angry, but then that was the point. "My neck hurts," Tibbs moaned. He tried hard not to smile. Several people were filming on their mobile phones. A little boy held a balloon in one hand while he pulled at the trousers of the police officer with his other. The officer patiently ignored him as he made notes of the number plates and asked the enforcers questions. They looked at each other nervously as they answered. The last thing they wanted was attention from the police. Tibbs smiled inwardly and looked through the driver's window.

"Open the door please," the traffic officer asked. Tibbs saw an ambulance pulling onto the car park. It was followed closely by a second patrol vehicle. "Try not to move your neck, Sir, just in case you've done some damage." Tibbs clicked the lock and the officer opened the door from the outside. "Can you tell me your name, please?"

"Richard Tibbs."

"What happened here, Richard?"

"Those men were trying to kill me," Tibbs said calmly. "I am in the witness protection program. I can't say anything else. I can only speak to DI Annie Jones."

The colour drained from the officer's face. He spoke into his radio, "three four two."

"Go ahead, three four two," the comms crackled.

"I need back up at Hunts Cross McDonald's"

"Roger that."

"And we need to get an urgent message to DI Annie Jones. I'm taking a priority casualty to the Royal. I'll stay with him until she arrives."

"Roger that."

"Steven," he called to the driver of the second patrol vehicle.

"What's up?"

"Arrest those two and take them to Canning Place."

"What's the charge?"

"Fuck knows," he thought aloud. "Using threatening

behaviour will do for now."

"Mr Tibbs," he leaned back into the Volvo where a paramedic was applying a neck brace. "I'll come with you in the ambulance. I've sent a message to the DI, hopefully she'll get back to me before we get to the hospital."

"Thank you, Officer," Tibbs nodded.

"Oh and Mr Tibbs," he added.

"Yes, Officer?"

"I hope you're not fucking me around."

"No, Officer," Tibbs frowned. "Of course not, Officer."

Chapter 20

The house was detached from its neighbours and the expansive garden was overgrown. It was a poor advert for buy-to-let landlords, who buy property in the hope that the real estate value will rise. This particular investment was losing equity year on year. The grass was knee high and the Hawthorne hedgerow, which encircled the property, was above head height and growing wild in all directions. Thorny branches reached out threatening to scratch any that dared to enter. All the curtains were pulled closed; the glass so grimy that she could barely make out the colour of the material. The window frames were made from wood; the green gloss cracked and pealing and the pebbledash was losing the war against climbing ivy, which sprawled over the front of the house.

Annie watched six heavily armed members of the Forced Entry Unit move silently to the front door of the rundown house. Their body armour gave them a robotic look. They looked almost indestructible. Her detectives looked on, ready to follow the unit into the building. Their uniformed backup was at the rear where the suspect's van was parked. All entrances and exits were covered. They were about to run through the final entry protocol when the screaming started.

"Can you hear that, Guv?" An anxious voice crackled on the comms. "We've got screaming coming from the house. It sounds like a male and a female."

"Green light. Go, go, go!" Annie skipped the protocol. "Standby all units. We're going in."

"Use the big key," the entry team leader hissed. The first FEU member struck the lock with a heavy metal ram. The door frame splintered and a second heavy blow sent the door crashing against the hallway wall. "We're in."

"Armed police!" Their entry calls echoed through the building. It was a big house and as the armed unit spilled into the front door, it seemed to swallow them up. She waved her team to move and they approached the front door as an organised fluid unit. Two long minutes ticked by as the sound of heavy boots resounded from the aging floorboards and cracked walls. She could hear a woman screaming for help and the sound of male voices; they were shocked, startled voices. "Armed Police. Put down your weapon!"

"Drop it, now!"

"Upstairs clear!"

"Downstairs clear!"

"Detective," the comms crackled. "You're clear to enter."

Annie walked up the hallway and turned into a long living room. The scene needed to be dissected in her brain, analysed and put into some type of context. The armed officers had a suspect face down on the floor. His nose was bleeding but he was cuffed and compliant. His eyes were bulbous and although he looked shocked, there was a sparkle in them; a hint of amusement. He seemed to be fascinated by what was happening as if he was an observer rather than a participant. He licked blood from his top lip.

"This guy was tied up in the chair," an officer said. Annie saw a smartly dressed man in his twenties slumped in a grubby armchair. There was a dark wet patch which spread from his groin area down the upholstery and finally pooled around his feet. His face was streaked with tears, his skin pale and drawn. It was a face of terror. "He's very shaken up. He says that his name is Francis Grant."

"Where is the woman?" Annie asked in the confusion. The high pitched screams for help were nerve grinding.

"She's in the cellar," Francis muttered. "I couldn't open the hatch. I tried but then that freak knocked me out. I tried my best but I couldn't help her. Honestly, I tried my best!"

"Calm down," Annie said putting her hand on his shoulder. "I'm sure you did all that you could."

"There's a padlock on the hatch." An armed officer said from the far corner of the room. "He couldn't have opened it without the key."

"Search him for the keys." Annie pointed to the suspect. "Mr Grant, what are you doing here?" The woman in the cellar began to scream again. It cut through the nerves like a dull blade.

"We're coming to get you," an officer called down to her. "Stay calm. What's your name?"

"Tasha." She sobbed. "Please get me out!"

"I've found a bunch of keys on him here."

"Do any of them fit that lock?"

"I don't have any keys to this house." The suspect smiled and spat a globule of bloody phlegm onto the floorboards. "None of those keys will fit any locks here."

"Shut up." Annie snapped.

"I'll be pressing charges for assault." Annie saw a glint in his eyes. He was playing games already. There was intelligence in his eyes and something else too. Cunning. "You won't find a padlock key on there. I hope that lady is okay."

"Is he for real?"

"She sounds very frightened to me, poor thing."

"Get him out of here," Annie said angrily. She nodded to her detectives to react. "Charge him with kidnapping, for now."

"Guv."

"Mark Weston?" One of the detectives hauled him to his feet roughly. The suspect looked blankly at him. "Are you Mark Weston?"

"Never heard of him," he grinned. "I think there's been a mistake. I just found this man here like this. I was going to let him go when your storm troopers barged in."

"He's a fucking liar!" Francis shouted. "He said he was going to kill me."

"Take him away," Annie snapped. "We can find out who he is once we're done here." The detectives bundled Weston through the door and into the hallway. He protested his innocence loudly and his shouts mingled with the woman's screaming. It was like standing in a lunatic asylum. Annie shook her head to clear her thoughts. "How are we getting on over there?"

"None of these keys fit the padlock."

"Bag the keys and force it," Annie ordered. She felt a twinge of concern stab at her detective's brain. The suspect didn't have the key to the lock. Not good. "Get her out of there for God's sake. She's grating on my nerves."

"You're all heart, Guv," the entry team leader joked. "Snap the clasp off it. Do whatever it takes."

"That did sound heartless didn't it," she chuckled dryly. Nervous energy made her twitchy and impatient when a big bust was in motion. There was no time to relax until the crime scene was cleared and the suspects were banged up. "There's only one thing worse than a baby crying and that's a woman screaming. I can't stand either."

"I take it you don't have kids, Guv." The officer cut the zip-ties from Francis's wrists and ankles. The young man rubbed at painful looking welts on his skin.

"That's one reason why I don't have kids." Annie shrugged. "One of about a thousand reasons not to have them. Okay, Francis." Annie smiled and tried to put him at ease. "Firstly, are you hurt?"

"I don't think so." He touched the burn on his neck instinctively and then went back to rubbing his wrists. "He hit me with a Taser. It knocked me clean over. I can't remember what happened afterwards."

"Yes they tend to do that to you," Annie smiled. "What are you doing here?"

"I work for Burnells estate agents," Francis explained. His hands were shaking and his voice was croaky. Annie could see shock setting in and she needed as much information from him as she could glean before it took a hold. "The owners want to sell the property. We have written to Mr Weston four times with no response so they sent me to gain access. They were going to put it on the market regardless, so I had to measure up."

"On your own?"

"We already have the original measurements that we used to advertise it before. All I had to do was check that he hadn't knocked any walls down." He paused, his lips twitched. "The tenant is listed as a sixty-five year old man." Francis shrugged. "I wasn't expecting a psycho with a Taser, and a woman locked in the cellar. This is like something off the television."

"Unfortunately, you've stumbled into it through no fault of your own," Annie said. "How are you feeling now?"

"Okay. I think," he muttered. His eyes were glazed. "I thought he was going to kill me. I honestly thought this was it," a tear broke free. "I wasn't expecting to be rescued like this. Thank you so much. I thought I was dead. I wasn't expecting to get out of here."

"No, I don't suppose you were," Annie nodded. "We'll get you checked over at the hospital and then we'll need a full statement."

"Okay," Francis grimaced. "Actually, I don't think that I feel too good."

"That's shock setting in." Annie touched his arm. "Nothing to panic about. It's perfectly normal after what you've been through." She turned to a uniformed officer. "Let's get him to the Royal."

"Guv."

There was a clattering from the corner of the room followed by the sound of wood splintering. The hatch was lifted and the woman's sobbing became clearer. Annie walked over to where the armed officers were gathered.

"There are no stairs, Guv."

"Get me out!" Tasha shouted.

"Are there any ladders down there, Tasha?"

"Do you think I would still be down here if there was?" Tasha shouted. Her fear had turned to anger. "Get me out!"

"He must have used ladders," Annie said. "Check the rest of the house."

"I'll drop down, Guv." One of the armed officers sat on the

edge of the hatch, passed his weapon to his colleague and then dropped into the cellar. Annie heard the officer talking calmly to her. "Tasha, I need you to drop the weapons onto the floor." There was a metallic clattering noise.

"We're going to lift her out, Guv."

"Good," Annie said. She stepped back while they lifted and dragged the terrified woman from the hatch. Her eyes were wide with fear, mascara streaked her cheeks. She looked frightened and confused; her bottom lip quivered and she hugged herself protectively. "Get her a blanket," Annie ordered. The tiny skirt and low cut top attracted the punters but did little to maintain body temperature. "Are you hurt, Tasha?" Annie neared her.

"Just my neck," she croaked touching the burn.

"We're going to take you to the hospital first," Annie smiled. "Once we know you're okay, we need you to identify the man who brought you here. Okay?"

"Okay. He had big goggle eyes." She murmured. "A proper fish face."

"Get her into an ambulance and send an armed officer with her."

"Guv."

"Thank you," Tasha said quietly, as she was lead away. Annie nodded and waited until she had left the building.

"What did she have in her hands?"

"A scalpel and a pair of scissors," the officer who had lifted her out said. "There's a trolley full of medical implements down there. Looks like something from a surgery."

"Any signs of blood down there?" Annie asked.

"No, Guv," he shook his head. "There's a table and the trolley, that's it. No signs of any blood."

"That's odd."

"Any fishing twine?"

"I didn't see any."

"Do you think he's the butcher, Guv?"

"It looks that way." Annie shrugged but she was unsure. "I want some ladders so that I can get down there and look around."

"We've got some on the way, Guv."

"Good," she turned to her detectives. "Take this place apart. Tell CSI to start in the cellar and work their way up the stairs."

"Guv."

"I'm going to look around here and then I need a long chat with Mark Weston."

"Guv, there's an urgent message for you from uniform."

"What's the problem?"

"Apparently Richard Tibbs has been involved in an RTA. He's claiming that two men were trying to kill him and he won't talk to anyone except you."

"Jesus," Annie sucked in her breath. "Tell them to take him to the station and wait with him. The way today is going, he could be waiting a while."

Chapter 21

"Brendon Ryder?" Stirling said gruffly. Drinkers and diners at nearby tables stopped whatever they were doing to look at the big man as he approached a table where three suited males were sitting. The table was positioned next to a panoramic window with a view of the giant Liverpool Ferris wheel and the Albert Docks beyond. It was the best table in the house used only by regulars who spent a lot of money and tipped well. His appearance was met with scowling faces.

"Who's asking?" John Ryder asked casually although he knew the answer already. He could spot a police officer a mile away.

"DS Stirling, Major Investigation Team. It's your stepson that I need to speak to, about the disappearance of Lacey Taylor." Stirling ignored John and stared at Ryder junior. The smell of steak, bacon and burgers filled his nostrils and reminded him that he hadn't eaten for hours. "Might be easier if we go outside. We need him to answer some questions."

"We?" John asked sarcastically. "You appear to be on your own, which is unusual."

"Not at all," Stirling replied calmly. "There are four detectives outside covering the fire exits in case he runs; nothing unusual about that when we're dealing with scumbags."

John Ryder made to stand up, his face reddened with anger, but a reassuring hand on the shoulder made him think again. "Are you arresting Brendon?" The third man asked calmly. Stirling didn't recognise his face but it looked lived in. "Asking him to step outside would indicate to me that you aren't in a position to make an arrest?"

"Not yet." he turned to face the greying male. Time had

etched deep lines at the corner of his eyes. "And you are?"

"Geoff Ryder," he smiled thinly. "I'm John's cousin and I'm also the family solicitor. You're interrupting our lunch, Sergeant."

"It won't take long and we can do it here now, or when we attain a warrant, we can do it later at the station." Stirling shrugged his huge shoulders. The Ryders shared furtive glances. Stirling raised his voice, aggression in his tone. "It's up to you, Bren. Are you coming for a chat or do I have to come back and drag you out?" Three well built men seated at the table behind them stood up and glared at Stirling, awaiting the order to attack. The big detective frowned and felt anger rising in his gut. He didn't take kindly to being intimidated. It seldom happened because of his sheer mass, but when it did, it pissed him off. "You had better have a word with the three stooges here before I throw them through the window and lock them up."

"We don't need a scene here, do we?" Geoff said quietly. "You don't have anything or you would have arrested my nephew already." He smiled and looked at the table of enforcers. "We're not going to allow Brendon to be bullied by you or anybody else. Is it worth smashing the establishment up and losing your job?"

"It really depends on your guard dogs here," Stirling shrugged. "Tell them to sit and we're all good."

The diner went silent. The aggression in the air was palpable. A table of six diners, seated near the door made for the till quickly. The restaurant manager nervously thanked them for their custom and asked them to return again soon, although he doubted that they would. It was a small intimate venue and all eyes were now focused on the big detective.

"Let's not make a scene here. You're out of line, Sergeant." Geoff wagged his finger. "Sit down, boys and enjoy your dinner. The detective just wants a chat." He pointed to an empty seat opposite him. Stirling grinned at the bodyguards and made a note of their faces for future reference. "You've got two minutes. Make the most of it." Geoff took a drink and waited for Stirling to fire an opening volley.

"We want to know what you know about the disappearance of Lacey Taylor." Stirling studied Brendon's reaction. His expression was nondescript. He didn't look in the slightest bit bothered by the question. There was no guilt in his eyes but the older men looked worried. "You do know Lacey Taylor?"

"Who?" He smiled unbothered by the question. "I've never heard of her."

"What about you?" Stirling turned to look at John. He did look bothered. In fact, he looked almost flustered. "Surely you've heard of her."

"Of course I have." John glanced out of the window as if looking for a good answer. "She's been all over the television, but we don't know her personally."

"She's been busy building opposition to the sale of government owned facilities in the city," Stirling tried to press the right buttons. "Before she disappeared, that is. I bet she's been a real pain in the arse for some people, don't you?"

"I don't know and I don't care." John shrugged but his eyes said something different. "Do you actually have a question, or are you going to piss about some more?"

"Questions?" Stirling rubbed his huge chin. "Oh yes, did you know that Lacey went missing with her dog?"

"Obviously wasn't a guide dog or she'd have found her way home, eh?" Brendon scoffed.

"Do you know what type of dog it was?" Stirling jumped on the comment.

"No." Brendon stopped smiling and glared at him. "Why would I?"

"We have a witness who saw you hiding her dog's collar in a litter-bin at Crosby Beach." Stirling knew that the existence of a witness would send ripples of fear through them. The tension in their eyes told him all that he needed to know. Their reaction was as damning as a confession unfortunately it couldn't be used in court. "That's why I'm asking you about her dog, you see?"

"Brendon says no comment," Geoff prompted. The vein at his temple throbbed and his left fist clenched and relaxed. He was stressed.

"No comment," Brendon echoed sarcastically. He smiled at Stirling and held his stare, challenging him. "I've never heard of her."

"This is all bollocks," John snapped. "What exactly are you doing here, Sergeant?"

"I'm investigating a murder."

"Is she actually dead?" Geoff asked. His eyebrows were raised and his forehead furrowed. Stirling thought that the question was disingenuous. "Call me old fashioned, but in the old days, to be charged with murder, there had to be a dead person somewhere." Geoff Ryder knew the answer to his own question. "Have you discovered a body?"

"Not yet." Stirling sat back and watched their faces. Brendon wasn't uncomfortable but his stepfather and his uncle were. He changed tack. "Do you know Charles Keegan?"

"I know him vaguely," John Ryder answered before Bren could. "We did a bit of business a few years back. The guy is a wanker."

"He's a dead wanker." Stirling searched for a reaction again.

"He's actually dead?" Geoff asked sourly. "As in, you have a dead body to verify it?"

"Yes." Sterling bit his bottom lip to stay calm. "We have a dead person with no head. He was tortured and decapitated."

"Ah." Bren put his thumbs in the air. "A proper murder. That's the type of murder where there's not many questions that need to be answered. It's basically a whodunit? Find whoever cut off his head and the chances are, he's your murderer. Job done. I could be a detective, eh Dad?"

"Shut up, Brendon," his stepfather growled. "Look, I can't say that I'm sorry to hear that Keegan is dead," John shrugged. "But what has it got to do with Bren?"

"His body was found in the vicinity of Crosby Beach, where your stepson was seen dumping the dog collar." Stirling didn't take his eyes from Brendon. The young gangster didn't flinch. He was a cool one. "He was found in a pond just a hundred yards from the collar. It's a bit of a coincidence, don't you think"

"We have no comment to make, Sergeant," Geoff sighed. "You've come on a fishing expedition. Your witness is mistaken. Now if you don't mind, our starters are here." He nodded to a waiter, who stood nervously holding a tray of food. "If you want to speak to Brendon again, make an appointment." Stirling held his gaze. He could see that he was rattled. "He doesn't know anything about a dog collar."

"Just one more thing and then I'll be off," Stirling stood aside to allow the waiter to distribute the hors d'ouevres. He put the food down and left quickly but nobody was keen to eat immediately. "A

Jeep Cherokee registered to you was involved in an RTA about forty-minutes ago." The three men looked distinctly uncomfortable with the news. "Someone drove into the front of the vehicle and made a complaint to the attending officers. He says that the driver of the Jeep and his passenger were following him. He alleges that they were going to kill him. Funny that isn't it?"

"We don't know anything about any RTA, Sergeant," Geoff snapped. "In fact, we don't have anything to say about anything. Understand?"

"Perfectly," Stirling smiled. Their discomfort was amusing. "I don't have all the details yet but I have a sneaking suspicion that it might be linked to what happened to Lacey Taylor and Charlie Keegan." The three men looked at him blankly. Stirling could feel the animosity oozing from them. "It's all to do with property deals. Do you know Boris Kolorov?"

"I think we're done here."

Stirling ignored him and continued, "You see, I know that you're connected to the Russian mob and they're a nasty bunch. Everyone knows, don't they?"

"We're just businessmen."

"Of course you are," Stirling grinned. "But let me tell you what I think. Go on, humour me."

"If you must," Geoff sat back and sighed. John Ryder was almost purple with anger.

"I think you were tipped off that we had a witness placing young Brendon here, at the beach." Stirling paused for effect. Keeping Tibbs' name a secret seemed to be irrelevant at this point. They had sent a vehicle to tail him. He hadn't mentioned his name so far and they hadn't asked who the witness was. Stirling got the impression that they already knew. "You asked around about who the witness was and maybe someone fed you a lead. After all, you're connected aren't you?"

Silence. The three men stared at him.

"What's up?" Stirling stood over the table and grinned like an idiot. "I reckon you asked around didn't you?"

Silence.

"Oh come on?" Stirling turned his palms skyward. "You asked around about who had been at the beach with the detectives and someone pointed you in the right direction."

Silence.

"Am I right?"

Silence.

"You heard that we had a witness, you panicked and now you're trying to cover your tracks. Our witness puts young Brendon here at the scene."

"At the scene of what?" Geoff scoffed. "You don't have a body therefore you don't have a crime scene to put him at!" he finished his drink and wiped his mouth. "If your witness could put Brendon anywhere near a crime, he would be in a cell already."

"It's a matter of time." Stirling countered.

"Our food is going cold." John Ryder picked up his fork and stabbed it into a garlic mushroom. "Fuck off, Stirling," he said through a mouthful of fungi.

"I am right," Stirling laughed dryly. "I can tell by your face."

"I'll be speaking to your DI," Geoff threatened. "You can't

go around making wild accusations, Detective. I'll have your badge for this."

"I think I've pissed you off." Stirling mocked. "I can tell that you're annoyed now, but I get carried away when I have an idea I just can't let it go." He shrugged but the gangsters were silent. None of them made eye contact. "Okay, you're mad. I'll get off. You enjoy your meal now." Stirling leaned over the table. "I'll see you soon." He whispered to Brendon. His left hand knocked a pint of larger into the young gangster's lap. "Oops, sorry!" Stirling faked an apology. "I'm so clumsy!"

Brendon stood up and wiped away the liquid. "You stupid bastard," he snarled. John Ryder glared at Stirling and grabbed his stepson's wrist. The three bodyguards sprang to their feet.

"Sit down!" John Ryder shouted. "Sit down now!" Brendon glowered at Stirling and his lips twitched at the corners. "He is trying to provoke a reaction so that he can pull you in, you idiot!"

"Just an accident." Stirling shrugged.

"Sit down now," Geoff repeated the instruction. "All of you sit down." The bodyguards slumped into their seats angrily. Brendon slapped the table and then followed suit.

"I'll ask the manager to get you a mop," Stirling turned to walk out and felt six sets of eyes burning into his back. He had gone to speak to Brendon Ryder on the strength of a weak identification, but he had left knowing beyond a shadow of a doubt, that the Ryders were involved in at least one murder.

Chapter 22

Alec Ramsay paced behind his desk. The raid at Breck Road had turned up trumps, but they had to make sure that they didn't make any costly procedural mistakes now that they had a suspect in custody. "Annie Jones is a good detective, Chief and from what I'm hearing so far, she could have the killer in custody," he explained. "You know the score, making an arrest is the easy part. As soon as we've pressed charges, I'll come back to you." Annie shuffled awkwardly in the chair opposite the desk and listened to the one way conversation about her, which was awkward at best. Alec always backed her but, the same couldn't be said for the top brass. They were generally obsessed with budgets, targets and compensation claims. "Yes, Sir, I'll pass on your comments. Okay, Chief, goodbye," he ended the call with a grin. "Sorry about that, but this is a pivotal moment," Alec frowned. "The Chief has got a squeaky arse on this one."

"He's not the only one, Guv," Annie nodded.

"He's impressed at how quickly you've made progress."

"Might be premature, Guv."

"Let's make sure he's not."

"I feel like someone is going to pull the rug from underneath me." She entwined her fingers and wiggled them. "All those poor girls buried and then Keegan in the pond, not to mention Lacey Taylor. It must look like shambles from above."

"It would if you weren't on top of it, but you are, so don't worry."

"If it wasn't for the tip on the van and Tasha Jenkins being taken, we'd have nothing, Guv."

"That's the way the wind blows, Annie. They all make mistakes eventually."

"We need to nail Weston for Crosby Beach. I can't settle until we've charged him."

"Is Weston talking yet?" Alec came around the desk and leaned against the window ledge. The world outside was oblivious to the severity of their dilemma. No one really appreciated what the officers inside the station faced on a daily basis to keep the civilians safe. He watched shoppers, office workers on their lunch breaks and a myriad of tourists from all corners of the globe wandering around the city below. Their most important decision would be where to eat for lunch and whether to have a dessert.

"No," Annie shook her head. "He says his name is not Mark Weston and he's refusing to give us his name and address or have prints and DNA taken. The only thing he has said is that he's not Mark Weston. He's talking to a lawyer," she sighed. "I didn't expect him to roll over to the murders, but we don't even know who he is yet."

"Tasha Jenkins identified him?"

"Informally, yes. We haven't completed a formal line-up yet but she described him to the letter," Annie smiled thinly. "We have her evidence and Francis Grant's statement so at least we can charge him with kidnapping and assault, threats to kill and false imprisonment."

"Good," Alec said thoughtfully. "That gives us plenty of time to cement the evidence against him for Crosby Beach."

"We don't have anything solid to connect him yet, Guv."

"I know," Alec said. "How long on forensics?"

"Kathy Brooks is working flat out. On top of Crosby Beach, she's got the house to examine now, too."

"Well we know that our killer didn't start out by sewing up his victims and burying them at Crosby Beach." Alec shivered as he thought about what he was saying. "He evolved to that. His MO has developed over time, becoming more intricate with each victim. Dennis Nilsen had murdered three men at Melrose Avenue before he moved to Cranley Gardens and killed fifteen more. The Butcher is up there in the sicko league."

"And then there's the Wests, both Midland Road and Cromwell Street were like boneyards," Annie nodded. "God knows what we'll find in the cellar and the garden at Breck Road. It's a big house."

"What did Kathy find on the initial sweep inside?"

"The luminol search in the cellar showed blood splatter on the floor and the walls, but it was localized." Annie checked the initial report on her phone. "There was more trace found in three of the bedrooms, the kitchen and the bathroom. She has blood and semen on a mattress, which she has made the priority. They'll be in there for a week before they start on the garden."

"A house of horrors, eh?"

"We can only imagine what happened there, Guv."

"How are they coping with the workload?"

"She's drafted in technicians from Cheshire, Manchester and Cumbria to speed things up. Uniform have given us everyone that they can spare. They've got two shifts working overtime. We've got masses to catch up on. The DNA results are starting to land. In the last hour she's identified four of the women found at the beach."

"Have their families been informed?"

"Not yet, Guv," Annie shook her head. "I'm waiting for Stirling to get back and then we're going to debrief the team and get up to date on the forensics. Once we've done that, we'll inform the families and you can bring the press up to speed."

"Great," Alec smiled weakly. "The less we tell them the better, for now. I'll need to sit in on your briefing," Alec frowned. "One wrong word to the press and my neck is in a sling." A knock on the door interrupted him. "Come in?"

"Guv." Stirling's oversized head appeared around the door. "Have you got ten minutes?"

"Step in, Sergeant," Alec waved his hand. Stirling filled the doorway as he passed through it and closed the door behind him. "We're just catching up anyway so we need your update too."

"How did it go with Ryder?" Annie smiled. "Was he pleased to see you?"

"No, Guv."

"Did he confess to killing Charlie Keegan and divulge where Lacey Taylor's body is?" Annie raised her eyebrows.

"No, Guv."

"Call yourself a detective?" Alec frowned.

"Shall I throw myself under a bus, Guv?"

"No," Alec smiled. "I'm already over budget and replacing the front end of a number ten bus won't be cheap."

"The number ten doesn't go past here, Guv."

"I'll bet the Ryders would gladly give you a shove."

"They had a hand in it, Guv," Stirling said frowning. "They were rattled enough when I turned up but as soon as I mentioned the incident with Tibbs, they closed shop. Have you spoken to Tibbs yet?"

"No," Annie gasped. "Shit, I forgot all about him!"

"No problem." Stirling shook his head and sat down. "They released him from the hospital and uniform brought him here for safe keeping. He saw me coming through booking and asked to speak to me. I wanted a word with him anyway, just to clarify what happened with Ryder's goons."

"He left a message with uniform saying that he would only speak to me." Annie rubbed her forehead and closed her eyes. The stress and strain were taking their toll and the lack of sleep added to the cotton wool feeling in her brain. "I totally forgot about him. What happened?"

"He thought that he was being followed," Stirling began. "He gave me the old soldier spiel about Iraq and how he used to teach counter-surveillance. He noticed a Cherokee following him and he clocked that the occupants were well-built males wearing shades. It was raining, so it raised his hackles and because he'd fingered Ryder, he surmised that they were affiliates."

"He was worried about them finding out from the moment he walked in, Guv," Annie explained to Alec. "It looks like his concerns were well founded."

"It does," Alec agreed. "Then what happened?"

"The wily old git did a u-turn on the dual carriageway, pulled into a McDonald's, made sure that they were following him and then rammed his Volvo into the front of their Jeep. Obviously he put them out of action and bystanders called the police. Then he declared that he was in witness protection and requested to speak to you."

"Clever guy," Alec said impressed.

"Bloody hell!" Annie muttered. "Do we know if he was right about it?"

"The Jeep is registered to a company linked to John Ryder."

"No way," Annie said aghast.

"Yes way," Stirling smiled. "Ryder is a director and so is Boris Kolorov."

"There we have the Russian link," Alec said. "What does the company do?"

"Demolition."

"So they're buying up properties and then bidding on the demolition contracts via their own company."

"Sounds like it."

"Probably a money laundering operation."

"Or a tax dodge."

"Or all of the above!"

"You think that they found out that Tibbs had identified Ryder?" Annie asked.

"No doubt in my mind, Guv," Stirling grimaced. "I went fishing and they took the bait. Their reaction was almost funny. I think they've been tipped off that we had a witness and then they've asked around and put two and two together and come up with Tibbs as the answer. If they silence him, we've got nothing to pin them to Keegan, or Lacey Taylor if we find her."

"It's a bit of a stretch coming up with Tibbs's name though, isn't it?" Alec was dubious.

"Not really, Guv." Annie stood up and walked to the window. "There were dozens of uniform at the scene when we took Tibbs there. He's on the register and a familiar face to a lot of them." Annie frowned. "Every one of them would like to see him swinging from a tree, because they don't know the real story."

"It would only take one careless conversation at the burger van and his name could have been picked up," Stirling offered another alternative. "The press have been drinking tea by the gallon there and mixing with CSI and uniform trying to pick up snippets of information. One wrong whisper over a burger and Tibbs's anonymity was dust. As soon as we took him to the scene his identity was vulnerable."

"Well it sounds like our Mr Tibbs can handle himself," Alec smiled. "I would have liked to have seen their faces when he rammed their Jeep."

"Priceless," Annie agreed. "Is he still here?"

"No," Stirling shook his head. "He said that he would go and stay with his sister for a while. He wrote her address down for me in case we need him for anything. I had a uniform take him there."

"Okay," Annie shrugged an involuntary shiver off. Something still didn't sit right about Tibbs. "We can't bring Ryder in on the strength of Tibbs's sighting anyway. He can't testify in court, so unless we find Lacey and some evidence to link them to her, we have nothing."

"Did you speak to his handler?" Alec asked.

"Who?" Annie asked confused.

"I know you checked out his change of identity and that checked out, but did you follow up by speaking to his handler at the

MOD?"

"No, Guv," Annie bit her bottom lip. "We got what we could, but if we wanted any more then we needed a court order. Things just snowballed and I didn't think it was relevant. Do you?"

"It might be," Alec shrugged. "You've got enough to think about for now. I'll make a few calls and get a warrant. We'll see if we can't find out exactly what his story is. At some stage, we're going to be asked about it. If we find out now, it might save us some considerable embarrassment later."

"I should have done it. Thanks, Guv."

"Where does that leave you with the Keegan investigation?" Alec asked Stirling.

"He was a crooked property developer backed by dirty money," Stirling shrugged. "We can assume his murder is connected to the acquisition of land in the city, which Lacey Taylor was protesting about. There's no doubt in my mind that they were both bumped off by the same outfit but until we connect names to bank accounts, we're stuffed. Ryder is in bed with the Russians and we know they're involved in everything from extortion to people trafficking."

"It doesn't strike me that it's John Ryder's style," Annie shook her head. Her top lip retreated to expose her teeth when she was thinking. "We know he's no angel but beheading the opposition and kidnapping community workers seems extreme for him; the Russian mob maybe, but Ryder?"

"I agree with you to a point," Stirling tilted his head, "but the stepson, Brendon makes me nervous. There's something about him that unnerves me."

"How so?" Alec asked. Stirling obviously had a hunch that he was more than willing to explore. "It's not like you to be unnerved by anyone."

"John Ryder and his cousin Geoff are career criminals, right?"

"Right."

"They were cool enough not to shoot me even though I tried my best to provoke a reaction, but the stepson just wasn't rattled by anything that I said. He made jokes, he was sarcastic but there wasn't even a glint of concern in his eyes. He was ice."

"Just another cocky young gangster working his way up the tree?"

"No," Stirling shook his head. "It was as if he really didn't care. He wasn't faking it, he wasn't worried."

"Maybe he hasn't done anything to be worried about," Alec offered. "Perhaps he isn't privy to the workings of the family yet."

"I'm not buying that." Stirling disagreed. "Geoff and John were concerned and they were shielding him. I think Brendon Ryder has gone outside of his remit and now they're closing ranks to cover up his mess. They will be more concerned about pissing off their Russian partners than us."

"Let's get everything we can on Brendon," Alec said. "If he's the weak link, then the family might just let him take the fall to protect the business. Good work, Jim."

"We need to get this briefing underway," Annie said anxiously. "I want the team brought up to speed on the forensics."

"Get yourselves organised and I'll be with you in five," Alec picked up the telephone. "I want to start the ball rolling with the Ministry of Defence. They won't do anything quickly."

Chapter 23

The atmosphere in the room was electric; rumours that identifications had finally been made passed from desk to desk. The detectives restocked their coffee cups and mineral water and waited for the DI to brief the team. Tension charged the atmosphere as Annie switched on the screens. She cleared her throat and looked at the faces before her. Her team was hungry for news, desperate for a breakthrough to work on. As the images appeared, a tense silence fell over the room.

"Our first victim is Mary Jackson, twenty-two years old and from the Huyton area of the city." Annie pointed to the bank of screens behind her. The faces of four young women were partnered with images of the abominations that they had become at the hands of the Butcher. The main screen showed an attractive woman with shoulder length brown hair. Her features were hardened by a sallow complexion and dark circles beneath her eyes. "We know that she was an addict and that she had form; shoplifting, possession and soliciting. She had no next of kin listed on her arrest jacket and the last known address we have is two years old, hence nobody noticed her missing. We need to know where she spent the last year of her life if we're going to work out where she was taken from."

"She was extracted from the dunes here," Kathy Brooks said pointing to another screen. It showed an aerial image of the beach and the surrounding nature reserves. "We're estimating that she was buried six to nine months ago. Her cause of death was suffocation. The breathing tube was blocked with seagull droppings."

"Poor woman, it's supposed to be lucky if a seagull craps on you," Stirling said sourly. No one laughed but then no one was supposed to. "If he went back to feed them, then surely he checked that the tubes were clear. Maybe she was lucky after all."

"If it quickened her death and ended her nightmare, then you could say she was lucky," Kathy agreed looking at the grim facial expressions around the room.

"We know from vice that she worked the Jamaica Street area for a few months but we don't know where she was taken from. Let's get her photograph out there and pin down where she was abducted." Annie looked around for DC Mason and spotted her at the back of the room. "We'll need Matrix to help us pinpoint where all these girls worked at the time of their disappearance."

"I've already passed the photographs onto Vice Squad," Alec added. "Between them and the Matrix Unit, we should be able to get a fix on them."

"Is Weston the killer?"

"We think so but we have to prove it."

"If we've got Weston in custody, why aren't we drilling him for information?" Amanda asked the question which every detective in the room wanted to ask. "Is he talking?"

"He's procedurally savvy," Annie answered.

Alec walked to the front of the room and stood next to Annie. "Here are the simple facts. We have a suspect who was arrested in a compromising position. He was in a house with a female locked in the cellar and a male bound in the living room. If you look at the evidence, all that we can prove is kidnap and assault. We can't connect him to the beach," Alec explained. "What we have is circumstantial evidence and nothing more. We can nail Weston for kidnapping Tasha Jenkins and for an assault on Grant, but if we want to nail him as the Butcher, we need to go at this as if we have no one in custody. I want this done with belt and braces, by the book, so that when we go to the Crown Prosecution Service it's an airtight prosecution. Forget Weston for now. Okay? We must find more evidence."

"All we have is kidnapping and assault," Annie agreed. "But we can hold him in custody while we find the evidence that we need."

"Guv." The gathering nodded and silence fell as they waited for the next batch of details. The image on the main screen changed. A rough-looking blonde with a piercing through her right eyebrow stared from the screen.

"Kerris Owens, thirty-three from Swansea," Annie moved on. "She arrived in the city two years ago. She was signing on from a bedsit in Kensington, but failed to show up for a benefits hearing eight months ago. We don't know where she's was between then and when she was murdered."

"Which ties in with her time of death," Kathy agreed. "She has been in the sand for at least six months. We found her in the dunes here." She pointed to the aerial image of the sand dunes beyond the beach. They seemed to stretch for miles.

"What are all the black spots on the map of the beach, Kathy?" a detective asked.

"Here are where the victims were extracted," she pointed. "Here are where the statues are positioned. I wanted to see if there was any correlation between the burial sites and the iron men."

"Is there?"

"Not that I can see, but I'm not finished analysing yet. Because of the way the victims are poised and their proximity to the Iron Men, we need to check every eventuality. I'm crosschecking high tides, low tides and phases of the moon, with the approximate time of burial. We may find a correlation and we may not."

There were some raised eyebrows amongst the detectives. "Kathy is right," Alec backed her up. "There is a weight of evidence that serial killers are triggered by high tides and the cycle of the moon. Bundy, the Zodiac Killer and Berkowitz were all more active during full moon phases."

"It doesn't help the women in my lab, but it may help you to figure out when your killer will strike again."

"Thanks, Kathy. This is Jackie Goodall, forty-two from Bootle." The image changed as Annie spoke. "Her last known address is a hostel in Sefton Park. She was on probation after a six month stint for distributing class A's. She went missing six weeks ago, which makes her our freshest victim. It should be easier to trace her whereabouts, so I want Amanda's team to take this one." Amanda Mason nodded her acknowledgement and her team swapped excited whispers. One of them began an internet search immediately. "Thanks, Kathy. Carry on."

"Jackie was pulled out of the sand here," Kathy pointed to the map. "It doesn't take a genius to work out that the killer was moving further away and deeper inland with each victim. At least, that's the pattern so far." The screen changed again and a pretty blonde smiled at the room. It wasn't a custody suite photograph and she had a different look to the others. Her eyes sparkled with life. Her teeth were pearly white and her skin was unblemished and healthy. Alive, she was a potential beauty queen. Dead, she was a mummified horror.

"The fourth victim is Tina Peters, nineteen," Annie grimaced. The tender age of the victim stung. "She is the only victim reported missing but she was a student studying in Brighton, so she wasn't on our radar. Her parents didn't hear from her for a few weeks but Tina had been erratic at keeping in touch, so they didn't panic at first. She had been talking about travelling and was a spontaneous kid, so they waited for her to contact them. That was in twenty-ten. She was never on our lists and we have no idea what she was doing in Liverpool, but using the timeline, we think she must have come here directly from Brighton."

"Tina was found here," Kathy said. "She's been buried for at least three years. The state of the victim is very different to the others. Her teeth were intact and her lips and eyes were not sewn shut. The killer broke her nose and her jaw before he strangled and buried her. Our killer could have been rushed into killing her, or he could have been nervous."

"This was an early kill. Possibly his first murder and he was still learning and still making mistakes," Alec interrupted. "If he has made any mistakes at all, then it was there with Tina Peters. All the other victims so far are anonymous working girls who won't be missed. If you can find out what she was doing here and who she was with, you'll find the link to our killer. Tina Peters is the key to catching the Butcher." Nodding heads agreed with Alec's summary of the victim. "Get out there and find out where these women were and we'll have a chance of linking Weston to the murders. I want two detectives in Brighton tomorrow to track down who Tina Peters studied with, lived with, drank with and went to bed with. I want to know everything about her from the day she was delivered."

"If she went missing in twenty-ten, Guv, most of her year students will be long gone from Brighton by now." DC Lewis raised his hand. His suit was dishevelled and his shirt was open at the collar. Alec liked him.

"I disagree," Alec said. "Brighton is a buzzing town with a thriving social scene and job market. There will be lots of students who don't want to go back to wherever they came from when they finish university there. Many get jobs in London and commute. Some of her classmates are still there. I'm positive that they are."

"Fair enough, Guv," Lewis agreed. "I'll go with Peters first thing."

"Good, thanks." Alec nodded. "Okay, everyone, let's find where these girls were taken from."

"One other thing," Stirling said. "We don't need to see any links to the Keegan murder or the disappearance of Lacey Taylor in the press. Be careful what you say or put in your emails. At the moment, they are completely unrelated."

"Good point," Alec said. "I don't want to see any mention of 'prawns' either. The press is running with the tag, Butcher of Crosby Beach, let's leave them with that. We need to concentrate on Mark Weston, the van and 163 Breck Road. Somebody out there knows something. Find them."

Chapter 24

Alec opened the door into the interview room and was taken aback by the suspect's eyes. He'd been told that they were distinctive, but that hadn't prepared him for how prominent they were when face to face. "He looks like Mesut Ozil," Alec pointed out loudly. "It's the eyes."

"He plays for?" Annie had heard the name before.

"Arsenal."

"Now you mention it, he does look like him."

"Do you mind?" Jeremy Cuthbert complained. His pink scalp reflected the light. A few ghostly white strands of hair clung desperately to his head, refusing to give up. "That is most uncouth."

"What's the problem?" Alec smiled.

"You're talking about my client as if he isn't here." Cuthbert removed his wire framed glasses and cleaned the round lenses on his handkerchief.

"I said the he looks like an Arsenal midfielder, Mesut Ozil," Alec explained aloofly. "Do you know who I mean?"

"Yes, I know who you mean." Cuthbert rolled his eyes skyward. "That's not the point. Talking about my client as if he isn't in the room is offensive."

"I think that the point is that before we sit down and begin recording the interview, you are trying to establish your legal prowess by pointing out my bad manners." Alec shrugged.

"Nonsense."

"I can understand why you would want to do that, however, what you need to understand is that I couldn't give a toss if your client feels offended by the fact that I think he looks like an Arsenal player." Cuthbert's mouth opened to speak but he couldn't think of a reply.

"I'm not offended. I've heard a lot worse." The suspect grinned. Alec made a quick assessment of his demeanour. He looked nervous but not overly so. He was almost savouring the prospect of locking horns with him. "The name Ozil is from Kurdish decent, as am I. Genetically we are prone to astigmatism, hence my eyes are unusual here, but not so much at home. At home I am a sex god, lady." He grinned at Annie. Annie frowned and resisted the urge to spit in his face.

"Whatever," Alec said as he sat down. He switched on a digital recorder. "Interview with Dazik Kraznic, arrested as Mark Weston on the twenty-fifth of November, twenty-fourteen. DS Alec Ramsay and DI Annie Jones, also present Jeremy Cuthbert. Can you confirm you name and date of birth for the tape please."

Kraznic sat back in his chair and folded his arms. His face looked impassive, "I'm Dazik Kraznic, born third of January, seventy-three in Gumbet, Turkey."

"Kraznic?" Alec asked.

"Your question is?" Cuthbert sighed, knowing full well that Alec would have researched it already.

"It isn't a Turkish name."

"My parents are Russian so I have dual citizenship."

"Great mix." Annie rolled her eyes.

"Do you mind, Inspector?" Cuthbert gasped.

"No." Annie smiled.

"Let's cut to the chase. My client is an illegal immigrant," Cuthbert added.

"Yet he can afford to retain your services?" Annie asked. "Are you being paid by him directly?"

"My payment is none of your concern, Inspector."

"If we find anything amiss with his finances, it will be our concern."

"Touché, Inspector," Cuthbert smiled. "I'm sure you'll find everything is in order. Shall we proceed?"

"Can you tell me if you were driving a van registered to Mark Weston of 163 Breck Road?" Alec began.

"I have never driven a van in this country," Dazik replied. He sat back and folded his arms. Annie noticed tattoos on both wrists. "I don't have a license to drive here. I haven't passed my tests." He smiled and shrugged his shoulders.

"Look, we're not interested in whether or not you're legal to drive," Annie said frustrated. She pushed a photograph of the van across the table. "We need to know about this van."

"I don't have a van." He didn't look at the photograph. He looked straight ahead and kept smiling. "I don't have that van or any other."

"You picked up Tasha Jenkins in this van."

"Who?" he grinned.

"Tasha Jenkins," Alec repeated. He pushed another photo

towards him. This time Tasha's pretty black face was on it. "This woman here."

"I've never seen this woman."

"You picked her up on Sheil Road."

"No."

"We have two witnesses who will put you in that van."

"Prostitutes?" Cuthbert scoffed. "Unreliable at best."

"Their statements are independent and concur."

"They're mistaken." Dazik said impassively.

"We don't think so."

"One of your witnesses, Janice Nixon?" Cuthbert frowned. "She said that the man Tasha Jenkins got into the van with had a hat and sunglasses on and that he only removed the glasses briefly."

"She's happy that she could identify him again."

"Really?" Cuthbert sneered. "It was dark. It was raining heavily. The man had a hat on and sunglasses and your witness has a drug habit."

"She'll pick him out of a line-up."

"She may do and I'll tear her to pieces in court." He ridiculed their evidence. "Do you have any forensic evidence to put my client in the vehicle?"

"Not yet," Annie snapped. "But we will."

"I'll ask you again. Have you ever seen this woman," Alec asked angrily. He placed another photograph of Tasha Jenkins onto the desk.

"No."

"She's identified you," Annie said quickly.

"Has there been a formal identification?" Cuthbert asked. He removed his glasses again and cleaned them unnecessarily.

"Not yet, she's under sedation at the moment," Alec said. "As soon as she's well enough, we'll have a line-up. Her description of you is very detailed."

"You mean she described a footballer?" Cuthbert sighed. "You said yourself that my client looks like somebody else."

"She'll identify him." Annie said trying to stay calm. Lawyers like Cuthbert made her blood pressure rise.

"So you deny picking up Miss Jenkins and assaulting her with a Taser gun?"

"Yes."

"You never drove this van?"

"No."

"How long have you lived at Breck Road?" Annie changed tack.

"I don't live there."

Alec rolled his eyes towards the ceiling and exhaled. "You don't live there?"

"No."

"Have you ever used the name, Mark Weston?"

"No."

"Do you know Mark Weston."

"No."

"Where do you live?"

"I share a flat with my friends," Dazik nodded. "It's in Sheil Road."

"The number?"

"Seven."

"Get your detectives and uniform over there," Alec said to Annie. Annie wrote the number down and walked to the door. She opened it and summoned the constable who was outside the interview room.

"Get two detectives to search this address," she whispered. "If they have any issues getting the warrant, I need to know. Okay?"

"Guv." She closed the door and smoothed her trousers before sitting down. Annie felt the suspect's eyes taking in her shape. He studied every curve from head to toe and he didn't do it discreetly. The scrutiny made her skin crawl.

"What were you doing at the address in Breck Road?" Alec asked as she sat down.

"I was looking for sex," Dazik grinned. "My friends told me that you can buy sex there."

Annie and Alec exchanged glances. "How did you get in?" Annie asked.

"The back door was open. They told me to walk in and that someone would meet me, like a receptionist," he smiled again.

"You did find a set of keys on my client?" Cuthbert asked a

rhetorical question.

"Yes," Annie blushed. She could sense her case slipping with every question.

"Am I right in saying that none of them matched any of the locks on the building?"

"Yes."

"Then we should move on, Detective."

"Why did you assault Francis Grant with a Taser?"

"The man who was tied up?"

"Yes."

"He was sitting in the chair when I arrived."

"Tied up?"

"Yes."

"So you didn't assault him?"

"No," Dazik shook his head emphatically as he answered.

"Did you hear a woman screaming in the cellar?"

"I didn't notice at first until I walked into the room."

"So you just stumbled into the situation?"

"Yes."

"Oh for God's sake!" Alec breathed deeply. "Is this the best that you can do?"

"This is my client's version of events," Cuthbert said. "His testimony is independent and will give any jury reasonable doubt."

"It's a load of bollocks is what it is!" Annie scoffed.

"It's the truth, honestly," Dazik said. "I walked into the house and one man was in the hallway. I asked him if I could get sex there," he shrugged. "He was a crazy man and he laughed and walked out of the hallway through to the back of the house. I don't know where he went. When I walked into the room, the electric thing was on the floor and everyone was screaming very loudly. I picked it up and then the army burst in and here I am."

"Am I sat in an alternative universe?" Alec slapped the desk.

"It is the truth."

"You don't have any evidence to connect my client to any assaults apart from the word of two prostitutes and a drug addict," Cuthbert rubbed his hands together. "I think that you should charge my client or release him."

"Wait a minute. What drug addict?" Annie asked. Her top lip retreated again.

"Francis Grant."

"What about him?"

"He has three priors for possession of class A drugs, Inspector, and he spent six weeks in a rehab last year." Cuthbert looked over his glasses patronisingly. "Surely you've checked out his previous?"

Alec looked at Annie and he could tell from her expression that she hadn't checked him out. She looked as if she had been slapped by an invisible hand. "He was stunned by a Taser, hogtied and traumatised. He was a victim here. We wouldn't check his record unless we thought that he'd committed a crime."

"Oh, I think the CPS will see it very differently," Cuthbert said. "Do you think that they would proceed to trial on the strength of your witnesses?"

"Yes."

"Good luck with that."

"The forensic evidence will back up the charges."

"Like I said, good luck." Cuthbert took off his glasses and stood up. He looked at his file and then looked at Alec. "I think that this has gone as far as it is going to go. Let's cut to the chase shall we?"

"Yes, let's do that."

"I didn't want to bring it up until I saw what evidence you have and you have nothing. You're desperate to find the 'Butcher of Crosby Beach' as the press has dubbed him, and you have my client in your sights," he said pointing the arm of his spectacles at Dazik. "You have an abducted prostitute locked in a cellar and my client was arrested at the scene. I'd think the same under the circumstances but you haven't a clue who my client is yet."

Annie made to speak but Alec touched her hand under the table. They were on the back foot and he didn't want any more punishment. "Well enlighten us."

"Dazik is an illegal immigrant so his records here are scant, however, he has only been in this country for nine months."

"Nine months?" Annie repeated quietly. She felt any hope of a conviction escaping from her body. "You can back that up?"

"My client was arrested three times in Calais last year for trying to stowaway on lorries. The paperwork states that in February, March and May, he was detained. He spent a month in a refugee camp prior to coming across the Channel. Before that, he can verify living and working in Turkey. We will produce mobile phone records, bank accounts and asylum application paperwork to establish that my client wasn't in the country when some of your victims were murdered."

Alec stood up and nodded. He indicated that Annie should too. "We'll need to see those documents and we'll be charging your client with abduction and assault. Interview terminated."

He opened the door with more force than was needed and stormed out. Annie followed him with a sickly feeling in her guts. What had seemed like a breakthrough had turned into a banana skin of monumental proportions.

Chapter 25

163 Breck Road was a three storey property under intense scrutiny. As dusk approached, every light in the house was burning and extra illumination was provided by spotlights. A coach-sized trailer was parked on the street; the interior was a laboratory designed to be used for major forensic investigations where multiple deaths were involved. A flatbed truck was next to it, loaded with ground excavation equipment. A mini-digger was being prepped by two mechanics in anticipation of searching the garden in the days to come. A gaggle of reporters stood chatting behind yellow crime scene tape and a television van was parked up on the kerb. Further down the close, the residents were safely locked in their houses, ignoring the relentless intrusive knocking at the door. There was only so many times they could answer the same questions, no matter who was asking them, or which channel they represented.

White-clad figures ambled from the house to the trailer and back again, delivering sealed bags of evidence and then returning to retrieve more. They too ignored the barrage of questions which were shouted from behind the tape. Four uniformed officers maintained the cordon and swapped serial killer jokes with the gathering as long as no one important was in earshot. Behind the close was a tree lined access road, which serviced the residents' bin sheds and garages. It had been closed off, much to the annoyance of the homeowners and was being used as a parking area. Four unmarked CSI vehicles and two marked police interceptors blocked the road. Behind number 163, the hawthorn hedges separated the close from an acre of Kensington, where the houses were waiting patiently to be demolished.

A lone-white clad figure moved furtively from the hedgerows

towards the back of the house. The row of garages hid him from sight. The rear windows of the house looked over the overgrown lawn and if he had been seen, it would look like a CSI was checking the outhouses and bin sheds. He knew that and it had always been part of his contingency plan. In the case of an emergency, the plan was straightforward. Sliding between the bins and the garage, he dropped to his knees and crawled to the back of the house. Three steps led up to the kitchen door and a coal bunker offered more shelter for anyone who wanted to approach the building unseen. To the left of the bunker was a skylight which opened into the rear cellar. There was nothing but darkness behind the glass. The police hadn't worked out that the cellar where they had found the girl had been adapted to purpose. He had built it as a cell. Beyond its walls, the cellar ran beneath the rear of the house and could only be accessed from the skylight. Had they studied the original plans, they might have spotted that the cellar on the drawings was much bigger than the one which they had found.

He slid down into the darkness and lowered himself onto the floor. His movement was silent and swift. On the far wall, the gas main entered the building, before climbing upwards through the kitchen floor to where the meter cupboard was fitted. A section of the lead pipe had been replaced with a reinforced rubber hose. It was an adaptation which he'd made when he reconstructed the cellar. He sat for a moment and studied the paving stones. Karla was beneath his feet, her friend Suzanne a few yards to the left. Diana was next to the wall on the right. The others didn't have names, or at least he didn't know what they were.

He could hear them sobbing in his mind, feel their tears on his cheek as he kissed them, taste their blood as he sliced them. It was always shallow and gentle at first but then as the excitement intensified, the cuts became deeper. Those precious moments as their sobbing became more frantic, as the realisation that they were going to die hit them, as their eyes sparkled with tears and fear and despair;

those deliciously sticky moments were what had driven him in the beginning, but their death was so final, so premature. He had tried to prolong their agony, his ecstasy, but they always went too soon. When he saw the iron men he knew. It was the perfect way to prolong that moment, that transition from unbearable suffering to peace. He closed his eyes and savoured their pain.

Footsteps above snapped him back to reality. He stood up and took a blade from his pocket. The rubber hose was sliced with a single movement. Gas hissed noisily into the cellar. He moved quickly to the far wall and switched on the single electric socket. A tiny green light indicated that the timer was on and in forty minutes it would switch on the electric hot plate which was plugged into it.

He took one last deep breath, savouring the decay which tinged the air. He could distinguish each woman in his mind, smell their rotting corpses and taste their unique odours. Then he slipped through the skylight and scurried back past the bunker, the bins and the garage, before crawling through the hedges into the sprawling desolation of the decaying streets beyond.

Chapter 26

"Major Bradshaw will see you now, Sir." A young officer stood from behind his desk and gestured to his senior officer's door. His uniform was crisp and immaculate; his cropped hair just a dark shadow on his skull. The brass name plaque with the Major's name engraved on it looked fitting against the stained dark wood. The Royal Military Academy Sandhurst was everything Alec had imagined and more. Every inch was polished, pristine and organised. It reeked of beeswax and bleach. Two units of officer cadets were being drilled outside, their boots making a rhythmical sound, which mingled with the urgent instructions shouted from their Drill Sergeants. It sounded like a foreign language to Alec. "Sorry for the delay," the soldier added chirpily. "These things take time I'm afraid."

Alec smiled and allowed him to open the door. He wasn't sure what 'these things' were but he was sure that he was about to find out. The brass-handle gleamed, worn smooth by years of polishing. "Thank you," Alec said.

"Detective Superintendent Ramsay to see you, Sir."

"Thank you, Corporal," the Major said. He stood and walked smartly around the desk. His boots were like black mirrors and he held himself bolt upright as if every muscle in his body were permanently tensed. His hair was shaven at number one, grey streaked the sides. "Superintendent, nice to meet you." His handshake was vice-like. "I only hope that your journey isn't a wasted one."

"Anything you can tell me will be a help."

"I'm not sure exactly what I can tell you but I'm certain of what I cannot." There was an awkward silence between them.

"Captain Nigel Dunn, alias Richard Tibbs has witnessed an incident which could identify a murderer. We're aware that we can't reveal his previous identity and we may be able to find a way around that in a court but there are other issues. I need you to clear them up."

"Issues?"

"You're aware that he's been put on the sex offenders register?"

"Yes, unfortunate, but hardly surprising," the Major said. His hands were peaked together as if in prayer. His face was like stone, giving nothing away.

"He has led us to believe that the entire business was some kind of mistake, due to his identity change?"

"He's a very resourceful man."

"When you say resourceful, you mean he's a liar?"

"Yes."

"Why was he put into witness protection?"

"That's classified."

"I have a warrant," Alec said calmly.

"Which we're honouring with this meeting, Superintendent; it's merely a courtesy. Your warrant has no authority here."

"It's signed by a Crown Court judge."

"Even your judge doesn't have the authority to access classified military information."

Alec sat and pondered the situation. Sandhurst was a four hour drive away. Falling into an argument which he couldn't win was pointless. He felt anger rising in his belly but displaying it would benefit no one. "Okay, I'm not here to argue with you. I'm asking for your help."

"And I'm trying to help you without breaking with military convention."

"Did he offend in Iraq?"

"I can't discuss Iraq."

"Is he a pedophile or not?" Alec asked impatiently.

"I can't answer that."

"You're happy for him to offend again?"

"Are there children involved this time?"

"Yes." Alec took a breath. "I am trying to protect them. Is he a pedophile?"

"Not exclusively," the Major frowned. He paused as he gathered his next words. "This is off the record."

"Understood."

"He's worse than that. He's a sociopath, a predator. His file indicates that he doesn't distinguish between his victims, although the majority were children. Iraq is a country where life is very cheap and anything is for sale at the right price. Dunn took full advantage of that fact, as did some others. He was part of a ring preying on the poor. When they were investigated, it opened a can of worms."

"I don't understand, Major. If he committed crimes, then why did you protect him with a new identity and allow him to return to civilian life where he's a danger to the public?"

"All I can tell you is that his crimes were not as bad as the ones committed by others. His testimony was rewarded with a second chance."

"His testimony or his silence?"

"His silence was another thing entirely. He receives a reduced salary for his silence."

"And a pension and protection?"

"It's not my choice. Neither is it yours. The decision was made by authorities far higher than ours. We have to manage the situation, not endorse it."

"My priority is the safety of the public, not keeping a lid on things."

"Has he committed any crimes?"

"Yes."

"Could you explain the circumstances?"

"He was put on the register for allegedly assaulting two young girls," Alec paused. "His bail conditions forbid him approaching those girls or any other minors. During the course of our investigation into a murder, Tibbs was found to have breached his conditions, by going to their school."

"And he was arrested for this?"

"No."

"Why not?"

Alec crossed his legs and thought about the best way to explain. He glanced at photographs of the Major in various uniforms and in different war zones. A familiar vehicle caught his eye. It was a

Challenger tank and the Major was wearing a uniform worn by British troops in Iraq. He must have served in Desert Storm too. "He came to us with information first."

"Why would he do that?"

"He said it was because he wanted to help us find a missing woman." Alec explained. "During our investigation, we discovered that he had been visiting a primary school and handing out sweets. My DI threatened to have him charged with breach of bail conditions and he clammed up for a while." The sound of boots pounding the drill square droned on in the background. "Then he revealed that he was in witness protection and was a former MP. The story that he gave my DI was that the girls at the school are his grandchildren and it's all a mistake, caused by the change of identity."

The Major stood and walked to the window. He ran his fingers along the ledge to check for dust. His expression indicated that there either wasn't any, or that it was at an acceptable level. "That is quite a story."

"Hence, I am here, Major."

"If you charge him with breach of bail, he will call his handler and threaten to expose others who were involved in a pedophile ring in Iraq so that we change his identity again."

"Obviously, I don't want that to happen."

"Off the record, Superintendent, the government and the military will never allow those names to be brokered. Dunn has a get out of jail free card, which will not expire. If you push it, they'll make him disappear again, new identity, new name."

"What can you tell me then?"

"Very little."

"Okay, Major," Alec said. He was boiling beneath the surface. "Off the record, was he married?"

"Yes."

"Did his partner commit suicide?"

"I don't know."

"Does he have grandchildren?"

"Not as far as I know."

"So he lied to my DI?"

"Undoubtedly," the Major said emphatically. "I am sure that your DI checked his story and hit a brick wall."

"She confirmed he was in witness protection. That was all they would confirm."

"That was all they are allowed to confirm."

"Is there anything else that you can tell me?"

"Dunn has pushed his luck before. If I had my way, we should bring back the firing squad, or we should have turned him and his co-conspirators over to the Iraqis. They would have done what we couldn't." The Major leaned on the desk and folded his arms behind his back.

"I can't compromise the safety of two little girls to protect anyone."

"You realise that if something like this came out, the image of our troops abroad would be tarnished beyond redemption?"

"I would have to be very careful that didn't happen," Alec said. "I have no wish to damage anyone except Tibbs."

The Major walked to the window and watched the cadets marching. He seemed to be mesmerised by their display of coordination. "Theoretically, if someone in witness protection was charged with a serious offence and processed quickly, the military may not be able to protect him."

"What if he threatened to expose people, theoretically or otherwise?"

"Then those others would have to take their chances. I think that the transparency which the digital age has brought to us is something that we should embrace, don't you?"

"I do."

"Incidents and events can be searched out by anyone in possession of a mobile phone."

"What are you saying, Major?"

"That once the theoretical 'cat' is out of the bag, you can't put it back."

"Theoretically."

"Indeed." The Major took a deep breath and turned to face Alec. "Richard Tibbs is not his first alias."

Alec sat forward and waited for the Major to finish but he didn't. A light switched on in Alec's brain. "That's why his file is so thin?"

"Yes."

"What should I be looking for when I get back?"

"Run a check for a Mark Weston." The Major coughed into his fist. "You know there's only so much that can be buried. Some things are just too big to be to be covered up. Details of national security and the names of secret operatives or black ops missions should never be revealed, but hiding the names of perverts because of their rank or who they're related to, is wrong, theoretically."

"I agree," Alec said confused. He was still reeling from the fact that Tibbs was connected to Breck Road. He was Mark Weston. "What are you saying?"

"Even the tightest vessel can leak."

"Secrets are only worth protecting while they remain secret." Alec smiled.

"Indeed, Superintendent." The Major walked to the door. "I hope that you can report how anally retentive and unhelpful the military were in this investigation?"

"Thank you for being unhelpful, Major." Alec made a mock salute and ran the facts over in his mind as he walked out of the door. He had made a mammoth breakthrough, but he would need to be very careful how he played the next few moves. If he was clumsy, he could bring the weight of departments that he didn't know the names, of down on his head. If he was smart, Tibbs would be exposed and at the mercy of the judicial system.

"Superintendent Ramsay." A voice dragged him back from his thoughts.

"Yes," Alec said. He stopped to face the young corporal.

"You should check you mobile, Sir," he smiled. "A DI Jones called and said that it's urgent that she speaks to you as soon as possible."

"Thanks." Alec turned and walked down the hallway, his footsteps echoing from the walls. "I hope it's good news for a change," he mumbled to himself although his gut feeling told him that it wasn't.

Chapter 27

Annie sat and stared at the phone. The main office was virtually empty. Her teams of detectives were responding to calls from the help lines while others were on their way to the explosion at Breck Road. She held a black coffee cup in her left hand, the contents now cold and streaky looking. The screen on her mobile flashed and it vibrated on the desk. She had no idea how to tell the caller the news. "Guv," she sounded out of breath. "I've been trying to get hold of you."

"I had to turn my mobile off while I'm at Sandhurst but it was worth the trip," he explained. He skirted the marching cadets and made his way to the car park, which was behind the main building. The sun was on its cusp but still had little warmth to offer. He was eager to tell Annie the news but her need to talk seemed greater than his own. "What's the panic?"

"There's been a gas explosion, Guv," she said. "At the Breck Road scene."

"Bloody hell," Alec spoke quietly, as he opened the driver's door and climbed into the BMW. The familiar odours of leather and pine air freshener drifted to him. The next question stuck in his throat. "How bad is it?"

"Bad," she sighed. "The building has collapsed. Only the front elevation is standing."

"How many casualties?"

"Brian Dooley is dead and Jenny Porter is missing. She's still in the rubble somewhere. They were the only two CSI in the building. A young PC who was carrying evidence packets is critical at the Whiston burns unit. Most of the technicians were working in the mobile lab at the time. We could have had ten officers in there."

"It could have been much worse, although Brian Dooley's wife and kids won't think so right now." Alec thought back to the night he was told about his wife's death. A sharp pain shot through him. It was a slicing pain which began above the groin and spread north. When he thought about her, he was always left with a sick feeling in his guts and nausea behind his eyes. It was grief and it never left him. It never waned but it became less frequent. "What do we know about the cause of it?"

"The building collapsed into the cellars where the gas main enters the house. We don't know if it was a leak or deliberate. It's all over the news, Guv. There are a dozen reporters and a television crew encamped there watching the recovery going on. One of them has the explosion on disk. We've got a copy already. The windows exploded on all three floors simultaneously. There was obviously a build up over time."

"We know it was gas?"

"Definitely," Annie said. "They had to isolate the gas main to put out the fire. As soon as the supply was cut, they had it under control."

"You had better get a family liaison to Dooley and Porter's homes. We don't want their families finding out from the BBC."

"That's already done, Guv." Annie swallowed hard. She felt as if the case was running away from her. "There are recovery teams from Manchester and Chester on the way to help with the search for Jenny. The fire was pretty intense, Guv. I'm not holding out much hope of finding her alive."

"We need to concentrate every resource on whatever was recovered from that house."

"My thoughts exactly, Guv," Annie said. "My gut feeling tells me that the explosion wasn't accidental, which tells me that we're onto something."

"Dazik is on remand, so either he's telling us the truth and he has nothing to do with the address or he has some very serious connections cleaning up after him."

"I think the same," Annie felt some confidence creeping back into her voice. "I'm having the press cordon moved back to the end of the close and I've ordered the forensic search of the gardens to begin. They're sweeping the lawns with Ground Penetrating Radar first, Guv. Once we've ruled out any bodies under the lawn, we'll move to the outbuildings and hedgerows."

"Good," Alec sighed. Annie had done exactly as he would have. She was a good detective but he was concerned how the brass perceived her investigation so far. Alec could see some flaws in the process. If he saw a flaw, the brass would see a gaping chasm. "You know what my next question is going to be don't you?"

"Yes, Guv."

"Okay. Who checked the services before the CSI search began?"

"I did, Guv," Annie replied nervously. "The gas cupboard was in the kitchen at the rear of the building. I had the supply isolated at the meter, Guv. We left the domestic electric supply running but all equipment was run through a bank of RCD switches. All the safety checks were signed off by myself and Kathy Brooks before they began their search."

"Good," Alec sounded relieved. "We're under the cosh as it

is but this is going to bring the rain down in buckets, Annie. We need to make sure that procedurally, we're watertight."

"I know," Annie sighed. "The investigation must look like a shambles from London, Guv. Maybe I should step down from the investigation."

"If you offer to do that to the Chief, he'll rip your hand off and you'll be working vehicle crime for the next twenty years. He needs a scapegoat or results." Alec had seen too many bright talents sacrificed to satiate public demand and the government's image. He'd seen the tough-on-crime politicians come and go and it made him sick to the core. It implied that the police were not tough on crime all the time. Was there ever a let's-be-lenient-on-crime week or a let's-be-reasonably-fair-on-crime month? Not in Alec's world and he wasn't going to let a good detective like Annie Jones fall on her sword to silence their critics for a moment. They would take the sacrifice and demand the impossible at the rising of the sun the next day. Pressure for results was always intense and it was also relentless. That was the way it was and Alec knew that it wouldn't be any different once they locked up their killer. There would be time for a quick breath of fresh air, a moment of self satisfaction, a bottle of single malt shared with a team of ambitious crime fighters and then the weight of expectation would return with a vengeance at nine o'clock the next morning. There was never any letup. "We'll give him results. If you are not up to the task then you'll hear it from me first, not the Chief. I don't want to hear you mention stepping down again. Am I clear?"

"Guv."

"Right. On the subject of results, I need you to arrest Richard Tibbs."

"Tibbs?"

"Tibbs is Mark Weston," Alec said. He didn't want to mention the details of what had happened in Iraq. It would cloud the issues that they faced. Annie had made too many mistakes already to muddy the waters further. He needed her focused on the facts that they had, which were few and far between. It would have been easy to let her stand down and take responsibility for the lack of progress, but that wasn't his way. Despite all that, it was difficult to keep the disappointment out of his voice when he spoke about Tibbs. "Find him and search all the details on Weston, the van, the house and anything else that he has that name on. We need to connect him to that house. Then dig into Tibbs himself. I want his bank accounts, his telephone records, his rental agreements, car insurance, his barber, his doctor, his dentist, understand?"

"Yes, Guv," she replied tentatively. Annie sensed his frustration with her. "Can I ask why the switch to Tibbs, what happened at Sandhurst?"

"What happened is we didn't check out his story properly," Alec said. He regretted saying it immediately.

"You mean I didn't check out his story properly."

"I meant what I said. We didn't." Alec paused. Destroying her confidence would not help right now. "You have one of the biggest cases this decade to handle and there are numerous priorities vying for attention at any one time. We will miss things, but as long as we sort them eventually, we won't go far wrong. Tibbs was a witness not a suspect."

"What have you found out?"

"Weston is a previous alias. He was married, but the Major wasn't sure if his wife killed herself or if those two young girls are his grandchildren."

"The lying bastard," Annie hissed. "We checked as far as we

could!"

"Look, he lied to the court the last time he was charged and they hit the same brick wall that you did. His information is classified. You could not have known. The fact is that we know now."

"Well I know now, but I still don't believe anything that I hear about Richard Tibbs, or whatever his real name is!" Annie was furious. "I need to see this information for myself. I need to run checks to see if Captain Dunn was ever registered as married here, Guv."

"You do?" Alec tried not to laugh at her anger. He needed her fired up.

"Something isn't right about the whole army cover up with him," Annie said angrily. "I'll have him checked through every registry office in the county. There will be records of his birth, his parents, any deaths and then I'll decide if what the army say is true. If there are any blood relations to those girls in his family, then I'll find it."

"Go and find him. I am almost certain that he's our killer."

"I'm on it."

"Oh, and Annie," Alec thought aloud. "Tibbs is connected to Dazik Kraznic."

"Via Breck Road?"

"The van, the house, Mark Weston?"

"They could be accomplices in the murders."

"That makes sense."

"I'm setting off now, keep me posted."

Chapter 28

Janice Nixon looked at the computer-generated images and thought back over the months and years that she had grafted on the streets. There were so many faces, that they seemed to merge into one long memory. The hours, days, months and years were speeded up like a time lapse film of her sad depraved existence. Wake up, take drugs, get dressed, sex for money, take drugs, sleep and repeat. Sometimes there was some food in there too. She couldn't remember the last time that she ate a nice meal. A meal that looked amazing when it arrived at the table and tasted even better than it looked. Her only clear memories were when she had been frightened and there were plenty of them. She had to break the cycle before the wheels fell off completely. It was as if the drugs softened her abusive daily routine into a soup of normality. To abuse drugs, she had to allow others to abuse her. Her circle of life was not the one intended by nature. Waking up with a type of hunger which was never really satiated became mundane. There were no highs anymore, only normal and lows so deep that she couldn't climb out without help. Drugs were her ladder to climb back to normal. She always had her first fix of the day ready for when she awoke. She would rather go to bed shaking and sweating than wake up with nothing to take. Her first hit was the most important. It allowed her to do what she needed to do to acquire the funds to feed the hunger which would stalk her through her waking hours. It never left her for a moment; a terrible itch which could never be scratched, a yearning so powerful that her body ached for it and yet when she took it, it was only mundane. The dazzling mind blowing highs that it once gave her were gone. Years of taking drugs made the week fade into a mash, so that she could function and no more than that. There was no clarity to her memories, no sounds, no smells just a mass of unpleasant sex and fuzzy faces.

The faces she looked at now were very lifelike; their eyes so alive that it was spooky. He had told her that they were images of what they thought the dead women might have looked like. There was something weird about that. The fact that they weren't real was one thing, but the fact that they were dead gave her the creeps. She repeatedly moved the three photographs into a triangular pattern and focused on the middle image for a few minutes, before repeating the process. "How long ago was she buried?" Janice asked. "This one is a maybe."

"The blond woman?" Stirling asked. "Our best guess is about twelve months, maybe less."

"She could be someone who worked briefly on our patch. I can't be sure though." She fiddled with her wrists as she spoke. Stirling noticed faint lines criss-crossing her forearms. Tiny raised scars, barely visible at a glance. He realised that she was a self harmer. The scars that he could see were near the wrist. They were old. Harmers evolved as people close became aware of their self loathing. Stirling guessed that she would keep the new scars where people couldn't see them. He felt the urge to roll up her sleeves and look for them. The fact that she was suffering bothered him. He felt the need to protect her. It was a dichotomy which had him baffled. His work made him tough, asbestos-like. He rarely had the emotions that an average human being would feel. Shootings, stabbings, overdoses, violent assaults and death were part of the job. Normally he dealt with, it yet here he was feeling concern for a tom. Cutting the skin and causing pain somehow released the pain within harmers. That was how he understood it anyway, although he felt like telling them to get a grip. Have a beer, have a cigarette, smoke a joint, kick the cat; do whatever it takes to unwind, but slicing your arms? Get a grip. He kept his opinions close to his chest. Expressing his theory of therapy for the mentally unwell would not get him promoted, nor would it endear her to him.

"Okay," Stirling smiled. "Anything that you can give us will help us to identify them. If we know who they are, then we can work out where they came from and where they worked. We need to know where he took them from so that we can find him and lock him up."

"Sick bastard," she hissed. "Were they all like, you know," she blushed, "like me?"

"No," Stirling replied with a shake of his big head. "One of them was a student from down south. She was nineteen."

"Nineteen," Janice said. "Her poor parents."

"They all had parents somewhere, but for whatever reason, no one knew that these girls were missing."

"It's so sad really though, isn't it?"

"What is?" Stirling asked. He was fascinated by her eyes. They were the greenest eyes that he had seen. The fact that she was a tom was more a hindrance than he cared to admit to himself but he couldn't deny being attracted to her. In his head, he could actually see himself taking her out on a date. When he said date, he meant for a curry. Jim Stirling, knight in shining armour and true romantic. Beer and curry. He had never been tempted romantically by a witness, but Janice made him edgy.

"Being murdered like that and no one even knows your name, or reports you missing," she said quietly. The corners of her mouth twitched to a half smile. A tongue stud glinted against the pink softness of her mouth. Stirling wondered what it would feel like to kiss her. "Makes you wonder if anyone would notice if you went missing yourself, doesn't it?"

"I know for a fact that the landlord of the Cherry would notice me gone," Stirling laughed. She laughed too and he liked the way the corners of her eyes wrinkled. "As would Murat from the curry house next to the pub. The loss of earnings would seriously threaten their livelihood. To be honest, I think that they would report me missing within twenty-four hours of my last visit." Stirling grunted when he laughed. He reminded her of a gorilla; a friendly gorilla but a gorilla none the less. "I have a few beers and a curry most nights after work. What about you?"

"I have a bath and some chocolate," she smiled sadly as she spoke.

"We all need to unwind somehow, eh?"

"Yes," she muttered, "drugs work for me but then you're a policeman so that's no good is it. You should stick to your beer and curry."

"Who would notice you gone, someone surely?"

Janice thought for a moment. Her eyes held his, smiling and mischievous. "I call my mum every Sunday morning before she goes for lunch. She meets my sister and my brother. It's a full Nixon family day out." Janice touched her lips with her fingers as she spoke. "My brother and sister take their partners and their children every Sunday without fail. They go to the same Toby Carvery, which my dad took us to every week since as far back as I can remember." Her expression took a sad tone as the memories replayed in her mind. "They always have the same table, week in and week out. She's a real creature of habit. If I didn't call she would think something was wrong. She would notice me gone, which is nice isn't it?"

"Do you speak to your sister or brother?" Stirling was shocked that she had such a normal sounding family background. He knew that it took all sorts but something about her meant he cared. Her family didn't sound broken beyond repair.

"Not for a long time." Her eyes dropped to the table. She

seemed to be staring the faces of the dead women. "It gets too complicated, birthdays, christenings, anniversaries. They're always inviting me to things and I'm always declining and making excuses that nobody believes. It got so awkward that I stopped going eventually."

"It's not safe out there at the moment. You're lucky that you have somewhere to go. You should go and see them," Stirling mumbled. He felt as if his efforts to impress were clumsy. "A lot of the girls out there don't have anyone. You never know what will happen, you might like it. It could get you off the streets."

"While I appreciate your sentiment," she spoke clearly, "you're verging on being patronising." She shifted uncomfortably in her seat. "I really need to get home."

"I'm sorry," Stirling said. He regretted mentioning it immediately. "It all sounded so normal, you know, the Sunday lunch and that. So far away from where those girls ended up. That could be you. I'm not patronising you, I'm concerned about your welfare. You don't need me to tell you how many lunatics are out there. Are things that bad that they can't be sorted?"

Janice smiled and took a breath. Her eyes fell on a silver crucifix which Stirling wore around his thick neck. His stubble was silver, flecked with black and the chain nestled where the stubble met his chest hair. She remembered wearing a crucifix that her father had given her as a child. She never took it off, but she lost it one day at school and cried for a week until he bought her a new one. "My mother tells me that I was always a difficult child. Things were said after my father died," she explained. "Things, which can't be forgiven or taken back. I tried it once. Playing the doting auntie to the little ones, while everyone chats about their perfect jobs and their perfect partners doesn't work when all anyone wants to know is if I'm still taking crack and sucking cocks to pay for it. Thanks for the concern but I can look after myself."

Her abruptness took him aback. He felt that he'd crossed a line into her private world and she'd slammed the door in his face. "Okay," Stirling said holding up his palms to the ceiling. "I get the message. I'll shut up. It's none of my business. I have no right to offer advice." He felt awkward and foolish. The only way Janice would be interested in a lump like him was if he had some money to pay for it. He cleared his throat nervously and tried to turn back to the job in hand. "Getting back to what you said earlier, do you think that you know her?"

"Maybe, but there's something different about her," she answered. "I like it that you care." A smile touched her lips. The frostiness seemed to melt slightly.

Stirling was taken aback again but felt a warm feeling spreading through his veins. "I do," he smiled. "Care that is." He nodded and coughed nervously, not wanting to encroach and be rebuffed again. "What's different about the image?"

"She had a turn in her left eye," Janice said. "We used to say she had one eye looking at you and the other looking for you. Her name was Nicola. Nicola Thomas. I might have a picture of her at home. We went to a party together once before she moved on. I could give it to you if it helps. You have my address don't you?"

"That would be really useful," Stirling smiled. He thought that she had invited him to her house. He wasn't sure but he thought that she had. A twinkle in her eyes confirmed it. He picked up his mobile and dialed. "Jim Stirling here," he said. "I need you to crosscheck victim four on the system with a Nicola Thomas. And can you check with Kathy Brooks if it's possible that the victim had a turn in her left eye, please. Thanks, let me know straight away. Thanks for that, it could be a really useful lead."

"You're welcome" she said, blushing.

"Listen," he said. "Can you remember what happened to her? Where did she go?"

"I'm not certain, but if I remember rightly her and a few others went to work indoors," she grinned. "You know, at a brothel."

"When?"

"Maybe eighteen months or more. It's hard for me to remember details."

"Where did they go to work?"

"It was hush hush because it was in a quiet close. The firm who ran it only used it for their own guys to party there. I never went there but I heard it was on Breck Road."

The significance of the address wasn't lost on Stirling, but he tried not to look excited. "Breck Road?" he nodded. "Did you know the number?"

"No," she thought aloud. "One hundred and something."

"One, six, three?"

"It could have been."

"You know, I don't know the area well, but I think I would remember vice mentioning a brothel there," Stirling lied. There was no mention in their searches of anything illegal going on at the property. "Are you sure it was Breck Road?"

"I'm positive, because I remember they said that it backed onto Kensington. That estate is all boarded up now but back then it was occupied." She laughed at the memory. "Proper shithole but people lived there; the type of people who didn't complain about cars parking in their street while the drivers climbed through a hedge to visit a brothel on the next estate."

"That's really helpful," Stirling said. "Why park on the estate though?"

"There was a cut through the hedges which separated the close from the estate. I remember dealers and junkies used the snickett to move from Kensington to Anfield, without using any main roads."

"On their mountain bikes?"

"Yes," she laughed. "Haven't they noticed that there are no mountains in the city, yet there are a million mountain bikes? I bet half of them are ridden by dealers!"

"You're right."

"I remember bumping into her and her friend once. They said the punters only used the back door, that way the neighbours didn't have a clue what was going on."

"Clever. We didn't know that it was a brothel."

"It wasn't for long though." Janice mused. "I heard they moved on somewhere else."

"When?"

"I don't know, just rumours, you know."

"Who did she work for? Did she say?"

"Now you're asking," she said uncertainly. "I know the Russian mob were in cahoots there. It was their men who used it but I can't remember the name of the guy who rented the place; Stringer or Strider, something like that."

"Ryder possibly?"

"Possibly," she shrugged. "I'm away with the fairies most of the time and the rest of the time I'm stoned."

"Hey, it doesn't matter. What you have told me so far is very helpful."

"Good, I'm glad. I hope you catch the bastard."

"Do you know any of the other girls who went to work there?"

"I can't remember."

"Do you recognise any of these women?" Stirling put the pictures of the women that they had already been identified onto the table. "Kerris Owens."

"Kerris, Kerris, Kerris," she repeated. "No. I don't know her."

"Jackie Goodall?"

She shook her head. "No. She was pretty though, wasn't she?"

"She was."

"Bastard."

"We'll catch him. Don't worry."

"Was it quick?"

"What?"

"When he killed them." Her top lip trembled. "Was it quick?"

"No."

"Bastard."

"What about this girl?" He changed the tack. "Mary Jackson?" Janice opened her mouth to speak but remained silent. She looked hard at the photograph. A memory pricked her mind.

"Yes, I know her." She smiled. "I do know her!"

"You do?"

"Yes, she's hairy Mary!"

"Hairy Mary?" Stirling almost laughed. The connotations of how she acquired the nickname were endless. It was one to repeat in the pub in the future. "She was a legend. She refused to shave her bits, you know, down there."

"Oh dear," Stirling frowned. "Not good."

"No!" she laughed. "It was good for her."

"I don't follow."

"Blokes are all different," she explained. "Some men like shaved and some like hairy. They get to know who their favourites are. Men travelled across the city to go with her."

"Where did she work, Janice?"

"I remember that she worked on Jamaica Street for a while. I had never met her then but everyone knew her nickname. 'Hairy Mary', I can't believe she's dead."

"Could she have worked at Breck Road?"

"I don't know but she could have I suppose. I doubt it though."

"Why?"

"She had her own clients."

"Maybe she'd had enough on the streets?"

"Look, it's a gamble that they take," Janice said. "Indoors can be warmer, drier, there's company and protection and a guaranteed customer flow."

"But," he smiled. "It sounds like there's a but."

"Some places it's almost like a job, you know, turn up, do your work and then go home when you've earned enough. I tried it once. The problem is, if you are into drugs then you could be making a deal with the devil. They treat you well at first, take a small cut and sell you gear at cost. Then the price goes up and so does the percentage that they take for the punters. You have to work longer hours for the same money and pretty soon all you're doing is working your tripe off to pay for your drugs, and the only winner is your pimp. He has ready-made addicts buying his gear and he's making a packet from the punters."

"You make it sound like a solid business venture."

"I'm sitting on a goldmine," she laughed. "I call it my moneymaker. If I didn't have a habit, I would be minted!"

"Drugs, eh. They have a lot to answer for. It's a slippery slope for the girls and a dangerous one."

"It is. I complained about his percentage and he knocked my front teeth out and raped me for my cheek." Janice put her thumb and forefinger into her mouth and pulled out a brace with three teeth fixed to it. She smiled a gummy smile and cocked her head sideways. "I never went back, but I couldn't work for three weeks either. I was broke. It took me months to get straight. Since then, I take my chances outside. Cold and wet beats black and blue."

"What was his name?" Stirling could feel his blood boiling.

"Gary Collins," she said. "Are you going to beat him up for

me?"

"No," he stuttered embarrassed. He felt his face flushing red with anger. "I'll keep my eye out for him, that's all."

"My hero."

"I'm not trying to be a hero," he shrugged. "Why didn't you report him for the rape?"

"Are you kidding me?" she asked with her mouth wide open.

"No!"

"I'm a hooker with a crack addiction."

"It's still rape."

"It wasn't always rape." She shook her head slowly as if she couldn't believe how naive he was. "Do I have to spell it out? I didn't always make enough money from the punters. I'm not proud of it but that's just the way it was. What do you think a jury would make of that?"

"I see your point."

"Do you?"

"Yes. He's scum." He couldn't meet her eyes with his. "I'm just saying blokes like him need taking off the streets. If I come across him, I'll make sure that he is."

"Fingers crossed that you do, Sergeant," she said smiling. She held up both hands, her fingers crossed. He noticed that she was shaking. She noticed that he had noticed and her smile disappeared. "I need to go. I'm beginning to feel that hunger. You know what I mean, or do I have to spell that out too?" Stirling nodded silently and slotted the photographs into his file. Their eyes locked for a second.

"I'll get someone to show you out," he said quietly. "Thanks for your help." He nodded and walked to the door. Opening it he paused to speak but then thought better of it. She needed to score. Delaying her would only cause her pain.

Chapter 29

Alec pulled his BMW onto the kerb, wheels half on and half off. Annie ended a phone call in the passenger seat and they sat in silence and looked at the terraced house that Tibbs had given as his mother's address. It was a two up, two down on the outskirts of the city. A single stone step before the front door was worn in the middle and painted white. Decorative net curtains hung in the windows, yellowed with age. The sash windows hadn't been painted for ten summers at least.

"I thought that he couldn't have any contact with his family because he's in the protection program?" Alec ducked his head to look at the upper windows. He was hoping that a full background check had been run this time around. There could be no more mistakes made with Richard Tibbs.

"After his crash episode, Stirling ran the address before he let him leave the station, Guv," Annie allayed his doubts. "Once bitten, twice shy. The house was registered to Mrs Dunn. She died three years ago and the house is technically still in probate because they can't trace her son, Captain Nigel Dunn. He must have a key and keeps it as a hideaway."

"And we know that he's in?"

"Yes, Guv," Annie said. "He came home an hour ago and hasn't left since. Shall I give the order?"

"Yes." Alec nodded and sat back in his seat. "Tell them to put the fear of God into him. Arrest him for breach of bail conditions."

"All units, green light, go, go, go!" Annie felt good sending in the armed forced entry unit. Tibbs would crap in his pants which would be a good thing; a small but tantalisingly delicious taste of revenge for taking the piss out of her. He had played her a merry tune and she had danced to it and made herself look incompetent to her seniors. That wouldn't happen again. She smiled inside as a heavy battering ram shattered the front door. The armed officers slipped inside one by one, their shouts audible even inside the car. Thirty seconds dragged by.

"We've got Tibbs, Guv," the comms unit crackled. "All clear."

"Let's go and speak to our number one suspect, Detective." Alec said as he opened the door. They climbed out and walked across the street. Two armed officers took up position on either side of the door. Annie noted three sets of curtains twitching, neighbours desperate for the latest gossip. She stepped into the house and it reminded her of her grandma's home. It had that old person smell. Mothballs mixed with damp and potpourri. The flavours of sterilized milk and strawberry jam on toast drifted back to her; her granddad's teeth floating in a glass of cloudy liquid on the windowsill in the bathroom. They were pleasant memories but unwelcome too. Remembering her past was often triggered by odours. Smells reminded her of the past far more than sights or sounds. A hideously patterned Wilton covered the hallway and the staircase directly in front of them. The walls were papered with a similarly hideous wood chip. A young schoolboy stared at them from the wall; a tear ran down his cheek. His tragic image was on the walls of a million people of that generation. Annie reckoned that most of them would be buried in landfill by now and the one on the wall could be the only one left.

"Where is he?" Annie asked. She mentally studied the interior of the house.

"In the kitchen," the entry team leader answered. "He's not

alone either," he added with a grin as he walked to the front door. "Caught with his pants down, Guv!"

Annie held her breath as she walked past a living room and a lounge. They would be searched later. For now she wanted to speak to Tibbs. At the end of the hallway, strips of multi-coloured plastic acted as a door to the kitchen. Annie knew that they were originally designed as a fly-screen but had become an epitome of household fashion. She poked her head through the gaudy plastic strips and stepped into the kitchen. More memories flooded back. A blackened kettle sat on an electric ring, its whistle still shiny and a bone china tea set sat on the stainless steel draining board.

"Here, Bugsy! There is no need for this," Tibbs shouted at her. "I'm trying to help you and you've shafted me. I gave you my fucking address!" Annie watched a very embarrassed woman dressing in a hurry. She had a tribal tattoo at the base of spine. Annie's teenage cousin called them 'slag tags'. Her eyebrows were shaved and penciled into a heavy wedge shape. When they went to town shopping, her cousin would nudge her, "look Auntie Anne, a 'scouse brow'." The woman looked around the uniformed gathering without making eye contact with anyone. She particularly avoided Annie's eyes.

"You've met someone your own age, I see," Alec said what Annie was thinking. She had expected the worst. "What's your name, luv?"

"Angel," she said climbing into a faux fur jacket.

"Angel?" Alec said. "Are they all called that?" he turned to Annie with a half smile on his face. "Were you here of your own accord?"

"What," she said. "Is he taking the piss?"

"Were you forced here, Angel?" Annie translated.

"No, of course not!"

"Of course not?" Alec repeated. "What are you doing here then?"

"Use your imagination, darling," she said sarcastically. "You'd be amazed what I will do for fifty quid. Richard is a regular aren't you, darling. You should give it a whirl sometime, might loosen you up."

"I'm as loose as I need to be, thanks," Alec mumbled. "Get her out of here."

"Oh," Angel objected loudly. "I haven't been paid yet!"

"The money is in my jeans," Tibbs interrupted.

"Normally you would have to wait, Angel," Annie nodded to a uniformed officer as she spoke. "But under the circumstances, this officer will give you the money, as you won't be seeing this scumbag for a century or more."

"That sounds bad," Angel tottered towards the door on heels too big for her. "What has he done?"

"Get her out of here."

"What did he do? Have I bonked someone famous?" The fly-screen fell off the doorway and clattered onto the linoleum. "This fucking dump is falling to bits," she ranted as she was led away. "I never liked this dump. It smells of old peoples' piss," she called, as they pushed her out of the front door.

"Nice lady," Alec commented.

"I thought so until you lot kicked my front door in!" Tibbs was furious. "What was that all about? I've done nothing but help you lot. I even gave you my address."

"You did but you didn't give us your other name, Mark Weston, did you?"

"I'm in the witness protection program. They have to change my name." Tibbs looked at Alec. "You know that don't you?"

"That's enough for now," Alec said.

"You're under arrest for breach of bail conditions." Annie read him his rights and let the uniformed officers take him away. When he was out of earshot, she spoke to Alec. "I'll have this place searched before we sit him down. I want the results from Breck Road and all the reports back from the registry offices before I talk to him again. He's not fobbing us off again this time."

Alec thought about what the Major had said. If Tibbs refused to talk and demanded to speak to his handlers, then he could slip through their hands again. He couldn't let this happen. Alec decided that he would leak it to the press about who he was and that he was a suspect in the Crosby Beach murders. The army would drop him like a bad smell and find another way to cover up his past. It would also blow away all credibility in anything he said. He had to keep his plan close for now, not even Annie Jones could know.

"While they process him, let's go to Breck Road and speak to Kathy," Alec suggested.

"Yes, we'll do that, Guv." They left the uniformed officers combing the house. Annie began to make a series of phone calls as they walked from the house to the car. Alec listened to each in turn and decided that he would have made them in exactly the same order. She was a chip off the old block, a good detective who needed some luck.

Chapter 30

The stench of burning reached them three streets before they actually set eyes on the smouldering ruins of 163 Breck Road. It reminded Annie of bonfire night. That memory triggered the thought of a baked potato, wrapped in tinfoil, roasted in the white ash as the fire burned down; the fluffy white interior a contrast against the blackened crispy jacket, with lashings of melted butter and way too much salt. Her memories reminded her that she hadn't eaten for twelve hours. Brushing the thoughts away, Annie broke the quiet. "Good news, Guv." A truck crane was lifting roof timbers from the rubble, while fire fighters sifted through the more manageable debris by hand.

"Good," Alec answered. "Don't keep it to yourself." He saw a JCB digger skimming the top layer from the garden as white-clad technicians studied the soil beneath. There was no scope for any more people on the site without compromising safety. Annie had organised things well.

"That was Stirling. He showed some of the enhanced images to Janice Nixon and she recognised one of them. We're running her name through the system. She also said that two of the dead women worked on the streets in Kensington and then moved to work at a brothel. Have a guess where it was?"

"I assume that I am looking at where it used to be?" Alec looked from the wreckage to Annie and back again.

"Yes, Guv."

"That changes everything. This pushes the cause of the explosion towards the deliberate option."

"It does, Guv." Annie swallowed hard. "We've opened Pandora's box here."

"Well let's hope we do a better job of closing it than she did."

"On a brighter note, Stirling said that Tasha Jenkins is awake and talking. Lewis is setting up a formal identification parade for first thing in the morning." Alec sighed and nodded. Slowly, slowly catches the monkey, he thought. One block at a time, the puzzle had to fit together. If they forced it, they would smash it and it would never take shape. The problem with their puzzle was that the pieces never remained the same shape for long. They morphed and altered into something else entirely if they didn't use them quickly. They exchanged a silent glance and opened the doors, climbing out before heading towards the mobile laboratory. The smell of scorched timber carried to them on the breeze. It was tinged with the scent of gas. The sound of diesel generators drowned out a hail of questions from the press cordon further up the street.

"Guv," Kathy Brooks called from the rear of the trailer-lab. "You need to see this. I'm glad you're here." The JCB engine gunned as it picked up a grab full of turf. The sound seemed to resonate through the ground. "I've had some very interesting results."

"That sounds encouraging," Alec said. "I hope you've got something solid, Kathy. We need a break." He caught the eye of the fire chief, fifty yards across the grass and waved. He returned the wave but shook his head and put a thumb down. "No joy with the search yet," he muttered beneath his breath. "I can't see anyone climbing out of that alive." Kathy held the door open and they stepped into a brightly lit lab. Halfway down the trailer, clear glass partitioned the sorting lab from the testing area. Alec watched as a scientist stood in a decontamination chamber between the two. "Tell me what you have," he sighed wearily. "If it's not good, make something up."

"You look tired, Annie," Kathy pointed out.

"Thanks," she replied sourly. "I've already been called Bugsy today, now you start."

"Who called you that?" Kathy frowned angrily. "The cheeky bastard!"

"No one that I'm worried about."

"Seriously though," Kathy whispered, "you look knackered."

"She's going to be having an early night tonight," Alec interrupted. "I need my DI fully rested to commence battle at zero, eight-hundred hours tomorrow. We've got a suspect to interrogate."

"Interview."

"Sorry," Alec saluted. "Interview."

"I'd get that in writing if I was you," Kathy winked at Alec. "If I had a pound for every time he said that I needed an early night!"

"You'd have less than a fiver," Alec finished the sentence.

"Okay, I can sense that Annie isn't the only one who needs some sleep," Kathy huffed. "Firstly the van, which Tasha Jenkins was allegedly abducted in." She brought up a report on her laptop. "It was cleaned superficially. Someone had a very good go at wiping it clean."

"No trace?" Annie asked confused.

"What I'm saying is that someone tried to remove all the trace."

"But failed?"

"Yes," Kathy nodded as she spoke and pointed to the screen.

"I can put Tasha into the front seat. I recovered her hair between the gearstick and the seat-belt anchor and skin cells beneath her finger nails belong to Dazik Kraznic."

"She scratched him," Annie smiled. "Good girl."

"It's a good start," Alec agreed.

"That's the kidnap charge sorted," Annie sighed with relief.

"I've also matched dead skin from Tasha and Francis Grant on the Taser spikes. They were assaulted with that weapon."

"Excellent!" Annie clasped her hands together.

"We also have Kraznic's hair in the weld of the Taser handle. You have your attacker connected to the assault weapon too."

"He doesn't deny picking it up," Alec pointed out. "He said that he picked it up just before the FET went in."

"Did he say that he tried to use it on them?" Kathy asked.

"No and they didn't report him trying to use it either," Annie added. "Why?"

"Because the hair has been frazzled, subjected to an electric source of substantial voltage. Most of it was carbon but there was enough to extract DNA." She explained. She pointed to a magnified image on the screen. "It's from his finger or hand and it was there before the Taser was discharged. He had it in his hand when it was used."

"That's a relief," Alec said. "So we have him in the van and using the Taser. What about in the house?"

"We don't have anything from the cellar, I'm afraid. We were processing it when the explosion hit," Kathy paused. Her hand went to her mouth. She took a deep breath and composed herself. "What I did get from inside before the explosion is very interesting."

"Good, we really need to get busy on whatever you've got," Alec replied.

"Oh, you'll be busy alright." Kathy handed them a print out, six pages long. "We found prints all over the house. Nine sets are in the system. There are their names. You've got some heavyweights on that list."

"Kolorov is on here, Guv," Annie said excitedly. "I recognise three of his men too."

"Look here," Alec pointed. "John Ryder. This ties in with what Stirling got from Janice Nixon. She said the place was a brothel for a time, backed by Russian money. That ties in with John Ryder working with them. We know they own property together."

"They are serious criminals, yes?" Kathy asked, concerned.

"Yes," Annie replied. "About as serious as they can get."

"Were my people blown up on purpose?" Kathy's voice broke slightly. "Was that explosion set deliberately?"

"We won't know until the fire officers have finished," Alec tried to reassure her.

"Annie and I turned off the gas at the meter."

"I know you did," Alec said. "No one is questioning that."

"Then if we did our jobs correctly, someone set the explosion deliberately?"

"My instinct tells me it's no coincidence and I can promise you that we'll find whoever did it."

"You can't promise that, but I know you'll do your best."

Kathy looked away and tried to clear her head. Vengeance was an emotion that she couldn't afford right now. The best thing that her and her team could do now was to process everything as quickly as possible. She sighed and gathered her track. "Okay, that's the easy bits to tell you," Kathy began again. "I took blood and semen off a mattress from one of the bedrooms on the top floor. None of the bedrooms had locks on the doors, apart from that one."

"So whoever managed the business lived there?"

"Maybe," Kathy agreed. "Makes sense. Well, the blood from the mattress matches one of our prawns."

"What?"

"Yes," Kathy said gravely. "We haven't identified her yet but it matches her DNA. The semen is also in the system and that's where things get complicated."

"I don't follow," Alec said. "If they're in the system, we can identify them."

"Oh their DNA is in the system alright but their name isn't. It's been erased."

"Who can be erased from the database?"

"Someone in witness protection," Alec answered.

"Richard Tibbs," Annie said beneath her breath.

"We know that Tibbs was once known as Weston. His name is attached to this place and now so is his DNA. But we can't prove in court that it's his."

"We've got enough to nail him in an interview, Guv," Annie said. "I want to nail the bastard to the wall. He was here, and so were some of the missing girls. I think this house is the missing link that we've been looking for. If those women all worked here, then we're even closer to nailing Tibbs than we thought."

"Don't get carried away," Alec warned. "It's early days yet and most of it's circumstantial."

"We've got him, Guv," Annie said excitedly. "I've had a feeling about him from the first time that I met him. All we have to do now is keep him locked up."

"Okay, let's plan this out," Alec held up fingers and counted as he spoke. "Firstly we need to get Kolorov and Ryder onside so we can pick their brains about what went on here."

"I think that's the key," Annie agreed. "I mean, why close the place down if they were making money?"

"We need them onside to ask them," Alec carried on. "Secondly we need to link the victims to this house and thirdly we need to link Tibbs to the victims."

"We'll struggle with step one, Guv."

"I didn't say it would be easy."

"No, but when step one is unachievable, step three becomes impossible."

"Go home and sleep for a few hours." Alec pointed his finger at her. "We'll meet later and get cracking on Tibbs. Thanks for all the hard work, Kathy. Keep it up."

"Guv." Kathy walked away checking results on digital screens as she went.

"Annie," Alec had an afterthought.

"Yes, Guv?"

"We came in my car."

"I know, Guv."

"I'd better drop you off at home on my way then," he laughed. "You've done well, Annie. We've got a killer in custody."

"Listen, Guv," Annie said as they reached the car. "I've got a million things running through my mind. I'm never going to sleep. Why don't we call Stirling and go for a bite to eat and a beer. We should talk this over, there's so much to take in."

"Sounds like a plan," Alec agreed. He opened the door and took one last look at the site. "They're not going to pull her out of there alive." He shook his head and climbed into the car. The urge to light a cigarette swamped him but he had given up again, for the third time since Gail had died. She would be spinning in her grave if she knew. This time he would stick to it, although sometimes there didn't seem much point in packing in. He lived alone and he enjoyed it. His main motivation was the fact that his office was on the top floor and it took nine minutes to take the lift and walk across the car park to the smoking shelter. That was a pain in the neck and worth packing in for.

Annie was on the mobile to Stirling as he started the engine and flicked through the stations looking for a decent tune. Teenage Kicks by the Undertones was playing on Rock FM. He turned up the volume a touch and let his head fall back onto the rest. His eyes were tired and felt gritty but he knew that if he rubbed them, they would feel worse. Tired eyes were up there with aching joints and the urge to pee in the middle of the night. Middle age was getting a grip.

"Stirling is busy, Guv," Annie huffed as she climbed into the passenger seat. "He reckons he needs to pick up a recent picture of one of our victims from a witness. It's just us I'm afraid."

"Which witness?"

"I don't know. I didn't think to ask."

"You should ask, Annie," Alec scolded her unconsciously. "You need to know every detail about everything in your investigation."

"Yes, Guv," she sighed. "I know, Guv."

"No problem. You have to be a sponge, Annie, absorb everything and give nothing away unless you're squeezed."

"I am a sponge, Guv."

"And don't take the piss out of your governor."

"Perish the thought."

Alec waited for his track to finish and then turned the music down. "I'll head to Coopers on the docks. Best burgers in town." He looked at Annie for a response but she was already asleep.

Chapter 31

John Ryder patted his breast pocket and wished that he had brought his Glock. Most meetings didn't warrant bringing a gun, but he felt that this one might. In his younger days, he wouldn't be without one but now his reputation alone was enough to terrify the majority of people, but not all. It was difficult to intimidate those who thought that they were tougher than you, and stupid people. Stupid people were different. They weren't scared easily because they didn't understand the danger that they were in, but that was when the muscle earned their money. His enforcers were built like bulls and had similar temperaments. When John waved the red flag, they attacked without question. Bones were often broken, faces sliced. Teeth pulled with pliers, finger nails ripped out. Whatever it took could be arranged and executed without incriminating the source of the violence. Victims knew exactly where the orders emanated from but daren't disclose it.

Unfortunately, bringing backup of any description was against their code. They had been partners for many years and they were wealthy and healthy because neither one had broken the code. Violence was part of the business that he was in but he rarely witnessed it anymore. It was carried out by others and he reaped the benefits from a distance. Stability was the key to their success. They didn't cross into anyone's territory. They didn't disrespect anyone. When others broke the code and crossed them, they were dispatched with swift brutality and stability was restored quickly. Now things were out of kilter and a member of his family was the cause. His stepson, Brendon, had caused no end of problems growing up but this time he had surpassed himself. The results of his antics had caused sleeping dogs to awake; nasty aggressive dogs with big teeth and now John had to try to calm them, or muzzle them. Stability had to be restored immediately.

He stepped out of the station and the wind sliced through his clothes and chilled him immediately. The lights from the harbour and the city beyond cast a yellow glow above the watery metropolis. John watched the other passengers leaving the station, scanning their faces for any kind of familiarity. Everyone was potentially a lookout, an assassin, his killer. He waited until most of them had drifted off and only a few stragglers remained. They were all strangers heading into the night. The woman closest to him looked Spanish; a hundred yards to his right a Japanese businessman drank coffee from a Starbucks cup and eyed him. John turned to get a good look at him but the man threw his cup into a bin and ran into the arms of a pretty red head. He picked her up and whirled her around. They laughed and kissed like a couple in love, parted for too long. He couldn't see or sense any imminent threats and decided to move on with his journey. A bank of cabs waited patiently for fares, but the tram stop was only a hundred yards to his right. It had always been part of their code, no cars, no taxis, they were too easy to follow and drivers could be bribed. Public transport was the only mode of travel allowed. He preferred the tram when he came here. Six sets of tramlines curved from across the canal to the station forecourt, where they loaded up passengers before distributing them all over Amsterdam. Snowflakes the size of postage stamps drifted down from graphite coloured clouds and his boots crunched in an inch of freshly fallen crystals. He could feel the excitement and taste the tension in the air. At night, the city had an aura. It was a living, breathing entity.

He saw his tram pulling into its stop and he walked quickly through the snow to meet it. The power lines above him buzzed and sparked as the trams trundled by in all directions. Waiting passengers boarded quickly and John slid his Euro note into the machine and took his ticket in return. He opted to stand and grabbed the rail as the tram jerked forward on its journey. A scruffy kid with dreadlocks and facial piercings stood next to him. The combination of body odour and the stench of stale cannabis made him feel queasy. John tapped him on the shoulder and pulled out one of his earphones to get his attention.

"What are you doing, man?" the kid whined. His accent was thick. John pitched him as a local.

"Move." John motioned with his head. "You stink."

The kid opened his mouth to speak but despite his age, John had a look in his eyes which made most want to back down. He decided against making anything of it. He had made the trip to sample the music and the dope, fighting an English dude in a thousand Euro suit on the tram wasn't on the itinerary. A couple nearby watched, an expression of distaste on their faces. John glared at the man for a second and he looked away quickly, fighting was not on the man's agenda any day of the week. If some angry guy on the tram wanted to bully a kid, so be it. John looked hard; not someone to mess with. He wasn't usually so openly aggressive but his nerves were making him tetchy. A glance sideways could have provoked an angry response. The tram swayed gently as it trundled though the city, rattling occasionally as it crossed switches. The next five minutes dragged by and took him down the Helgernstraat to the De Wallen district of the city, the network of canals, alleyways and narrow lanes which formed the famous red light district. He stood near the door and waited for the tram to stop.

As the doors opened, an icy blast of wind hit him. He stepped onto crunchy snow, instantly regretting not bringing an overcoat, but there was a good reason why taking a coat to a meeting like this one was a bad idea. He buried his hands deep into his pockets and tucked his chin to his chest to keep the chill out. The bar where he had arranged to meet his business partner was fifty yards away. Stepping off the pavement, he crossed over the tramlines and then paused as a herd of cyclists whizzed by. Not even the snow could stop the Dutch riding their bikes around the city. The cycle lanes were gritted religiously creating a black slushy strip next to the snow covered pavements. At the corner of the alleyway, an attractive blond gyrated in a window, a red light above her flashed 'sex show'. She was at street level, but stairs led up to a bar above. Murphy's Irish Bar, one of millions of similar bars worldwide which bore little to no resemblance to any bar in Ireland, save that they sold the black stuff.

John took the time to appreciate her curves with his eyes as he entered the alleyway walking towards the main island in the De Wallen. It was one of ninety such islands linked by fifteen hundred bridges, which crossed the three main canals, the Herengracht, Prinsengracht, and the Keizersgrach. He loved the city, he loved its culture and most of all he loved its anonymity. It was his idea to meet here for the first time, which was eight years prior. Whenever there was a major issue, John and Boris met alone to discuss it. It had worked for years. The same city, the same bar and always alone; no weapons and no muscle.

He could see his own breath as he ducked beneath an illuminated Guinness sign and pushed open the door of the bar. Inside was bright and warm, the floorboards were spotted with wet footprints and the odd puddle where a lump of snow had fallen from a shoe tread and melted. A group of men stood huddled around a Juke box, laughing and arguing about their choice of selections. Their language and accents told him that they were Geordies; one of a hundred stag-do trips in the city at any moment in time. He spotted Boris sat in their usual booth, on a raised area next to a window. It offered a view over the canal and the busy lanes where red lights glowed and women danced in the windows, trying to attract the eye of a passing male with a pocket full of Euros to enjoy.

John walked to the bar and checked every face on his way.

He studied every booth and every table full of tourists, looking for a familiar face. Suspect everyone, trust no one; it was the secret to a long life. All he needed was a whiff of an ambush and he would turn around and disappear into the night the way he came. The glimpse of a face or the hint of a Russian accent would give away a set-up. There were none, which was good. He couldn't be too careful. If anyone resembled any of Boris's men, then there would be trouble. Trouble in his business usually ended up with a winner and a loser; one dead person and one alive. The key to success was never being the dead one.

"Large malt, please," John smiled at the barmaid. She returned his smile as she reached up to the optic. "No ice," he added. The barmaid placed the glass onto a green napkin. John folded it around the glass. He made one more scan of the customers as he paid then climbed the steps to where Boris was waiting. The Russian stood up and they shook hands and shared a brief embrace, before sitting either side of the table. "Have you been here long?"

"No," Boris replied. "I took the tram and then had a walk around the canal. It's nice out there in the snow. Cold but nice, yes?"

"Yes, it's nice." John raised his whisky. "It's been too long. Cheers."

"It is always too long, my friend," Boris sounded genuine. They held each other's stare for a moment. Both of them knew that there was a serious problem, yet they wanted to enjoy the company of the other for as long as possible before business was broached. Boris smiled but he looked thoughtful. His eyes were full of melancholy. "You know that in a different world, we would be good friends, you and I."

"I think that we are anyway; given the circumstances of our friendship."

Boris grinned. "How old are you now, John?"

"Pushing sixty," he laughed. "I'll be having a get together at our place in Marbella. You can come to my party."

"I will."

"Don't bring that mad girl you took to London," John laughed again at the memory. "Where did you get her from?"

"I don't remember."

"She was sick on my trousers."

"I paid for them to be cleaned."

"I never got the smell out of them, no matter how many times they were cleaned."

"She was crazy, yes?" Boris agreed. "I promise not to bring her."

"Then you're invited."

"Thank you!" Boris raised his glass again. They clinked them together and then sat back, the smiles gone and the joviality lost for a moment. "Do you know how old I am, John?" his grey eyes narrowed as he spoke. His cheeks were full and reddened by vodka and there was no distinguishing line between them and his neck. "Let me tell you and then there is no pressure trying not to offend me. Shall I?" he smiled but there was no mirth in it. He loosened his tie with two sausage-like fingers and rolled up his cuffs to reveal thick hairy wrists and equally thick gold bracelets. "I will be sixty-five this year."

John nodded and smiled. There was an underlying tension between them. Boris was building up to something, that much was obvious. They respected each other, even liked each other, but it had always been obvious that Boris Kolorov didn't just call the shots in their Liverpool business ventures, he called the shots everywhere. "Sixty-five and still kicking my friend. A lot of people don't make it that far."

"They don't," Boris nodded. "That is very true. We have both lost people along the way, haven't we?"

"We have."

"And we will lose more before we are finished."

"Not too many, I hope."

"Hope is a commodity that we can seldom afford, John."

"Sometimes, hope is all that we have."

"Only for the weak, John and we are not the weak." Boris raised his empty glass in the air and the barmaid acknowledged that she wold bring a round over. "We cannot hope that things work out. We cannot hope that people don't try to steal from us. We cannot hope that a problem will fix itself." Boris paused as the barmaid put down two glasses. John wiped his empty glass and let her take it. She smiled and left in a blink, leaving the faint smell of Alien behind her. John liked that perfume and he made a mental note to buy some at the airport duty free shop on the way home. "If we allow ourselves to rely on hope, then we're finished before we begin."

"What is the problem, Boris," John asked casually.

"What do you think is the problem, John?"

"Okay, we both know what the problem is and I'm handling it."

"Are you?"

"Yes."

"I don't see any evidence of you handling it, John." Boris shrugged. "It's one thing disposing of a problem at a tourist spot. I mean that's unforgivable, but after the house? I mean, when is enough too much?"

"Is that what it is? Is it Breck Road that's the issue here?"

"Of course it is," Boris snapped. "Breck Road and your troublesome stepson. He has caused so much trouble for you, for us, for everyone!"

"So you burned it down without a thought to tell me and then you summon me here to give me a bollocking?"

"What the fuck are you talking about?"

"You know what I'm talking about."

"I didn't burn it down," Boris said slowly. His eyes narrowed to slits as he studied John suspiciously. "Do you think that I would bring any more attention to that address?"

"Do you think that I would?"

"Are you telling me that you didn't arrange it?"

"I thought you had."

"That's ridiculous," Boris sighed. "What the fuck is going on?"

"How much do you know?"

"I know that your stepson has brought every detective in Liverpool to our door," Boris said quietly. "What I want to know is why and how you intend to fix it. We should have used dynamite on that shithole the first time around."

"You're as much to blame as I am for that. We should have

tidied that mess up properly when we had the chance."

"How do you lay any of this at my feet?"

"Dazik Kraznic," John raised his index finger and wagged it at Boris. "He's yours. He took the police to Breck Road, not Brendon."

"He was told not to take women there."

"He didn't listen."

"What is he being charged with?"

"Kidnapping and wounding with intent," John leaned forward as he spoke. "And false imprisonment. He's looking at fifteen years. Do you think he's going to keep his mouth shut?"

"He'll be persuaded."

"I can't believe that you let him recruit from that address."

"Recruit? Are you mad?" the Russian snapped. "You know me better than that, John." Boris emptied his glass and waved it to be refilled. "I have acquisition teams all over the world. Do you think that I would use a lowlife like Dazik Kraznic to capture girls?"

"Are you telling me that he isn't on your payroll anymore?"

"Yes. Not since we closed the place down."

"Then he's making acquisitions for someone else and using that address, or he's entertaining himself."

"What about Weston?" Boris frowned. "The rent is still in his name?"

"Yes but he disappeared when we closed the place. We had called the letting agents in to measure up and put it on the market so that it looked legitimate. Then the next thing is Dazik Kraznic gets busted. The police suspected that he might be connected to the murders at Crosby Beach, so they began a forensic search of the place. The next thing is it exploded."

"There's more to it than that. There must be."

"It's complicated enough."

"Something is missing."

"Dazik Kraznic is your man, yet you say you didn't torch the place."

"Brendon is your stepson, yet you deny that he did it too."

"Touché."

"How is this connected to Keegan and the woman? What was her name?"

"Lacey Taylor."

"Explain it to me." The barmaid dropped a wooden tray onto the table and unloaded their drinks. John wiped his empty glass and placed it onto the tray. "Keep the change," Boris said handing over a ten Euro note.

"It's eleven Euros," she laughed.

"I'm sorry, forgive me," Boris sounded genuinely embarrassed. "You can tell how often we buy our own drinks, eh?" he gave her a twenty and waved her away. "I'm sorry. Get yourself a drink with the change."

"Keegan was giving us the heads-up on some of the sealed tenders for the properties we've been buying and he was signing off on some grants for us. He was visiting a youth centre in Allerton, a three acre site when something happened between him and Lacey

Taylor. She knew that he was being investigated for corruption." John held his whisky glass in both hands and turned it slowly, holding it with the green napkin. He stared into the amber liquid as he spoke. "She had been investigating the sell-offs and talking to local kids and their families. I don't know where she got her information from, but Taylor threatened to report Brendon to the drug squad for dealing crack though some of the teenagers there. Keegan told Brendon that he was under surveillance and he took the situation into his own hands."

"What a mess, John." Boris looked out of the window and watched a bouncer snatching a phone from a tourist stupid enough to take a photograph of one of the prostitutes through a window. He wasn't sure if he would just delete the image or smash the device. The tourist stood with his mouth gaping open as the bouncer tossed his phone into the canal. "How did the police connect Brendon to Keegan's body?"

"They don't have any evidence."

"They don't?"

"No." John shook his head. What evidence there is will be used to our advantage. I've seen to it."

"I'm confused." Boris shrugged. "I heard that the police paid you a visit. They questioned him about Keegan in public?"

"They were fishing. They have a witness who saw Brendon's partner dumping a dog collar into a litter bin near the dumpsite. Their witness has no credibility."

"This sounds like amateur hour."

"Brendon's partner has been dealt with." John finished his whisky and signalled to the barmaid. "He won't make any more mistakes. We put eyes onto the witness but he was smarter than we thought. He slipped us but the last thing we heard, he'd been picked up by detectives himself, which has given us a perfect opportunity to lay the blame at his door. You see, his being at the scene places him there too. After all, he found the dog collar and took it to the police. I'll clean this up and make sure that we're not implicated in anything except making money out of a failing economy."

"You can contaminate him enough?"

"Yes."

"You know what the alternative is, John?"

John looked hard at Boris. He bit his bottom lip and shook his head. "I can't let anything happen to Brendon, Boris." John grimaced as the drink arrived. He wiped his empty glass and took the new one. "He's my brother's son and my wife's child. She worships the kid, couldn't live without him. If I thought for one minute that he could be removed from the equation, then I would have done it myself years ago. It would kill her if anything happened to him. I can't let that happen."

"Are you becoming sentimental in your old age, John?"

"I don't give a toss about him, but I love my wife."

"I know that you do. Look what you did to your brother to be with her." Boris grinned and pointed a fat finger at John. "You had your own brother killed, yet you can't remove his pain in the arse son?"

"Leave it, Boris," John sat back as he spoke. "Brendon is out of bounds."

"We're back to square one, John." Boris paused as another round arrived. John left a twenty Euro note on the edge of the table and nodded towards it when the barmaid arrived. He used his napkin to pass her his empty glass again. "Do we hope that all this goes away and that Brendon doesn't mess up again, or do we make sure that he doesn't?"

"You will have to trust me to solve this."

"I trust you implicitly," Boris said. "We wouldn't be having this conversation if I didn't. Your stepson is a different issue. He was part responsible for what happened at Breck Road and as for the body of Charlie Keegan, I am simply flabbergasted."

"Who torched Breck Road, Boris?"

"You tell me."

"Dazik Kraznic is locked up," John said. "Brendon hasn't been out of the house since this happened. I've made sure of that."

"Are you sure, John?"

"Yes."

"Do you know where he is right now?" Boris reached into his inside pocket. John stood up quickly. Boris smiled and took his phone from his jacket. "Jumpy?"

"What are you playing at, Boris?"

"I had a text message from Liverpool half an hour ago," Boris held up the screen. The writing was in Russian. "Brendon is following a man called Jim Stirling through the Kensington area. He is a detective sergeant, I believe?"

"For fuck's sake!" John hissed. "Your men are following him?"

"They are making sure that he doesn't make any more mistakes," Boris shook his head as he spoke. His many chins wobbled. "Business is business. What the fuck is he doing following a detective?"

"I don't know." John was genuinely flummoxed. "He's a proud lad and wants to do well. Stirling embarrassed us last week. Brendon will see it as his job to iron things out."

"Iron things out against a sergeant in the Major Investigation Team?" Boris laughed. "He is more talented than me and you combined, John."

"He's impulsive."

"He's a fucking liability!" Boris slapped the table with his right hand. "What is he going to do, shoot a police officer? Beat him up? What is he thinking?"

John held up his hand and opened his jacket slowly. "I'm getting my phone." Boris nodded and let out a long frustrated breath. John dialed and waited for an answer; his face was red with anger. "What are you doing?" he asked in a low growl.

"Two things, Bren," John hissed. "Number one, go home and don't let that copper see you following him and number two, Boris is very pissed off with you, so if I were you, then I would go home right now." There was a gap of ten seconds or so before John said, "just do it Brendon or you had better have your things out of my house by the time I get home." He ended the call and shook his head. "I'll deal with him, Boris. He means well."

"Brendon is the cause of this. Yet he doesn't seem to have learned anything from his mistakes?"

"What can I say?"

"Nothing."

"I will fix this."

"You must."

"Don't make things difficult, Boris," John shuffled down in his seat as he spoke. "I will make this go away."

"Fine, but if you don't, I will have to disassociate myself from you and there's only one way to erase any evidence."

John picked his next words very carefully. He sipped his malt and sighed. "You have men following my stepson." John sighed. "Boris, if you threaten my family, then I must make sure that you can't fulfill your threats. Do you really want us both to be looking over our shoulder for the next decade until one of us dies of old age?" He looked at his old friend and smiled. "Leave this with me, Boris, let me handle it and the equilibrium will be restored quickly. Trust me."

"The damage is done, John," Boris raised his voice as the alcohol took effect. "Our business deals are under scrutiny. There are detectives searching the charred remains of one of our buildings and we're being connected to the murder of a council officer who signed off government grants for development. How can you restore all this, John?" Boris drained his glass again. Before he could order another one, the barmaid was there with charged glasses. His earlier tip had motivated her somewhat. John wiped his glass clean and took his new drink. "We take a scapegoat down and wash our hands of him. That way we're clean."

"Our scapegoat is already in custody, Boris," John whispered. He smiled and raised his glass. "Whoever Richard Tibbs is, he's about to do us a huge favour. Don't complicate things, Boris. Let me handle this my way. If it all goes pear-shaped, I'll look the other way while you step in and Brendon is fair game. I can't say anything fairer than that."

There was suspicion in the Russian's glazed eyes. The vodka was catching up with him. He sat back and mulled over what they had discussed. "Okay, my old friend." He waved to the bar. "One more for the road, eh? Large ones this time!" They waited until the drinks had been delivered. "I'm sorry that we're in this position, John. It brings me no pleasure to threaten those people that you love, but we cannot hope that this goes away. Hope is for the weak."

"Cheers," John clinked his glass as he spoke. He sipped his whisky rather than downing it. The Russian had crossed the line for the first time ever. They had come across situations where they disagreed before, but neither had threatened the other. Boris had basically told him that he was going to hit Brendon, regardless of the protestations of his partner. Although he hadn't said it, he was warning John that it was going to happen, regardless. John had refused to sanction it. He had said that it wasn't going to happen. He couldn't allow it to happen. That meant that he would be a target too, in fact, he was certain that if Boris interpreted their conversation the same way, he would have him taken out before Brendon. "Are you going to have me hit tonight, Boris?" John stopped laughing and put his glass down. "I haven't booked a hotel yet because I didn't know how the meeting would pan out. I didn't want to waste the deposit if I'm going to end up in the canal with a bullet in my head."

"John, John, John," Boris sighed. His bottom lip hung limply like a fat pink slug. "If this Tibbs man wasn't in custody, then I would have no choice but to silence Brendon. As it stands, I trust that you can make sure that the man stays inside. I'll take your word as your bond, John. I trust you, my friend."

They shook hands and then stood and embraced across the table. "I need the toilet," John said, breaking the hold first. He reached for his glass and emptied the burning whisky from it using the napkin to hold it. "Order more drinks and I'll be back in five minutes." Boris grabbed his chin between his finger and thumb and squeezed his face as if he were his favourite nephew. He patted him on the shoulder excitedly. "Get the drinks in, you old piss-head," John laughed. "I should call you 'Boris Onemoreski'."

"Onemoreski?" Boris thought about it. "I see, you're right."

"I'll be back in a tick."

"One more for the road, old friend!" He waved to the barmaid, who was already on her way over. The bar was thinning out; the stag party gone but their tunes were still blaring from the juke box. John walked down the steps and headed along the bar towards the toilets, which were at the rear of the pub. Boris sat down heavily and looked out of the window. A small man in a black puffer jacket leaned against the railings above the canal, staring into the blackness. His steel rimmed glasses and bobble-hat made him inconspicuous amongst the other tourists. He was slightly built and unremarkable. Boris raised his glass to the man and nodded. He turned away as if he hadn't seen a thing, before walking down the alleyway at the side of the bar. He didn't seem interested in the gyrating women nearby, unlike others who paid too much attention to the flesh on sale. His appearance belied his lethal reputation. The Russian had used his services many times before. Boris looked across the inky black water to the opposite bank. An ancient barge, as old as the city itself was half submerged, only the mooring ropes stopped it from slipping beneath the surface. It seemed to hang from the canal wall, clinging on for dear life, desperate to escape its watery grave. Above, a row of crooked buildings stood five storeys high. Three of them had bars at street level with guest houses above, while the others were brothels, every window and cellar light had a scantily clad woman in them. Some of the women were pretty and would be a fine addition to Boris's own prostitute stables, but others were borderline freaks. He looked at one bloated figure and tried to distinguish which sex it was. Male, female, lady-boy, transvestite or transsexual? They were all out there in the De Wallen; it could have been any, or even a mixture of them all and he wouldn't have been surprised. Above the window where the overweight 'thing' danced, floor to ceiling louvre doors opened onto a crooked balcony. There were plant pots at either end, the vegetation reduced to stick like growth, bare and dead.

Movement from the balcony caught his eye; movement and then a quick flash. There wasn't time for it to register as a muzzle flash before the bullet smashed through the window. There was a second of white hot pain as the bullet flattened and ploughed through his brain, before blowing the back of his skull off. As the barmaid arrived with her tray of drinks, she was hit by a cloud of pink goo. A lump of grey matter hung from her chin. She looked down and realised that her apron was dripping with blood and brain matter and then she started screaming.

John Ryder heard the glass smashing and then the screaming but he didn't turn around. His shoes crunched the snow as he walked. He pulled his jacket lapels together to keep out the cold and headed down the alleyway which led to the main canal where he could blend into the tourists in the red light district. The baselines of a dozen songs drifted out of the bars and down the canal, reverberating off the dark bricks. The multi-coloured neon lights flashed and strobed and the sickly sweet smell of cannabis mingled with the aromas of burgers, Bratwurst hotdogs and Argentinian steaks. He smiled as he mingled into the crowds. Relief flooded through his soul. The whisky had soothed his jangling nerves but now it was over, he really needed a drink. He thought about booking into a hotel and making a night of it, but something inside told him to get home as quickly as he could. If he was sharp, then he could get the last flight into Liverpool. He decided to walk to the end of the canal before taking a right turn back to the Heldenstraat. From there he would take a taxi to the airport. There was no need to take public transport any longer; their code was no longer gospel. It hadn't just been broken, it had been shattered. John felt that he could relax for a while, before he dragged Brendon around Liverpool by the scruff of his neck, cleaning up the mess he had made. Thinking about him made him worry and he felt a pang of concern. He took out his mobile and pressed the redial key.

"What now?" Brendon snapped like a petulant teenager. "I'm

nearly at home."

"Make sure you shut the electric gates and switch all the alarms on and phone your uncle Geoff." John said as an afterthought. "I want a few of the boys to stay at the house with you and your mum tonight. There could be some trouble coming our way."

"Why? What's happened?"

"Just do it. Okay?"

"Okay," Brendon moaned. "Don't talk to me like I'm stupid. I'm not stupid. I did that thing. Funny. I'd love to be there when they tell him."

"Funny isn't the word that I would use to describe any of this."

"I'm going," Brendon snapped. He had no idea what his stepfather had done to protect him. "I don't need a lecture from you."

"Phone Geoff, straightaway. Okay?"

"Okay!" The line went dead. John looked at the screen blankly and then scrolled through to find Geoff's number. He decided to make the call himself, just to be on the safe side. A loud bang retorted off the walls and echoed down the canal. There were a few high pitched screams and a flash of bright light arced through the sky. The crowd looked towards the source as another rocket exploded and whistled skywards noisily.

"Fireworks!" a male voice shouted. "Someone has put fireworks into that bin!" Another bang exploded and a blue light shot across the canal and landed on the roof of a houseboat. "I thought I was tripping for a minute there!"

"Excuse me," a voice nearby said. John looked up. "I think you've dropped something." John looked down at the floor instinctively. There was a glint of silver and then searing pain across his throat. He dropped the mobile and put his hands to his neck. Thick hot blood squirted between his fingers and soaked down his jacket and through his shirt to his skin within seconds. He tried to scream but it was nothing more than a gurgle. The blade had sliced through his trachea, severing the vocal cords. Blood filled his mouth choking him and the coppery taste of his own life force made him gag. His lungs filled with his own liquids. His vision blurred and his eyes began to fail. As he staggered aimlessly trying to gain attention, he saw a slender man wearing steel rimmed glasses picking up his phone. He slipped it into his pocket and then disappeared into the crowd. John felt his knees buckle and he collapsed onto his back. Blurred faces leaned into view, frightened voices shouted things that he could no longer comprehend. As the last few beats of his heart spurted blood onto the snow covered cobbles, he saw his brother's face drifting to him from the darkness.

Chapter 32

Coopers was frequented by tourists visiting the Albert Docks and by law enforcement officers stationed at Canning Place, which was adjacent to it, across the dark water of the inner docks. As its name suggests, the theme was barrel making in the eighteen hundreds and it was almost a shrine to dark stained wood and brass rails. Behind the bar, wine was pulled from wooden vats, ale from barrels and ciders from oak kegs. It was a busy restaurant but partitioned booths allowed some privacy if it was needed. Alec was well aware of how many headlines had been picked up from Coopers by journalists with acute hearing. When there was a big case running in the local press, every second stool at the bar had a paparazzi perched on it. They sat and drank and listened. Many an officer's lips had been loosened with the liquor sold there.

"Dazik Kraznic kidnaps Tasha Jenkins, takes her to Breck Road and then locks her in the cellar," Annie surmised. She sprinkled salt and vinegar on her fries and eyed the juicy cheese burger which filled the plate in front of her. "Then what was going to happen next?"

"Unless he decides to tell us himself, then we may never know." Alec took a swig of cold Tiger beer and savoured the flavour as he swallowed. His burger looked too big to pick up and bite without the contents exploding across the table. He cut it in half with his knife. "Did he take her for his own gratification, or was she taken to order?"

"Ordered by who?"

"Whoever was renting Breck Road."

"Richard Tibbs," Annie sounded sure. "Was she destined for a hole on Crosby Beach, or is Kraznic a pervert of a different kind?"

"You're convinced that Tibbs is our killer?"

"One of our victims has left DNA on a mattress at the house on Breck Road. A mattress with DNA on it which has been removed from the database?"

"But we can only surmise that it was Tibbs DNA."

"Granted, but we know two more victims worked there for a period of time and were never heard of until they were found buried. Richard Tibbs's alias is on the rent book." Annie shrugged as if it all made perfect sense. "He first alerted us to Crosby Beach." She paused to bite into her burger and then wiped her mouth with a napkin. "He took us there knowing that we would look for Lacey Taylor and find his victims. He wanted us to stop him."

"Do you actually believe that psychopaths, like the killer, want to be stopped?" Alec slugged his beer again. "I'm not convinced, Annie."

"What they want, is for everyone to know what they have done. They want to show off how clever and 'special' they are."

"Even if that results in them being caught?"

"Look at the facts," she placed her palms flat on the table. "He was involved in some sick shit in Iraq. We have no idea what the hell went on there but we know that it was serious enough for the army to hide him and protect him. They changed his name. He is the man Mark Weston, who rents Breck Road and has the lease on the van, that Dazik Kraznic was driving. His DNA is on a mattress, alongside one of our victim's blood." She raised a finger and took a sip of cider from a half-pint glass. "He came to us voluntarily and took us to Crosby Beach, where he knew that we would find the bodies."

"Why though?" Alec glanced out of the window. Across the docks a school party was queuing to gain access to the Tate Gallery. Their yellow jumpers made them difficult to miss and hard to lose. They were enthralled by the tall wooden ships which were anchored in the docks. Some of them were play fighting with invisible swords, pretending to be pirates. "We have to assume that if he worked and lived at Breck Road, then he knows the Ryders. He must have worked for them, or for people that they knew?"

"There's a good chance that they never met." Annie said. "The Ryders are clever men. If they were running a brothel from Breck Road, then the chances are that the hired muscle did the dirty work. They may not even know what Tibbs looks like. They may not know that Weston is indeed Tibbs."

"Yes." Alec agreed. "I can swallow that. So why finger Brendon for dumping the dog collar?"

"Revenge, money, sick sense of humour?" Annie shrugged. "We only have his word for it. We have no evidence of the Ryders being at the beach and we still haven't found Lacey Taylor."

"Yet we know they are connected to Breck Road, Keegan and Tibbs."

"What about Dazik Kraznic?" Annie chewed her food and washed it down with cider. "How does he slot in?"

"Ethnically, he's more likely to be linked to Kolorov."

"And we know that Kolorov has business interests with the Ryders."

"And they own Breck Road."

"And it's rented by Mark Weston, Tibbs."

"Why take Tasha to Breck Road then?"

"Maybe you're right and he was taking her there for someone else."

"Tibbs."

"It has to be."

Alec felt his phone vibrating and held up his hand. "I had better take this." He held the screen up to Annie. It flashed 'Kathy Brooks'. "Kathy," he answered. Making the most of the break in conversation, Annie took another bite of her burger and shoveled some fries in with it. Alec had stopped chewing. His mouth was wide open and the contents were on show for a moment until he realised. He wiped his mouth with the back of his hand. His eyes widened and he shook his head. "And you're sure?" He ended the call and put the phone on the table, pausing for a moment before meeting Annie's curious gaze with his own.

"I think we'd better eat up, Annie."

"What's she found?"

"The CSI at the Tibbs arrest found a dog buried in his mother's garden."

"Taylor's dog?"

"Looks like we've got him," Alec nodded. "Lacey's daughter identified it as her mother's dog, Cilla, five minutes ago."

"Fucking hell, Guv!" Annie sprayed burger as she spoke. "We've got him."

"I'm not hungry, any more," Alec stood up. "Let's go and charge him."

"I'm right behind you." Annie said taking a last bite from her burger. "She's absolutely positive?"

"Ask her yourself," Alec warned, "I won't repeat what she said to me when I asked her if she was sure."

Chapter 33

Jim Stirling parked up and turned the engine off. Across the road, a row of shops stood empty, their shutters covered with graffiti. It was impossible to distinguish what type of business they once were; their hand painted signs were now nothing more than cracked and blistered planks. They were once the hub of a small section of the community, newsagents, fruit and veg shop, hairdressers and bakery. It was a town planner's blueprint which worked for decades, until the big supermarkets began their insidious spread throughout the inhabited world, decimating small businesses the planet over. Now they were nothing more than decaying shells, already stripped of copper piping and electric wiring sold on for scrap. The first floor windows were blackened rectangles, all apart from one, which had a low wattage light bulb burning inside. It looked like an oasis amongst the dereliction. He checked his phone for the address and then looked up at the only occupied flat on the block. As he did, Janice appeared at the window. She scanned the street and saw him almost immediately. He waved and smiled and she did the same. She gestured to a doorway beneath her. It was set back between two shops. He nodded and climbed out of the car. A single-decker bus trundled by, the lights inside burned brightly. The passengers looked depressed and forlorn. Tired from a day's work, or a day's shoplifting. Some were asleep, some almost asleep and the rest wished that they were in the first group.

He crossed the street and knocked on the door. It opened immediately as if she had been waiting eagerly behind it. "Hey," she said smiling. "I didn't think that you would call around."

"I said that I would."

"You did," she agreed. "And here you are too!"

"I came for the photograph," he lied. He had but he had called because he wanted to see her too. It was madness and he knew it, but he couldn't help it.

"Of course you did," she flushed red as she spoke. He hadn't meant to but he had made her feel silly. "Come in and I'll find it for you."

"I don't think that is a good idea, Janice," Stirling mumbled. "I could get into trouble because I'm on my own. You know how it works."

"Oh, yes," she stuttered. "Because I'm on the game?" She looked disappointed. "Of course that makes senses. I'll go and get it." She looked hurt and mildly offended. "Wait there then." She turned to walk up the stairs.

"Why don't you get your coat as well," he said after her. "We could go somewhere else."

"What?"

"Why don't you get your coat and I'll take you for a beer, maybe a curry if you're hungry?"

Her face lit up and she smiled. Her complexion was blushed once more. "I'm always hungry," she laughed, "and I love curry. I'll be two minutes."

"Great," he stuttered. "I'll be in the car just over there."

"Which one?" she looked confused.

"That one," Stirling pointed to the only car on the block, "the BMW." He looked at the empty street and smiled.

"Gotcha," Janice laughed again as she ran up the stairs.

Jim Stirling couldn't stop smiling as he crossed the road. He reached the car and opened the door, then squeezed his huge frame into the driver's seat. Janice slammed the door of the flat and ran to the edge of the pavement. Her coat was over one arm and she had the photograph in her hand. She had pale blue jeans on and a long white jumper. Stirling thought that she looked like anything but what she was. She looked normal. She looked pretty like the girl next door. Janice waited impatiently for a gap in the traffic and then skipped across the road.

As she ran around to the passenger's side, Brendon Ryder took her picture from a hundred yards away. "Got yourself a girlfriend, have you?" he whispered to himself as he looked at the image on his phone.

Chapter 34

Richard Tibbs was agitated as he sat and waited for the detectives to enter the interview room. The atmosphere was dry and still. He knew that they had turned off the air conditioning to make it more uncomfortable for him. They seemed to forget that he had been a police officer for a long time. He may have worn a different uniform but the job was the same. Arrest criminals, interrogate them, hand over all the evidence to the prosecutors and go to the pub to celebrate. There were many books on how to make a suspect talk. Tibbs had read them all. He had even thought about writing one himself when he was put into the program but it would have breached his anonymity clause. Every detective had a grasp of the basic techniques of interrogation and they usually had a trick of their own up their sleeve for interviewing the bad ones, murderers and rapists. Tibbs had seen it all and more. They weren't going to stitch him up. Not again. His life had been ruined once.

Turning off the air conditioning was common practice. Turning it back on was usually done as a favour for the suspect. Are you hot? Tell me about this and we'll switch on the air con. Are you thirsty? The same rules apply. He looked at the clock on the wall. Since they had sat down, only five minutes had passed. It felt like fifty-five minutes. That was another trick, a big clock on the wall where the suspect can see it. They were positioned so that the suspect could see time dragging by, feel the agony of every single second of captivity ticking away. An hour-long interview would feel like days if you stared at the clock every few seconds and most suspects did. You can't help it. It is there in front of your face, tick, tick ticking away. It puts all time into perspective. If you can't handle a few days of interrogation, can you survive years in prison?

"Relax, Richard," Alan Williams said. He was the best that the legal aid system could offer him, which wasn't much. "Relax and tell them everything that you've told me and you'll be out of here in a few hours."

"Relax?" Tibbs scoffed. What he had told his brief was a pack of lies. All he had to do was make them convincing. He was good at lying. He always had been. "That's easy for you to say. You're on the clock."

The door opened and Annie Jones walked in, followed closely by Alec. Tibbs noticed how her trousers hugged her hips and Annie noticed that he had noticed. She scowled at him in disgust. Cursory glances were exchanged with the brief and Annie switched on the recorder. "Interview with Richard Tibbs, DI Anne Jones, DS Alec Ramsay and for the tape please?" she said to the brief.

"Alan Williams, representing Mr Tibbs."

The detectives sat down and positioned their files in front of them. Tibbs knew that the files were padded with blank pages. The thicker the files, the more evidence against him, or that's what they wanted him to think. Been there and done that, he thought. "How many pages are blank then?" he couldn't contain himself. It had been his problem all of his life, his temper. That was how he was stitched up in Iraq and he couldn't let them do it again. No way. He would die before they sent him away. "I'm not going to be intimidated by your thick files, Inspector. It's the oldest trick in the book!"

"You can look at them in detail once we're done," Alec said calmly. "Your brief will be given copies of everything that we have here. Not a blank page in sight." Annie stood up and put four bottles of mineral water onto the table, smoothed her black trousers and sat down. Alec loosened his tie and ran his fingers through his tousled sandy hair. They look calm and confident, which bothered Tibbs immensely.

"It's a thick file. Must be full of your colouring-in then? Have you been sketching?" Tibbs nudged his brief and snorted. "Either that or it's your 'how to stitch up a suspect' guide, the extended version, eh?" He laughed but his laugh was nervous. His throat was dry. He reached for a water bottle and twisted the lid off. There was something different about the detectives. They viewed him through different eyes today. Something had changed dramatically and it wasn't in his favour. He thought that Annie had bought his version of events, but now she seemed to be looking at him with contempt again. "Don't look at me as if I'm shit on your shoes, you snooty bitch."

"Language, Richard," Williams advised.

"I've cooperated with you from day one." He looked from one to the other and then at his brief. Their confidence was making him even more nervous than he already was. "I came to you, remember?"

Alec looked at Annie and nodded. He fingered the deep dimple on his chin and said, "We can start there if you like." Tibbs looked confused. "Why did you come to us with the dog collar?"

Tibbs lowered his head to the table and put his chin on his hands. He smiled. "This isn't about breaking my bail conditions any longer, is it?"

"Answer the question, Tibbs," Annie snapped. "Why did you bring us the dog collar?"

"Because you weren't getting anywhere, I was helping you."

"You lied about why you were there."

"I was giving you that scumbag, Ryder, on a plate!"

"But you lied about why you were there." Annie repeated.

"Yes, but I was scared. I've explained that to you and you checked my story." He tapped the table with a shaking finger. "You checked my story, so what has changed, eh?"

"We checked as far as we could." Annie passed some notes typed up by Alec from his visit to Sandhurst. "Major Bradshaw had a slightly different take on your story."

"Major fucking Bradshaw?" Tibbs picked up the notes and read them. His hands trembled and his lips moved as if he was reading the words silently. "He's a conniving bastard. I can explain this."

"Sure you can," Annie said sarcastically.

"I didn't tell them that we had a daughter. I didn't trust any of them and I knew that they would use it against me if they found out."

"So the Major lied?"

"No," Tibbs snapped. "He didn't lie. He didn't know about our daughter, so how would he know about my grandchildren?"

"Why would you hide that from them? They were protecting you."

Tibbs drained half of his water in three long gulps and wiped his mouth with the back of his hand. He thought about his reply. The second hand on the clock moved from the five to the twenty before he spoke. He knew that the detectives would wait for his reply. They were trained to wait. Silence is uncomfortable and suspects don't like silence. "You have no idea who they are."

"So tell us."

"I arrested an Iraqi interpreter in Basra. He worked inside the base but lived off base. Many of them wouldn't do that because they became targets. He was never touched. We thought he was passing information to the resistance. He was injured during the arrest and he died from his injuries."

"I'm listening," Annie said.

"One of my friends was kidnapped and tortured with a drill. I blamed him. Looking back, I had anger issues. The death was brushed under the carpet by my superior officer but then he started asking for favours in return."

"Favours?"

"We worked closely with the Iraqi police. I've never met a more corrupt bunch of bastards in my life. They knew all the bad men. My superior and some of his friends wanted introductions into certain circles. Life is cheap there."

"And you facilitated these introductions?"

"Yes."

"They got caught?"

"Red handed. I was given the choice to testify or go down with them. They were powerful men."

"So you went into witness protection and hid your daughter from them?"

"My handlers were faceless. I never met them."

"Where was the birth registered?" Annie asked. "Which registry office?"

"I can't remember."

"Personally," Alec interrupted, "I think the old soldier routine is a cry for sympathy. Major Bradshaw wouldn't piss on you if you were on fire. He thinks that you're a very accomplished liar."

"Fuck you," Tibbs hissed. Anger flashed in his eyes and then disappeared just as fast. He took a deep breath and tried to control his breathing. "I don't care what you think."

"Why lie about it when you came in?" Annie asked. "If you had come clean, we could have avoided all this in the beginning."

"I was worried that this would happen!" He tapped the table with his index finger. "I was frightened that you wouldn't believe me. I gave you Lacey Taylor's kidnapper and now you throw it in my face. I was helping you."

"Of course you were," Annie agreed, "because you're a registered sex offender and you had just visited a primary school with a pocket full of chocolate."

"I've explained that to you." His face twitched and reddened. Annie could see that he was becoming stressed. "I am not a nonce."

"Oh yes," Annie checked her files. "You were visiting your grandchildren."

"That's right," Tibbs stuttered. Annie didn't want him to shut down yet. She had to keep him talking. She decided to back off a little to see if he would slip up. "I explained all this to you. I love those kids."

"Then you saw someone who resembled John Ryder, dumping the dog collar into the litter bin?" Annie changed tack. "Because you had seen John Ryder on the television, wasn't it?"

"Yes. It was the bloke who was with him that dumped it."

"The man you say that you saw, Brendon Ryder, is his stepson."

"Okay," Tibbs quipped. He shrugged. "I told you he looked like him and look what happened when I did. They found out that I had told you and followed me. I told you they were bad news."

"I think you were worried because you know that they are dangerous men," Alec added. He sat back and took off his jacket.

"I said that already."

"You told us that, because you know them well." Alec said. He placed a picture of Breck Road onto the table. "You know them from this address. In fact you rented the building from them. I think that you managed the place for them."

"What are you talking about?"

"What is this?" Alan Williams asked. He scrambled to put on his glasses and looked at the photograph. Tibbs sat back and sighed. He shook his head and looked at the ceiling. The solicitor studied it but it meant nothing to him. "What has this building got to do with my client?"

"It has nothing to do with me." Tibbs turned to the brief. "It's a brothel that I went to a couple of times." He shrugged. "So what?" His face was purple with rage.

"I don't see the relevance," the brief said.

"You did more than visit the place, Tibbs. Your client rented this property under his first alias, Mark Weston," Annie said, as she put a copy of a tenancy agreement onto the table. "It is still in his name."

"Bollocks!" Tibbs shouted. His face was red with anger. "I visited the place a few times when I was drunk. Someone has cloned my details. Let me see that document." He snatched the tenancy agreement and studied it. "That is never my signature. Wait a minute," he said excitedly, "I remember now!"

"Remember what?" Annie frowned.

"I had my wallet stolen there once. I went back the next day but the place was closed up. I cancelled everything and forgot all about it."

"So you don't know Brendon Ryder?"

Tibbs looked at the clock for inspiration. He thought about his answer which told Alec it was a lie. "I might have seen him there once or twice but I didn't know who he was then. My memory isn't great."

"You said you didn't know him."

"I didn't."

"But you may have seen him at a property rented in your name?"

"That's not my signature."

"It's purely a coincidence then, that months later you bump into him at Crosby Beach and spot him dumping the dog collar?"

"Must be," Tibbs stuttered. "He's a bad one. Take my word for it."

"I wouldn't take your word for anything," Annie gasped. "You tried to set Ryder up didn't you?"

"What are you talking about now?" Tibbs sighed. "Set Brendon Ryder up?"

"Yes. You brought it here and then pointed us in his direction."

"The man is a nutcase!"

"What makes you say that?"

"I've heard stuff about him. He's a nutter."

"I thought you didn't know him," Alec said.

"I think I need a moment alone with my client," Alan Williams interjected. "Don't say anything more, Richard."

"You should listen to your brief," Annie said smiling. "We can link you to the disappearance of Lacey Taylor, which means you've been lying to us all along."

"What?" Tibbs stood up and pointed his finger at Annie. "Are you off your head, you stupid bitch? I tried to help you!"

"You're up to your neck in it, Tibbs. We've found her dog." Annie tapped the end of her nose. Tibbs' eyes rolled skyward. His face darkened with anger again. He looked as if steam was about to erupt from his ears.

"Good!" Tibbs shouted. "It's about fucking time. It took you long enough to find it!"

"Don't say anything else, Richard," Williams flapped. "I must insist that we take a break."

"Is she there, too?" Tibbs asked in a calm but concerned voice. His eyes narrowed. He had spittle on his chin and a confused look on his face. "Did you find Lacey Taylor with her dog?"

"Not yet," Alec replied. "Is she in your mother's garden, too?"

"What?" Tibbs whispered. "Mum's garden?"

"I must insist that we stop this interview now!" Williams stood up. "Shut up, Richard!"

"You shut up," Tibbs spat as he spoke. "In my mother's garden?"

"That's where we found Cilla."

"Are you fucking mad?"

"No, but then I didn't bury a dog under the roses."

"In my mother's garden?"

Annie looked at Alec and they nodded at the same time. "Cilla was underneath your mum's roses where you buried her. What did you do with Lacey?"

Tibbs put his hand to his mouth and closed his eyes. He shook his head back and forth and muttered incoherently. "No, no, no, no, not again."

"What, nothing smart to say, Tibbs?" Annie laughed. "Watching you implode is almost amusing."

"You can't do this again." Tibbs muttered. He banged his head on the desk. "There must be someone up there who hates my fucking guts because this can't happen to me again. Not again." He leaned back and squeezed his eyes together tightly. "Please tell me that you haven't found Lacey Taylor's dog in my garden."

"We have found her dog in the garden of the house where you were arrested." Annie shrugged. "That is a fact; a fact which gives us enough to charge you with her murder, without finding a body."

"In light of the evidence, I must insist that we stop here," Williams said slowly and clearly. "I am insisting on record that we stop."

"That's up to your client," Alec glared at him. "Unless you're not clear, we're investigating the murders of eight women here. The dog connects your client to Lacey Taylor's kidnapping, and we're assuming, her homicide."

"Surely you're not trying to connect my client to the Butcher's murders too," Williams scoffed. "That is a stretch isn't it?"

"He's done this!" Tibbs slammed the table with his hand. "He's a nutcase! He killed Lacey and he's framed me. I cannot believe this."

"Who has?" Annie asked.

"Ryder!"

"I think you tried to frame him." She sat back and raised her eyebrows. Tibbs glared at her angrily. "It was all part of your plan."

"I didn't kill anyone," Tibbs said flatly. He stared at the table, his hands by his side. "How the hell can you connect me to the Butcher's victims? This is a joke."

"We've recovered blood from one of the victims from a bedroom at Breck Road," Alec changed direction. He placed a photograph of a mattress on the table. "It was taken from this mattress, along with samples of your semen."

"That's a connection right there," Annie said.

"You've got nothing!"

"We have blood and your DNA," Annie laughed sourly. "It's pretty damning evidence, Tibbs."

"So you have a mattress? So what?" Tibbs shook his head. "The victims were all prostitutes weren't they?"

"Not all of them," Annie said.

"I told you that I went there for sex. So what if you found my semen there? If you found her blood, big deal; women bleed every month but it doesn't stop some of them working. Know what I mean?"

"Come on, Richard," Annie coaxed. "You wanted to stop. You wanted us to stop you, so you took us to Crosby Beach."

"No!"

"You knew that we would search for Lacey and find the other victims there."

"I did not kill anyone."

"Who did it then?"

"Ryder."

"We found the dog in your garden."

"I didn't bury her there."

"So someone randomly buried Cilla in your mother's garden?"

"I've had enough of this." Tibbs folded his arms and buried his head in them.

"How many times did you 'visit' Breck Road?" Alec took over.

"I don't remember."

"How many of the woman did you sleep with?"

"I don't remember?"

"Four, five, more?"

"Is there a point here, Detective?" Williams intervened again. His face was pale and drawn. Watching his client drowning beneath the flood of evidence was mentally draining.

"Yes there is. You see, three of our victims worked at Breck Road. The house with your client's name on the rent book. The same house where we've removed semen from a mattress. Can you see the pattern forming here, Tibbs?"

"They're stitching me up for the lot?" Tibbs shook his head and sat back. He stared at the ceiling tiles for a moment. "I don't believe this." He sat up and reached over the table, touching Alec on the hand. "I came here to help. I wanted you to find Lacey because Ryder is an arsehole. I didn't kill her and I didn't kill those women."

"I need to make it clear here," Annie said. "We will also be investigating the arson of Breck Road, which resulted in the deaths of two officers."

"And I suppose I did that too?"

"You're familiar with the building and you knew that your DNA would be found."

"You bitch," Tibbs said under his breath.

"We're going to charge your client with the murder of Lacey Taylor, Mr Williams," Alec said. He felt Annie's eyes on him. It was a pre-emptive strike before Tibbs claimed he was in witness protection and complicated things. Now he was being charged, the MOD wouldn't touch him. "Unless he has anything further to add?"

"This is madness," Tibbs sighed.

"It certainly is," Annie agreed. "How many more will we find, Tibbs?"

"God knows," he whispered.

A knock on the door interrupted them. A uniformed officer peered around the door. "DC Mason needs a word urgently, Guv."

"Interview suspended while we have an update," Annie said stopping the recording. "I suggest you use the time to speak to your client. Tell him to save the families of the victims any further pain by pleading guilty."

"Fuck you bitch," Tibbs muttered.

"You've got ten minutes," Annie called as she slammed the door behind them. Her nerves were on edge, excitement tinged with fear. It was a compelling case but just not as tight as she would like it to be. Alec had walked ahead and was down the corridor leaning against the wall drinking a bottle of water. DC Mason stepped from the lift, file in hand and an air of excitement about her.

"Has he coughed yet, Guv?" she approached them in a flurry of arms and legs. "We've got the bastard now," she added. Her scouse accent made her words seem slurred. "Kathy has got the lot at the lab, Guv, but he can't wriggle out of it now. Not a chance!"

"Slow down," Alec said. "One thing at a time please." He could see from her excited state that something big had broken. His heart quickened as he waited for confirmation that they had something solid.

"Twine," she said quickly. "The second search team has found twine at his flat. The bastard had spools in a sports bag. We'll find the needles soon. Sick bastard is nailed to the wall now, Guv."

Annie felt her knees wobble and she could hear the blood pumping through her ears. Had she just heard what she thought she had heard? They had the body of Cilla linking him to Lacey Taylor and now the twine. It was nearly game over. Nothing else mattered. Alec looked thoughtful for a moment while the information sank in. "I want to hear it from his own lips." Alec rubbed his hands together.

"We have got him but a confession at this point will take us to trial by express."

"Let's get back in there," Annie agreed. She hugged Mason and walked briskly back down the corridor. "Do you want to tell him, or shall I?"

"It's your case, Annie. I'll take great pleasure in watching his face."

They opened the door and stepped into the room. Tibbs had his fingers locked together as if in prayer. His eyes were closed and his lips moved silently. Alan Williams held up his hand. "Mr Tibbs is in shock," he said. "He won't speak to me. In fact he won't say anything at all. I think that he's had a psychotic episode."

"The man is one long psychotic episode," Annie snapped. "We've found spools of twine at your client's home address. CSI are running the DNA as we speak, to see if it is the same brand. Do you want to take a bet that they match up?"

The brief removed his glasses and let out a long sigh. He shook his head in the negative. "I'm not a gambling man, Detective but if I was, I would say that the odds are stacked against my client."

"I can't blame anyone but myself," Tibbs stuttered. His hands clenched into fists and then relaxed again repeatedly. "This is my own fault!"

"Felling sorry for yourself, Tibbs?" Annie goaded him.

"They all asked for it, fucking bitches."

"What did you say?" Annie was aghast.

"The sluts here are the same as the sluts everywhere. They get everything that they deserve!"

"You sick bastard," Annie said sitting down opposite him.

"No one cares how many whores are slaughtered. Why should they care?"

"Charge him," Alec ordered. He had heard enough of his ranting.

"Fucking sluts!" Tibbs snatched the Parker pen from his solicitor's hand and launched himself across the desk. He swung it down hard, striking Annie on the forehead. The nib pierced her flesh to the bone, ruptured her left eye and tore a deep rent down her lower face. She cried out in agony and reached for her ruined eye. "My eye!" she screamed. Alec was shocked by the attack, frozen to the spot for a second. Vitreous jelly ran down her hand, mingled with blood. The shiny orb looked like burst ping-pong ball. Alec sprang to her aid and reached for Tibbs.

"You fucking bitch!" he screamed like a lunatic. He brought the makeshift weapon down again piercing her temple. Blood splatter hit the ceiling tiles. Alec grabbed at his wrist, but Tibbs was enraged. His momentum broke his grip easily and he stabbed again. Alec hit the panic button and a deafening siren reverberated in the corridor. He punched Tibbs hard in the face splitting his lip and cracking his front teeth. A second blow cracked his jawbone but did little to stop the onslaught. Alan Williams grabbed at his client's collar trying to wrench him away from Annie, but Tibbs broke free easily. She was pinned to the chair, the floor bolts stopping it from tipping. Tibbs was on her, flailing his arms like a demented windmill.

"You slut!" Tibbs stabbed. The pen ripped through her cheek and into her gum. He tugged it free, leaving a ragged black circle in her face. Annie howled in pain. Alec saw terror in her remaining eye as he stabbed again. He tried to deflect the blow but the pen punctured her neck below her ear. A fountain of blood jetted against Alec's face, blinding him. He tried to wipe the blood from his eyes but his vision was nothing but a red blur. The blood made it impossible to gain purchase; everything was too slippy to hold. Tibbs was writhing out of his grip and Alec tried desperately to keep a hold of him. "Fucking whore!" He stabbed again. Alec threw himself between Tibbs and Annie. The nib pierced his shoulder and he kicked out hard. "Bitch!" He stabbed again but Williams grabbed his sleeve from behind. Alec kicked him against the wall and he banged his head against the stud wall. His eyes rolled and then cleared quickly. The door opened and three burly uniformed officers piled into the melee. "Bastards!" He let out an ear piercing scream, "Bitch!"

"Fucking bitch!" The officers flattened him against the floor. His legs kicked out wildly as they cuffed him roughly.

"Get an ambulance now," Alec called over the shouting. He looked at Annie and felt vomit rising in his guts. Her left hand covered her ruptured eye and he guided her right hand over the jetting wound on her neck. "Keep pressure on that, Annie," he said loudly. "Get a paramedic in here, quickly!"

"They're on their way, Guv."

Tibbs was bundled away kicking and screaming every step. Alec swallowed hard and assessed her injuries. She was savaged. "Stay with me, Annie." He pressed his hand over hers against her neck. The jet of blood pulsed with her heartbeat and it was so powerful that it squirted between both sets of fingers. Alec tried desperately to stem the flow.

"Help me," she hissed. Blood and saliva spurted from the hole in her cheek, mixing with the aqueous fluids from her eye. "Please, Alec. Don't let me die!" Her breathing was fast and deep. Alec felt helpless as he watched her blood pooling on the floor beneath her. The light in her remaining eye was dimming fast. Alec pressed harder, closed his eyes and prayed that the paramedics would make it before it was too late.

Chapter 35

Alec woke up with a crick neck and a head full of cotton wool. He screwed up his face and moaned softly and tried to remember where he was and what had happened. It had become a daily routine for him. Wake up and work out where he was. He had lost count of the number of mornings when he had awoke and reached over to Gail's side of the bed, just to make sure that it wasn't all a bad dream and that she was actually dead. He wasn't sure what he would do if he ever reached over and found that she was actually there next to him. That would mean the he was dead too, or something equally confusing. It wasn't such a bad idea to be next to her again, if the transition from alive to dead was quick and pain free. He could only wish that he had told her that when she was alive. The smell of disinfectant drifted to him and the constant chatter of strange voices reaffirmed that he was in hospital. An aching pain in his shoulder confirmed his location. The memory of being punctured by a ballpoint was fresh. He rubbed his tired eyes and sat up.

"How are you feeling, Guv?" the gruff voice of Jim Stirling greeted him. "I put a coffee next to you a while ago. It might be cold now but I didn't want to wake you up." Alec looked around the relatives' room. He had fallen asleep in an armchair; Stirling was draped on a settee opposite him. Sunlight was filtering through the blinds, which must have been closed by a nurse. Alec could remember staring at the stars before he finally drifted off. He felt guilty for sleeping while his Inspector was fighting for her life. The truth was, he felt responsible for her attack. He had tried to stop Tibbs, but had failed miserably. The man went berserk. His strength had been frightening. In the confined space of the interview room, with all the furniture bolted down, maneuverability was impossible. Wrestling himself between Tibbs and Annie had taken only seconds but it was long enough for him to pummel her pretty face with a sharp metal instrument in his fist. In the hands of a psychopathic killer, a twenty-pound Parker pen had become a lethal spike.

"How's Annie?" Alec asked. He reached for the coffee and guessed from the streaks on the surface that it was a half an hour old at least. He slurped at it gratefully, regardless of the temperature.

"She's in a bad way, Guv."

Alec put his head into his hands and sighed. "I should have been quicker."

"There was nothing more that you could have done, Guv. You broke his jaw and knocked two teeth out."

"I should have seen it coming. We kept prodding him for a reaction and we got one."

"He's bashed his own head in against the wall of the cell, Guv. They had to strap him to the cot. Personally, I'd have left the bastard to brain himself."

"It won't get Annie her eye back." Alec stood up and stretched. "I'm going to go and see how she is."

"They've taken her back into surgery, Guv." Stirling said. "They can't get her blood pressure stabilized. She's bleeding internally somewhere."

"That's not good."

"No."

"Tibbs?" Alec walked to the blinds and opened them. The fourth floor window looked out over the university district. The catholic cathedral dominated the view like a huge metal wigwam on the horizon. Below, the streets were crammed with hundreds of students making their way to lectures in the dozens of historic buildings which made up the campus. He yearned for their youth, their blind ambition and their innocent nonchalance as they faced the rest of their lives, oblivious of the horrors which it held. They were excited by the latest album, the next big fashion accessory and each other. "What have they done with the bastard?"

"He's being assessed at Risley. No doubt his brief will claim that he's lost his marbles." Stirling knew that they wouldn't section him unless absolutely necessary. He could butt as many walls as he wanted to, but that didn't make him mad. "There's been some developments while you were sleeping."

"You should have woken me up," Alec sounded annoyed.

"There was little point," Stirling shrugged. "Boris Kolorov and John Ryder were murdered last night."

"What?" Alec felt adrenalin coursing through him. News like this was bound to have an impact across the city. The death of one gangster would cause a reaction and it was not always a good reaction. Two deaths could turn a ripple into a Tsunami.

"Kolorov was hit by a sniper as he sat in a bar in the De Wallen district of Amsterdam."

"Amsterdam?"

"Yes, one shot through the forehead. Definitely a professional hit. Ryder had his throat slashed a half mile away about the same time. The Dutch police haven't got any leads on either murder yet and they're asking us for information on Ryder. Kolorov is on their system but Ryder isn't."

"Were they together?"

"Bit of a coincidence if they weren't, Guv, but the Dutch haven't pieced it together yet."

"What do you think?" Alec swigged the cold coffee and grimaced at the taste.

"Looks to me like they've upset someone further up the food chain."

"Connected to Breck Road burning down?"

"Maybe but I doubt it. They both have bigger fish to fry," Stirling said. "Somebody torched Breck Road to slow up our search and my money is on Tibbs doing it." Stirling paused. "A double hit in the centre of Amsterdam stinks of drugs, or trafficking to me. They've crossed the wrong outfit and been rubbed out."

"Let the Dutch have everything we have on Ryder and Kolorov." Alec turned away from the window. "I think that we should go and have a word with Kraznic to see exactly what went on at Breck Road." He turned as a doctor walked into the room. She had her corkscrew hair tied up at the back of her head. Her teeth looked uncannily white against her Asian skin. A silver pen glinted from her clipboard and Alec felt a pang of guilt.

"Your Inspector is in our ICU. We found the bleed and we've managed to stem it for now, but she's very poorly."

"Can you save her eye?"

"Not a chance," she grimaced. "There was nothing left to save. Her sight is almost irrelevant at the moment. She might not make it."

"What are her chances?" Alec asked.

"Fifty-fifty, at best." She turned and opened the door. "I'll call you if there is any change."

"Thanks," Alec said quietly. The door closed and he turned to Stirling as the big detective's mobile buzzed.

"Stirling," he answered. The caller spoke a few sentences which made his face darken. Alec thought that it wasn't just bad news, it was very bad news. "What about the assault?" he seemed incredulous. "Get vice to bring her in. Let's see if being charged with soliciting might change her mind. Thanks for the heads up." Stirling sighed and shook his head. Alec waited patiently for him to calm down enough to speak. "Tasha Jenkins has identified Kraznic as the man that she got in the van with, however, she's saying that she went of her own free will and was paid for what she did. She's saying that she was a willing participant in everything that happened."

Alec breathed deeply and then expelled the air through pursed lips making a faint whistling sound. He felt a knot of anger strangling his guts. "Come on, let's get out of here. I need some hot coffee on the way. Maybe Kraznic can make some sense out of all this mess before they let him walk."

"Guv."

"I'll buy us a do-nut to cheer us up," Alec opened the door as he spoke and let the big detective amble past. "On second thoughts, I'll buy you two."

Chapter 36

After making a few phone calls, Alec was afforded a visit to Walton Jail. HMP Walton has eight wings which date back to 1854, surrounded by a much more modern mushroom topped wall. The site of over sixty hangings, its gruesome Victorian legacy lingers in the very bricks and mortar. It is a desperate place, depressing, dank and oppressive. It was built when a jail was a gaol and the noose was used freely. They checked their belongings in at reception and were allowed to forgo the indignity of a full search because of their rank. Normal visiting time was not for five hours and the waiting room was empty. Alec didn't like being parted from his mobile while Annie was in ICU. He felt out of touch. Prisons always made him edgy, despite being able to leave at any point.

They were led through a series of interlocking barred gates to the waiting room, which had a tiled floor; the edges were blackened where the residue of years of mopping was allowed to build up. It had the smell of a towel left in a sports bag too long; a mixture of damp and sweat. The door between the waiting room and the visiting area rattled and then opened on squealing hinges.

"Ready when you are, Detectives," a thin guard called them in. His shoulders looked like someone had left the coat hanger inside his shirt. "I'm Officer Davis and I'll be facilitating your interview."

"Thanks," Alec nodded curtly. There was no love lost between prison officers and the detectives. Both viewed the other with resentment and suspicion.

"Is it true that you're the detectives working on the Butcher case?" he asked excitedly. "My missus is going mad for it. She's watched every bit of news available online, twice at least. She's buying every newspaper which is carrying the story; costing me a bloody fortune!" he nudged Alec with his elbow, "It's not every day we get a serial killer on the doorstep is it?"

"Whatever keeps her happy? It's cheaper than her going to the bingo every day," Stirling grunted. "Where is our man?"

"He's on his way down," the guard replied chirpily. "So is this to do with the Butcher then, or not?"

"Not," Alec said shortly. "We're speaking to Kraznic on a completely unrelated matter."

"You have to say 'no' though, don't you?" he nudged Stirling but this time the withering look he received deterred him from doing it again. "Is it to do with the murders?"

"No."

"Oh well," the guard shrugged, "I'll tell the wife that I met you anyway."

"You do that," Alec smiled thinly.

"She thinks that you look like the other Ramsay fella," he joked. "You know the chef bloke who swears all the time. What's his name?"

"Gordon," Stirling laughed. "Never had that before have you, Guv?"

"Never."

A door at the far end of the visiting area opened and a guard walked in guiding Kraznic by the elbow. He shuffled along the row of tables and sat down with a bump. His bulging eyes were almost hidden by swelling. The lids were purple with hues of blue at the corners. He didn't look at either detective as he sat down nervously.

"What happened to your face?" Alec asked.

"I fell." He didn't look up as he answered. His voice was thick as if his lips were swollen inside.

"What happened to him?" Stirling asked the guard.

"He was found in the showers," he shrugged, "if he says that he fell, then he fell. Nothing more we can do about it."

"I bet a lot of people fall in here, eh?" Stirling mumbled. The guard grunted and walked away. He leaned against the wall and pretended not to listen to their questioning.

"Do you know a man called Mark Weston?" Alec sat down opposite him.

"Yes," he replied without looking up.

"How do you know him?"

"I did some work for him."

"What kind of work?"

"All kinds."

Alec nodded to Stirling and he placed six photographs onto the table. They were black and white images of males of various size, age and race. "Do you recognise any of these men?"

"Him," Kraznic pointed to a picture of Tibbs. "That's him."

"What were you doing when you were arrested at one six three Breck Road?" Alec studied him as he thought about his answer. He didn't twitch or move. His hands remained still and he kept his voice clear and calm.

"Delivering the girl to him."

"He hired you to kidnap her?"

"He hired me to bring him a girl. She was a prostitute. Locking her in the cellar and waiting for her trick was part of the deal. She would have been paid well for it. It was a game and she was part of it."

"That's a different story isn't it?" Alec asked.

"I've had time to think."

"So now she was paid to be in the cellar?"

"Yes. I think she'll say the same when she decides to tell the truth." Kraznic shrugged and continued to look anywhere but at Alec. Alec couldn't let on that Tasha had already recanted her compliant. "All she had to do was wait in the cellar."

"Until Weston arrived?"

"Yes."

"Did you know that he had changed his name?"

"Yes. He changed it to Tibbs when it kicked off at Breck Road."

"What happened there?"

"The girls kept leaving. Something fishy was going on." Kraznic shrugged. "They didn't stay longer than a few months and the owners got pissed off with him. They closed the place and kicked him out, but he still has keys."

"They got pissed off with Tibbs?"

"Yes. He managed the place."

Stirling frowned and shifted heavily in his seat. "So he stayed at the house?"

"Most of the time."

"Were the girls held there against their will?"

"No, they were on the game but they came and went as they pleased. Problem was that after a few months of working there, they kept on leaving and never coming back."

"Why was that?" Alec asked. "Were they mistreated?"

"Some of the punters got rough sometimes, but that was part of the job."

"So what do you think happened?"

"Tibbs is a pervert. He was always after freebies. If they said no then he paid them and hurt them. You know what I mean."

"What makes you say that?"

"I heard stuff from some of the girls. Even when the place closed down, he still wanted me to bring girls to him."

"For what exactly?"

"Use your imagination. What do you think?"

"So you took girls there for him to hurt?"

"Never, I always dropped them off when he was done." He sniggered and looked at Stirling skittishly. A sneer creased his lips. "That bitch will tell the truth and I'll be walking out of here any day now."

Alec sat back and folded his arms. He frowned as he thought about his next question, deep lines creased his brow. "Okay, you've clearly stated that you had nothing to do with harming any of the women. I understand you wanting that to be made clear but we think Tibbs did more than just use their services," he leaned closer and whispered, "We think he may have killed some of them. Someone connected to that house did. Do you understand how important it is that we don't blame the wrong man?"

Kraznic rubbed his hands together and bit his lower lip. He considered his next words carefully. "If I was you, I'd look in the cellar."

"We did."

"You looked in the front cellar, not the back."

"Wait a minute," Stirling snapped. "How do you know where we searched?"

"I read the newspapers. He wouldn't let anyone go down the back stairs under the kitchen. If you didn't know where the entrance was, then you would never find it. If there was any funny business going on, it happened down there."

Alec nudged Stirling and he stood up and headed towards the waiting room door without questioning him. He understood immediately that the search of the ruins needed to focus on the rear of the house. The remains of Breck Road had been levelled but not removed. Stirling walked over to the exit guard and gestured to the door. "I need to get to a phone quickly," Stirling said. He looked over his shoulder at Alec, but his superior was otherwise engaged. "Is Kraznic in segregation?" he whispered to the guard.

The guard put the key into the lock and turned it noisily. "No, he's in general population, why?" The door opened and Stirling lumbered through.

"I'm concerned if anyone found out that he might be connected to what you mentioned earlier," Stirling winked, "he could become a target." The big detective walked away without another word and the guard slammed the door shut behind him. He positioned himself as close to the prisoner and the visiting detective as he could, without looking suspiciously like he was ear-wigging. He knew at least two of the cons on C wing were related to one of the Butcher's victims. They would be very interested that Kraznic was connected to the deaths, however tenuous the connection. He tried to listen to their conversation.

"My colleague has gone to inform our investigators to change their focus to the rear of the house." Alec nodded and studied Kraznic's bruises. "Did you know that your boss, Kolorov, was hit last night?" Alec watched his response with interest. It was the first time that Kraznic looked him in the eyes. His legs twitched with nervous energy. He was shocked by the news. "You didn't know did you?"

"No."

"He was shot through the head."

"I hadn't heard."

"John Ryder was murdered too, throat slashed."

"Messy."

"I should think so. Not a coincidence though, do you think?"

"How would I know?"

Alec let the news sink in for a minute. He took a pack of Lamberts from his pocket and slid them across the table. "You look like you might need a few of them. The warden said it was okay to bring one pack in."

"Thanks."

"Did the Ryders ever go to Breck Road?"

"John?" he shrugged. "Once or twice maybe, but I never saw him there."

"What about the others?"

"I wouldn't know." Alec saw a flicker at the corner of his lips. His hand came up to his face. He was lying.

"Tibbs said that he saw Brendon Ryder there a few times."

"Tibbs is a liar. I never saw Brendon there."

"You're sure?"

"Positive."

"You know that we found some evidence to connect Tibbs to other murders," Alec said. "He's in big trouble."

"Good," Kraznic muttered. He looked rattled. "I hope that the freak rots in hell."

"He may have had an accomplice."

Silence.

"You know, someone to help him capture victims; someone with a van and a stun gun. Would you know anything about that?"

"I'm not saying anything else without my lawyer."

"That is sensible."

"I wasn't in the country when these terrible things happened."

"So you've said," Alec agreed. "I can count on you giving evidence in court?" Kraznic looked down at the floor and nodded his head. Alec stood up and gestured to the guard. "Thanks for your help. Try not to fall over again, eh?" Kraznic nodded and held his cigarettes tightly. "One more thing," Alec thought out loud. "Did he ever mention his grand-kids?"

"Yes," Kraznic shrugged. "He said that they lived in the city but that he couldn't see them."

Alec turned and walked away. He wasn't sure if he had more questions than he had before he arrived. There were some answers but they certainly were not clear and he wasn't convinced that they were true either.

Chapter 37

"Can you tell me where the Dorset is from here?" DC Lewis asked a traffic warden who was stalking a blue Nissan. The parking meter was about to run out, just seconds left on the clock. Traffic heading downhill towards the pier, on his left, was slow. He wondered if they would have time to walk along it before their flight back.

"What?" The warden turned irritated by his presence. Lewis flashed his warrant card and grinned.

"How do I get to the Dorset?"

"You're a long way from home," the warden commented on his identification. Lewis watched the driver of the Nissan tottering as fast as she could, on heels which were far too high for her. She was marooned in the middle of the road, as the traffic wouldn't let up long enough for her to cross.

"I'm on a case down here and I need to find the Dorset."

"I see. It's in the heart of the North Laines, situated on the corner of Gardner Street and North Road. Walk though this lane here," he pointed as he spoke. Lewis could see a narrow entrance between two buildings, "keep going straight on for a few hundred yards and you can't miss it."

"Thanks," Lewis said walking away. He smiled as the woman opened her door and climbed into her Nissan. The traffic warden turned around and his face visibly showed his disappointment as she started the engine and drove away.

Entering the Laines, Lewis could see the attraction of Brighton as a resort. The narrow streets were buzzing and packed with tourists. Ten minutes on, DC Lewis spotted the green canopies which shade the outside seating areas of the Dorset and headed through the busy narrow lanes towards it. It had a welcoming appeal to it; the ideal place to sit and watch Brighton life going by. The resort is a melting pot of students, wealthy commuters, tourists from across the world and a large gay community which creates a busy, exciting and socially tolerant society next to the sea. The Dorset is a huge Victorian building, which was once a traditional pub. It has reinvented itself many times, but has always been a popular landmark and meeting place for groups of all ages and demographics.

The afternoon sun was dipping but he noted the remarkable difference in temperature between Brighton and the banks of the Mersey. The tables outside of the Dorset were full, business suits drinking martinis and continental lagers mingled with art students and day trippers alike. The atmosphere was alive. He felt like buying a beer and sitting amongst them, watching the world walk past, but socialising wasn't on the menu on this trip. The Laines were lined with curiosity shops, vintage clothing shops and antique stores which resembled museums. If one was easily distracted, then progress could be slow. Lewis focused on reaching the steps that led up from the cobbles to the main entrance.

Inside, the wooden floorboards were stripped and bleached and chalk covered blackboards were updated daily with the specials. Compared to the packed tables outside, it was quiet. He approached the bar and looked for an employee who appeared to be old enough to be the manager. The four members of staff visible to him looked barely out of school. One of them spotted him waiting and rushed over. He was young and camp, his shirt sleeves were rolled up and a white canvas apron protected his clothing and projected an image of hostelry.

"Hi! Can I help you?" he smiled. His fringe was caked in gravity defying gel giving him what Lewis called the 'I've just seen a ghost' look.

"I'm looking for the manager," Lewis said showing his warrant card. "Are they around?"

"Liverpool?" he frowned. "You're a long way from home, handsome!"

"Yes," Lewis said seriously. "The manager?"

"Josie!" the young man shouted, almost singing her name. "The police want to know if you're here. What have you been doing showing your arse in the tavern window again?" he skipped off to the other side of the bar to serve, leaving Lewis with a smile and a cheeky wink. "I'm Jac, if Josie can't help, I finish at six!"

Lewis blushed and looked around nervously to see if anyone had noticed his discomfort. No one had because no one cared. Brighton was akin to a human zoo, interesting and varied species of every description on view. In comparison to most, Lewis had little to attract the eye of a bystander. "Thanks, Jac," he mumbled.

"Can I help?" Josie asked disturbing his thoughts. She was mixed race with a ring through her left nostril and a million dollar smile. Her left arm was a tattooed sleeve of religious iconology. She could see that Jac had been interacting with him. He had a knack of making straight men blush. "Have we done something wrong? Jac overcharging again?"

"Not that I know of," Lewis joked, regaining his composure. "I am looking for some information about a young girl who I believe worked here." He showed her a photograph of Tina Peters. "It was a few years ago, do you know her?"

"No, I'm sorry. When did you say she work here?" Josie

shrugged.

"Two years ago, we think."

"I've only been here six months, sorry."

"Would anybody else remember her possibly?"

Josie put a painted nail to her full lips and thought about it. "I know someone who might do, but he doesn't actually work for us although he does work here." She frowned. "Does that make sense?"

"Not really," Lewis laughed.

"Pink Pete has been the DJ here since the early eighteen hundreds, according to him anyway," she laughed, and pointed to a poster on the wall, "he gets on with all the staff. If anyone might know her, it will be Pete."

"That's great," Lewis said looking at the poster. Pink Pete was featured wearing heavy makeup and a pink wig cut into a sharp bob. His false lashes more akin to those of a camel than a human. "How can I get hold of him?"

"You can't until next week."

"Why not?" Lewis was confused.

"He's gone to work at a music festival in Ibiza," she shook her head. "I think he's back on Friday, sorry I can't be of more help."

"I don't suppose you have a mobile number for him do you?" Lewis leaned closer so that the customers nearby couldn't hear him. "I wouldn't ask but Tina Peters is one of the victims recovered from Crosby Beach. I'm sure you've seen it on the television?"

"Oh my God, the place with the iron statues; what are the papers calling it, the Butcher killings?" she covered her mouth with her hand. "Oh that's terrible! The poor girl and she worked here?"

"We think so," Lewis explained. "I spoke to her old landlady and she remembered that she worked here up until she left Brighton."

Josie touched his arm. "I'm not supposed to give out his mobile. He's very fussy about it but under the circumstances. I'll go and get it. Give me five minutes." She disappeared through a paneled wooden door into the backup areas leaving Lewis to take in the surroundings. The aromas of garlic and bacon drifted from the kitchen and a waitress walked by with a sizzling skillet of spiced meat of some description. His stomach rumbled reminding him that he hadn't eaten since they had left Liverpool. The bar was lined with real ale pumps and mulled cider taps. He checked his watch. They had five hours until their return flight. If Josie came up with a number which gave them some valuable information, they may have time to sample some of the Dorset's wares. His partner was checking a lead across town at a secondary school where one of Tina's housemates had become an English teacher. Between them, he was sure that they would find something concrete to take back to the MIT.

"Here it is." Josie reappeared through a different door. She held out a business card which had the caption, 'Pink Pete, getting wed? Think pink, think Pete'. Lewis raised his eyebrows and shrugged. "He hosts a lot of gay weddings and the like," Josie explained, "that's what he's doing in Ibiza. Someone is getting married over there."

"This is very useful, thank you." Lewis took it from her and held it up. "I'm going to try one of your ales and ring him straightaway. I'll take that table by the window and I'll have some food too if you could send me a menu over?"

"Take a pew. Try the Blue Bird bitter; it's our bestseller at the moment." Josie said as she went back through the hatch, leaving a whiff of Calvin Klein behind her. "I'll bring it over."

Lewis slid along a high-backed church pew and put his mobile onto a heavily marked pine table. The deep scratches and cracks in the wood added character to the furniture, despite the fact that none of it matched. A window looked out over the outside seating area. He put the business card next to his phone and waited for his ale to arrive. Josie placed a pint of dark beer on the table and handed him an oversized laminated menu. He scanned both sides quickly. "I'll have the gammon and eggs please," he pointed. "Can I have chips with it and the yolk runny?"

"Of course," she said taking the menu from him. "I hope that Pete can help you. He knows the staff better than anyone."

"I'll give him a try now." Lewis picked up the mobile and punched in the numbers on the card. There was a pause of static noise and then the unfamiliar sound of ringing abroad. It rang without being answered for long moments. Three men wearing suits were seated at a long table outside his window. They thought that they were being discreet as they snorted white powder from a compact mirror. Lewis resisted the urge to bang on the window and wave his warrant card. It would be mildly amusing if nothing else, but all he would achieve was losing the custom of three of Josie's wealthy customers. He knew that cocaine in Brighton was like Guinness in Dublin; for sale everywhere and enjoyed by the locals and visitors in equal quantities. One of the men made eye contact with him and said something to his friends. They put the compact away quickly and laughed amongst themselves. Lewis was about to hang up when a voice answered.

"Hello."

"Is this Pete?"

"Who is asking?"

"I'm DC Lewis of the Merseyside Major Investigation Team,

but I'm calling from Brighton," Lewis explained. "I'm sorry to bother you while you're on holiday, but I'm in urgent need of some information and I think that you may be able to help."

"Merseyside?" Pete's voice wasn't as camp as he had expected. "You're a long way from home, Detective. What is this about?"

"Tina Peters," Lewis said. "Do you remember her?"

"Yes. I was friends with her."

"I'm afraid that she was murdered."

"I saw her face on the news. Shocking stuff. Have you caught the bastard yet?"

"We might have. We're making progress."

"How on earth can I help?"

"We need to know why Tina went to Liverpool, so we're tracking down anyone who might have been friends with her before she left."

"Tina was a lovely girl, Detective but she was a sucker for a handsome guy. She was always falling head over heels for someone and then a week later, she would get bored and move on. I used to call her the butterfly."

"Can you remember any of her boyfriends?"

"No," Pete paused to think. "There were so many."

"You can't remember anyone with a link to Liverpool?"

"Oh yes," Pete sighed.

"You can?"

"Her friend from Liverpool?" he chuckled. "I remember him well. His name was Charlie. She was crazy about him."

"Charlie who?" Lewis asked excitedly. "Do you remember his last name?"

"Have you got a pen there?"

Lewis reached into his jacket and rummaged for his pen. Opening his notepad, he poised expectantly, "Go ahead."

"C for Charlie. O for Oscar. C for Charlie. A for Alpha. I for India. N for Nero. E for Echo," Pete paused. "She met Charlie every night, Detective and Charlie was usually from Liverpool in those days. Most of it was back then, if you get my meaning?"

"I see," Lewis dropped the pen on the table. "She had a habit?"

"A bad one, Detective." Pete sounded sad. "I was really shocked to hear that she was one of your victims but not completely surprised. I'm sorry that I can't be more help."

"Thanks, Pete," Lewis sighed, deflated, "if you think of anyone who she might have been hanging around with before she left, you could call me on this number?"

"Look, I have hundreds of photographs on memory sticks from my theme nights at the Dorset. I'll look through them and see if there are any of Tina. I can't do it until I get home though."

Josie arrived with a large oval plate piled with a thick gammon steak and homemade fries. Two runny eggs sat on the meat, the yellow too yellow and the whites, too white. "Thanks. That would be really useful," Lewis murmured as he ended the call and stared at his food. It looked tasty but his appetite had disappeared with his enthusiasm.

Josie left him with a smile and stepped outside to clear empty glasses. She chatted to some of the regulars and then placed the empties near the hatch. After emptying the glass washer ready for a new load, she walked behind the bar to the other side of the pub and cleared glasses from a raised seating area.

"Who is the guy asking all the questions, Josie?" a sharply dressed man in a dark blue suit asked.

"He's a detective from Liverpool. Would you believe it?" Josie said, leaning closer so her customers couldn't hear her. "That's your neck of the woods. You must have heard about the serial killer up there?"

"Yes, of course."

"Well one of the women that he killed used to work here when she was at university!"

"Really," Geoff Ryder said feigning surprise. "What a small world it is. What did you tell him?"

"Nothing, Geoff," Josie said smiling. "I never met her but I put him onto Pete. If anyone will remember the staff, it's Pete."

"Good work, Josie. Thanks. Tell him that his lunch is on the house. Don't make a fuss, but it's the least we can do under the circumstances."

Chapter 38

Alec approached the rear of the house where the dig was well underway. The top layer of garden had been taken away and the cellars to the rear of the house had been excavated by huge yellow plant machines. The smell of burnt wood lingered stubbornly in the air. "Morning, Alec," Kathy waved from behind a digger. "I hope you have brought coffee?"

Alec held up a cardboard tray which held two large cups of McDonald's latte. "Of course. Would I dare to approach in the morning without caffeine?"

"Not if you know what's good for you." Kathy smiled from behind her long fringe. Her hair masked scars left from a vicious assault that she had suffered years before. Alec could barely see them anymore but Kathy was convinced that she was deformed. He cringed inside when he thought how Annie would deal with her injuries in the long term, if she survived them. Facial scarring was a terrible legacy for anyone, but for a female? Alec thought they must struggle far more. "How is Annie?"

"Still in ICU, no change," he shrugged. "Tell me we can lock Tibbs away for good?" He handed her a coffee and looked around. "Anything in the garden?"

"No. The lawns and the backyard are clear," she said dismissively, "however we have another dump site in the cellar." She took his elbow and guided him along the path to where the excavation was busiest. Ladders protruded from the ground and four white clad figures were busy in the pit. Alec could make out the rear wall of the house, above and below ground. Paving stones had been uncovered and lifted. "We've found two skeletons beneath the slabs.

They pre-date the beach victims by at least two years, maybe more."

"So this is where the Butcher learned his trade?" Alec mused. "Annie knew that he had more victims somewhere. She'll be pleased when she wakes up and I tell her that she was right."

"She will say, 'I told you so'."

"She will indeed. I take it our victims are female?"

"I don't have any identities yet and there could be more of them."

"The twine at Tibbs's house, it does match our victims?"

"Yes it's the same brand and one of the reels matches up with two of the victims exactly. You've got enough to convince the CPS to prosecute him."

"I'm going to charge him with the murder of Lacey Taylor first; then with the assault on Annie. That will give us enough time to piece together all the forensic evidence. There will be a mountain of it by the time you've finished here."

"We may never have enough to charge him with each individual victim, but I'll make damn sure that you have enough to lock the bastard up and throw away the key." They looked into the excavated cellar and sipped hot coffee, their breath making clouds in the cold morning air. The thoughts of the victims below, what they suffered before they died and who was left to mourn their disappearance, were mutual yet unshared. Some things were best kept inside. Alec had the feeling that things were coming to a close, yet there was no comfort or satisfaction in that thought.

Chapter 39

Dazik Kraznic stayed in his cell until the last convict on the third tier of C wing had gone for the slop that they passed off as food. The smell of cabbage and boiled beef drifted up to him but despite always feeling hungry, he couldn't rush to get his food. If he went anywhere near the other inmates they attacked him. Being spat at was nothing. There were far worse things in prison than that. He had asked to be segregated but the governor had refused on the grounds that he was only in for kidnapping and assault and also because he hadn't been convicted. He was still on remand, awaiting trial. Despite keeping a low profile, he had been kicked black and blue every time the guards turned their backs. There had been threats of worse to come too. If Cuthbert pulled his finger out of his arse, he should be out before anybody had the chance to bring their threats to fruition. Kolorov must have reached out before he was shot. The slut had been convinced to change her statement, so it was a matter of days at worst until he was released. Until then, he had to be extra careful.

He peered through the narrow gap between the door and the frame. He could see the back of a con's head turning onto the second landing. As he turned to walk down the next flight, the con looked up at his door and spotted him peeking out. He stopped and smiled but there was no mirth in it. A tattooed dragon ran from his left eye, above his ear and down his neck. He ran his forefinger across his throat and his smile turned into a twisted sneer. Dazik hid quickly, waiting a few seconds before checking if the skinhead had descended. The metal staircases and landings were empty, although the chatter of the inmates echoed off the walls making it seem as if they were close. There were voices everywhere, yet no one was there. C wing had over one hundred inmates and ten guards, but he had never felt lonelier in his life. Kolorov had promised him protection if he was jailed, but his reach was limited. Walton was a local prison with few foreigners. He was branded as a rapist, a woman beater, a nonce, and as such, he was prey for the predators inside. There would be no protection for him here. Here he was alone. Totally alone. Alone and frightened. Just like the women he had taken for him. Guilt spread from his stomach outwards, creeping through his veins. It mingled with regret and sorrow and a dose of self loathing. Why had he ended up in this shithole? Why had he chosen to do those things? For money? It wasn't as if he had made a lot of money. He threw him crumbs when he felt like it; just enough to make walking away difficult, but not enough for him to walk away for good. Once he was out, things would be different; he would brush the streets before he would go to jail again. He took a deep breath and opened the door wider and checked both directions before stepping out onto the landing. A plate smashed somewhere below, making him jump. The sound was amplified by the vaulted ceilings. A chorus of jeering followed the breakage. "Sack the juggler!" drifted up to him. "While you're down there butter fingers." A harsh scouse accent echoed above the other catcalling. It sounded like the man had a throat full of phlegm.

He tucked his towel under his arm and headed for the showers, keeping close to the wall so that the peering eyes below wouldn't spot him. Fear had designed his schedule for him. Showering was infrequent and had to be done while the others were eating. Eating had to be done when the others had finished their food and were moving into the recreational areas. He would shovel whatever slop was remaining onto his tray as fast as he could and then rush back to the relative safety of his cell to eat it. Despite being careful, they had still managed to get to him but that day, he had been stupid enough to walk into the yard. He had been feeling claustrophobic and the draw of fresh air had dulled his survival instincts and he'd been attacked before he reached the outer door. When the guards finally intervened, his nose was broken and his eyes were swollen shut. He couldn't allow anymore lapses before he was released.

The shower room was silent apart from the dripping sound of water. He was so scared that a drop of water from the showerhead hitting the tiles sounded like a cricket ball hitting a pond. It looked to be unoccupied although the further reaches of the wet area were hidden in dark shadows. In the recesses of his mind, blood crazed inmates lurked there, wielding cut-throat razors and craft knives. The thought of a craft knife slicing his bare wet flesh while he showered was enough to never bathe again but he stank. Timers controlled both the lighting and the length of time the hot water flowed for. He hit the rubber covered switch and the lights flickered into life with a humming sound. The bank of fluorescent tubes chased the dark shadows away and replaced it with a harsh white glare. He blinked to focus. The shower nearest to him hissed into life and he jumped back against the wall, his breath trapped in his chest. A second shower jet hit the tiles and steam began to rise. As the airlocks in the pipes settled, the water stopped. He laughed nervously and hung up his towel. His nerves were taut, to say the least. He removed his boots and socks in one, placing them onto the bench which lined the wall beneath the clothes hooks. Instinct made him check three hundred and sixty five degrees before he unfastened his belt and pulled off his underwear and jeans together. Nakedness heightened his feeling of vulnerability. His skin was unprotected, there to be slashed or burned, stabbed with a shank of metal, or punctured by a sharpened object. He tried to push the thoughts from his mind. His shirt remained buttoned as he pulled it over his head and hung it on a hook. The smell of his body odour was foul. He couldn't stand it anymore. Showering was the priority over eating.

He took three steps and pressed the shower button, tipping his head back to allow the water to hit his face. Waiting for it to warm up was a luxury that he couldn't afford. When the general population wanted to rape and kill, time was precious. He lathered cheap green soap into his bits and pits and rinsed as quickly as he could. A clanging noise from his left made him stop. He held his breath and listened. Had he heard a footstep on the landing or was it a cell door closing? The jet of water was all he could hear and as it was on a timer, he couldn't turn it off. Two more sounds echoed off the tiles, louder this time; louder and closer. They were footsteps, two sets or maybe even three, or were they downstairs on another landing? Noise travelled on the landings. Maybe he was being paranoid. A scraping sound cut through the air. He looked to his left where the noise had come from. Something metal clattered on the tiles, out of sight somewhere. The noise was from the right and he turned to face it. There was no one there. He could feel his blood pumping through his ears. His temple pulsed in rhythm with his frightened heart. More footsteps, this time from both directions. Another scraping sound came from the left and the sound of boots. Two sets? They weren't creeping anymore; they were at both ends of the shower area. A clatter of metal in a sink and then glass shattered and tinkled across the tiles.

"Is there a rapist in there?" a voice whispered. "You're going to learn what it feels like, nonce."

"A murdering scumbag rapist?" another voice drifted to him.

"Attacking defenseless women and raping them?" a third hissed.

Kraznic turned to run. His feet slipped in the soapy water and his legs tried to do the box-splits without informing his brain. His hips screamed in pain and his hamstring muscles felt like they might snap. He scrambled to maintain his balance but the more he panicked, the more frantic his movements became. Although his feet were running, he wasn't moving an inch. He looked like a cartoon character running on fresh air. His left hand grabbed for the shower pipe and his fingertips gained purchase for a second, allowing him to adjust his body weight over his knees. He placed his feet flat onto the tiles as wide as he dared and steadied himself against the wall. His chest was heaving as he sucked oxygen into his constricted airways. He swallowed hard and braced himself for an attack. His vision was blurred by the steam in the air and the water in his eyes. He blinked it away and turned full circle to face his attackers, but there was no one there. His breathing was fast and shallow and his entire body was tensed ready to defend himself.

No attack came. He couldn't hear anything but the water hitting the tiles and the thumping of his heart in his chest. His sense of hearing was ultra-aware but there was nothing but his breathing and blood pulsing in his inner ear. Reluctant to let go of the wall, he walked arms out, zombie-like to where his towel and clothing was. Fear was far more powerful than modesty and he grabbed his belongings beneath his arms and wrapped the towel around his waist. A piercing scraping noise stopped him in his tracks. It was the sound of broken glass being dragged over a mirror, or a nail scratching a window, both rolled into one. He froze and stared into the steam. The water cut out with a deep gurgling sound and he knew that the lights would go out soon afterwards. He opened his mouth to scream for help but a huge hand covered the lower half of his face. Kraznic felt himself lifted off the tiles and saw the wall heading towards him at speed. As his forehead connected with a sickening thud, his brain shut down to protect itself and the lights in his mind went out.

Chapter 40

Chief Carlton stepped out of the lift. Two familiar faces looked surprised to see him entering the MIT office unannounced. The detectives stepped in to the lift as he exited. They wouldn't speak until the doors had closed. Visits from the Chief usually coincided with times of great success or times of total calamity, but were almost always preannounced. They nodded a silent hello to each other and he headed for Alec's office. The office space was full of detectives who stopped working at their desks for a moment as the senior uniformed officer walked briskly through the office. Phone calls were momentarily muted and the typing of emails paused. Raised eyebrows and whispered expletives were passed amongst the team. A dark cloud hovered over the investigation and the tension in the room was palpable. The early editions of the newspapers and broadcasts on local radio stations were the obvious reason for his presence. His face was ashen and his shoulders were stooped, as if he carried a great burden upon them. He paused before knocking on the door but didn't wait for an answer before entering. Alec looked up from his laptop and sighed. Stirling stood from his chair and plunged his hands into his pockets like a nervous schoolboy. The door closed and the team exchanged theories about what would be said and then went back to their business.

"Chief," Alec stood and greeted him formally. He wasn't sure what the purpose of the visit was yet, although he had a good idea. Chief Carlton had his uniform on, as always, but he didn't have his hat. He must have left it in his office, which was a good thing. If he had come on official business, he would have brought his hat. Alec relaxed a little. "You've heard the news then?"

"Heard it, seen it, read it and had it relayed to me by the

Home Secretary, who then quizzed me on what she had told me!" he sat down with a sigh and gestured for Stirling and Alec to sit too. "Please tell me that this is news to you too."

"It was one hell of a shock," Alec said. There was a knock at the door and DC Lewis poked his head around the gap. His smile vanished when he saw the Chief. "Oh sorry, Guv. I didn't know you had a meeting going on."

"And I suppose no one out there told you either, did they?" Stirling chuckled. It was almost a ritual in MIT. If anyone asked if the Governor was busy, everyone replied 'no'.

"I did ask if you were busy, Guv," Lewis blushed purple. "The tossers out there said you weren't."

"It's a never ending source of amusement," Alec shrugged. "Don't worry about it. What's up?"

"I just wanted to tell you that I've downloaded the footage that has been sent from the pub in Brighton where Tina Peters worked."

"Good," Alec said. "Get on it straight away."

"One question." Lewis raised a finger and smiled. "I don't want you to think that I'm thick, but who exactly am I looking for?"

Alec looked at Stirling and then back to Lewis. "Good question."

"Tibbs would be a good start, although very unlikely," Stirling offered. "Otherwise you're looking for someone who shows up on our facial recognition system." He shrugged and winked at Lewis to leave it at that.

"How is the new system going?" the Chief asked. He had championed it, despite its teething problems. Stirling rolled his eyes to the ceiling and gestured for Lewis to leave it. He had entered a picture of the Prime Minister, David Cameron and the system identified him as a fraudster from Prescott called Nathan Giles. Apt, but flawed at best.

"I'll crack on with it, Guv," Lewis took the hint, evaded the question and closed the door behind him.

"I take it that there are still issues with the program," the Chief smiled wryly. "Back to my earlier question, did you know about this?" His eyes looked watery and tired. There was no aggression or disdain in them. "The early editions have set tongues wagging but when the daily nationals hit the shelves I would like to have answers." Alec turned his laptop towards the Chief. He removed his reading glasses from his pocket and put them on. As his eyes focused, he shook his head and closed his eyes. "Oh dear," he sighed. "Have you spoken to the Governor?"

"Yes," Alec said. "Five minutes before you walked in." He stood and stretched his back, then walked to the window. The Liverpool Ferris wheel was turning slowly. It was a magnificent attraction to add to the waterfront quarter. The views from the top were spectacular. It was also a safe addition to the attractions, unlike the yellow duckmarines, which had been withdrawn from service. They were yellow amphibious vehicles that ferried tourists around the streets of the city before sailing around the docks. They kept sinking. Alec had been watching from the window when the last one went down a few months earlier. Imagine a yellow bus which floats, full of tourists and suddenly stops floating. Alec recalled the almost comical images of people climbing out of the windows as it began to sink. His mind drifted back to the point at hand. "They found Kraznic hanging upside down in the showers. He had been beaten and slashed repeatedly, sodomised and then they shoved a sharpened toothbrush into his right ear, puncturing his brain. His lips were sewn together anti-mortem."

"I'm seriously concerned that the inmates at Walton not only knew that he was vaguely connected to our investigation, but they also knew details like the stitching of the victim's lips. How the hell does something like this happen in a prison?" The Chief shook his head. "More to the point, how have the press got a hold of that picture?" He pointed the front page of the Echo. The early edition led with the headline, 'Is the Butcher Dead Meat?' and a close up photo of Kraznic covered the page. His eyes were blanked out but it was clear to see that it was him. "It had been taken inside the prison sometime before the attack. There's no doubt about it."

Alec leaned against the window ledge and rubbed his eyes. They were sore and tired. "We've been blindsided good and proper. Someone in the prison leaked the story to the press and they were probably well paid for it too. The first we knew was a report on the radio this morning." He frowned. "It's no big surprise though. Walton is full of local guards and local cons, right?"

"Right," Stirling agreed. He knew that if the inmates got wind that Kraznic was linked to the murders, he would be attacked, but he hadn't expected Kraznic to be quite so badly beaten and certainly not murdered. "They will have family members in the local press and probably in this building too. As soon as they got a sniff that he was linked to the murders, he was a target." He was keen to deflect any blame from their interview. "One of the guards asked us if we were questioning him in connection with the Butcher. He might have said something on the wing and bingo, Kraznic is toast."

"I can see that," Carlton agreed, "but the photo for heaven's sake! It was as if it had been planned all along. How did they take that?"

"Mobile phone," Alec said. "Mobiles are like gold dust in clink but they're there nonetheless. Killing him is a message of solidarity to the victims' families on the outside." He took his seat behind the desk and folded his fingers together. "We need to take the initiative back from the press. You need to distance Kraznic from the Butcher investigations, Chief. Call a press conference. Once the link is denied, it will fizzle out quickly. We will charge Tibbs today with the murder and kidnap of Lacey Taylor and leak that he's our number one suspect in the Crosby murders. Their focus will change before the teatime news. This nonsense will be gone before breakfast tomorrow."

"Are you sure you're ready to charge him?"

"It would have been nice to wait for Kathy Brooks to finalise her search, but now we don't have the privilege to do so. We make the press look like they have jumped the gun and play it down. Charging Tibbs will take the spotlight off this shambles. We nail him today."

Chief Carlton brushed imaginary dust from his trousers with trembling hands. He'd noticed that they were trembling more these days and it frightened him a little. His father developed tremors in his fifties and he was sitting in a nappy full of his own waste ten years later. The older he became, the more perspective life gifted him. What was it all about anyway? He had spent decades locking up criminals anyway that he could. Now he had to make sure that they locked up criminals the right way, without infringing on civil rights and such bollocks. He had a chance to wipe out the Kraznic issue and wrap up the Crosby Beach murders in one day. "Do it," he said. "What can go wrong?"

"Don't tempt fate," Alec said wagging his index finger. A knock on the door interrupted them for a second time. "Come in," he called.

"Sorry to interrupt again, Guv, but we've had a phone call and I thought you would want to know immediately," Lewis said poking his head around the door. "Laura Ryder has been admitted to the Royal. Uniform are on site and they have been informed by the doctors that she has either attempted suicide or she's been poisoned. Do you want me to go down there and see what's going on?"

"Yes, and I'll come with you," Alec said. He looked at Stirling and the big man shrugged. Her second husband had been assassinated. It wasn't beyond the realms of belief that she had had enough. "What do you think?"

"Who knows," Stirling grumbled. "It doesn't affect our plans does it?"

"No," Alec agreed.

"Is it something that we need to worry about?" Carlton asked. He stood and shuffled uncomfortably.

"Not right now," Alec said reassuringly. "We'll charge Tibbs. You sort the press out."

Chapter 41

Alec and Lewis waited patiently at the nurses' station for permission to enter the intensive care unit. Entry was monitored and limited in order to combat infections being carried in by visitors. After what seemed like an age, a uniformed officer opened the door and gestured for them to come in. Compact anti-wards were on both sides of a narrow corridor. The lighting was subdued and Alec thought the air felt dry to breathe. It was an unnatural atmosphere generated to make those who teetered on the edge of this world comfortable, before they slipped into the next. Some would recover and stay but most of those wheeled into the unit would cross. It was quiet, apart from multiple beeping noises which drifted to him from the various life monitoring machinery. The floor shone like glass and the smell of antiseptic mingled with the sickening odour of human waste. He wrinkled his nose at the offending aroma.

"Stinks doesn't it," the uniformed officer commented. "The bloke in the first bed exploded a few minutes ago."

"Exploded?" Lewis frowned.

"That's the best way to describe it. I've never seen so much shit in my life," he began to explain.

Alec held up his hand to stop him. "I get the idea, no need for the details."

"Sorry."

"Where is our patient?"

"Fourth room along on the right." The officer pointed. "The doctor is with her now."

"Any of her family there?"

"The husband's cousin, Geoff Ryder, brought her in last night. He's still in there but he's not saying much."

"Thanks," Lewis said walking down the corridor behind Alec. A pretty black nurse wiggled out of a ward, almost colliding with him. Her look of surprise quickly turned into a smile. She stepped sideways, mouthed the word 'sorry' and disappeared into the next ward. Lewis took the opportunity to watch her wiggle from behind and he wondered how she had squeezed all of that ass into one tunic. "Keep your mind on the job in hand," he whispered beneath his breath. Further down the corridor, they came across a name plate with Laura Ryder's name written on it in felt tip. Alec knocked gently and opened it. An Asian doctor was filling in his notes. "DS Ramsay," he introduced himself and walked in. The man that he assumed was Geoff Ryder stood up and walked towards him. He looked tired and very concerned. "Are you Geoff Ryder?"

"Yes," he answered. "I'll let you talk to the doctor alone. I need a coffee anyway."

"We will need to talk to you too." Lewis tried to gauge his level of involvement from his reactions but he didn't give anything away.

"I'll be outside once I've bought a drink." He opened the door and stepped out without looking back.

"What is wrong with her, Doctor," Alec asked bluntly. "Did she jump or was she pushed?"

"Sorry?" The doctor frowned confused.

"Suicide or attempted murder?"

"I am a doctor. I don't know." He shook his head stepped towards the door.

"Hold on a minute," Lewis said stepping in front of the door. "We need you to tell us exactly what is going on here please. This could be a murder investigation."

The doctor sighed loudly and removed his thick glasses. He rubbed the bridge of his nose with two fingers and then replaced them, blinking to focus. "Mrs Ryder was brought in last night in what we thought was an intoxicated state. She was disorientated and vomiting but when her condition deteriorated we ran blood tests and found that she had ethylene glycol poisoning caused by the ingestion of ethylene glycol, the primary ingredient in automotive anti-freeze."

"So she drank it?"

"I assume so," the doctor shrugged. "It is a toxic, colourless, odourless liquid with a sweet taste. It wouldn't be difficult to swallow enough to kill yourself. It is occasionally consumed by children and dogs due to its sweetness."

"What if she drank it without knowing?"

"If it was in a sweet drink then she wouldn't know it was there, Detective. She vomited so much that we have no way of knowing how she ingested it." The doctor ran his hand over his thinning hair. A few stubborn strands was all that was left. "I really must get on with my rounds."

Wait a minute," Alec said impatiently. "How bad is she?"

"Bad."

"Will she live?"

"Following ingestion, there is cardiovascular dysfunction, and finally acute liver failure." The doctor spoke quickly and without emotion. "The major cause of toxicity is not the ethylene glycol itself but its metabolites. Treatment consists of initially stabilizing the patient, followed by the use of antidotes." He picked up his notes. "We have administered them and now we need to put her on dialysis."

"Dialysis?" Lewis said, shocked by the severity of her condition.

"Hemodialysis is also used to help remove ethylene glycol and its metabolites from the blood. As long as we can do it in time, the prognosis is generally good, with most patients making a full recovery."

"And are you in time?"

"I don't know. Only time will tell. She may have suffered irreversible damage to her kidneys, her brain, even the lungs can be effected. Obviously, we'll keep you informed of her progress." He stepped around Lewis and reached for the door handle. Alec placed his hand over the handle and smiled. In close proximity to the doctor, he could smell saffron and cumin on his breath.

"One more thing, Doctor," Alec tilted his head as he spoke. "If you had to make an educated guess, did she jump or was she pushed?"

The doctor shook his head and frowned. "I cannot be drawn on that. I refuse to speculate."

"Humour me," Alec pushed. "Your opinion will not be repeated to anyone."

The doctor sighed. He realised that Alec was a pedantic man. "In my opinion, she was pushed." With that he reached for the handle again. Alec stepped aside and allowed him to leave.

The door closed and Lewis walked over to the bed and looked at Laura Ryder. She was a pretty woman. He could see why two brothers fell for her but he couldn't see why anyone would poison her. The door opened and Geoff Ryder came in. He looked at Lewis, who was standing over Laura and something flashed in his eyes. Was it jealousy? Lewis could see that he was angry about something. "Shall we talk outside?" he said flatly. "They say the hearing is the last thing to go."

Alec thought it was an odd thing to say. "They do?" he said walking out of the door.

"People in comas," Geoff explained. He held the door and then walked alongside the detectives. Lewis was head and shoulders taller and twenty years his junior. "They say that people in comas can still hear. That's why people play music, or recordings of loved ones." Lewis nodded and waited until they had left the ward before asking any questions. The uniformed officer waved a hand and as the detectives left the ward, he walked into the ICU to guard Laura.

Alec headed for a quiet seating area at the rear of the building. The windows offered a view of both cathedrals, the river and the Wirral beyond. Geoff kept pace with him, his Gucci shoes squeaking on the highly polished floors. Alec guessed that his suit was Hugo Boss and cost a thousand or more. "Can you tell me what happened exactly?" Alec asked. He pointed to a row of chairs well away from other visitors. They sat down with one empty seat between them. "Take your time," he prompted, "from the very beginning, everything that you remember."

"Since John's death," he said with his hands clasped tightly together. "I've been calling around to see her every day. She's been very down, you know, depressed."

"Her first husband committed suicide?"

"Yes," Geoff nodded as he spoke, "she had a hard time getting over James. In the end their mutual grief brought her and John together."

"I bet it caused a few raised eyebrows?"

"Obviously becoming involved with her husband's brother immediately after his death wasn't acceptable to some; others questioned John's motives as she was about to become a rich widow," Geoff looked him in the eyes as he spoke. There wasn't a flicker of deceit in them. "People made spurious allegations against John. The brave ones actually voiced their opinions. None of them were right. John loved his brother as much as Laura did. James wasn't happy in his own skin, Detective. He couldn't admit who he was and he couldn't face living his life in denial. Laura knew. She never said anything but she knew."

"He was gay?"

"Well and truly entrenched in the closet. I heard rumours that a filthy little rent boy was bribing him and that's why he jumped, but we'll never know."

"What happened to him?"

"Who?"

"This rent boy?"

"He was found dead shortly after James was."

"Coincidence?"

"Like I said," Geoff said calmly. A thin smile touched his lips. "We'll never know. The fact is that his death almost killed Laura. John's murder could finish her off."

"Tell me about last night?" Alec asked. Lewis stared at Geoff. His profile was sideways on. He was cool and Lewis could see no reason to disbelieve him, although there was something that he couldn't put his finger on. He studied his profile as he spoke.

"I called around to see her. She was behaving strangely and complained of feeling unwell."

"Had she been drinking at all?"

"She didn't drink alcohol. Not ever."

"Was she drinking anything, tea, coffee, juice?"

"Not that I could see." He shook his head thoughtfully. "Laura was slurring her words. She began to vomit and hallucinate so I called an ambulance and brought her here."

"Did you notice any note, or signs that she might have tried to kill herself?"

"Note?"

"Suicide note."

Geoff shook his head and stood up. He walked to the window and put his hands in his pockets. "I don't buy the suicide thing."

"Okay then. Who would want her dead?"

"The same person who had John murdered." He answered without turning around. "We both know that John was involved in some unsavoury business." He turned to look at Lewis. Lewis nodded in the affirmative. "There's a lot of money involved and things are up in the air at the moment. His property interests were run by a holding company, New Generation Holdings. Boris Kolorov was also a director and as you know, he's dead too."

"So does control of his interests pass directly to Laura?"

Geoff laughed. "We're not talking about a legitimate corner shop newsagents here, Detective. His investments were as varied as they are numerous. Ownership of such businesses rarely comes down to contracts or wills."

"I'm assuming that there are no binding contracts attached to most of those businesses, so the sharks must be circling now that there is blood in the water?" Alec said bluntly. He knew that most of Ryder's business deals would have been sealed on a handshake. Mutual respect and the fear of brutal violence were both far greater incentives not to renege on a deal.

"John was slowly moving everything into the legitimate business world, mostly property. That was the side which I had an interest in. He would never have divulged any of his illegal shenanigans to me." Geoff raised his eyebrows as a wry smile crossed Alec's lips. "I can see why you would be sceptical, Detective, but if you think about it realistically, if my reputation was tainted by any illegal activities then I would have been of no use to him."

"You're very resourceful people," Alec countered sceptically. "There are ways around most things."

"What about his stepson?" Lewis asked. Geoff sat down near him and rubbed his chin thoughtfully. "Would he be in a position to take over?"

"Never in a million years." Lewis studied his face as he answered. "To say he was a disappointment to his mother and John, would be an understatement. John tolerated him simply because he was his brother's son. He was blood."

"So poisoning his mother would be futile?"

"In terms of running the family business, yes but financially he is set to inherit all their liquidated assets, in the event of both parents dying. Killing Laura would be very lucrative in the short term. However, Laura is very well liked and Brendon is not. If anyone suspected that he was involved in hurting his mother then he wouldn't have very long to spend his new found wealth."

Alec had the feeling that Geoff was feeding him bait; just enough information to make him suspicious. The solicitor knew how to walk the very fine line between legal and not. He hadn't made a threat, yet one was implied. His thoughts were nothing more than speculation yet they carried so much more than that. Alec baited him. "Do you think he's capable of killing his own mother?"

"Brendon Ryder would kill his own mother without blinking an eyelid," Geoff said quietly. "The man isn't right in the head. He never has been."

"Are you going to elaborate on that?" Alec asked.

"No."

"Okay. You represent the family so I understand your obligation to them, but do you think he poisoned Laura Ryder?" Alec asked.

"I don't know," Geoff mumbled. "Maybe whoever killed John wanted the entire family wiped out. That's usually how these things pan out. If you don't leave anyone alive then you can sleep soundly in your bed. In that world, relatives seek revenge."

"We'll need access to her house," Alec said. "Unless you're happy to accept that she tried to commit suicide?"

Geoff nodded and Alec thought he saw his face muscles switch. It was an involuntary reaction to his request, but Alec couldn't read it. "No problem. They are putting Laura on dialysis soon, so I can meet you at the house."

"Do we need to get a warrant, Mr Ryder?"

"That won't be necessary. You may have access to the main house only," he stood up as he answered. "I'll waver any legal requirement. I want to know what happened to Laura as much as you do and if Brendon has had a hand in it, then I hope you lock him up for his own safety." Geoff Ryder nodded and walked away back towards intensive care. Alec felt a very strange vibe coming from him. "I'll be there in an hour, maybe less."

They sat in silence until he had gone out of earshot. "There's something not quite right here, Lewis," Alec said thoughtfully. "Did you get the impression that he wants us to search the Ryder home?"

"I did, Guv, and there's another thing too." Lewis took out his phone and held it up. "I took a picture of Geoff while you were talking. I'm going to send it to Mallon straight away."

"Why?" Alec was confused.

"I am certain that he is on some of the footage from the Dorset in Brighton," he explained. "The last place that Tina Peters worked. That would give us her link to Liverpool."

"Do you know who owns the place?" Alec frowned and though about the implications. "I'll put money on it that if you're right, the Ryders' holding company owns the real estate."

"I never thought to check who owned it; I had no reason to," Lewis sounded disappointed with himself. "I should have checked, it but if the Ryders have property down there then it would explain a lot."

"Go on."

"The DJ that I spoke to said that Tina had a cocaine habit, a bad one and that most of the cocaine in the town came in via dealers from Liverpool. We know that John Ryder was a heavy hitter in the drug world. If they were distributing in Brighton, then where better to have a base, than one of the busiest pubs?"

"Good work. Lewis," Alec patted his shoulder and stood up. "Get that picture checked out with your footage so that we're sure, and verify who owns the Dorset. I want the answers to both before we search the Ryder home."

Chapter 42

Jim Stirling stared at the screen and then looked at the image of Geoff Ryder. He turned to his colleague and patted him on the back. "You're right. That's him there. No doubt about it." Lewis clicked on the image and used the mouse to enlarge it as much as he could without losing the clarity. "I searched the land registry and New Generation Holdings have owned the real estate for nearly eight years. Geoff Ryder is retained by the company to deal with legal matters, property conveyancing and the like." Several members of the investigation were looking on as the developments unfolded. DC Mallon approached with a tray of cups and a full jug of coffee. The detectives passed the cups along as they were filled.

"See this one here," Lewis pointed at the screen as he spoke. The smartly dressed lawyer was pictured in an embrace with an attractive young brunette. They were cheek to cheek, smiling at the camera. "Geoff Ryder with Tina Peters at the bar of the Dorset. They look pretty cosy there."

"So she came to Liverpool to visit Geoff Ryder?" Lewis mused.

Stirling shrugged. "It gives us a positive link between Tina and Tibbs. Ryder is the link to Liverpool and obviously Richard Tibbs was an employee of theirs in some capacity, although he's denying that."

"We need to know when Ryder last saw her and why he didn't come forward when she was identified as one of the victims." Lewis answered. "If we didn't have Tibbs bang to rights, then we would be looking at Geoff Ryder right now." The team exchanged glances and nodded in agreement. There was an uncomfortable silence as the implications hit home.

"Look at it like the CPS will," Stirling said to the group. He pointed to the evidence board for Richard Tibbs. "He brought the collar to us. He claims that Brendon Ryder dumped it, but we have no evidence to support that. Add to that the fact that Lacey Taylor's dog was buried in his garden and he's guilty of murder without a body."

"Surely Tibbs's defense will claim that Ryder set him up by planting the dog?" Mallon played devil's advocate.

"We have nothing to worry about there," Sterling countered. "He stabbed a female detective in the eye with a pen during an interview. Tibbs is the only witness to seeing a van or Brendon Ryder at the beach and he lied to us about why he was there. I don't think that his sole testimony is enough for reasonable doubt."

"I think the CPS will agree with that," Lewis folded his arms and nodded. He looked around the other detectives and no one disagreed. "But should we be looking for someone else for Tina Peters and the others?"

"Same rules apply here then," Stirling pointed to a picture of Breck Road before the explosion as he spoke. "Mark Weston was the lease holder and he rented the van which Kraznic was driving when he abducted Tasha Jenkins. His DNA was found on a mattress, alongside DNA from one of our victims. Kraznic pointed us towards the rear cellar where we have three more victims and he told us that he often picked up women for Tibbs. Okay, he's dead, but his interview evidence counts in our favour, but the hammer falls with the twine which matches the twine used on the victims and he took us to Crosby Beach."

Alec listened to his detectives debating the information and he had to agree. It looked as if Tina Peters was inadvertently introduced to her killer by her boyfriend. There were decades between Peters and Ryder but he was a handsome man, he was wealthy and he had a never ending discounted supply of her best friend, Charlie. What he needed to know was how it all fitted together. It was another nail in the coffin of evidence which would bury Tibbs. Circumstantial or not, it all added up, but something bothered him about it. Something just didn't fit. "I'm going to delay charging Tibbs until we've searched the Ryder place."

"Are you having second thoughts, Guv?" Lewis asked.

"The evidence is overwhelming, but I think it would be foolish to charge him until we have finished the search. I am hoping that we might find more damning evidence to nail him." What Alec really meant was that he wanted to be convinced, beyond a shadow of a doubt, that Tibbs was the Butcher himself.

"Better safe, Guv."

"You have a particular knack of winding up the Ryders, don't you?" Alec said to Stirling. Stirling nodded and grinned. "I want you to lead this search."

"Okay, Guv."

"If Brendon Ryder is there, then I want you to push him to the limit," Alec said calmly. "You said he was wired, so push all his buttons and let's see what he's wired up to."

"That'll be a pleasure, Guv."

"The rest of you, this is a one off opportunity to search John Ryder's house. The drug squad, vice and uniform have all been trying to get in there for years. Let's make the most of the chance. Remember that we still need a link between Keegan and his murderer and he did business with John Ryder, although they didn't like each other. Keegan was bumped off and now so has Ryder. Eyes and ears open; soak everything up."

Chapter 43

A tree-lined avenue led the small convoy of police vehicles to Woodend, the home of the late John Ryder. There were no streetlights as the road was unadopted by the local council and the residents couldn't be bothered hiring a contractor themselves. They had their own lights inside their grounds. All eight properties off the mile long avenue were valued in the millions, surrounded by high walls and protected by electronic gates and armies of surveillance cameras monitored acres of landscaped gardens. A few minutes research had informed Alec that the entire street was owned by three footballers, two pilots, a judge and two drug dealers. Woolton is on the outskirts of the city and it had become an exclusive area for the mega rich. Strawberry Fields, made famous by the Beatles, was a part of its heritage, as were the expansive Jewish graveyards which occupied vast parts of the outskirts of the village. The village was founded in the 1800's by rich merchant seamen, quarry owners and Jewish money brokers. Money attracts money, Alec thought as they reached the end of the road, to be confronted by gates which were three metres high and topped with elaborate wrought iron spikes. A maneuverable camera studied the entourage as they stopped on the drive.

"There's a speaker box on the wall there, Guv," Stirling pointed out. As he spoke, the gates rattled and began to open without any communication to the house. "We are expected, of course," he joked.

"Where are the machine-gun towers?" Lewis muttered. "Too

much fucking money, in my opinion." They crawled through the gates and a well maintained tarmac driveway weaved through the trees, then curved to the left. The main house was nearly half a kilometre further on and as they approached, reproduction Victorian gas lamps illuminated the way. "See what I mean. They say crime doesn't pay. What a load of bollocks that is."

"What you have to think about is, Lewis," Alec turned slightly to look at him, "where has all his money gotten him to exactly?"

"Still a joke, Guv." Lewis mumbled sulkily.

Alec continued the lecture unabated. "He's on a trolley in a fridge in Amsterdam, with his throat slashed. Most of his blood spilled onto a cobbled street and the contents of his lower intestine emptied into his boxer shorts before he took his last breath." Alec held his palms upwards and shrugged. "Now I don't have electric gates and a heated swimming pool but I should be able to draw my pension and spend a few weeks in the sun every year sipping rum from a coconut. Think about it, Lewis. Where would you rather be?"

The trio fell silent, each with their own thoughts on the subject. The truth was that a career in drug dealing was a lucrative one, yet invariably it was also a very short one. The driveway curved around and they pulled up in front of a mock Tudor house with two wings, four bedrooms in each and a three vehicle garage built on to the right-hand side. Apart from its unusual size, it was tastefully designed and quietly unassuming. As they pulled up, Geoff Ryder opened the front doors. Floodlights turned night into day. A slate-covered porch sheltered the double door entrance. He was silhouetted by the interior lights and Alec could make out a figure lurking behind him. "It looks as if Brendon Ryder is at home too."

"Bonus," Stirling said, as he reached for his seat-belt "I'm looking forward to pushing his buttons."

"Geoff Ryder is smart," Alec said. "Try and coax Brendon away from him if you can. I don't think he'll cope as well under pressure, without his uncle there to support him." Stirling nodded and opened the door. The car shifted noticeably as he climbed out. "Jesus, I'm sure he's putting on weight," Alec said to himself as the vehicle shook.

"I heard that," Stirling said slamming the door. He breathed in subconsciously and walked towards the second vehicle. Kathy Brooks exited the passenger side and two other white-clad figures climbed from the rear. "Where are you going to start? The kitchen?" he asked. She nodded and smiled thinly. They walked towards the front door, where three more CSI officers met them. Geoff Ryder gestured for them to enter and stepped back to allow them to pass. "We need to start in the kitchen," Stirling said to Ryder. He looked at Brendon and grinned. "Hello Brendon, nice to see you."

"Fuck off, fatty," Brendon grinned back at him. He was about to speak when Geoff raised his index finger in his face.

"You can be quiet, Brendon, or you can leave. It's up to you," Geoff warned him calmly. "I will not have any dramas while your mother is fighting for her life. Understand me?" Brendon tutted and walked away. "Please come in and do whatever you need to do. Anything you need, just ask me."

Kathy Brooks and her team entered and set down their cases. She looked around the cavernous hallway. Polished wooden floors led off in three directions. One to each wing and one headed towards the rear of the house. A wide carpeted staircase hugged the left-hand wall, snaking to a landing which overlooked the hallway. "Which way to the kitchen?"

"Follow the corridor towards the rear. It leads directly into the kitchen. The living areas are to the right and the library and office are to the left. All of the doors are open; nothing is locked."

"Dad would be spinning in his grave," Brendon sneered. He leaned against the doorway which led to the left wing, his Puma tracksuit was unzipped to the waist. "Opening the doors to the filth and he's not even in the ground yet."

"He would be spinning in his grave if he thought that someone had tried to kill your mother," Geoff turned on him. "And God help anyone who has!"

"While I have you both together," Alec interrupted their domestic. He smiled at both individually. "Can you account for your whereabouts yesterday?"

"I was at work," Geoff began calmly.

"Brendon?"

"How does fuck off sound to you?" Brendon snapped over the top of him. "This pussy might be happy to bend over while you do him up the arse, but my dad taught me not to talk to the pigs, unless it involved telling them to go and fuck themselves."

"Brendon!" Geoff shouted. "Grow up, for God's sake!"

"This is not your house, Uncle Geoff. Get fucked!"

"Maybe we could talk through here?" Alec guided Geoff down the corridor towards the rear, which left Stirling strategically alone with Brendon. "This is a formality, Geoff, but we have to ask the question. You do understand?"

"Of course," he puffed. He didn't look comfortable leaving Brendon but his anger had the better of his judgment. "The quicker we resolve this, the better for everyone." They walked down the hallway and Geoff diverted them into an expansive living room. It was split level, with picture windows along one wall. Three, four seater leather settees seemed almost lost in the room. A fifty inch plasma was fitted above a well stocked bar. Alec thought it looked more like a hotel lounge than a home. "Let's talk in here. That ungrateful little shit can fend for himself for once."

"He's a difficult character to deal with?"

"Impossible."

"He's not a teenager any more, so why pander to him," Alec tried to draw him.

"He's pushing thirty yet, he dresses like a schoolboy and talks like a retard. He's not the sharpest tool in the box by any imagination."

"Yet he seems to be reasonably intelligent."

"Appearances can be deceptive, Detective. He hasn't got the sense that he was born with." Geoff seemed to compose himself. "I'm sure you don't want to waste time discussing Brendon unless he becomes a suspect, so shall we crack on?"

Alec had the impression that he was being spoon fed again; just enough to give him a taste but not enough to satisfy. "Okay, where were you yesterday?"

"I was at work until six-thirty, all my staff can verify that I didn't leave the office and then I came here and found Laura," he shrugged, "I called an ambulance and you know the rest already."

"We'll have to check with them, of course, but that sounds simple enough."

"Fine."

"Was Brendon home?"

"No."

"Do you know where he was?"

"I spoke to him earlier in the day and he said that he was going out drinking in town with his friends."

"Okay, we can check all that easily enough."

Geoff nodded and turned towards the door. "I'll keep an eye on the search if you don't mind?"

"There are just a couple more questions," Alec stopped him. Geoff rolled his eyes to the ceiling and sighed, but it didn't deter Alec. "About one of the properties that John had an interest in, the Dorset in Brighton." Recognition flashed in Ryder's eyes and Alec spotted it. "You know where I mean, don't you?"

"Of course I do," Geoff answered flatly. "You're going to ask me about Tina Peters and my relationship with her."

His answer took the wind from Alec's sails. He was hoping that he might deflect the question or beat all around the bush before answering, but he cut straight though the issue. Alec nodded and watched his eyes. "Are you aware that she was one of the murder victims found on Crosby Beach?" There was little to no reaction from Ryder. He remained calm.

"Not until the other day when one of your detectives turned up at the Dorset," Geoff replied. "I heard the name, but I hadn't seen any photographs and so I didn't associate her with the murders. I was shocked when I realised it was the same Tina." He looked at his shoes and shook his head. His eyes seemed distant for a moment, glazed and unfocused. Alec detected genuine regret. "She was a very beautiful young woman."

"She was," Alec agreed. "How long were you two an item?" Ryder's reaction seemed genuine. He hadn't denied knowing her which counted for a lot. "You were dating, weren't you?"

"Dating?" he scoffed. "Tina didn't date anybody. She went

with whoever she fancied, whenever she wanted to and then she moved on. I was one of her fancies for a while, which suited me fine. She was young and attractive, but we didn't have a lot in common outside of the bedroom, if you know what I mean. I enjoyed being with her when she was straight, but she liked the Charlie a little too much for my liking."

"Did it cause problems between you?"

"Not really. It was a casual thing. If she crossed the line, I went home without her. She was more than capable of looking after herself."

"When did you last see her?"

"A few years back." He looked thoughtful. "She came up for the weekend and we did the whole tourist thing. She was mad about the Beatles museum and Mathew Street and then she spent the rest of the weekend buzzing off her tits on coke. I was getting a little tired of financing her highs, so we had a row. I went home and she stayed in the nightclub with Brendon and some of his friends. He made sure she got on the train the next day and I never saw her again."

"Brendon saw her to the train?"

"Yes."

"Was he alone?"

"I don't know, to be honest. He might have put her in a cab or got someone to give her a lift. I can't be sure." Ryder backpedaled. Alec saw a chink in the armour. "I hope you're not trying to implicate Brendon in her murder?"

"I'm asking questions, that's all for now."

"He may be a massive pain in the arse, but I am retained by the family, Detective."

"I am not trying to trip you up. I just need to find out what happened to Tina Peters and the others."

"I understand," he said calmly. "I'm sorry for snapping."

"Don't worry," Alec waved it off. "Did you ever hear from her after that weekend, phone calls, emails, text messages?"

"I had a few text messages from her and I tried to call her when I had calmed down but the number flipped to voice mail all the time. After a few weeks, I gave up."

"Did you ever actually speak to her?" Alec asked. "It's very important that you are sure."

"No, I didn't and I'm positive," Geoff Ryder looked straight into Alec's eyes as he answered and Alec believed him. "If I'm honest, I was confused by the text messages which she sent. When I replied, she didn't answer for days, which wasn't like her. With hindsight they didn't make sense and they didn't seem like they were from her. You know what I mean?"

"Yes," Alec nodded. "Did she ever go to the property at Breck Road?"

Geoff Ryder looked surprised by the question. His lips parted silently and his eyes widened. "Breck Road?" He said slowly. "Good God, no. I wouldn't have let her anywhere near that shithole. What on earth makes you ask that?"

Alec could see genuine surprise on his face. "Some of the other victims worked at the address for a time before they disappeared." Alec watched the lines on his forehead deepen as he analysed the information. "Did you know any of the women who worked there?"

"No," he shook his head slowly and sighed. "I only ever saw pictures of the place. I did the conveyance on the property, but it wasn't somewhere I would have put myself, purely on a professional standpoint." He paused and put praying hands in front of his mouth. "Although the real estate value was the main reason to purchase the property, John wanted to give Brendon a start. At least, that was the plan."

"What?" Alec smiled. "He set his son up with a brothel?"

"No, Detective," Geoff laughed. "The place had six bedrooms and a couple of cellars. The idea was to convert the bedrooms into bedsits and rent them out to generate a decent monthly income for eighteen months, before gutting the place using government grants and reselling it. It was supposed to be a step on the property ladder for him."

"What went wrong?"

"Brendon," Geoff scoffed. "The kid isn't all there."

"So it was Brendon who turned it onto a brothel?"

"Sort of," Geoff shivered involuntarily. "He rented to rooms to some dodgy tenants. They were working girls and one thing sort of led to another. Brendon was like a kid in a sweet shop until he was bitten. After that he hardly went near the place. That's when he sublet the building."

"He was bitten?"

"I thought you would know," Geoff grinned sourly. "Check his records. He was a bit rough with one of the girls and she damn near bit his cock off. It took surgeons four hours to stitch him together. He was lucky to keep it at all, although he was left with a very embarrassing kink. Some of his friends used to call him 'right turn' because it looks like a road sign. That was until he glassed one of them and it hasn't been mentioned since."

"He is violent then?"

"Very."

"Did you know Mark Weston?"

"Jesus," Geoff hissed. He walked to the windows and looked out into the night. "Mark Weston was Brendon's idea of a parachute. He railroaded him into putting his name on the rent book. The man was an alcoholic. That's when it all went out of control. John stepped in in the end and we were about to put the place back on the market. He's locked up isn't he?"

"Yes," Alec said.

"You found Lacey Taylor's dog in his garden, I believe?"

"Yes."

"But you haven't found her body yet?"

"No."

Geoff turned and headed for the door. "Everything we have discussed is off the record, obviously."

"Obviously."

****

"That leaves us all alone," Stirling smiled. He could see the hatred in Brendon's eyes. They were like tiny cauldrons of boiling poison set in a piggy face. Stirling identified that he was a very angry man and angry men are dangerous, but they also make mistakes. "You can start by telling me where you were yesterday."

"I was out all day." He sneered.

"Where?"

"Drinking in town."

"Who with?"

"Just some mates."

"Where did you go?"

"Along Lime Street, then down to Wetherspoons. I didn't get home until after midnight. You can check it out."

"We will," Stirling tilted his head. "You can count on that."

"Is that it, Sherlock?"

"Did you know that your uncle was screwing Tina Peters?" Stirling jumped in with both feet. Brendon's eyes widened and his moth twitched at the corners. "She was murdered and buried on Crosby Beach."

"Who?" Brendon said sarcastically. His voice was almost a snarl. "He's always screwing somebody half his age." Brendon seemed to be thinking. "She was seeing my uncle? What was her name again?"

"Tina Peters. She was one of the victims from Crosby Beach?"

Brendon flushed red. He obviously recognised the name. "She was from Brighton."

"Was she a whore?" He scoffed. "Most of the victims were whores weren't they?"

It was Stirling who felt uncomfortable now. He shifted his bulk and took a deep breath. "Most of them were, yes."

"Was Tara?"

"Her name was Tina."

"Okay then, was Tina a whore?"

"I don't think so."

"I don't recall her name."

"Do you think it's a coincidence that she was found near where Tibbs said he saw you dumping the dog collar?"

Brendon shrugged. His eyes darted around the hallway as if looking for a way out. "Tibbs is a fucking liar. You found her dog didn't you?"

"Yes," Stirling answered.

"In his garden?"

"Yes."

"I'm no detective, but that's enough for me to think he probably killed Lacey Taylor?"

"Lucky for you that we did find the dog. Why do you think he was trying to stitch you up?"

"To take the focus off him, obviously." Brendon tutted childishly.

"But the focus wasn't on him." Stirling shrugged. "It wasn't on anyone at the time. So I don't understand why he would draw attention to it in the first place."

"Because he's a horrible old pedophile and as mad as a box of frogs."

"You know that we searched high and low for a white Mercedes Vito," Stirling saw a flash of recognition in his eyes as he spoke. "If we had found that van, you could have been in big trouble. He could have framed you big time, because we wouldn't have looked for the dog. We probably would have taken his word that you were there; especially when we found Keegan in the pond." Brendon shuffled uncomfortably. "I mean there were business links to your family with him."

"Well he's a liar, so it doesn't matter anyway. There was no van so how could you find one?"

"Good point," Stirling conceded. "He had us chasing our tails though."

"That's because you're stupid," Brendon smirked.

"Seriously though, do you think he killed the girls that we found in the cellar at Breck Road too?" Stirling raised his eyebrows and asked the question as if he was really interested in his opinion. "I mean there is another connection to your family business."

"Another connection to that pervert, nothing to do with us."

"So you do think he killed them?"

"Probably," Brendon looked up at the landing as he spoke. He couldn't maintain eye contact and he folded his arms defensively. "Or it might have been someone who had the house before we bought it. Or someone else who lived in one of the rooms there."

"Really?" Stirling asked seriously. "You can't think it was someone else. I mean he killed Lacey Taylor and her dog and then tried to blame you. Horrible lying pedophile like that must be capable of anything?"

"He is. I'd shoot them in the back of the head." Brendon made a gun with his fingers and pretended to shoot them. "Kiddie fiddlers are all the same. Scumbags."

"Why do you think he killed her?"

"Who?"

"Lacey Taylor."

"Because she's a woman?" Brendon said sarcastically. "There were no men buried on the beach were there?"

"Apart from Keegan."

"Different kettle of fish altogether."

"But she didn't fit the profile of the other victims, so why would he target her.?

"Fuck knows," Brendon frowned. His frown turned to a sneer. "Who cares why he killed the stupid bitch."

"Last time we met, you said you didn't know her." Stirling prodded.

"I don't."

"You said she was a stupid bitch, which sounds like you know her to me."

"I know of her." Brendon gulped; his Adam's apple jumped up and down. "From the news and stuff. She was always ranting about saving this shithole and saving that shithole, but at the end of the day, that's all they really were, shitholes."

"You never met her?"

"No."

"Do you think Tibbs knew her?"

Brendon shrugged and kicked the soles of his trainers against the door-frame. His hands were deep inside his tracksuit pockets. "I don't know. I haven't seen him for a long time."

"Did you know him?"

"No. I think I saw him once or twice, but I never spoke to him. The guy gave me the creeps, to be honest."

"Where did you last see him?"

"At Breck Road." The young man became animated as he spoke. "He was all over the brasses at that house. He's a pervert. Most of the girls upped and left because of him, the weirdo. He's the reason they went." His eyes darted around the hallway. He was lying but he was excited by his lies. "My dad got rid of him in the end."

"Did you know that some of the girls who worked there are victims of the Butcher?" Stirling watched his eyes. He wasn't surprised at all.

"No way," Brendon feigned shock. "Really?"

"You didn't know?"

"No!" Brendon laughed cruelly. "Pedo Tibbs is the Butcher?"

"I didn't say that."

"You fucking did," Brendon pointed his finger and grinned. "You did, you fucking did!" he turned around and clamped his hands together gleefully. "Just wait until I tell the lads that. They'll wet their pants laughing!"

"I didn't say that he was the Butcher."

"Oh, you fucking did," he scoffed. "You didn't mean to but you did. That is priceless. No wonder he was trying to point the finger at me, wanker!"

"Did Tibbs ever meet Tina Peters?" Stirling pressed.

Brendon stopped laughing and glared at the big detective. His eyes narrowed. "I know what you're up to, pig. Who did you say?"

"Tina Peters," Alec added walking into the hallway with Geoff Ryder. "Sorry to interrupt, but I overheard your conversation. Your uncle said that you all went clubbing in Liverpool together."

His voice startled Brendon and so did the insinuation that he was lying. "What did he say?" He asked incredulously. "What have you said, you fucking worm?"

"You knew Tina," Geoff pointed his index finger angrily. "And you said that you took her to the station the last time she came to Liverpool. You better hadn't deny it either." Something flashed between them. Brendon didn't like his uncle, that was obvious, but he was wary of him. "Did you take her to the station?"

Alec and Stirling studied his every movement as his uncle put him under pressure. "No."

"You told me that you did."

"I didn't," Brendon whined. "I said that I made sure that she got there."

"What does that mean in English"

"After the club we got into taxis and all crashed out at Breck Road," he shrugged and kicked his trainers. "I pulled a woman and she stayed the night in my room. Tina made a fuss in the morning because she wanted to get the early train from Lime Street but that was because you fucked her off," Brendon pointed at his uncle accusingly. "One of the lads must have taken her because she wasn't there when I got up. It wasn't my job to babysit your girlfriend, Uncle Geoff," he sneered. "So if Tibbs the pedophile buried her on the beach, you can blame yourself not me!"

"Was Tibbs at the house at the time?" Alec asked.

"I don't remember. I was wasted and it was a long time ago."

"So you don't know who took her to the station?" Stirling asked gruffly.

"Not a fucking Scooby-Doo."

"I don't suppose you can remember who was there that night?" Alec asked.

"Let me think," Brendon put his index finger to his lips, "erm, nope!"

"I think you've got as much as you're going to get from him, Detectives," Geoff shut them down. Alec had the same feeling that he was letting them peek underneath the covers and then pulling them back down again. Geoff turned to Brendon. "Now, I would suggest that you shut your mouth, unless you're asked a question about your mother being poisoned. Understand me?"

Brendon looked at the floor and nodded meekly.

"I said do you understand me?" Geoff repeated calmly.

"Yes, I understand you," Brendon muttered.

"Alec," Kathy Brooks appeared at the end of the hallway. "Have you got a minute please?" The four men exchanged glances and then headed towards the rear of the house. Alec walked alongside Kathy, while Stirling walked behind and used his size to slow the Ryders down. He wanted a few seconds distance between the home owners and the governor. "We have some interesting results," she said chirpily. "You might want to keep the psycho family out of here for now," she added quietly. Alec turned to Stirling and gestured to the living room. Stirling turned and blocked the hallway with his shoulders.

"You can wait in there if you don't mind," he smiled coldly.

His granite jaw clenched signaling that arguing was futile.

"Actually, I do mind," Brendon snapped.

"It wasn't a request," Stirling glared at the younger man. "Go in there and wait."

"Do as the officer asked," Geoff said assertively. Brendon looked at his uncle and followed his instruction without question. Stirling waited until they had gone in, before following Alec. He walked down the hallway into a huge open kitchen area. The ceiling was vaulted and made from glass, giving the impression of airiness and space unlimited.

"This kitchen is bigger than my house," he commented sourly. Wine racks, full of bottles, lined one wall and light oak units covered the other three. The extensive flooring was made from Egyptian marble tiles. In the centre, a granite topped island formed the central focus of the kitchen. Kathy and Alec laughed at him as he looked around open-mouthed. "The cocaine business must be booming."

"This place has been sanitized," Kathy said quietly. "There are no prints, no hairs and no residue. Someone has cleansed the place from a forensic point of view." She opened a Smeg fridge which was the size of a double wardrobe. "Apart from these." She pointed to two sports bottles which contained a well known brand of isotonic drink, "I've swabbed them."

"And?" Alec prompted.

She picked up one of the bottles, "most of this bottle has been drunk and it has antifreeze in it. If it was full when she drank from it, then she consumed enough to kill her."

"What about the other one?"

"It's sealed," she said picking it up with a gloved hand. "But look here beneath the label." The corner of the label was slightly darker than the rest. "A tiny pinprick through the plastic. Probably made by a syringe. I haven't tested the contents yet, but I'm expecting to find antifreeze in this too."

Alec sighed and shook his head. He looked at Stirling for a reaction. "A sealed bottle?" Stirling read his thoughts. "Whoever did this knows that we can't prove that the bottles weren't compromised prior to purchase."

"Exactly," Alec smiled thinly. "Unless we can find a syringe full of antifreeze in the house, then we're stumped again."

"Shall I call uniform, Guv?" Stirling asked.

"Yes," he agreed. "We need more hands. Kathy, I need your team to complete an initial sweep of the house, starting upstairs in the bedrooms. Then move down back to here."

"Two of my team are up there already," she nodded. "Once we realised the kitchen has been cleansed, I sent them to start in the bedrooms." She paused. "We're looking for a syringe, so I'll have Ken search through all the bins too although anyone who takes the care used to sterilise this kitchen, is hardly likely to leave a syringe in the bin."

"Then why leave the bottles in the fridge?" Alec frowned. "They wanted us to find them."

"That's my guess," Kathy agreed. "No doubt about it."

"Guv," a voice called from the far end of the kitchen. "Have you got a minute please?"

They walked over to where a CSI officer was kneeling in a doorway. Through the adjoining door, Alec could see the interior of a double garage. The walls were covered with bicycles and sports equipment and parked on the left, a bright red BMW Tourer gleamed. "I opened the door to see where it led to." The white clad figure said. "These were next to the wall here." He pointed to the left just inside the garage. "I thought it was odd."

Alec stepped into the garage and the temperature dropped a few degrees. He looked around, absorbing the details. A powerful jet-ski, four canoes, skis and carbon fishing poles and camping equipment; the Ryders obviously enjoyed the outdoor life. He looked at the items which had attracted the attention of the CSI. A pair of green Hunter wellington boots stood next to a sharpened spade. "See here," the officer pointed to the blade. "Sand and soil. There are both on the soles of the wellingtons too."

"Good work," Kathy said. "Bag them for analysis. What size are they?"

"Eleven, Guv."

The tiny hairs on the back of Alec's neck prickled. Brendon was about an eleven. Why would sand be on their spade; sand and soil? He walked around the BMW and studied the items on the walls. Shelving units held smaller sporting items and the accessories which matched the different pieces of equipment. The fishing tackle looked familiar. At least the twine did. It was the same brand as the Butcher used. The same brand which had been found at Tibbs' home. "Bag this twine too," Alec ordered.

"It's the same brand, Guv," Stirling said from behind him. His observation reassured him that he wasn't thinking off on a tangent. "Shall we take Brendon in, Guv?"

"What have we got?" Alec shook his head. "Without forensic evidence to confirm what we're thinking, we have nothing."

"Whoever poisoned Laura was either part of the family, or it was a totally random act of corporate terrorism, which I'm not having. This place is like Fort Knox. No one broke in here and tried to assassinate her. Brendon Ryder did it and I'm betting that the sand on that spade is from Crosby Beach. He dumped Keegan in that pond."

"I agree but what chance have we got of proving that?"

"What about the twine, Guv?"

"Could be a coincidence but I don't like coincidences. Someone is playing games but I can't work out who it is."

"Me neither."

"I want to see inside the BMW," Kathy said. "Could you get the keys, please?" She said, looking through the rear window. Stirling gestured for the CSI to wait while he stepped into the kitchen to get the Ryders. "I'm guessing that this belongs to one of the males in the family. Estate car for towing jet-skis and the like. There's a two seater Mercedes out front, which I'm assuming is Laura's."

"How can we help?" Geoff appeared in the doorway. He looked calm but concerned. Brendon stood behind him looking sheepish and pale. "Have you found something?"

"Step inside," Alec waved them in. Brendon hesitated but Stirling loomed behind him blocking any exit. "We have found two sports bottles laced with anti-freeze. They were in the fridge."

"Bollocks!" Brendon looked surprised. "There's no way!"

"I'm sorry" Alec shook his head. " What do you think? That we made it up, or planted them there?"

"Fuck knows!"

"You don't believe us?"

"In the fridge?" Brendon was incredulous. He glared at Geoff. "Are they having a fucking giraffe?"

"Shut up, Brendon," Geoff said calmly. "Listen to the detective."

"Did she use isotonic drinks regularly?"

"Yes," Geoff said. "She jogged around the grounds every day."

"We think the anti-freeze was injected into the bottles," Kathy added. Geoff looked thoughtful while Brendon went pale. "It has a sweet taste, so she wouldn't have noticed the difference."

"Obviously, this is very concerning. I'll increase the security at once," Geoff said sternly. "After what happened to John, we can't be too careful."

"I don't think that anyone breached your perimeter, broke into the house and then injected antifreeze into two bottles in the fridge. Do you?" Alec said flatly.

"It would seem improbable," Geoff agreed, "but not impossible."

"Who do these wellingtons belong to?" Kathy interrupted.

Geoff looked at Brendon. Brendon shook his head slowly and bit his bottom lip. "They're my dad's."

"Your dad was a size nine," Kathy said matter of factly. Everyone turned to look at her. "I had to read his autopsy report which was sent from Amsterdam. He was a nine, they are a size eleven."

"He wore thick socks," Brendon mumbled. He looked at the ceiling for inspiration which made him appear both a little low on intelligence and guilty. "What does it matter anyway?"

"It doesn't, unless the DNA says they belong to someone else and the sand and soil samples are traced to crime scenes, then of course, it will matter a great deal." Kathy said aloofly.

"The footprints we cast at the pond were an eleven weren't they?" Stirling feigned doubt.

"They were," Alec nodded and stared at Brendon. "The pond where Keegan was dumped."

"Right next to where Richard Tibbs said that you threw the dog collar into a bin," Stirling added. "Maybe he saw you dumping Keegan and decided to fit you up."

Brendon was about to speak but Geoff held up his hand to stop him. "Be quiet, Brendon, they're fishing for a reaction."

"Can you open the BMW, please?" Kathy changed tack.

"That's my dad's car." Brendon was defensive. He folded his arms across his chest. "Why do you need to look inside that?"

"Just open the car, Brendon," Geoff advised. He looked sternly at the younger man.

"I don't have a key."

"You do," Geoff Ryder pointed to his pocket. "They are on your house keys."

"Tosser!"

"Just open it!" Geoff snapped.

"Do you go fishing?" Stirling asked. He walked to a bench where the fishing twine had been bagged for examination and held it up. "We found some of this very same brand at Richard Tibbs's home."

"What is he going on about?" Brendon flushed red with

anger. "I've had enough of this shit." He tried to walk out of the garage but Stirling blocked his path. "Let me pass."

"Open the vehicle, please," Stirling smiled. Brendon began to tremble with anxiety. His temple pulsed visibly, as his frustration intensified. "Open the BMW, now, Brendon," he added calmly.

Brendon stepped backwards a pace and took a bunch of keys from his pocket. He seemed to stare at them as if they were alien to him. The alarm fob was part of the bunch, clearly marked with the manufacturer's branding. "I don't see why you want to search my dad's car. He's not even buried yet, and you," he pointed a shaking finger at Geoff, "You're supposed to work for him. You let these bastards into our home. You're a conniving leach!" The indicators flashed as the locks clicked audibly. A loud beeping confirmed that it was open. "I remember him buying this car," he added, as if in a dream. "I wanted a BMW but he said that they were too fast for me. He always put me down. He always thought that I was stupid, but I'm not stupid." He shook his head and looked at the faces around him. They stared at him as if he was stupid too. "He said that we could have a family BMW, which was the nearest that I would get to owning one. We saw this and thought that it was ideal for towing the ski and storing the camping gear. Although it's an estate model, it's a high powered M3 class with a V10 supercharged engine. I had a hundred and sixty out of it once. I took it whenever they were away."

Kathy opened the driver's door and reached inside, popping the tailgate. It opened slowly, in one fluid movement. She looked in and sprayed Luminol across the dark material. A mist settled across the fibres and she waited for what felt like an age for it to react. Brendon stood rigid as she took an ultraviolet torch and shined it into the rear. Purple blobs appeared, concentrated in the centre and becoming less prevalent near the edges. Alec and Stirling nodded to each other. "It's positive for blood, lots of it," Kathy said without turning around. She continued to spray inside. The more she sprayed, the more blood she found. Kathy scraped samples and put them into specimen pots.

"Don't say anything," Geoff Ryder said. He looked pale and drawn, shocked by the implications of what was about to happen. "Not a word, Brendon, until I can work out a way to sort this out."

"Arrest him," Alec said solemnly.

"For what?" Geoff asked.

"The murder of Charlie Keegan."

"Don't say anything, Brendon," Geoff touched his arm and looked solemnly into his eyes. He tried to reassure him. "I'll be at the station when you get there."

His nephew smiled and shook his head. "Fuck off, Uncle Geoff," Brendon said. A gunshot rang out; the noise was deafening in the confined space of the garage. Geoff clutched his lower abdomen, blood poured between his fingers as he grabbed at the wound. He stared at the blood in disbelief, his eyes widened and his lips moved silently. His legs gave way and he sat down hard on the floor. "Put your hands up!" Brendon aimed the pistol at Alec. It was a Sig Sauer, 9 mm. Alec knew that if the clip was full, there were enough bullets to shoot them all, without reloading. "Hands up now!"

"Don't do this, Brendon," Geoff groaned.

"Shut up, you snake!"

"We're not armed, Brendon," Alec said raising his hands. He kept his voice calm and kneeled next to the older Ryder. Blood was running between his fingers profusely and pooling around him. "Your uncle needs an ambulance or he will die."

"He needs a backbone," Brendon replied curtly. He activated

the garage door with the key fob and it opened quietly, little more than a hum. Stirling moved quickly for a big man. He ducked beneath the wing of the car and edged along it towards a tool rack. Brendon was on to him immediately. He bent down and looked beneath the car and then fired off two rounds.

"Okay, okay!" Stirling shouted. He stood up with his hands raised. His face was as dark as thunder, but there was nothing that he could do against a nine millimetre automatic.

"Get inside the kitchen, all of you!" Brendon shouted. He gestured towards the door with the gun. Stirling and Alec picked up Geoff Ryder and Kathy pressed a large gauze pad over the wound. Brendon climbed into the driver's seat and started the engine. Alec heard the engine roaring and the tyres squealed, as it reversed rapidly out of the garage. It stopped for a second as Brendon steered it towards the driveway and then a wave of gravel clattered against the doors as he sped away into the night.

Chapter 44

One Year Later

The Iron Men stood stoic in the face of the oncoming storm. Gale force winds were combining with high tides to smash the North West coastline. The sky was gunmetal grey and the low clouds tumbled, twisted and turned themselves inside out as they raced inland. Alec marvelled, as breakers the size of buses crashed over the statues, enveloping them and then retreating as a ton of white foam, before being replaced by the next powerful wave. The Iron Men would be battered and swamped, submerged and battered again but they would remain in place, undamaged by the relentless elements. Annie Jones stood next to him, enjoying the display of power which Mother Nature was putting on. She could feel the rumble of the breaking waves vibrating in her chest. It was something she had only experienced at the point of take off, or in close proximity to a speeding express train. The familiar scent of the sea was like a tonic and she breathed it in deeply and held it in her lungs as long as she could, before releasing it.

Her eye patch had taken some getting used to, but she found it infinitely more comfortable than the glass eye that they had offered her. She couldn't get on with it and hated the way it looked. They offered her eye patches in different shapes and colours. She felt more comfortable in them. The doctor advised her to give the glass eye a chance, but in the end she settled for the patches. Although it attracted a few odd looks, she preferred the fact that the patch made it obvious that she had suffered a traumatic eye injury, whereas the glass eye encouraged the curious to stare. She hated being stared at, so the patches won. The force had been incredibly supportive, to the point where they had offered her early retirement on full pension, but she refused. Annie couldn't sit at home and fester. She was an active woman with an active brain and more to the point, she was a damn good Detective Inspector. Having one eye wouldn't change that in the slightest.

Brendon Ryder was still in the wind. During her recovery, Annie had followed the case intently and upon her return to work, she immersed herself in the Crosby Beach Murders. Richard Tibbs had proved impossible to interrogate. His mental condition was deteriorating daily and he flatly refused to talk to Annie, who he blamed completely for his plight. Just the mention of her name sent him into a violent rage. Alec had managed a fifteen minute interview with him, during which he belligerently denied murdering Lacey Taylor or the Butcher's victims and he stuck vehemently to the story of his wife and child. Annie wasn't convinced either way. All the signposts were pointing in different directions and Richard Tibbs had become an enigma. He was a puzzle with no solution.

When all the requested information had been gathered, Annie discovered there were no records of a marriage, a birth or a suicide. What had really happened in Iraq had been buried so deep that it was lost. His multiple identities had muddied the waters further, to the point where she doubted if even Richard Tibbs could remember the truth. The fact was that he was unstable and a danger to society. He had been sectioned and incarceration only added fuel to the fires that had destroyed his sanity. One thing for certain was that if the Iron Men could speak, she would have the answers that she sought so desperately. She shivered against the wind and hunched her shoulders, then smiled thinly at Alec. He smiled back with sympathy in his eyes. Sympathy was something she rarely gave and she definitely didn't require any herself.

"I am not sure that I want to do this?" Alec said. "I feel like we're scratching the scab from a sore."

"If it gives us answers, then bring it on."

"I feel like we're about to step into the weird world of the psychopath again, where nothing ever adds up or makes sense," he shook his head and shrugged, "I suppose that's what makes them so special. Are you ready?"

"There's nothing else that I would rather do right now," Annie replied assertively. "I lost an eye, not my nerve."

"That's a good job, because Kathy is coming," he gestured towards the white-clad figure approaching. "Let's hope this is the breakthrough we've waited for." They turned from the sea and walked towards the path which weaved between the huge sand dunes. Grains of sand filled the air and Annie could feel it in her hair, in her ears and even in her mouth. "Hi, Kathy," Alec greeted her.

"Hello," she smiled and tilted her head into the wind. "Admiring the view? It's impressive isn't it?" She looked at the mountainous waves. "There was a guy windsurfing earlier, believe it or not."

"He's probably reached Prestatyn by now," Annie joked. "What have you found?" she asked, eager for the news.

"The dogs found a female. They found her between the dunes and the woods," Kathy shouted over the howling wind. "Follow me," she waved a gloved hand and trudged off over the sand. Alec zipped his bubble jacket beneath his chin and dug his hands deep into his pockets before following her. "She was just under a mile away from our first search area and the pond, but when we expanded it to include the area where Geoff Ryder told us to look, the dogs found her almost immediately. I'm beginning to think that we've been played all along on this one."

"Well, hopefully this will throw some light onto it all," Annie shouted.

Alec nodded and kept his thoughts to himself. Until he was sure what they had found, he couldn't commit to one theory or another. As they weaved between the massive dunes, the wind became less powerful but it carried minute grains of sand which were painful on the face. The treeline loomed closer and a white crime scene tent flapped wildly, threatening to leave the beach and take to the skies in a hurry. Yellow crime scene tape, bowed by the wind, formed a perimeter around it. "Are you sure it's her?" Alec asked as they reached the gazebo.

"As sure as I can be, until we get her to the lab." She opened the flap and Alec ducked beneath it. Annie paused and took a deep breath before following them.

Stirling was already at the scene and he looked up from the victim, without removing the gauze from his nose. "Alright, Guv," he said, allowing the singular greeting to apply to both of his senior officers. "This is crazy," he said. "I think we need to rethink the entire case."

"I agree," Annie said. "Brendon Ryder fitted up Tibbs. We know that the sand on the shovel at the Ryders' house matched the sand from the beach and the soil samples matched Tibbs's garden, therefore it was used to dig at both places."

"And the samples from the wellingtons matched too," Kathy reminded them. "The DNA inside the boots was Brendon's."

"Brendon Ryder dug up the dog and planted it for us to find, so that we would focus on Tibbs?" Alec asked.

"He had no choice once Tibbs had put him at the scene," Stirling said. "Once we found Keegan in the pond, it was only a matter of time before we looked at the Ryders."

"The chances are that he disposed of Keegan and Taylor at the same time roughly?" Kathy said.

"The blood in the BMW matched Keegan and Taylor. He

brought them out here, buried her and then dumped Keegan in the pond." Annie thought out loud. "Tibbs must have spotted him at the reserve just like he said that he did. If he hadn't come to the station, we never would have found the others. It's no wonder he flipped."

"Just remember what he did to you, Annie," Kathy commented.

Annie shrugged and pointed to her eye patch. "I'm hardly likely to forget it, am I?"

"Sorry, I didn't mean to be flippant."

"No offense taken." Annie nodded at the body for her to continue.

"It's the same MO as the other prawns," Kathy said as she pointed to the half buried victim. "Medical tubing glued into the nostrils and stitching of the eyelids and lips with fishing twine. I can tell from the way the cheeks have sagged that her teeth have been removed. The blue rose tattoo on her left shoulder matches the distinguishing marks given to us by her daughter."

"Is that enough?"

"Her hair matches and so does this sovereign ring," Kathy pointed to her hand as she spoke, "Meet Lacey Taylor."

"I don't know whether to be surprised, or not," Alec mumbled. "I am somewhere between disappointment and relief."

"She was under our noses all this time," Stirling sighed.

"We couldn't search the entire coastline," Alec said.

"We wouldn't have found her without Geoff Ryder talking. I think he had a lot of time to think while he was recovering from the bullet in the guts," Stirling said gruffly. "Having said that, he didn't really give us anything until you came back to work, Guv," he said to Annie.

"Maybe he was sympathetic to another invalid," she said sarcastically. "Losing six inches of your large intestine and suffering a broken pelvis can change your outlook on things, I suppose. If he had been more forthcoming originally, we would have got to this point twelve months ago."

"I got the impression that he wanted us to find out about Brendon," Alec added. "I honestly believe that if he hadn't been a blood relative, he would have informed us of his concerns much earlier. I think loyalty blinkered him; loyalty to his dead cousin and to John Ryder."

"When he told me that Brendon came here night-fishing regularly as soon as he could drive," Annie sighed, "I knew we had it wrong."

"Tibbs tried to stitch him up and he lied about why he was here," Alec said. "If anyone else had told us that, we would have believed them immediately."

"All the way," Annie agreed. "From the moment Richard Tibbs walked into the station, we've been chasing shadows but now we know that Brendon Ryder killed Lacey Taylor and that he's the Butcher."

"All we need to do now is find him," Alec frowned as he spoke. The wind seemed to become more intense, ripping at the canvas as if it was desperate to get inside. "We still don't have a clue where he went to."

"I check the information daily," Annie agreed. "No phone calls and no activity on his bank accounts. He has simply disappeared."

"Now we have cast iron proof, we can crank up the media campaign. I hope he's become complacent, because I'm going to make sure that his face is on every television screen and front page from lunchtime until doomsday. Somebody must know where he is."

Chapter 45

Annie Jones sat patiently and tried to ignore the receptionist who repeatedly walked past the doorway to look at her. She couldn't have made it anymore obvious if she had tried. Annie thought that the white eye patch was less striking than the black one, but it had obviously fascinated the young lady who worked on reception at Ryder, Lawrence and Barclay solicitor's office. The waiting room had been furnished by someone who loved Ikea; Annie recognised the bookshelf and coffee table from the last catalogue she had seen, as were the prints on the walls. She glanced at her watch and wished that there was a window to look out of. The stack of legal magazines and glossy gossip publications held no interest for her. She took out her phone and scrolled back through her emails, making a mental note of which ones to prioritise when she finally had some admin time. Most of her admin was restricted to her settee with a bar of Dairy Milk and a large glass of Shiraz.

"Hello, Annie," the familiar voice of Geoff Ryder greeted her. "I'm so sorry that you've been kept waiting, but one of my best clients promised to settle his account this morning. I couldn't really take his cheque and then bum rush him out onto the street."

His presence brought with it the scent of Hugo Boss. Annie knew that it was the one in the red bottle, although she couldn't remember its name. "It's no problem. You look like you have put some weight on," Annie said. "In a good way obviously, you looked ill the last time we met."

"Thank you, young lady," he said with a theatrical bow. "I have been visiting the gym again. The pain has become more manageable but I'm getting there slowly," he said smiling. Annie thought that he had had his teeth whitened. His suit was immaculate and a crisp white shirt was open at the collar. "Please come through. Can I get you a coffee? Milk and two sugars, right?"

He gestured to the nosy receptionist and she nodded that she understood. "I'll bring it right in," she mumbled staring unashamedly at Annie.

"Good memory," Annie replied. She leaned over the reception desk and smiled. "It isn't a fashion accessory," she whispered to the young girl, as she passed. "I really am a pirate." The girl looked as if she had been slapped, as Annie followed him through reception and into his office.

"Please forgive our secretary," Geoff smiled coyly. "She's an agency placement. Finding someone who doesn't mind turning in Monday to Friday, being civil to our clients and being able to speak English is becoming more difficult."

"Ah, the dreaded 'agency', that would explain it," she smiled. "She's forgiven."

"They were called job centres in my youth, but now I believe the job centres have no jobs to advertise."

"No," Annie agreed. "The agencies have all the jobs."

"Therein lies my dilemma," he walked around his desk as he spoke. "I hope you don't mind me saying, but I love the white eye patch," he smiled charmingly. "It suits you. Please take a seat."

"I'm not quite Gabrielle, but I've got used to it," she blushed a little as she spoke. "It feels strange to take it off now."

"We have to adapt, don't we?" Geoff said, as he sat down behind his desk. "It amazes me how resilient the human condition can be. I honestly thought that Laura would implode after all that happened, but she dealt with it better than I did." He paused and made a steeple with his fingers. "Are you here about Brendon, or do you need legal representation?" The door opened and the receptionist walked in and placed a cup of hot coffee next to Annie. "Thanks, Tammy." He waited for her to leave before continuing. "Seriously, how can I help?"

"We found another body," Annie said bluntly. His face twitched as if he had a sharp pain in his tooth. A flinch like when metal hits a filling. She was surprised by his reaction. Surprised and confused.

"Oh, dear God." He whispered. "At the beach?"

"Yes," she studied his face. "It was the body of Lacey Taylor."

"Really, now that does shock me." he sat forward sharply and frowned. "Wow." His reaction confused Annie. His surprise was faked. She was sure of that but she couldn't understand why he would overreact. "On the bright side, if I may suggest that there is a bright side in all this, at least her family has some closure."

"They were prepared for the worst but it was still a terrible shock for them, especially her daughter."

"I am assuming that you are looking for Brendon in connection with this new finding?"

"Yes," Annie sat forward as she spoke. She folded her hands over her exposed knees. His eyes were drawn to her thighs momentarily. She shuffled uncomfortably. "We're not looking for anybody else in connection with her murder."

"What makes you so certain that Brendon killed her?" He frowned. "I am aware that Richard Tibbs was your prime suspect for a time."

"That was largely because her dog was buried in his garden,"

Annie said flatly.

"Yes, of course it was."

"Buried there by Brendon."

"Clearly."

"We found Brendon's DNA under her nails and inside her. She was raped." She paused as he took in the information. His eyes narrowed and he took a sip of water from a chunky glass. His shoulders seemed to dip, as if he was suddenly tired, or as invisible hands pressed down on him. "The MO is the same as the other victims which we found at Crosby Beach."

"The Butcher's victims?" He said aghast.

"I'm afraid so."

"That poor woman," he shook his head. "So there is now no doubt that Brendon is the Butcher?"

"None," Annie said. An awkward silence settled between them. "Have you or his mother heard from him?"

"Not a word. I can assure you of that. My phone records are always available for you to check."

"Thank you," Annie said. "What about Laura; can you be so sure about her?"

"As sure as I can be." He paused to think about his next words. "This has been very difficult for her, but she has been surprisingly resilient. Laura is under no illusions about Brendon's position. She is disgusted by his actions but she is still a mother. She wants him locked up, but alive."

"And you're convinced that she hasn't heard from him?"

"Nothing," he said sincerely. Annie believed him. His eyes didn't flinch. "If we had, then you would have been the first person that I would have called. I want him caught for his own safety, Detective." She noted that his use of her first name was omitted. "And there is no doubt that the DNA belongs to him?"

"None."

"You know how dreadful I feel about all this." He shook his head and sighed into his hands. "John knew that he wasn't right in the head and he knew that something bad had happened at Breck Road, but he never divulged his suspicions to me fully." He was almost choked by his words and his eyes filled. The display of emotion wasn't lost on Annie. "I don't suppose he could tell me that he thought his stepson was a stone cold killer, really, could he?" He paused at the painful memories of his beloved cousin. "Jesus, he would be devastated if he had been alive to witness this. John was no angel, but this?"

"I know that this must be very painful for the family, but we're about to launch a huge media campaign to find him."

"I see." His eyebrows were raised in concern. "I appreciate you informing me. At least I can warn Laura to avoid the television."

"It might be wise," she nodded her agreement. "There's to be a Crimewatch Special tomorrow night and of course the big news channels are already carrying the story. The nationals are leading with his photo and the Echo and local rags will follow suit. Momentum is building, so if he's still alive then we'll find him."

"Good. The family wants an end to this."

"We have been waiting for Brendon to make a mistake and reveal his whereabouts, but he has fallen off the planet." She tilted her head and watched his reaction. "He is abroad, dead, or he's being helped by people far more intellectually gifted than he is. We know that he isn't stupid but he couldn't mastermind disappearing. I need to be completely clear on this," she paused, "are you or his mother hiding him?"

Geoff Ryder sat back and whistled through his teeth. He grimaced and then smiled thinly. "I can understand why you would think that. He has surprised us all, to be honest. He has been spoon fed and led by the hand from the day he was born. How he has survived on his own wits is beyond us!"

"John was a powerful man, with contacts both here and abroad."

"Absolutely right, but they were contacts that would have jumped through hoops to help John, but not Brendon." He shook his head emphatically. "John tried to introduce him into the business but he was a square peg. I can't think of one single person who warmed to Brendon, in fact he managed to generate quite the opposite reaction. People disliked him immensely."

"What about outside of the family circle?"

"The same. He had no friends at school or college. His achievements were none existent but he had a knack of causing trouble. He lived on his stepdad's reputation."

"I thought he had a group of friends who he drank with in town?"

"No," Geoff laughed. "He was so desperate for friends that he would buy everybody's drinks for their company, but he wasn't liked. Nobody offended him because of who he is." Geoff paused and rolled his eyes skyward as if something had just dawned on him. "Wait a minute! There was one friend, Gary."

"Gary who?"

Geoff tapped his fingers on the desk and screwed his eyes

tightly closed. "Gary, Gary Gary." He shook his head. "Bloody hell, it has slipped my mind."

"Take your time."

"Bissell!" he slapped the desk top. "That's it, Gary Bissell like the carpet cleaning machines!"

Annie sat forward and took out her mobile. "Gary Bissell, and where did he live?"

"Don't get excited," Geoff said raising his hand to stop her. "He died in a boating accident, a year or so back. They recovered his body from the sea near Heswall, or what was left of him, anyway."

"Boating accident?"

"I think so."

"What type of boating accident?"

"I can't remember. They think he had been hit by a propeller. It was a small piece in the Echo."

"What was he doing in the river?"

"That was never explained."

"Where did he live?"

"Formby, if I remember rightly."

"That's a stone's throw away from where we found Lacey Taylor."

"It's a stone's throw away from Crosby Beach too," Geoff shrugged. "Do you think that there's a connection?"

"I don't know, but it could be very useful. Thank you," Annie said, standing up. "I need to call his name into the station and get an address. Thanks for the coffee." She smoothed her pencil skirt and straightened her jacket as she stood. Geoff ran his eyes over her admiringly. "I'll be in touch."

"Of course, Annie," Geoff held out his hand as he stood. "Nice to see you again. You take care. I hope you find him soon."

Chapter 46

Janice Nixon pushed her shopping trolley along the meat aisle. The refrigerators made the air uncomfortably cool so she walked quickly. She could have gone faster but for the front left wheel, which wobbled annoyingly when she picked up speed. It was like having a restrictor on it. Maybe they did it on purpose, she thought, so that you could only travel at browsing speed. Being six months pregnant had changed their grocery list dramatically. Jim Stirling still ate his beloved spicy curries but they had both cut back on red meat, caffeine and alcohol. Their romance had been a whirlwind but for the first time in her life she finally felt as if all the trauma of her previous experiences were behind her. Janice hadn't worked the streets since the first night they went out for a beer and a curry. In fact, she had only been back to her crappy flat twice; once to get her stuff and the second to hand back the keys and take the utilities' meter readings. Within two weeks of meeting Jim, she was totally clean of drugs. A month later, she had a job at the local supermarket. She gave up smoking and began to see her family every Sunday. After the first visit, which was understandably emotional, it was as if she had never been away from them. Her life as a drug addicted whore seemed to belong to another and her memories of those dark days faded fast, although they were still there taunting her. In the darkest moments of the night, they came to her and warned her what still awaited if she screwed up.

Six months later she was absolutely sure that she had ruined everything and terrified that Jim Stirling would kick her back into the gutter where he had found her. When she realised that she was three weeks late, she panicked. She had always been regular, even when she was on the drugs. Her menstrual cycle was like clockwork. She berated herself for getting caught and dreaded telling him. She envisioned him flipping out and telling her that he wasn't the paternal type. He wasn't. She knew that and she should have been more careful. He was a detective in one of Britain's toughest cities. His career was his wife; his colleagues, beer and football were his family. She was amazed that they had fallen in love as hard and as fast as they had, but fall they did. The thought of losing him made her feel physically ill. It took days of agonising over telling him or having the baby aborted secretly but she couldn't do that. She would rather have become a single mother. She eventually gathered the courage to tell him and in typical Jim Sterling fashion he had surprised her with his reaction. Her ribs had been sore for three days he had hugged her so hard. They were married at a civil ceremony, a month to the day that she told him, and the rest was history.

Here she was filling a basket with their favourite foods and considering what nutritional value they had for their unborn child. She had a craving for Marmite, which prior to being pregnant, she hated. The week before, she had eaten a family sized jar by herself. Deciding whether to buy one jar or two was the most pressing decision that she had to make at the moment. Life had gone full circle for her. She had been to hell and back without actually dying. Now she was in a place which only a few really found. A place where that initial burning passion and unswerving attraction never faded. Many experience it fleetingly, but for most the intensity fades at some point without your knowledge and never returns. You look back one day and think, 'When was the last time we made love all night without once thinking about sleep?' Or the sudden realization that you no longer get butterflies in your stomach when they walk into the room; the white hot burning of sexual attraction which for most is unsustainable for more than a few months. It fast becomes a warm cosy place where comfort and companionship try to fill the emotional void but fail miserably. They were the lucky ones. Janice was enveloped in a love that she had never felt before. The thought of becoming a mother only added to her euphoria.

Janice floated up and down the aisles never giving a thought to the cost of the goods. Money had always been the only driving force in her life. She had barely managed to exist before. The drugs stole every penny that she earned. Now she could buy what they needed without worrying. They weren't rich by a long chalk, but they didn't need to scrimp either. She put four tins of Boddingtons into the trolley as a treat for Jim. She was carrying their baby, so it wouldn't hurt if he had a few tins while he watched the football. There was no need for them both to abstain totally. A smile touched her lips as she pictured him on the settee shouting at the referee. When she had gathered everything on her list, the trolley was half full. She made her way to the shortest queue and quickly decided that the girl on the checkout was in the wrong job. She was a rusty coloured automaton with blusher and lip gloss on. Each fingernail was a miniature work of art and her eyelashes would have looked at home on a camel.

"Do you need any carrier bags?" She asked in a monotone voice without looking up.

"Yes please," Janice replied as she loaded her shopping onto the conveyor belt. She wondered how she was going to get six litres of milk and four tins of Boddingtons into a carrier bag and then into the house without making multiple journeys to and fro.

"Disposable or bags for life?"

"What?" Janice laughed.

"Disposable carrier bags, which are five pence or canvas bags for life, which are seventy pence?" She scanned the goods faster than Janice could pack which caused the shoppers behind her to grumble as they waited for conveyor belt space.

"The bags for life aren't really bags for life are they though?" Janice said sarcastically. "They are more like bags for the week, aren't they?"

"I don't make them, luv," the assistant chirped. "I just scan the stuff and take the payment."

"I can see that."

"Which is it to be then?"

"Disposable please," Janice tried a smile as she shovelled her shopping into the trolley as fast she could. Her back ached as she paid for her goods and then packed them into her newly purchased carrier bags. Although she enjoyed the experience of foraging for her man, the baby was taking her strength and shopping made her weary. With her trolley packed, she headed for the exit. Outside was grey and blustery; the storm had almost blown itself out. A light drizzle fell and she shivered at the memory of freezing on her street corner. Sympathy squeezed her insides as she thought of the others stood in the rain, waiting for a punter to come along. Sometimes the memories haunted her but they came to her less frequently now. She pushed the trolley to the back of their Mazda and used the fob to click open the boot.

"You've come up in the world haven't you?" A voice startled her. She turned to see a man in a tracksuit grinning at her. A black baseball cap covered his head and dark glasses masked his eyes. "And you're up the duff too, dirty bitch," he laughed hoarsely.

"Do I know you?" Janice asked. She racked her brain for the slightest memory of his face. She couldn't remember him as a customer, but she knew him from somewhere. He was familiar in a bad way. She looked around for other people but it was quiet.

"No, you don't know me," he said with a smile tinged with evil. "But I know you. I didn't think it would last between you and him but here you are. Fancy him shacking up with a whore." Janice frowned and swallowed hard. She was beginning to feel frightened by his presence. His tone was acidic and he knew too much about her for her liking. He was enjoying her discomfort and confusion. "You live with the big fat copper don't you?"

"Fuck off!" Janice snapped. She tensed, anger and anxiousness grappled inside her. "Jim would kick your teeth in, if he heard you talking to me like that."

"Oh, but he's not here is he?" Brendon took his hand from his pocket and pointed his nine millimetre at her unborn baby. Her mouth opened in a silent scream but no sound came out. "Now, me and you are going for a drive." He gestured towards a white Mercedes Vito with the gun. It was parked next to her car. "Get in," he said staring at her. Janice looked around for help but there was no one nearby. "Scream and I'll put a bullet through your little piglet there. Now move!" As he turned sideways, she recognised his profile. He was the man that Jim had been ranting about for weeks. She couldn't remember his name but she was convinced that it was him. Jim told her that he was responsible for all the murders on the Beach at Crosby. He was the Butcher.

Janice let go of the trolley and walked towards the side door, which was already open. Leaving a trolley full of shopping which she had paid for stressed her more than it should under the circumstances, but she guessed that was just a natural emotion. With legs that were full of lead, she stepped towards the van. Her bottom lip quivered and she felt a trickle of urine leaking down her thigh as she climbed into the van. As he slammed the door closed and locked it, in the near total darkness the tears started to flow.

Chapter 47

Annie climbed out of the minibus and looked around. She heard the rear door sliding open as the uniformed search team was deployed. The trees and hedges on both sides of the roads were untended and overgrown. Once a busy thoroughfare, Mother Nature was reclaiming the tarmac and concrete, inch by inch. "Comb the extended area around the buildings while we wait," she ordered the team of officers who were exiting from the rear door. Above them a corrugated iron canopy branded with the faded and peeling Esso logo was supported by two crumbling brick columns. Beneath the canopy, the skeletons of four petrol pumps stood like rusty sentinels guarding the derelict fuel station. Thistles and nettles protruded through cracks in the concrete forecourt and oil stains, decades old, spotted the area around the pumps. A barely readable 'no smoking on the forecourt' sign made her smile on the inside. She envisaged the service bays full of greasy mechanics working with hand rolled cigs hanging from the corner of their mouths. That was way back in the days when health and safety was nothing more than an a sensible idea. "Start on the left of the property and sweep right to the stream."

"Roger that, left to right, Guv," a uniformed officer said. "What exactly are we looking for?"

"Until we can get inside, look for signs of recent activity, for now." She sighed and watched Alec's BMW pulling into the forecourt, closely followed by Stirling in a marked police car with an armed unit behind him. "I'm hoping this is our warrant arriving to search inside," she explained to a uniformed sergeant as she studied the building. The main structure was a one storey unit with a double service bay at one end and what would have been a shop, selling car parts, newspapers, cigarettes and sundries, at the other. Although she couldn't see it from the front, Annie knew that there was a bungalow attached to the rear where the owners dwelled. "Records showed that Gary Bissell was the only son of Gary senior and Carol. They were the owner-occupiers of the service station, until it closed down when the local planners built the Crosby bypass, diverting their traffic and strangling their business."

"I remember this place being open, Guv," he pointed to the old shop as he spoke. "I've stopped here many times to buy crisps for the kids on the way to the fair at Southport. They must be getting on in years now. I am surprised they're still here."

"We know that the Bissels stayed in the bungalow. They're claiming disability allowance and their council tax and utility bills are paid up to date. We've tried to contact them but all efforts have failed." They turned as Alec approached in a huff. The wrinkles in his face deepened when he was angry.

"We can't get a bloody warrant," Alec held his hands up in the air; his face like thunder.

"What?" Annie gasped.

"The judge says that no crime has been committed by them and he can't see any connection between the Bissell's property and our case. The fact that their son was friendly with Ryder, is negated by the fact he is long since dead. He is not prepared to allow forced entry into their home when they could be visiting relatives or taking a cruise."

"Was he stoned?" Annie whined. "We need to get access to this building."

"This station hasn't been open for how long?" Alec asked. He walked across the forecourt and peered into the old shop unit. The reinforced glass was threaded with wire mesh, which made it almost impossible to see through. Decades of grime compounded visibility. He rubbed the glass but it made no difference. "The bypass was finished twenty years ago, right?"

"Right," Annie agreed.

"I would be surprised if the structure is still intact and secure all the way around."

"Me too," Annie agreed. "Places left empty like this are vandalised all the time."

"Especially when the owners are not there."

"We had better check if they are, or not."

"Let's give it a once over and see what we can find, shall we?" Alec moved towards the opposite end where the service bays were. The bays were separated by a metre wide column of brick and secured by metal concertina doors. A tin sign was screwed to the brick, rusted and faded by time. "The Michelin Man," Alec said pointing to the battered tin. "It's a tyre pressure guide. Do you remember them?"

"No, Guv," Annie grimaced. She looked preoccupied.

"Ford Granada, Escort, Cortina, Capri," he read from the list. "I had all of them at some point in time," he mumbled to himself. No one else was interested. He checked over the service bay doors. The blue paint was cracked and flaky. Thick padlocks the size of grapefruits fastened the doors to the concrete supports. Annie touched one of the padlocks and lifted it up to inspect it. Rust spots covered it and it felt pitted by the weather but the keyhole itself was shiny. She showed it to Alec. "That has been used recently." He commented.

Annie rubbed her foot against the floor in a semicircle. Her toes scraped against the concrete. "Look here," she pointed at the dirt and debris. "Blue paint flakes. These doors have been opened as recently as today."

"Today?"

"The wind and rain would have washed this away otherwise."

"This side has been used but not as recently." Stirling said from the next bay. "The keyhole in the lock is shiny but I don't think the door has been opened for a while." He rattled the door hard but although it was noisy, nothing gave. "I'll take a look around the back. You never know."

"Under the circumstances," Alec said. "I think that we should start with the living areas. If there are vehicles in there, they can only open the doors from outside. They're not going anywhere."

"Agreed," Stirling said. "I'll take a team this way, you take the other."

"I'll keep you company, Guv," Annie agreed. They walked along the front elevation of the service station and stopped when they reached the corner. A concrete path hugged the walls and led past two bedroom windows before reaching an arched porch built from red brick. The wedge-shaped keystone, which supported the arch, had the numerals 1960 chiselled into it. The bungalow's roof was thick with green moss and the window frames were cracked and peeling. Tall chimney pots reached skyward from a central stack. Patterned net curtains hung in the windows, greyed with age and frayed at the edges. The windowsills inside were spotted with mold. Annie could almost smell the damp through the glass. "There's condensation inside the glass here," Annie said as she past a bedroom. "There is some type of heating on inside."

"Maybe someone is at home, after all?" Alec stepped into the porch and knocked hard on the door. "Mr Bissell!" He shouted through the letterbox. "This is the police. Please open the door." He peered through the flap into a hallway which hadn't been decorated since the eighties. "Mr Bissell!" he tried again. Suddenly his body tensed. "Oh, shit!"

"What is it?" Annie asked concerned. Alec sniffed the air coming through the letter box.

"I can smell gas," Alec snapped. "He caused the explosion at Breck Road. He's trying the same thing again. Get everyone back."

"I'll find the meter box, Guv," Annie shouted as she ran for the corner of the bungalow. "You break all the windows; I'll cut off the supply."

"You heard her," Alec said to the uniformed officers nearby. "Break the windows! I need an armed officer on each room, in case anyone in there has a weapon." Two officers drew their batons and stepped forward. Covering their eyes, they shattered the windows with a series of heavy blows. The armed officers ripped down the curtains and aimed their weapons inside. As Annie turned the corner, she heard the glass shattering and ran as fast as she could around the side of the building. The side wall was solid, no doors, no windows and no sign of any utilities entering the building. She slipped in knee high grass and stumbled around the next corner. Stirling was a hundred yards away behind the service bays. "Look for the gas meter!" She shouted to him. "It must be on one of the outer walls. We need to cut off the supply, quickly!"

Stirling frowned and looked along the foundation walls. The rear was overgrown and resembled a scrapyard. Grasses and brambles grew to waist height. The rusting hulk of a Commer van was surrounded by scrap wheels and used tyres. Half a dozen car doors of different shapes and sizes were rotting against the rear wall of the service bays. He sent a uniformed officer back the way that they had come, to check for the gas supply. "I can't see anything," he called. "It must be at the front."

"Bollocks!" Annie muttered as she turned and ran around the side of the bungalow, back towards the front of the house. Alec had his arms folded and looked unworried. The uniformed officers waited patiently for orders. "Mr and Mrs Bissell don't seemed bothered that you have smashed their windows," Annie said catching her breath. She was surprised that there had been no reaction from inside the house. "We can't find where the gas supply enters the building. It must run underground and be connected to a meter inside."

"I agree," Alec nodded and winked. "As soon as the smell of gas has cleared, send the armed unit in first. We know he's armed so it's best not to risk it."

Annie signalled to the armed unit and they moved in line to the front door. They knew that there was little danger. A frightened criminal would have opened fire, or bolted for freedom as soon as the windows were smashed. "Do you think that the gas will be cleared by now," she asked. Her eyebrows were raised.

"Should be."

"There was no gas was there?" She said quietly.

"I don't know what you mean, Inspector. I clearly smelled gas."

Annie frowned and waved the armed officers in. A heavy metal battering ram took the door from its hinges with a single blow. The structure was as fragile as the exterior. "Armed police!" Their shouts reached them. "Armed police!" The backup unit moved in formation and Annie waited impatiently until the calls were all clear.

"Clear." There was silence for a moment and then uniformed shapes filed back into the hallway and porch. "You need to get in there, Guv." The senior officer said from the ruined front door. His face was pale and ashen. A second armed officer staggered out of the door and dropped to his knees. He wretched onto the path and the sound of vomit splattering onto the concrete seemed unusually loud. Seeing a hardened police officer forced to the point of nausea didn't bode well for what was inside. "I'll call CSI," he added with a grimace.

Alec and Annie exchanged glances and walked to the porch. There was no lingering odour of gas in fact Annie was now sure that there was no gas supply at all. The building was old and isolated. She guessed that Alec had used the ploy of gas leaking to gain access to the bungalow. His ethics were sometimes questionable, but on this occasion, she admired his ingenuity. Annie stepped through the door and the smell of damp hit her first, followed quickly by the sickly sweet smell of rotting flesh. As she stepped inside the hallway, the stench of urine and excrement mingled with decay to inform her that this was a murder scene, before she had even seen a body. They took latex gloves from their pockets and put them on. She looked around. A low telephone table sat near the wall to the left. A green telephone sat on it, the hand piece connected to the main body with a coiled flex; the circular dial was well used, the numerals beneath worn by friction from a dialing finger. The table had a padded faux leather seat attached, so that the phone could be used in comfort. Annie thought it was like stepping back in time. The museum-like image was topped by a seventies style pop-up telephone index sat next to the phone.

The carpet was mustard coloured with deep swirling patterns cut into it. The walls were painted chocolate brown and covered in matching Artex swirls. To the right a doorway led into a small lounge. The stench of death thickened to the point where she could almost taste it. "They were home, after all," Annie covered her mouth and nose with her hand. She took a jar of eucalyptus, unscrewed the top and smeared a blob under her nose. Handing it to Alec, he followed suit. A threadbare Wilton covered the floor, the once vivid colours jaded by time and the presence of a coal fire in the room. The scent of cinders and sulphur were detectable beneath the smell of dead bodies. A Welsh dresser covered in blue Delftware plates and brass ornaments dominated the rear wall. "They haven't been dead long. The blood here is still congealing." She pointed to a crease in Mr Bissell's trousers where his blood had run down his torso and pooled in the material around the zipper. The surface of the blood was thickened but it was clearly still liquid beneath.

"I'm thinking the same here," Alec said looking at Mrs Bissell. "She's been nailed through the hands and wrists to the armchair, with a nail gun, at a guess. The nails are too deeply embedded for anything else. Her throat has been slit from behind." The old woman didn't look real. She looked like an extra from a zombie movie. A shock of frizzy grey hair defied gravity. Her eyes were wide and accusing, her tongue discoloured and hanging from the corner of her blackened lips. The rent in her throat looked like a huge second mouth. Her dressing gown was soaked in her blood. It was a scene from a George A Romero film. Alec looked at Annie for details from her side of the room. She looked sickened yet enthralled as she circled the old man.

"Mr Bissell is the same, Guv." She sighed. "Nailed to the chair through the wrist and forearm, beaten and his throat is slashed. Looking at the arterial spray on the wall, he was very much alive when that happened."

"It wasn't quick," Alec added solemnly.

"I'm going to look around the rest of the house," Annie said. She couldn't wait to get away from the carnage in front of her. The vile stench was oppressive, making it difficult not to gag. "We should leave the real evaluation of how they died to Kathy, or we'll be on the receiving end of a tongue lashing." She stepped out of the lounge and felt a wave of relief flow over her as she left the murdered couple behind. The heartbreak of the situation wasn't lost on her. Their life would have made some of Shakespeare's tragedies seem like a comedy sketch. Married young, decades ago, they went into a life of matrimony together, lived and breathed a business together, had a child, then through no fault of their own, lost everything together. In the twilight of their lives, their son died and then to top things off, they were tortured and slain together in their own armchairs. Probably by someone they were trying to help. If there was some kind of cosmic macabre irony in that, Annie couldn't see it. "What a waste of two lives," she muttered. Her stomach was knotted with angst. There were days when she wished there was an off switch or at least a fast forward option. Alec touched her shoulder sensing her distress. "I'm dissecting the tragic lives, of a tragic couple, who were slaughtered in tragic circumstances and the only word that I can think of to describe it all?"

"Tragic?"

"Pointless," she sighed. They both laughed but it was nerves making them find humour in the sadness. "Completely fucking pointless."

"It is a difficult one to get your head around," Alec said concerned. Annie was normally titanium coated. Nothing much ruffled her, or even scratched the surface. Sometimes it was difficult to remember that she had suffered a major trauma and then returned to work as if she had recovered from the flu. "Best not to dwell on it, Annie. Stay focused."

"It's not just their murder, Guv," Annie said with a sigh. "Look around. They worked all their lives, to get fucked by the highways department and end up living in a shithole while their world disintegrated around them. Makes you wonder where the justice is, doesn't it?"

"Yes."

"I mean, what is it all about?" Annie stopped and took a deep breath. She felt her emotions bubbling beneath the surface. The sight of such evilness, the smell of violent death, the certain knowledge that they would have been more frightened for each other than they were for themselves, shook her to her soul. Her knees felt weak and she had to slow her breathing down. Not only did they have the time to contemplate their own hideous demise, they had to watch their soulmate screaming in agony before they died. Annie wasn't sure which was worse. "What could they possibly have had that was worth doing that to them?"

"Looking around, nothing," Alec touched her elbow. The ridges in his forehead deepened. "Maybe they knew something. The best thing we can do for them is to catch the bastard and lock him away for life. Come on, we've got a job to do," he said guiding her towards the bedrooms. "I'll take this one, you take the other."

Annie breathed deeply and then exhaled. She tried to expel the cloying aroma of death from her lungs but it wouldn't budge. She knew from experience that it would stick to her for days. There wasn't a soap on the planet which could cleanse the stench from her nostrils. A dull ache niggled from behind the eye patch. She knew that it would build and build and become more intense as the day progressed. If she didn't take her painkillers now, there would be no stopping it. The doctors had told her to expect it. She waited for Alec to step into the bedroom, before taking out her pills and slipping two from the bottle. She placed them under her tongue and then swallowed them one at a time. Her throat felt dry and the capsules took long seconds to slide down into her stomach. Annie pulled herself together, pushed away from the wall and stepped into the other bedroom.

Her jaw dropped open as she looked around. There were black and white images of the Iron Men on the wall above a single bed. A crumpled pillow and navy blue sleeping bag were the only bedding. The mattress was mottled with stains; lots of them. She stepped in and looked behind the door. That wall was covered in coloured images of the familiar statues. Some were from magazines, but most of the images were photographs. Whoever took them was a keen photographer and Gorman's Iron Men were obviously their favourite subject. Clothes were discarded in piles, mostly tracksuits, dirty sport socks and boxer shorts. A walnut veneer dressing table stood to her right. It had an oval mirror which was attached to a swivel, fixed to the back of it. A brush sat next to a tin of deodorant and a bottle of Aramis. Although it was sparse, it looked lived in. The clothing was akin to Brendon Ryder's style. Next to the bed was a pizza box with one slice remaining. It looked days old, rather than weeks. Three empty quick noodle pots sat on the window ledge and an ashtray overflowed with ash and handmade filters. The sweet smell of cannabis lingered around the bed and that part of the room. The sleeping bag and minimal number of grooming items made it feel like his presence was only supposed to be temporary, yet the dirty laundry showed that he had been staying there for some time.

"Nice pictures," Alec's voice made her jump. "Obviously a fan of Crosby Beach?" Alec mused. "It looks like someone was staying here doesn't it?"

"Yes," Annie agreed. "The clothing, aftershave, smell and small mountain of pot noodles next to the bed make me think they had a male guest."

"Don't women eat pot noodles?"

"Not while there is any alternative available."

"It would appear that the Bissells offered Ryder a safe haven?"

"And look at the thanks they got for it," Annie said flatly. "Maybe the media surge spoiled the arrangement. The Bissells saw something on the television and confronted Ryder, or maybe he realised that he couldn't stay here any longer and didn't want to leave witnesses."

"We need something that tells us where he has gone to."

"A doorway at the end of the hall leads through to the shop and the garage. We've found the BMW, Guv," Stirling announced from the doorway. "It's in the service bay. The other side of the bay where you think the door was opened recently," he paused and raised his eyebrows, "is empty now, but there's an oil patch where a vehicle has been parked and someone changed the oil. I looked around and there's an old oil filter on the bench and an empty box for a new one. The box says the filter fits all Mercedes vans including the Vito." He grinned. "Tibbs was telling us the truth about the van that he saw at Crosby Beach."

"So it's been hidden here ever since." Annie said. "Gary Bissell must have been the man that Tibbs saw with Ryder."

"Bissell didn't have a boating accident," Alec scoffed. "Ryder topped him and dumped him in the river."

"And then when the shit hit the fan, he sought refuge from his grieving parents," Annie snapped. "I really hope that he doesn't come quietly when we find him. If anyone deserves a bullet between the eyes, it's that bastard."

"Well, we know that he is here in the country and that he's driving a white Vito. Get that out to all points," Alec ordered. Stirling took out his mobile to pass on the information to headquarters. He looked at the screen and a strange mewing sound came from his throat. Alec wasn't sure if he was joking. "What's wrong?" Stirling grabbed for the door handle to steady himself. His knees seemed to buckle slightly. He wobbled visibly and his face turned purple. He held up his hand as if to say 'hold on a minute I'm struggling here', and his eyes narrowed as he looked up from the screen. His other hand flung the mobile away as if it had suddenly become white hot. Alec couldn't fathom what had happened. "Jim?"

"Are you okay?" Annie frowned confused by his catatonic state. "Jim what is it?"

Stirling pointed to the phone on the floor. Annie stepped forward and picked it up. "That bastard," Stirling growled. "The fucking bastard," he screamed and swung a huge fist at the bedroom door. The impact sent fragments of hardboard flying across the room. His arm disappeared to the elbow and he had to tug hard to retrieve the limb. "I'll kill the bastard," he snarled like a wounded animal and punched another huge hole in the door. Annie looked at the screen and showed it to Alec. Uniformed officers ran into the room, startled by the sound of violence. "No!" Stirling roared and turned his face to the ceiling. "No, no, no. no, no," his roar became a pitiful whine.

The screen showed an image of a young woman bound and gagged. She was sitting with her knees up, her ankles taped and her hands fastened behind her. Blood trickled from both nostrils. Her eyes were wide open and full of terror, black mascara streaked her cheeks. The face of Brendon Ryder grinned over her shoulder, part of his arm visible. He had taken the bizarre 'selfie' using her phone. "Brendon Ryder has taken Janice Stirling," Annie said to the panicked officers. They looked at each other confusion on their faces. "Jim's wife!" She explained. "Brendon Ryder has taken Jim's wife and she's six months pregnant."

Chapter 48

Janice tried to remain calm for the baby's sake. She was far from calm but trying to control her breathing helped. The alternative was to lose control and panic and that would cause distress for her unborn child. The journey from the supermarket had been a nightmare so far. She tried kicking and screaming to raise the alarm but the bastard stopped the van, punched her hard in the nose and tied her up like a stuffed pig. The congealing blood in her nose combined with the gag made breathing very difficult. She was frightened that if she panicked, she would suffocate. Her childhood was dotted with panic attacks, which she had learned to control as she reached adulthood. Controlling her breathing and taking herself away to another place helped but the urge to scream until her voice snapped was overwhelming. If she hadn't been pregnant, she didn't think that she would have got into the van. She wasn't scared of being shot, if she died then she died, but she couldn't be so blasé with her child's life. Six months earlier, she would have run. He may have caught her; he may have beaten her and he may have shot her. All those things would have been far better than allowing him to force her into the van. He was a serial killer, a psychopath, a nutcase, a fruitcake, a fucking raving lunatic but he had a gun pointed at her baby. She had no choice. At the time, the chance of survival if she cooperated was far greater than if she resisted.

A series of sharp turns and violent bumps in the road bounced her around the back of the van. Janice knew they were speed ramps, which was a good thing, as speed ramps indicated they were in a built up area. She had no idea where they were but there had been traffic noises all the way until they hit the ramps. It had been quiet since then. She felt the van take another sharp turn and then it stopped. A door opened but the engine was still running. He had climbed out of the van for some reason. She cocked her head and tried to listen for clues. Metal rattled and she heard the sound of heavy chains being dragged and pulled. All sorts of images ran through her mind. Was he going to wrap her up in chains and dump her in the river? Maybe he would chain her to a dungeon wall and leave her to rot in the dark. There was a clang similar to a garage door opening. It would make sense if he had stopped to open a garage door, but what was he planning to do once they were inside? The sound of his footsteps stopped the nightmares from flashing in her head for a moment and she felt him climbing back into the driver's seat. The door slammed shut with a thud.

"We're here," he shouted chirpily. He could have been talking to his kids in the back seat on the way to the zoo for a day out. Anger rose in her throat. She wanted to shout back but the gag was painfully tight. Wherever they were, she wasn't as happy that they had arrived as he was. Janice wished that she had a gun or a knife or a hammer, or anything that she could use to kill the bastard. She wouldn't hesitate. She wouldn't blink and she wouldn't give him a second thought when he was dead. Jim had waffled on about the murders for hours on end. The case had been his life for over a year. He lived and breathed it. She wished that she hadn't listened so intently. The detail had fascinated her but now she was in the clutches of the Butcher, knowing what he had done to all those women was not a bonus. He pulled their teeth out for God's sake! Janice hated the dentist. She always had since she was a kid. How did those poor women suffer that amount of pain without dying of a heart attack? She couldn't fathom it. Tooth after tooth after tooth; the enamel and dentine splintering and cracking, exposing the nerves. The ripping and tearing of the roots from the gums and all that blood. How could she survive such torture? She didn't think that she could and she was certain that her baby wouldn't. If she got one chance, no matter how slim, to run, then she would take it. An agonisingly slow lingering death would cause her baby to suffer unnecessarily and she couldn't do that. He would have to put the gun down at some point and when he did, she would use every ounce of strength in her body to escape. She would run, kick, scratch and bite anyone that came into striking distance.

The van stopped and the engine died. There was silence for a while. She waited for him to move but nothing happened. Then she heard a beep and another polyphonic sound. He was using a mobile, texting or something. She couldn't tell which. She hoped to God that he had sent that picture he had taken to Jim. He said he was going to. Jim would go ballistic. He would be sick with worry, but he would look for her. She knew that he would search day and night until he found her and when he did, she wanted to watch what happened to that bastard. Jim would pull off his arms and legs one at a time and Janice would film it and replay it for him while he bled to death. She prayed to a God that she didn't believe in that Jim would work out where they were and come and find her. Her emotions were swinging from intense anger to devastating despair. Part of her wanted to kill him but the other part was happy to comply with anything he said, if it meant that she could survive and bring up her baby with Jim.

"Your husband is very rude," Brendon chirped. "You should see the message he has just sent to me. Very abusive, he's got a warped mind." Janice heard the driver's door open and felt the vehicle rocking as he climbed out. The side door slid open and she could see cracks of light seeping through the blindfold. "They know where we are. He'll be here soon enough," he said grabbing her ankles. He dragged her painfully across the van and grabbed a handful of her hair. He pulled her upright, tearing some of the hair from the scalp. Janice whelped. She was determined to be brave but she was both in pain and terrified. He twisted her head violently and ripped off the blindfold.

Janice looked into his piggy eyes. They were like marbles, glassy with a glint in them but also cold and lifeless. She prayed that his weren't the last eyes that she would look into. He grinned and pulled her hair tighter still. She could smell tobacco on his fetid breath and feel its warmth on her cheek as he spoke. He looked at her intently, studying every line. "I bet you were half decent ten years ago. Still, I wouldn't pay to fuck you, not a chance." He dragged her to her feet. "I don't mind paying for a decent looking woman, but you, nah!" He snorted. He bent low and grabbed her around the thighs, picking her up over his shoulder. Her body weight was centered on her stomach. She let out a muffled scream and kicked out. "Fucking hell!" He dropped her onto her feet. "Worried about squashing the piglet, I bet?" He looked into her eyes and she could see the amusement in them. He took an evil-looking hunting knife from a sheath which was strapped to his leg and licked the flat of the blade. It was over a foot long and had a razor-sharp blade on one side and a wicked serrated blade on the other. The jagged teeth were split like a wood saw, designed to rip and tear flesh. He held the cold steel to her face. Janice tried to lean back but he had her in his grip. The blade felt cool and sharp against her skin. She could smell the oil that he had used to sharpen the blade with, as he ground it against a whetstone repeatedly until it could shave the hair from his skin. It had a compass built into the handle, which she thought was odd. He slid it against her cheek a few millimetres and she felt the sting as it sliced. She squeezed her eyes tightly together so that he couldn't see her pain and prayed that death would come swiftly. She felt a warm trickle of blood run from beneath her eye. "Don't be awkward, or I'll have to hurt you. Okay?" She kept her eyes closed. "I said okay?" he shouted in her face.

Janice snapped her eyes open and nodded furiously that she understood. He took the lethal blade away and grinned. Emotion replaced adrenalin. She tried to fight the rising sobs, but they beat her and escaped her lips. Her legs trembled and felt like jelly. She couldn't hold her own body weight. Tears flowed from her eyes, mingling with her blood and the smeared mascara. Sobs racked her body and she felt like she was suffocating. She couldn't get her breath. Her body began to twitch and writhe. She had never had a seizure but she was pretty sure she was having one now. Her eyes rolled back into her head and a clucking noise came from her throat. She felt herself falling backwards onto her arms. As she hit the floor, the pain in her shoulders was excruciating. Janice felt her teeth clamping down hard on the gag and her body went into involuntary spasm. The sensation of suffocating combined with fear was too much. Her body went into a state of sheer panic.

"Fucking hell!" Brendon muttered as he watched her twitching violently on the floor with a sense of curiousness, surprise and frustration. "You're no good to me dead, stupid bitch."

He reached behind her, unfastened the gag and then rolled her onto her side. Removing the gag had an instant impact on her. She opened her mouth and sucked huge gulps of air into her lungs. There was a wheezing sound as her brain tried to compensate for the lack of oxygen, by forcing her lungs to work overtime. She spluttered and coughed as her heart rate settled and her limbs stopped trembling. Pins and needles set into the extremities and a layer of cold sweat formed on her skin. Her throat felt dry; her lips were numb and she needed to drink. "Water," she mumbled. Her voice was barely audible.

"You can have some water when we get upstairs," he snapped as he slipped the huge blade into its sheath. He slammed the door of the van closed with a bang. Janice realised that they were in a garage of some kind. The floor was bare concrete and the ceiling was open wooden joists, which appeared to be supporting a floor above. In the far corner, a staircase climbed upwards. Brendon took the knife out again and cut the binding from her ankles with a single slice. He dragged her to her knees but she was still very weak; too weak to stand. "Get up!" he growled, pulling painfully hard on her forearm. "Move or I'll gut you here."

Janice stamped her feet to get the circulation going and made an effort to walk but her legs were like lead. She didn't like the idea of climbing stairs. The higher they went, the more difficult it would be for Jim and the police to rescue her. Brendon tugged her, half pulling and half carrying her to the bottom of the staircase. "Walk, you stupid bitch!" He paused and snarled at her before dragging her upwards. She tried to make it as difficult for him as she could without becoming a dead weight and making him angry. Janice was thinking about escape and the stairs were not a good sign. Not many buildings in the city had garages beneath. She knew that some of the developments near the river did. They were tall, to offer views of the water. Riverside townhouses, the architect called them. If they were in a townhouse then there could be three or more floors. She really didn't want to be dragged up to the upper floors where escaping would be virtually impossible. Jumping through a window wasn't beyond her physical ability although she didn't fancy that from more than a floor up. Her options flashed before her eyes as they climbed. Brendon flicked on the light and took a bunch of keys from his pocket. He supported Janice with one hand and unlocked the door with the other. Dragging her through the door, he released her while he turned to lock it behind them. She dropped to her knees and looked around. The beige carpet was thick and was mostly wool in content. Janice didn't know much about carpets but she knew an expensive one when she saw one. Thick curtains blocked out the light from the windows and black and white prints of Liverpool's landmarks decorated the walls. A black leather corner settee dominated the far end of the room and a huge plasma screen was attached to the wall in front of it. The room was clean, neat and tastefully furnished. Behind them she saw a dining table with black veneer and six matching chairs around it. Brendon dragged the table up against the door and then piled the chairs on top of it. He stacked them so they filled the space between the door and the rear wall. There was no way that the door could be forced open. He clapped his hands together and sneered. "Even your fat husband won't break that down," he snorted. "Get up," he said gruffly. Janice thought about running at the curtains as fast as she could but she didn't know what was behind them and she was too weak. For all she knew, it might be a solid wall behind them. She would have to wait for her moment.

"I need water," she gasped. Janice looked around for a kitchen. There was a door to the right and another staircase directly above the first one. "I feel faint."

"Stay there," he sighed. "One wrong move and you are dead. Understand?" He looked at her suspiciously. She remained kneeling while he walked to the door and opened it. Switching the light on, Brendon disappeared into the kitchen. Her mind turned everything into makeshift weapons, a heavy vase, a small table, a marble ashtray, but with her hands tied they were all useless. She heard the clink of glass and the sound of running water and then he was back within seconds. He held out the glass and then tutted when he realised that she was tied up. It angered him, despite the obvious fact that he had tied her up. "Here!" He held the glass in front of her face. She moved forward slightly to drink and he moved it away, tormenting her. He put it suggestively close to his groin. "Here!" He laughed sourly, moving it again as she neared. "I thought you wanted a drink?" She wavered, nearly losing her balance. Her thirst overwhelmed her shame as she desperately followed the water.

"Please, I can't do this. I'm exhausted." She sighed heavily and sat down on her heels and waited for the taunting to stop. He lifted the glass an inch above her forehead and tipped it slightly. Cold water splashed onto her face. It ran into her eyes and then down her neck, trickling beneath her neckline.

"I bet you've had a few facials in your time, eh?"

"Hundreds," she replied flatly. "I even enjoyed some of them. Now can I have a drink or not?"

"Not!" He hissed and threw the water into her face. She squeezed her eyes closed tightly and lapped at the water which ran near her lips with her tongue. "You've got a smart mouth on you, slut. Well you can gasp."

"Arsehole," she said beneath her breath. The little water that she had salvaged helped but was not nearly enough to quench her thirst. "I can't wait for Jim to get a grip of your scrawny neck. He'll snap you like a twig." Janice couldn't help herself. Insulting him was all she had left. Brendon grabbed her chin between his thumb and forefinger and tilted her head back. He smiled and his eyes seemed to glaze over. It chilled her to the bone.

A flash of white hot pain shot through her brain. A concussive blow stunned her. A millisecond later she felt the fragile bones in her nose crack under the force. The coppery taste of blood filled her senses. She didn't have time to scream, unconsciousness took her instantly. Somewhere in her subconscious, she wondered if she would wake up buried in the sand.

Chapter 49

Brendon grabbed her by the ankles and dragged her to the second flight of stairs. It was impossible to drag her up the staircase with her hands still tied behind her back. It crossed his mind to drag her face down but he thought that her chin would crack against every step. At best, that would break her teeth and choke her and at worst she may bite off her tongue and bleed to death, or break her neck. He needed her alive for the time being. Taking the survival knife from its sheath, he sliced through the tape and grabbed her wrists tightly with both hands. He took a deep breath and then dragged her up to the next floor. Her chest wheezed as her back hit each step. It was harder than he thought it would be. His thigh muscles burned with the buildup of lactic acid and his breathing became labored. Pulling a limp body up a flight of steps would have taxed a fit man, let alone a slouch like Brendon Ryder. Keeping fit had never been his thing. He spent his life wearing tracksuits and sportswear, yet the only time he visited a gym was to sell drugs. His passion for football only extended to watching it from a bar stool. The last time he had seen a football outside of television was at school. His stepfather used to say that the only thing he wasn't addicted to was exercise.

On the way up, he paused twice to rest and groaned in agony when he reached the top. He dumped her on the carpet and slumped on the floor with his back against the wall, while he caught his breath. Sweat trickled from his brow into his eyes and tiny rivulets ran down his back. He sighed and looked around for inspiration. He had half an idea forming in his mind. All he had to do was stop anyone from following them. It sounded simple enough. Along the hallway, three doors led into the bedrooms, two doubles and a single. He had been using the master bedroom so he was familiar with the furniture in there but he had a good idea what was in the others. There was more than enough to block the stairs and slow down any potential pursuers. He didn't have much time.

"Don't you go running off anywhere now, will you?" He prodded Janice with his boot. Her face was swollen and bloody. She moaned but she didn't move. He stood and walked into the spare double room. It took him four trips to toss the mattress, the base and the wardrobe down the stairs. The wardrobe wedged sideways at an angle which was more luck than judgment but with the weight of the mattress and its base behind, it would difficult to shift. By the time he had emptied the single room too, his impromptu barricade was complete. "No one is coming up here fast," he said smiling at his achievement. He rested for five minutes before dragging Janice to the top floor. In his opinion, it took a heroic burst of strength to pull her up to the top floor without stopping once and he clapped his hands together when he dropped her. When they reached the top, she was coming round slowly although her eyes were so swollen it was difficult to tell. He sat her on a chair and used curtain tiebacks to fasten her around the waist. It wasn't the most secure binding but they were four floors up and the stairs were impassable. He had an automatic and the knife. She was going nowhere.

The helicopter was the first sign that they were coming in force. Brendon heard the rotors approaching. He walked to the balcony doors and slid them open. It was warm outside and the air was tinged with the scent of the sea blowing in off the river. The sound of gulls squawking drifted on the breeze. He looked up from the balcony and protected his eyes from the glare of the sun with his hand. It flew over the St John's Tower towards the river and appeared to drop as it neared. Above the sound of the helicopter, sirens wailed in the distance. They seemed to be coming from all directions, although they would only be able to approach from one. His stepfather had owned the townhouse from new and it was used as a safe house for his employees who were on the run, or for visiting business associates. It had four floors which overlooked the river and a single garage beneath. Within walking distance of the Pier Head and the city centre, it was the centre property of a terrace of seven houses. Brendon was on the fourth floor looking down, when the helicopter took its second sweep overhead.

The ground support would arrive soon but he wasn't too concerned. He wasn't trying to escape or hide any longer. It was his idea to tell them where he was and so far things were going to plan. If indeed you could call it a plan. He wasn't sure that you could but it was the best that he could come up with. He had taken a valuable hostage; not just a random but someone who meant a lot to his adversaries. His defensive position had height, which historically meant that he had the advantage over his enemies and he had blocked the stairways to protect his rear. They wouldn't be able to rush him up here and he would have the option to negotiate with them for days, if he felt the need to. He wasn't sure what he wanted to achieve yet but taking a position of strength increased his choices. There would be no point in demanding a plane or a boat. Escape wasn't an option. His twelve months in hiding had drained all his cash reserves. He had no money, no passport and no friends. The only people that he knew who were willing to help him had done all that they could. The police news blitz had pushed him over the edge and out of hiding. That was what made him angry and so he took something that he knew was precious to his pursuers, Janice Stirling.

The first police vehicles came into view and he smiled as the convoy of flashing blue lights grew longer. He felt flattered by the size of the taskforce that they had dispatched to catch him. They poured into the access road and then fanned out to form a semicircle on the car park in front of the townhouses. Armed officers sprang from the vehicles, took cover behind them and trained their weapons on him. As the last vehicle deployed its officers, he counted thirty weapons pointed at him. It might have been overwhelming for some but Brendon didn't feel intimidated by the show of force. Yes, they had more men and more weapons, but it hardly mattered. He wasn't going to try to shoot his way out; there was no point in that.

Brendon thought that weapons were strange things, as they were only dangerous in the hands of someone who was totally willing to use them against another. Brendon had seen many armed men in his time, yet only a few actually used them to hurt or kill. Few of the young men that carried knives could actually slash or stab another human being. They were carried as a deterrent, in the hope that the mere presence of the weapon was enough to avoid an attack. He wondered how many of the men and women below would happily shoot him if they were in a one on one situation, without questioning the moral issues which surrounded taking a human life. Most of them probably, yet he knew that some would not. There were many weapons threatening him but in this instance, the only weapon that mattered was the one which was in his hand. That single firearm could be used to determine the outcome of his stand. Brendon Ryder was the only one who would decide if the hostage lived or died.

He looked along the line of vehicles and stared at the faces of the plain clothed officers but he couldn't see Stirling. They were some distance away and some were covered by dark glasses, some with balaclavas but none of them had his size or stature. Movement to his left caught his eye. A sniper team had reached the roof of an adjacent building. The shooter and his spotter bent low as they ran across the roof, before taking up position behind the cover of a low safety wall. The sniper shouldered his rifle and Brendon grinned as he imagined the cross-hairs being lined up on his forehead. He raised his middle finger and spat in their direction. The wind took his globule of phlegm and blew it back at him. The green goo landed on his right sleeve and he brushed at it wildly. "Eeeh, dirty bastard," he hissed as he wiped it off. He blushed red and wondered if the sniper had watched him spit on himself. The spotter had binoculars on him. He didn't think they would shoot him yet, not without some dialogue.

His attention returned to the assembled force below. Their

numbers were growing. A white articulated lorry turned into the approach road. He guessed it was the mobile incident unit. Once that was deployed, they would try to make contact. That's what happened on the television anyway. Get set up, put the kettle on and then call the baddie and persuade him to give up. Nine times out of ten everything turned to shit and the baddie gets blown to bits, but hey ho, that's television. It would be boring if they gave up straight away. He was almost looking forward to talking to them. It would be fun making Stirling squirm and beg for the life of his whore. His options were limited, that was a fact, but this way he could force Stirling to beg and at least he could find out the answers to some burning questions. They would ask him what he wanted and he was struggling to come up with an answer. Most baddies had a list of demands but Brendon didn't want anything. That would baffle them. Even Morgan Freeman couldn't negotiate that one.

Chapter 50

Alec looked at the HD screens which were fixed to a bank of surveillance equipment on the left-hand side of the incident unit vehicle. Officers from the Tactical Firearms Unit were debating points of access and exit to and from the townhouse. The trailer was crammed with senior officers from different departments, all eagerly waiting for orders. "How's Jim holding up?" a familiar face asked him. He couldn't place a name to the face but he knew that he was TFU. "I haven't seen him around yet, where is he?"

"I've sent him to Canning Place," Alec replied seriously. "However this goes down, I can't have him on scene."

"We could do with him here to break a hole in the wall."

"Let's hope we don't need to call him down here, shall we?" Alec humoured him. He meant well but he wasn't in the mood for jest. "Are the Surveillance Team on scene yet?"

"They're here now." Annie pointed to four men in black body armour who were entering the vehicle. She waved them over and they made their way to the screens.

"He's on the top floor," Alec pointed to the main screen. The camera images changed. "Can we get eyes on the rear fire escape again?" The camera tech nodded and brought up the rear of the townhouses again. "Okay, we have to assume that John Ryder used this place for business, as it's never been rented out. If it was a bolt hole, it will be well prepared as such." He indicated a series of metal landings attached to the rear elevation. "There are landings which are connected by a series of folding ladders. There's access to the fire escape from every floor."

"Correct," the tech agreed. "There are four landings, which run the full length of the terrace. Someone escaping from the rear landings could reach the ground at these three points, here, here and here."

"Which means they could have a vehicle or some form of escape in place at the back," Annie said.

"Right." Alec agreed. "Check the alleyways to the rear for a vehicle or a motorbike, which looks like it may have been parked there for a long time. Annie is right, Ryder may have keys stashed in the house for an escape vehicle parked behind."

"We're on it, Guv. There's a team searching the alleyways, here and here and the access roads here and here," the tech nodded. "My concern is an exit built between the townhouses. If Ryder did use it as safe house, there is a high probability that they built access between them. There could be conjoining doors between them on any of the floors, the garages or the loft space. We're waiting for the Land Registry to tell us who owns the other townhouses, just in case."

"Don't wait for them," Alec said. "I want them all evacuated and send our teams in to search for any possible exits. He brought one property down with a gas explosion. We have to assume that may do that again. Evacuate them immediately."

"Guv."

"What about the sewer system?"

"We're waiting for detailed plans but the planning permission drawings don't show any large networks beneath that area."

"We need eyes inside that townhouse," Annie said turning to the surveillance unit. "Can you get us eyes on every floor, starting with the top and working down?"

"We can get snake-cams in there immediately. As soon as we have access to the adjoining properties, we're up there." The four men turned and left to collect their equipment and get to work.

"We'll get them into those houses now," Alec said. "I'll have my teams start with the evacuation of adjoining properties and work outwards. We need those cameras in place."

"Is there a negotiator on the way?" Annie asked from the rear of the group. "We have the number for the landline, Guv," she added.

"We're not waiting for them to arrive," Alec said. He reached for the number and glanced at it. "We need to get Janice Sterling out of there. Are we all live with the sniper teams?"

"Yes, Guv," the tech said patching them in. "Alpha team ready?"

"Roger that." A voice crackled. "No clear shot."

"Beta team ready?"

"Roger that." A second voice answered. "No clear shot."

"Roger that, Alpha and Beta teams, standby." He looked at Alec and nodded. "They're set and ready, Guv."

"I want them patched in at all times," Alec ordered. "If they get a clear shot at any point then I want to know about it. I have a feeling that this bastard knows that he is leaving there horizontally and that's fine by me."

"Guv."

"Get him on the phone," Alec said rubbing the dimple on his stubbly chin. He had a bad feeling about the situation. "While we get set up, let's see what he wants."

Chapter 51

Brendon heard the telephone ring and it gave him a start. His heart jumped as the shrill tone echoed through the house. Janice Stirling stirred. She was tied securely to a stiff back chair, her head lolled loosely onto her chest. Blood ran freely from both nostrils. He looked at the phone and weighed up if he would be in the line of fire if he answered it. It was situated on a small table next to the settee. The sniper team was making him nervous. He decided that he could reach it safely without making himself too much of a target. Picking up the cordless handset, he walked across the room and looked out of the rear window and listened to the caller.

"Brendon Ryder?" Alec asked. Brendon watched uniformed officers scouring the streets behind the house. If climbing down the rear fire escape had crossed his mind, which it hadn't, it was no longer an option. "Is that Brendon?"

"Yes." He scanned the surrounding buildings to the rear. A second sniper team was positioned on the roof of an old leather mill to cover any escape down the fire exit.

"Is Janice Ryder still alive?"

"Stupid question," Brendon scoffed.

"Why is it stupid?"

"If I say no, you'll kick the doors in and shoot me. So I am not likely to say anything but yes, am I?"

"That depends if you're planning on living much longer or not."

"Does that matter to you?" Brendon laughed. "Because it doesn't bother me one way or the other."

"Janice is pregnant."

"Nothing gets past you does it, Detective?"

"I am obviously concerned about her well being."

"She's alive for now."

"Can I speak to her?"

Brendon looked at her and grimaced. Blood was congealing on her face; her lips and mouth were blackened with it. "Not just now, but she is alive."

"I'll take your word for it," Alec said calmly. "Why have you taken her? What do you want, Brendon?"

"What do I want?" He paused and grinned to himself. "I want an airplane fully fuelled at John Lennon airport and a million Euros in used notes."

"I can't see that happening, to be honest," Alec said flatly. He could sense that Brendon was taking the piss.

"You're not taking me seriously are you?" Brendon giggled.

"Not really," Alec played along. "No one in their right mind would ask for Euros. They might crash next week and you'll be broke."

"True."

"You dropped off the map for a year," Alec said trying to turn the conversation back on track. "I assume you have kidnapped Janice Stirling for a reason. So what do you want?"

"Well firstly, it will really piss off her fat husband. It's been worth the effort just for that."

"Okay, so you have scored a point against Sergeant Stirling. Is that what this is all about?"

"I want to know what my options are," Brendon flopped onto the settee as he spoke. He thought that he would be feeling pumped and aggressive but he just felt knackered. The adrenalin had worn off and the excursion of dragging Janice up the stairs had sapped his energy. He almost wished he had just turned himself in. It wasn't as much fun as he thought that it would be. "I heard some of your news reports and realised that I can't hide forever. Some of the coverage was entertaining. I especially enjoyed the Crimewatch special, which you appeared on, although it was mostly bullshit."

"What was bullshit, Brendon?" Alec tried to engage him in dialogue. He didn't know where Brendon was mentally. Talking to him was the only way to explore his mind and determine if he was suicidal or not. A suicidal kidnapper was not something that Alec wanted to encounter, especially when he was a killer and the hostage was pregnant.

"Your bullshit about the Butcher!" He shouted. "Trying to stitch me up with killing all those women and burying them on Crosby Beach, you should be ashamed of yourself." He sounded genuinely offended.

"You didn't do that?"

"No."

"Who did you kill, Brendon?" The line went quiet and Alec looked at Annie. She shook her head and shrugged and then waved her finger in a circular motion near her forehead. Alec had to agree with her, he was a lunatic. "You didn't kill Lacey Taylor?"

"No."

"We found your DNA all over her, Brendon."

"I didn't say that I didn't kidnap her," he paused. "I did." Alec left the line silent to prompt him to continue. "And I fucked her, but you know that anyway, don't you?"

"Yes."

"But I didn't kill her."

"Who did?"

"Gary Bissell topped her." Brendon had thought about blaming Gary many times. So many that he thought it might actually be true.

"Okay, let's say that I believe you for now," Alec said slowly. "Did Gary kill Charlie Keegan too?"

"Yes," Brendon laughed. His hand went to the hunting knife at his side. He remembered how easily it had sliced through the muscle and how difficult the sinews in the neck were to sever. It was the weight of the blade which allowed him to chop as well as slice, otherwise his head wouldn't have come off. "Gary was mad. He cut his fucking head off. He was a nutter!"

"When we were investigating the poisoning at your house, we took some samples before you raced off in the BMW, you remember?" The line remained silent so Alec continued regardless. "Their blood was in your car," Alec sounded confused. "Help me out here and tell me why that was?"

"It's not that fucking difficult to work out, Sherlock. Is it?" Brendon felt smart for a change. "I helped him to dump the bodies, of course. He made me do it. He was always bullying me, ever since school."

"What about her dog?"

"What about it?"

"Did he make you dig up her dog and plant it in Richard Tibbs's garden?"

"Yes."

"Why would he do that when Tibbs had fingered you?"

"Because he was my mate."

"Why did he kill them?"

"Who knows?" He snorted. "He was a fucking looney tunes!"

"He must have had a reason."

"Ask him," Brendon's tone soured. He was bored with the line of questioning.

"He's dead."

"Is he?"

"You know that he is."

"Tough."

"We found his parents this morning," Alec said. He was fishing for a reaction.

"You leave them alone," Brendon said. "They're nice people."

"You liked them?" Alec asked. He turned to Annie and frowned. He wasn't sure if Brendon was playing dumb, or if he had actually lost the plot. What he didn't want to do was anger him.

"They didn't know about any of this. They're nice people." He repeated angrily. "They are old and they didn't know anything. They just let us hide the vehicles there."

"Did they let you stay there?"

"A couple of nights and they didn't know that I was in trouble with the police."

"They didn't know you were on the run?"

"No!" Brendon shouted. "If you even think about charging them for harbouring a fugitive, or whatever other shite you can come up with, I'll toss this bitch off the balcony!"

"Calm down," Alec said soothingly. "We can't charge them with anything." Alec frowned and looked at Annie.

"You need to keep it that way too."

"He sounds concerned for them," Annie whispered. She shook her head and shrugged her shoulders. "He's in total denial," she said quietly. "Or he's gone over the edge."

"What do I do?" Alec turned off the microphone so that Brendon couldn't hear him. "I have to be straight, or he'll think I'm playing him." Annie nodded and agreed. "We think he killed them but if he really doesn't know they're dead, then watches the news, we've got problems."

"We have to be straight," Annie said.

Alec thought about his next words carefully. "I don't understand why you would do that if you thought that they were nice people," Alec said. He was risking provoking him but couldn't see any option. "I mean they helped you, so why?"

"You don't understand why I would do what?" Brendon

snapped.

"The Bissells."

"What the fuck are you talking about?"

"They're dead, Brendon."

"Bollocks."

"It's true."

"When?"

"We found them today."

"You're lying."

"I am telling you the truth."

"What happened to them?"

"When did you last see them, Brendon?" Alec ignored his question.

"I haven't been there since Sunday," he said excitedly. Alec could hear his breathing, quick and shallow. If he was feigning surprise then he was doing a good job. Alec couldn't get a handle on what was happening. "They were fine three days ago. You're winding me up!"

"Why would I?"

"Because you can," Brendon scoffed. "You lot don't need a reason."

"They are dead." Alec rubbed his chin and frowned at Annie. She looked as baffled as he was.

"What happened to them?"

"They were found in suspicious circumstances, Brendon. That's all that I can say."

"Does that mean that they were murdered or what?"

"We think so."

"This is a game of some kind. You're taking the piss out of me, aren't you?"

Annie nudged Alec and scribbled on a piece of paper. He read it and nodded. "Unfortunately not," Alec said sadly. "Have you got the television on?"

"No why?"

"Take a look on the North West news. The camera crews will be at their petrol station." They had taken a gamble pressing the point but Annie had pointed out that if he watched the news later and knew that they hadn't told him that they had discovered their bodies, then he would think that they were lying to him. He had to know that they were being completely honest and open with him. The life of Janice Stirling and her baby depended on it.

Brendon grabbed the remote and switched the television from standby. He clicked on the news channels and he selected BBC North. The screen was split between images of the Bissells' garage and the siege at the townhouse. A reporter was trying to find a sound-bite which described the tenuous link between the two crime scenes. The headlines read, 'Elderly Couple Found Slain'. He swallowed hard and banged the remote against the side of his head. "No, no, you are setting this up," he shouted down the telephone. Brendon was furious. "You have set this up, you arsehole!"

"Why would we do that?"

"To fuck with my head."

"I don't want your head messed up, Brendon," Alec said quietly. "I need your head to be clear and calm. We want you to let Janice Stirling go and walk out of there yourself. We can talk things through, once everyone is safe."

"Bollocks," he shouted. "This is another one of your games, like linking me to those women. You can fuck off, you bastard!"

"Brendon, this is not a game."

"I don't believe you," he growled. "You get Stirling on the phone in the next ten minutes, or this bitch is dead."

"I can't do that, Brendon."

Brendon slammed the phone against the settee. "You must think that I'm stupid. Well I'm not. I never have been and I never will be." He shouted at the handset despite it being disconnected. "I'll show you how stupid I am." Brendon grabbed Janice's mobile phone and dialed Jim Stirling's number.

Chapter 52

"What is he playing at?" Annie asked confused. "He must have killed the Bissells. I mean who else would have any reason to?" She continued. "We need to get him to talk, Guv."

"Get Jim down here immediately," Alec ordered. "It might keep Ryder on the ground for now. We don't want him going over the edge." Annie picked up her mobile and dialled without any further discussion. It made sense to send him back to the station, but they couldn't deny Ryder's demand either. The comms unit crackled and the camera tech answered. After a brief exchange, he turned to Alec and pointed to the screens.

"Here we go," he said. "We've got eyes and ears on the top floor." The screens showed the inside of the townhouse from different angles. Brendon Ryder was holding a mobile phone to his ear and pacing up and down. His lips were moving but there were no words coming out. He was muttering incoherently. His face was dark and angry. In the middle of the room a petite female was slumped in a chair. Her head dangled against her chest, her clothing was smeared with blood. The gathering stared at her intently. "She's breathing," the tech said. "I can see her chest rising and falling. She's alive."

"Look here at the staircase on the first floor," an officer from the firearms unit said as he pointed to another screen. "The stairwell has been barricaded. There's no access from the ground floor."

"We could potentially gain entry on the second floor balcony at the front of the building, or from the fire escape at the rear." Another officer added. "Either of those options are going to give him advanced warning that we're rushing him. Janice Stirling would be dead before we got to the stairs."

"We might not need to go in at all."

"Let's hear it," Alec said enthusiastically. The tactical team, were right in the fact that there was no way of rushing Brendon Ryder without giving him enough time to kill Janice. It was either a long range shot from one of the snipers or nothing. Having another option was a bonus.

"Our surveillance boys are telling me that the walls between the houses are timber frame and breeze-block construction."

"We could knock a hole in that with a hammer, Guv."

"We could punch through that, never mind a hammer!"

"Are we aiming to take him alive, Guv?" The TFU officer spoke quietly. "Because if we're primarily concerned with getting Janice Stirling out of there unharmed, then we should be looking at using a thermal imaging scope and some 7.62 ammo. A Heckler and Koch HK33 could penetrate that stud walling easily. One quick burst of fire would take him out. He wouldn't even know that we were there."

Alec sat back and sighed. He looked at Annie and shrugged. She smiled thinly and he could see from her expression that she favoured that as an option. As long as Ryder was two metres or so away from Janice, Alec agreed with her, although he had to try to negotiate him down first. Part of him was hoping that they would have no choice but to take that option. "Get your men in position to do that," Alec said to the firearms officer. "I want every option available to us ready to go." He looked at Annie as the specialist left the vehicle. She nodded her support of his decision and nothing more needed to be said. "If he thinks that he's safe in there, he's sadly deluded."

"He's not the brightest bulb on the tree, Guv."

"Obviously."

"Did you get hold of Jim?"

"He'll be here in five minutes," Annie replied. "He's asking for permission to switch on his mobile," Annie raised her eyebrows. "We told him to switch off after the text from Ryder?"

Alec nodded. His face crinkled with concern but any communication was better than none. "Tell him to answer it, but spell it out that Janice is in mortal danger if he pisses that lunatic off."

Chapter 53

The sirens wailed as the police interceptor raced through the traffic towards the river. It was less than a mile from Canning Place Police Headquarters to the riverside developments. It lurched to the left as the driver swerved to avoid a lumbering cement truck which pulled out, despite the blue and twos being deployed.

"Sorry, Sarge," the driver apologised as the vehicle lurched wildly. Jim Stirling frowned and held on tightly. His mobile vibrated in his hand. He glanced down at the screen and his heart nearly jumped out of his chest as he saw that it was a call from Janice's phone. The Albert Docks went by in a blur and he only glanced at the Liverpool Wheel as they sped along the dock road. The officer tutted and shook his head. "I would stop and book that fucking idiot if we weren't in a hurry!"

"Turn off the sirens."

"What?"

"Turn off the siren!" Jim shouted holding up the mobile. The driver saw the screen flashing and blushed. He switched off the blaring noise and made a thumbs up gesture. "Slow down," he added. "I need to think clearly." The uniformed driver took his foot off the accelerator and the vehicle slowed. Jim looked at the screen and remembered what Annie had told him. 'Switch your phone on but remember that Janice is in mortal danger if you piss him off. Mortal danger. Mortal danger. Mortal Danger.' It seemed to echo around his mind. He took a deep breath and answered the call. "Stirling."

"Finally!" Brendon snapped. "I was about to give up and take it out on your missus." Brendon instantly felt better. He knew anything that he said about Janice would cut Stirling to the core. "She's not looking her best, if I'm honest. I had to give her a slap or two, might have been three or four actually, but she has a sharp mouth doesn't she?" He cocked his head in anticipation of what Stirling's response would be. Anger, aggression, threats to kill? Who could tell so early in the game?

"She can be a little sharp if you get on the wrong side of her." Stirling felt anger rising like burning bile in his throat. The urge to scream and vomit at the same time was incredibly strong. He knew that whatever happened, he had to bow down to Ryder. "Please don't hurt her."

"I'm sorry," Brendon said sarcastically. "I couldn't quite hear that."

"I said please don't hurt her." Swallowing his pride wasn't an issue. If Ryder told him to stand on one leg naked and sing One Direction songs, then he would. "Did you hear me that time?"

"Yes, I heard you." Brendon said slightly deflated. He wanted a confrontation. At least, he had thought that he wanted a confrontation. Now he was here, he wasn't so sure.

"I am very sorry about that day in the diner," Stirling said as genuinely as possible. "I was out of order to try to embarrass you in front of your family."

"You were," Brendon sounded almost surprised. "I was going to shoot you for that." He tried to sound like his stepfather but failed miserably. John Ryder never threatened anyone. A rival would never know that he was going to be shot, until he was on the floor bleeding to death. "I could have had you shot anytime."

"I know that you could have and I'm grateful that you didn't," Stirling said, trying to sound as contrite as he could. The giant Anglican Cathedral loomed up on the left as they turned towards the riverside developments. Puffy white clouds, tinged grey at the edges, ballooned across the sky above it. He watched them and remembered climbing up the bell tower with Janice a few months earlier. They were both born and bred in the city but had never been inside either cathedral. Stirling was embarrassed by his lack of knowledge about his home. The view from the top had been worth the muscle-mashing walk up the hundreds of stone steps that led to the roof. "I've changed a lot since I got married to Janice. It's opened my eyes."

"I bet it has," Brendon laughed, "marrying a hooker will do that to a man. I bet she's showed you things that you didn't think possible, hasn't she?"

"She's a lovely woman who got hooked on drugs and couldn't find her way out of it for a while," Stirling tried to remain calm as he spoke. He needed Ryder to see Janice as more than an ex-prostitute. "You must have seen a hundred women in the same boat, haven't you?"

"Probably more than that."

"They weren't all dirty, were they?"

"I suppose not," Brendon sighed. He sounded bored with the conversation. "Do you ever wonder how many?"

Stirling sensed that Ryder was going to try to provoke him but he had to go along. "How many what?"

"You know, when you're kissing her," he paused. "Do you wonder how many cocks she's had in her mouth?" He paused again for an effect. "You must think about it. I know that I would. Shall we ask her?" Brendon bent down and pushed her head back. She groaned. "Hey, time to wake up," he slapped her face as he shook her. "Wake up!"

Stirling could only bite his lip as he listened to what was happening. "Don't hurt her, Brendon," he kept his voice even and tried to remain calm. "What is it that you want from me and Janice?"

Janice opened her eyes as wide as she could. She blinked and looked around. Brendon Ryder was grinning at her. His piggy eyes had madness in them. He had a mobile to his ear. "Hey, she's awake," he said down the phone. "Say hello to your husband," he cooed. "Hiya, Jim, I'm a little tied up at the moment," he taunted them.

"Janice," Stirling said. "Are you okay?" Stirling felt tears in his eyes. The police interceptor turned into the approach road to the estate and came to a halt next to the mobile headquarters. A small army had their weapons trained on the fourth floor balcony of the middle townhouse. The reality of his wife's perilous position hit him. "Can you hear me, Janice?"

"Jim," she croaked. Her voice sounded gravelly.

"Are you okay?" he asked and immediately felt ridiculous for asking the question.

"I've been better," she muttered. Janice licked her lips and swallowed, trying to get her natural juices flowing. Brendon put the call onto speaker mode so that he could hear everything. "My nose is sore but I've been hit harder than that many times." She watched Brendon's face darken at her jibe. It was like flicking a switch from light to dark. "I am joking, sorry," she said to him directly. "I'm nervous and I never know what to say when I'm nervous, so I revert to sarcasm."

The apology seemed to stave off any physical retribution, for the moment at least. "See what I mean about her mouth, Jim?" Brendon spoke loudly so that he could be heard, but it made him sound unbalanced. Stirling shivered at the thought of her being in close proximity to a man as dangerous as Brendon Ryder. "She doesn't know when to shut up, does she?"

"Sometimes she doesn't think about what she's saying," Stirling answered cautiously. He climbed out of the interceptor and walked over to the trailer. The door was opened by a uniformed Inspector who nodded a silent greeting as he climbed in. "She doesn't mean to be insulting. It's just her sense of humour, isn't it, Jan?" The tech took the mobile from him and fitted a jack-plug lead into the speaker slot so that everyone could hear. "She doesn't mean any offense, do you, Jan?"

"No," her voice was weak but he thought that she might get the message to shut up. Alec and Annie pointed to a chair and Stirling walked over and sat heavily in it. He couldn't take his eyes from the screen which showed his wife tied to a chair, her captor leaning over her. Her eyes were blackened and swollen and the blood from her nose had run down the front of her tee-shirt. She looked like she had been beaten badly. The anger inside him threatened to boil over. He stood rigid and breathed deeply. His fists clenched and unclenched and his eyes filled with tears as he stared at the screen.

"I was just asking Jim if when he's kissing you, he ever wonders how many cocks you have had in your mouth," he paused. "Wasn't I, Jim?" Alec put a comforting hand onto his wrist and nodded grimly. Stirling looked around at the faces in the room and all stared back at him with pity in their eyes. Some were so uncomfortable that they couldn't meet his gaze. He puffed up his cheeks and blew out slowly. "I said, wasn't I, Jim?" Ryder shouted.

"You were," Stirling replied flatly.

Janice felt burning tears in her eyes. They spilled over and made fresh tracks in the smudged mascara and congealed blood. She didn't cry for herself, she cried for Jim and how excruciatingly embarrassed he must have been. If his colleagues were listening and she was sure that they would be, he would be traumatised by Ryder's cruel questions. "I think that you should guess, Jim," Ryder said. "You have a guess and then I'll guess."

"What do you mean?" Stirling felt his fists tighten. His face was purple with anger. He gritted his teeth and closed his eyes waiting for the inevitable.

"We'll have a competition," Ryder said. "We'll both make a guess and then Janice can tell us who is closest shall we?"

"What do you want, Brendon?" Stirling tried to end his sport. He had had enough of his game.

"You know what I want, Jim," he taunted, "I want you to guess."

"What do you really want?"

"I said fucking guess!" Ryder sounded angry. "Guess or I'll have to smash Janice in the face again." He grabbed her hair and twisted her head back. Janice cried out and closed her eyes anticipating another blow to her already painful swelling. It sounded animal like. "Guess!"

"Okay!" Stirling shouted. "Don't hit her!"

"Guess."

"Fifty," Stirling said quickly. He shrugged and put his head into his hands. His stomach felt like a giant hand was twisting his guts. He was totally helpless and at the mercy of a lunatic.

"Fifty?" Brendon repeated. "Fifty?" He waited for another answer but Stirling remained silent. He couldn't bring himself to guess again. Alec sat back and folded his arms. He regretted bringing Jim Stirling into the equation. How could he operate rationally when the kidnapper was crucifying him over the telephone? "Fifty? Are you taking the piss out of me?"

Annie could see that Alec was struggling with his decision. They made eye contact and Annie cringed inside. Brendon Ryder was ready to torture Stirling. She could see it coming and so could everyone else in the unit. "I'm not trying to take the piss."

"I hope not, or I'll be insulted."

"I don't want to insult you."

"Good," Brendon said. "I'll give you another chance, okay, but let's do some maths first okay?" Jim stared at the screen and bit the back of his fist. He squeezed his eyes closed tightly to make the image disappear but it was still there when he opened them "Jim, I said okay?"

"Okay."

"Good," he paused and spoke to Janice. "How many days a week did you work when you were a whore?" Janice shivered and felt her lips quivering. The tears ran freely and a sob stuck in her throat. She closed her eyes before she answered. She had to think about the baby. "How many?" He said impatiently.

"Please don't do this," she sobbed.

"Answer the question or I'll have to think of another game." He slid the survival knife from its sheath. "One which involves my knife."

Stirling stood up at the sight of the fifteen inch blade and closed his eyes. He took a sharp breath. "Answer him, Jan, it doesn't matter anyway," he said calmly. "Don't hurt her, Brendon, I'll play your game. Put the knife away."

Alec and Annie reacted as one. They grabbed Stirling by the arm and put their fingers to his lips to shush him. Annie shook her head anxiously and they waited for Ryder to pick up on what he had said. The tech turned off the microphone. Alec felt his breath trapped inside his chest. If Ryder realised that they could see what he was doing, it could be all over very quickly. Stirling rolled his eyes to the ceiling. He couldn't believe what he had done.

"Okay," Brendon said slowly. He slid the knife back into sheath. His expression hadn't changed. He didn't seem to realise what Jim Stirling had said, "so answer the question."

"Seven nights," Janice muttered. Her expression was different. She had noticed and her eyes darted around the room.

"Good," Brendon said happily. "How many men did you do in a night?"

"About ten."

"Ten!"

"Yes."

"That's seventy a week, Jim!" Brendon laughed. "Seventy cocks a week, fifty-two weeks a year is," he paused to do the calculation, "three thousand six hundred and forty cocks." He waited for a response. "Did you hear me, Jim?"

"Yes."

"That's disgusting, Jim," Ryder said patronizingly, "how can you go near her?" Janice sniffled, trying desperately to clear her nostrils. Congealed blood and mucus conspired to make her breathing difficult. "How many years were you a whore?"

"Nine."

"Work that out, Jim," Brendon sounded ecstatic. "I can't do that in my head. Work it out on your phone."

"I am talking to you on my phone." Stirling was at boiling point.

"Don't be difficult. Work it out on your mobile."

"I'm using my phone to talk to you!"

"Work it out now, or Janice here is going over the balcony." Brendon's voice sounded clinical and cold. He was almost monotone. Annie rushed forward, handed her phone to Stirling and he found the calculator app and entered the numbers. He closed his eyes and put his hand to his mouth. Tears ran from both eyes. "Hurry up!" Brendon shouted.

"Thirty-two thousand, seven hundred and sixty," Stirling said quietly. The words seemed to stick in his throat.

"How many?"

"Thirty-two thousand, seven hundred and sixty."

"Thirty-two thousand, seven hundred and sixty what, Jim?" his voice was thick with sarcasm.

"Cocks."

"Amazing isn't it?" Brendon smiled widely. "I mean you married a whore, right? So you have some idea what she's been up to but this is amazing," he whooped with glee, "when you analyze the numbers, it is mind blowing isn't it?" He waited for a response but Stirling wasn't forthcoming. Ryder raised his voice. "I said it's mind blowing, isn't it Jim?"

"If you say so."

"I do, I do, I do," he said laughing. "Your wife has had over thirty thousand cocks in her mouth. Oh my god, how dirty is that?" Ryder paused. "I said, how dirty is that, Jim?"

"I heard you."

"Over thirty thousand, Janice." Ryder turned his attention on her. "Well it's your problem I suppose but personally I think she must be crawling with germs. Horrible dirty filthy germs," he reinforced his point by speaking slowly, pronouncing every syllable. "Now your guess of fifty was just silly, wasn't it?"

"Yes."

"Do you think I should make it thirty-two thousand, seven hundred and sixty one, Jim?" Brendon pushed him harder.

"No."

"No, I don't either, because I would probably catch something nasty." Ryder paused again. "I wouldn't fuck her with yours, Jim. She's a skanky bitch but I could make her do other stuff while we're here. What do you think, Jim?"

"I think that you should tell me what you really want."

"You embarrassed me, Jim, now I've embarrassed you in return. The difference is, that every time you look at her you'll remember that number and better still, so will she. Won't you, Janice?" Her body trembled and she whimpered. Saliva dribbled from the corners of her mouth. He had taken what little pride and dignity she had left and twisted it into something vile. She believed that every time Jim looked at her she would be thinking about what he was thinking. "She's not answering because she's a little bit upset."

"Okay, you've got what you wanted and hurt her and embarrassed us, so what's next?" Stirling asked. "What do you really want?"

"I want the truth."

"You wouldn't know the truth if it crept up and bit you on

the arse," Stirling scoffed. "What is it that you think we're lying about?"

"Mr and Mrs Bissell for a start."

"We found them dead. That's the truth."

"I don't believe that."

"I can't make you believe it, so what's next?"

"What is next, Jim?" He went quiet for a moment. "That depends really."

"On what?"

"On what Janice has to say," Ryder sounded distracted. "I'll call you back." He hung up and the line went dead. Stirling wondered if he had suddenly realised his glaring mistake earlier. They watched as he crouched down in front of Janice Stirling and looked up into her swollen eyes. The tech turned up the microphone in the townhouse. "You two are very close, aren't you," he said to her quietly. He seemed to be thinking about something. "Does he talk about work at home?"

Chapter 54

Brendon kept close to the wall and pulled the front curtains closed. He peered through a gap between the material and the wall and saw the army of armed police officers encamped outside. They didn't appear to be making any plans to storm his position and although he was no military mastermind, he didn't think that they could. He stepped back and leaned against the wall with a sigh. What a mess he had made of everything. He felt sick inside. His life of privilege was gone, taken from him by his own actions. Stupidity was the one constant through his life, his stepfather had reminded him of that fact often. John Ryder didn't really like him and he certainly didn't love him as his own but he made sure that he had money. He always had new clothes, decent cars and enough money to do as he pleased. As a result of his own decisions, that life was gone, never to be seen again. The time to pay the piper was near but he needed answers before he could face the repercussions of his actions. He wasn't sorry for what he had done. He was sorry for getting caught. He had tried to impress his stepfather by silencing a snitch but the situation ran away with him. Everything always did. The results were catastrophic.

"Here," he handed Janice some water. "There's not much left but it's better than nothing. I blocked the stairs with furniture and then remembered that the kitchen was on the floor below." He laughed coldly as he grabbed another chair and sat facing Janice. "I never plan anything properly. I think that I have thought of everything and then shit always goes wrong and it's usually my own fault."

Janice listened to him as she drank greedily from the glass. She thought about smashing it in his eyes but he was just a little bit too far away. His attitude and demeanor appeared to have changed. He looked focused. There was curiosity in his eyes and his voice. "We can get water from the bathrooms," Janice said. "I assume the bedrooms in a house like this have en-suite bathrooms?"

His face brightened and he smiled. Nodding his head he chuckled, "See what I mean?" He sighed. "I never would have thought of that until we were desperate. Then I would have gone for a piss and realised that there was water there all the time!"

Janice half smiled to humour him but it hurt her face. "So what are you going to do next?" She drained the water and looked at his face. He was volatile, angry one minute and contrite the next. She had met people like him before. Some said they were bipolar, massive highs followed by deep lows interspersed with long bouts of depression, but Ryder was different. His unpredictability was dangerous. Even his smile oozed malice. She genuinely feared for the life of her unborn child. How she interacted with her captor would determine much of what happened next. She knew that, but she had no idea what he was thinking or how he thought things would pan out. "How do you think this will end?"

"God knows." He put his hand to the gun instinctively. Janice shivered visibly. Although the room was reasonably sized, there was little furniture to hide behind, she was tied around the waist to a chair and Ryder was a serial killer. If there was a shoot-out, she was certain that he would kill her first. "Those bastards are trying to fit me up."

"You said that you didn't kill anyone." Janice licked her lips. The water had refreshed her. "If that's true, then what have you got to worry about?"

"Prison," he scoffed.

"I thought that your stepfather had a reputation. Big boy like you would be okay in prison," Janice smiled thinly. "If you haven't done anything really bad then you won't do long, will you?" She didn't know what game Ryder was playing but if he believed that he hadn't killed anyone, who was she to argue with him? If she could reassure him that he wouldn't be in prison long, then he might be more inclined to give up. He could be trying to convince her that he was innocent, or he could be trying to convince himself, or he could just be completely fucking puddled, she couldn't decide which.

****

Jim Stirling wasn't so sure that engaging Ryder was wise. Janice was too straight sometimes. Her honesty could be cutting. He sat glued to the screens, watching his wife prodding the devil with a stick. She really didn't realise what she was saying. Or maybe she did but didn't care. Life had made her tough. Alec and Annie watched and listened. Although they were in charge of the operation, containing Ryder didn't seem nearly enough. While he had Janice as a hostage, they were little more than helpless. Ryder was too close to her for them to take him out. They would have to wait patiently for a break. Annie felt the familiar throbbing pain behind her eye patch. It was building ominously. Waiting was stressful for all concerned, but for Jim Stirling? She could only imagine what agonies he was suffering.

****

Ryder lifted his index finger and wagged it at her playfully. "Sometimes it is not what you have done but what they say you have done that counts," he sneered. "They can make you guilty if they want to, and they want to make me guilty of just about everything."

"I don't follow," Janice said; her voice thick with phlegm. "Things are more transparent nowadays, so how can they set you up?."

"They make things up, your fella and his cronies," he smiled sourly, "they nick you for one thing and then clear up a load of other shit by pinning it on you. They find evidence wherever they need to find it, if you know what I mean."

"I am not sure that I do."

"Did he tell you about my mum being poisoned?"

"Well," she frowned. "It was a long time ago but I remember him talking about it."

"A year or so ago."

"Yes, I remember."

"Someone spiked my mum's sports drinks with anti-freeze," he became animated as he spoke. His arms waved around like a weatherman on acid. "Did he tell you that bit?" He paused and Janice nodded that she knew that. "Someone poisoned her and then as if by magic, they found two bottles in the fridge that tested positive for chemicals and I could tell that they thought that I had done it." He waved his arms again. "I could just tell!" His face darkened as he spoke. She could literally see the anger rising in him. He studied her eyes as he spoke. "Did he say that they thought it was me?" Janice tried not to react but she must have done because Ryder slapped his knee with his hand. He stood up and pointed the finger in her face. His hand went to the gun for a moment but he left it tucked into his belt. "I fucking knew it! I can tell by your face that he said that I had done it." He turned around and sat down again. "Tell me what he said. Tell me exactly." He leaned forward and waited.

Janice swallowed hard and licked her lips. There didn't seem to be much point in making things up. She didn't know what he wanted to hear the most, that they did think it was him or that they didn't. It was all that she could do to tell the truth. "I remember that he said they found evidence in the fridge and that the bottles had been injected with a syringe, I think," she paused. His expression was calm for now, although his eyes were boring into her as if he was searching inside her skull for the answers. She felt her hands trembling as she recounted what she remembered. "I remember that he said you shot your uncle and escaped in your car." Ryder wasn't satisfied with her answer. She could see it on his face. He wanted more. She took a breath before continuing. "He said that he was sure that you had done it."

"He said that I had poisoned my mother?" He frowned.

"Yes."

"No doubt about it?"

"No," she shook her head.

"They never suspected Uncle Geoff?"

"Never."

"He was positive that it was me?"

"He was positive."

Brendon covered his mouth with his hands and shook his head in disbelief. "Why, why, why, would they think that?" He seemed to be asking himself. Suddenly he punched Janice on the left thigh. The heavy blow deadened the muscle instantly. Janice rocked back, both shock and pain battling for supremacy in her brain. She grimaced against the pain, her breath hissed between her teeth. He carried on as if nothing had happened. "Did he say why they were so sure?" He asked curiously as if seeking directions from a pleasant-faced stranger.

Janice had to ask questions of herself. Her own sanity was being brought into question. Brendon Ryder had just punched her hard enough to floor her, yet he hadn't even paused to take a breath.

She knew that he was a mad man and that she had to try harder not to say anything that would rile him. Her brain raced for words which were chosen carefully. "They found your prints on a bag in the rubbish, I think," she paused and waited for another blow. He seemed to be processing the information.

"A bag?" He frowned.

"Yes. The bag had a syringe in it."

"What bag?" He snapped and punched her leg again. Her mouth opened in a silent scream, saliva dribbled from the corner of her mouth. He screamed in her face. "What fucking bag?"

Janice recoiled in fear. His eyes narrowed and she was holding her breath waiting for another punch to come her way. "I can't remember exactly what bag it was, honestly, but I do remember that it was a carrier bag, just a plastic shopping bag in one of the bins."

Ryder stood up again and growled at the ceiling. Janice cringed and held her breath waiting for another attack. "How can I deny anything when the bastards come up with stuff like that, hey? How can I deny anything?" Sitting down, he leaned towards her, his voice hushed. "You see?" He shrugged. "This is exactly what I am talking about. It is not what you have done. It's what they say you have done." He wagged the finger in her face again. "They think that I poisoned my mum and hey presto, they find my prints on a carrier bag which happens to have a syringe in it." He shook his head and grinned. "Oh come on, Janice. I am not Einstein, but I am not stupid either. Would I leave the syringe in the rubbish?" His expression told her that he required an answer. He asked the question again, very slowly. "Would I be stupid enough to leave a syringe in a carrier bag in the bin?"

"I doubt it."

"Doubt it?" He whistled and clapped his hands together. "Janice doubts it everyone!"

"I mean that it wouldn't make sense to go to those lengths to poison someone and then make such a simple mistake," Janice tried to placate him. Her thigh was throbbing incessantly and she could feel the muscle swelling beneath her jeans. The pain was sapping what little energy she had remaining.

"My point exactly, Janice!" He sat back and folded his arms. His expression said that he was deep in thought. "Why would I poison my mother?" He stood and leaned on the chair. "She is about the only person who really gave a shit about me. Her and the Bissells and now they're telling me that they're dead?" His eyes glazed over and Janice felt her knees trembling. "What exactly are they trying to do?" Ryder shook his head and sat down again. "You can see what they're doing, can't you?"

Janice didn't have a clue what he meant but she nodded that she did.

****

In the trailer, Annie looked at Alec and frowned. "Is that for our benefit, or his?" she asked. "I can't make my mind up with this lunatic. Is he trying to convince himself that he hasn't done anything because if he is, then he is far more dangerous than we thought." Jim Stirling nodded his head and sighed. He couldn't take his eyes from the screen and what he was hearing wasn't doing anything to give him any hope of his wife being released any time soon. "It's like listening to three people in there."

Alec shook his head and turned to the screens which showed the thermal imaging that was being sent from the conjoining building. The two green shapes were overlapped, no matter which angle the firearms officers looked from. There was no clean shot to take him out. "As long as he is talking, Janice is valuable to him," he turned to Stirling. "It doesn't matter if he talks all day, as long as Janice is unharmed," he tried to reassure him.

"Unharmed?" Stirling pointed to the screen which showed Janice's bloody face. "Are you watching the same thing as me?"

Alec felt embarrassed but he knew what he meant. Janice Stirling was breathing, which when taken in comparison to most of the females who came into contact with Ryder, was a bonus. "She's a strong woman. She's doing well and we'll get her out of there." He patted Stirling on the shoulder. "Trust me."

******

"Surely those days have gone," Janice shrugged. "They can't plant things and get away with it any more, can they?" She turned her palms to the ceiling as she spoke. "DNA and forensics nowadays separates the guilty from the not guilty, don't they?" Brendon eyed her suspiciously. Janice felt like she was sitting next to a firework. The blue touch paper had been lit and she knew that it was going to explode; she just didn't know when, or how loud the bang would be. "They either have the proof that you did it, or they don't. If they don't, then you'll be fine."

"What about the prints on the bag?" He snapped. "I didn't poison my mother, yet they have my prints on a carrier bag. Explain that!"

"In my mind, it can only be one of two things."

"Really," he said sarcastically, "would you care to expand that comment."

"You said that you didn't poison your mother," she said calmly trying to keep her voice conversational despite being terrified, "if I take that you're telling the truth for granted, then either the police planted the evidence or someone else put it there."

"Correct!" He clapped his hands slowly and tilted his head. "If you were on a jury that would be brilliant but now look at it from the other side, where I am a liar plain and simple?"

"The truth usually comes out at some stage."

"Maybe I can convince them that I didn't poison my mother but they'll stitch me up for the murders anyway," he said, matter of factly. Janice noticed that his eyes glazed over, as if he was somewhere else completely. His eyes had that glassy look that junkies get straight after a hit. It's a look that Junkies and psychopaths share; one was caused by mental imbalance, the other by chemicals, either way it was a detachment from planet Earth. She was scared anyway but when he seemed detached from reality, she was more scared than she had ever been.

"They can't say you murdered anyone without solid evidence," she tried to convince him.

"It's not that simple. I was there, you see," he shook his head vigorously, "just because I was there, doesn't mean that I killed anyone but they will try to pin it on me."

"Pin what on you, exactly?"

"They'll start with Charlie Keegan and Lacey Taylor and take it from there," he snorted, "that's bad enough but then on Crimewatch, the bastards were saying that they suspect that I am the Butcher!"

"You didn't kill any of them?" Janice asked curiously.

"It's complicated."

"I don't see how it can be." She shook her head. "You did or you didn't."

"What does your fella say about it?" He leaned forward, his elbows on his knees. His piggy eyes had that sparkle in them and Janice thought that he would be really crap at poker. When he was calling, his eyes were full of anticipation. He wanted to switch the conversation back onto her every time it became uncomfortable. "I'm very interested in what he had to say about it at home."

Janice didn't want to get into this conversation. Her options were zero but she had to be considerate of the fact that he was unbalanced. She sighed and said, "He said that Charlie Keegan had his head removed and was dumped in a pond," Janice said flatly. "How complicated can that be?"

"Very."

"They think that you had a motive," she added. "Your stepfather did business with him."

"He was a grass," Brendon snapped. "That isn't tolerated in this city but I didn't actually kill him."

"I don't care what he did and neither does anyone else. The fact is he was murdered and they think you did it," Janice answered sharply. "So you killed him because he was a grass, what has this got to do with me?"

"I didn't kill him," Brendon repeated. "We were asking him some questions and my mate Gaz went too far and he died."

"Too far," Janice was exasperated. "Too far is putting a guy in hospital, breaking his legs or something. Your definition of too far is very different from what the vast majority of people would think." She shrugged. "He cut his head off, for God's sake!"

"Afterwards, yes," Brendon protested. He pushed his hands into his tracksuit pockets and looked at the floor. Janice thought he looked almost embarrassed. "That was to stop them identifying his body."

"And your friend is where?"

"Dead," Brendon said quietly. The brooding look on his face warned her not to pursue that unfortunate fact.

"In which case, you will have nothing to worry about," Janice said impatiently. "If you say that you didn't do it and there are no witnesses because your friend is dead, then they won't be able to prove it one way or the other, will they?"

"That was what my uncle said at the time," he snorted as he thought back to when they snapped Gary's neck. Brendon stood up for a moment and walked around his chair. He leaned on the back of it with both hands and bit his lip. "Maybe I can swerve Keegan's murder, but I did kidnap Lacey Taylor with Gaz." He fiddled with his fingers and wouldn't make eye contact. Janice had seen enough liars in her time, to know another one when she met one. He was manufacturing this bit. "She was going to grass my stepfather to the police. Her and Keegan were in cahoots." He frowned as if that justified double murder. "She was a lippy bitch, so I roughed her up."

"You raped her." Janice regretted saying it as soon as she had said it. "I mean, that is what the evidence says," she tried to soften the blow. "I read that much in the Echo."

Ryder sat down and nodded. He messed with his fingers again. Janice thought that he was almost childlike when he was uncomfortable with a subject. She didn't think that he would last long under interrogation from the likes of Jim Stirling and his colleagues. "I have a bad temper," he explained. "It runs in the family." He was almost apologetic about the fact. "She made me very angry and I lost my temper with her. She needed to know who was boss, you know?"

She ignored his excuses. Mental abuse, physical abuse, rape, it was all the same psycho babble that was used to explain why some men were animals. "They have your DNA on her, don't they?" Janice said quietly. "So you can't exactly say the sex was consensual, can you?"

"No."

"They'll nail you for that then, won't they?" There was little point in beating around the bush. She was hoping that he wouldn't mention Lacey and the other women. A conversation with the Butcher of Crosby Beach about his victims was not something she relished, without an axe in her hand. "You can't swerve that, can you?" His face darkened again and she wished that she hadn't answered him at all, but not answering him could make him even worse.

"This is my dilemma," he looked her in the eye. The glint was gone. He blinked. "I fucked her but I didn't kill her." He was lying. She could see it in his eyes. "What do you think they would give me for kidnap and rape?" He paused. "If they nail me for Keegan too, maybe even conspiracy to murder?" She bit her bottom lip and looked down at the floor. He was staring at her intensely, studying her reaction. She could feel his beady eyes boring into her skull. "What has Stirling said to you about her murder? You had better tell me the truth. I can tell when you're lying."

She sighed and rocked back slightly in her chair. She wrung her hands together as she thought about her next answer. He had her backed into a corner. She was damned if she answered and damned if she didn't. If she thought that she could break the double glazed units in the patio doors by sprinting at them, then she would have tried. Janice felt like a rat in a trap. There was nowhere to run and nowhere to hide. He was pressing her for the information that had become the key to the entire case. How could she answer him without risking riling him? She exhaled and smiled thinly. It was a nervous smile. "They know that whoever killed Lacey killed the others too."

He frowned. His expression was one of genuine surprise. "How do you mean?"

"The other women." Her voice was almost a whisper.

"The Butcher's victims?"

"Yes."

"Because they're on the beach?"

"Not just that."

"You're telling me that the police are saying that whoever killed Lacey Taylor is the Butcher?" Janice remained silent and nodded almost imperceptibly. Brendon frowned and put his head into his hands. He picked up the empty glass and looked into it, then put it down again. His throat was suddenly dry. He laughed but there was no mirth in it; it was a harsh hoarse sound. Suddenly, he picked the chair up and swung it over her head. It whistled through the air. He spun through a full circle and grunted like an Olympic athlete. Janice cried out in fear and ducked.

****

Stirling stood up and held his breath as he watched. Alec and the tech watched the view from the thermal imaging cameras. There was no clear shot. He was directly in front of her. Annie took a sharp intake of breath and bit her nails as the scene played out on the screen. "Get her out of there," Stirling muttered. "For fuck's sake, get her out of there!" He put his hands to his face but he couldn't take his eyes from the screen.

*****

Ryder slammed the chair down onto the floor and sat on it.

His face was like thunder and he glared at Janice. He shook his head and took a breath before speaking. His voice was surprisingly calm. "Whoever killed Lacey Taylor killed the other women?"

"That's what they think," she said meekly.

"That is one hell of a jump in assumptions isn't it?" He cocked his head and studied her reaction. Janice couldn't look at him in the eye. She was terrified. "What the fuck makes them think that?"

"The way they found her."

"I don't understand how they have come to that conclusion," he shook his head, his expression incredulous as he spoke. "That is impossible."

"I'm just telling what I was told."

"I know you are," he said coldly. Impatience crept into his tone. "Why do they think that?"

"The MO," she muttered staring at her feet. If ever she had needed to be teleported to another place it was now. "The MO was the same."

"What are you talking about?"

"They call it the MO," she explained as calmly as she could. "It means modus operandi."

Brendon jumped to his feet and kicked Janice hard in the shin. She cried out like a wounded dog. The veins in his forehead pulsed blue beneath the skin of his temples. "I know what it means, you cheeky cunt!" He stepped backward and kicked out a second time. She screamed as the toe of his training shoe ripped the skin from her shin. He grabbed her hair and stamped on her toes hard, cracking several and bruising her instep. She cried out and tried to throw herself backwards away from him but he held her tightly. "Do you think that you're clever?" He grabbed her chin and put his face inches from hers. "Anyone who watches the television on a Saturday night knows what an MO is, you twat!"

"I am sorry!" She sobbed in pain. "I was trying to explain!" Her explanation was cut short by a stinging slap to the right cheek with the back of his hand. She felt a tooth crack and the inside of her mouth split against the edges of her teeth. The taste of blood filled her mouth and she tried desperately to hang onto consciousness. She felt desperate in the knowledge that if she failed to answer his questions, he would kill her. "Please let me explain!"

"You filthy whore!" He screamed. "You think you're smarter than me don't you?"

"No!"

"You do!" He twisted her hair painfully.

"I'm sorry!" she sobbed. Her words were nothing more than an incoherent blubbering. "I'm sorry. I was trying to explain what he told me, that's all. I didn't mean to offend you!" She put her head to her knees and covered her face with her arms. "I'm sorry!"

"Shut up," he shouted. Her sobbing subsided. "I said, shut up!" Janice held her breath to quell her cries. "Don't you dare talk to me as if I'm stupid, you dirty skanky bitch!"

"I don't think you're stupid," she sobbed. "Honestly, I don't."

"Good," he hissed. His breathing was labored and she could see sweat forming on his forehead. "Now, you tell me exactly what he said about Lacey Taylor's murder and I mean everything." He loomed over her as he spoke. "Look at me. Look me in the eyes, so that I can see if you're lying to me." He took the survival knife from its sheath and pushed the serrated edge against her throat. She could feel the jagged cold steel pressing into her skin. Whatever her answer was now, she knew that this was the end. If she lied, he would know. If she answered him honestly, then his psychotic episode would escalate. Of that she was certain. The pressure beneath the knife increased and she felt a trickle of blood run from below her ear, down her neck and onto her shoulder.

****

Jim Stirling watched the onslaught on screen and slammed his fist against the desk. "Send them in, Guv!" He turned to Alec. Tears streaked his face and the tendons in his neck looked like wires ready to snap. "Give the order!"

"We can't breach the barricade, Jim," Annie touched his arm as she spoke. "He'll kill her if we enter the house."

"Our only choice is to wait for him to step away from her," Alec sighed. "As soon as she is clear of him, we'll take the shot, I promise you that!"

"He's going to slit her throat, Guv!" Stirling was shaking. "Send them in!"

****

Janice wiped spittle from her mouth with the back of her hand. She tried to control her breathing but she could feel panic gripping her. "They found her body not far away from the others," Janice blubbered. His eyes drilled into hers as she spoke. Her tears blurred her vision but she could feel the intensity in his glare. "She was the same as the others."

"What do you mean?" He hissed.

"She had the tubes taped to her face, so that she could breathe under the sand," she sobbed as she spoke. "Jim said that the tubes made them look like prawns."

Brendon's face contorted into a mask of evil. He raised the huge blade and roared with anger. "A fucking prawn!" He screamed and kicked her in the chest with the sole of his foot. Janice flew backwards on the chair. Her head cracked against the floor with a thud. She screamed too, their voices mingled to a cacophony of fear and rage, panic and anger. Janice was flat on her back attached to the chair. Brendon stood back and turned his face to the ceiling; his arms were raised in the air. He screamed as loud as he could, so loud he felt his head would explode. "Bastards!"

******

"Take the shot!" Alec ordered.

"Aim high and take the shot." The order was repeated on the comms

Janice heard his deafening screaming and then her face and body were splattered with blood and viscera. A globule of grey matter ran down her cheek. She saw Brendon Ryder's head and chest explode outwards as bullets pierced the back of his skull and then smashed their way out of his face. Blood, bone and breeze-block showered the interior of the room as the wall and Brendon Ryder disintegrated beneath the burst of machine-gun fire.

Chapter 55

18 Months Later

Geoff Ryder sat in an interview room beneath Canning Place. It was cramped and smelled of sweat. Claustrophobia made him feel like crawling up the walls. He wanted out but he couldn't just walk out of the custody suite. He was stressed to the limit about being there. It brought back too many bad memories. His years of defending the Ryder family had included regular visits to the police headquarters but this time the pressure was intense. Never in his wildest dreams did he envisage being there under these circumstances. He just never thought it could happen. His sense of invincibility had been shaken from him. He always felt that he could wriggle and manoeuvre out of anything but not this time. This time there was no getting out of it with a technicality.

The death of Brendon Ryder, no matter how shocking, had been a type of blessed relief. With his demise, the murders of eleven people were buried and laid to rest. That took the pressure off his mother, the extended family and Geoff himself. The police weren't looking for anybody else. They were convinced that Brendon Ryder was a serial killer. That aside, here he was waiting for detectives yet again but this time he couldn't explain things away. They had the woman. They had the DNA and they had witnesses. Sweat trickled down the small of his back and he felt incredibly nervous.

The door opened and Jim Stirling ducked into the room, shifting his bulk with remarkable ease for such a big man in an enclosed space. He looked at Geoff with a stern expression and nodded a silent greeting. His face was stony as he dropped a photograph onto the table and pointed to the battered face of a woman. Her eye was black, six stitches clearly visible along the eyebrow. The cheek was bruised a purple colour and was swollen as if she had a golf ball in her mouth. Her top lip was split, the cut reached upwards towards the left nostril. "She's a mess," Stirling said. "This pretty much says everything doesn't it?"

"What can I say," Geoff shrugged and a shiver ran down his spine. There was no getting away from it. The woman was badly hurt and he would have to deal with the fallout. He touched the photograph and felt a burst of adrenalin spreading through his veins. His fingers touched the split lips and he could almost taste her blood in his mouth. "My client has suffered a lot of abuse because of her son's crimes. This woman attacked her in Tesco and she's defended herself with a large tin of potatoes in her hand and it has caused a lot of damage." Geoff shrugged and smiled. "If the CPS proceed, we'll plead not guilty, via self defense and diminished responsibility." He smiled thinly. "I believe that the woman was a relative of one of the Butcher's victims. She recognised my client and attacked her without provocation. There are only losers on this one, Detective."

"She can't react like this or she'll finish up in jail," Stirling warned gruffly. "She'll end up with an assault conviction on her record, if she cops for it and apologises profusely."

"I'm sure if we throw in some voluntary counselling, we can convince the CPS to opt for the lower end of assault."

"It will still go on her record."

"I know," Geoff Ryder agreed. He sighed and smiled. "It's been a long time since I've seen you. How is your wife now?" He added.

"She's fine," Stirling seemed uncomfortable discussing Janice with a member of the Ryder family. "She's enjoying being a mum. She's a natural."

"Good, good," Geoff said genuinely. "I'm glad no long term harm was done to them. Truly I am."

Stirling nodded and turned for the door. Ryder's kind words held little to no meaning at all to him. "We'll get Mrs Ryder charged, processed and then you can take her home. I can see no point in holding her any longer. You can take her home once we're done."

"Thanks very much," Geoff said extending his right hand. Stirling shook it and then ambled back through the door. Geoff breathed a sigh of relief as he left. The last thing that he wanted was attention from the police. He had had to wait a long time. A very long time indeed but now that the focus had shifted, he could indulge himself once more. He had missed it. There had been times when he didn't think that he would be able to contain his urges but he had been strong. Brendon had nearly ruined everything with his amateurish attempt at hiding Keegan and Lacey Taylor, near to his beloved Iron Men. Luckily, his blunder had allowed Geoff to point the finger of guilt for the women in his direction. Recovering Lacey's body and altering her to make her the same as the others hadn't been the chore that he thought it would be. In fact it had been enjoyable.

The entire sorry string of events had been a trauma which he had overcome, but now he was free to continue to create. The brief intermission had given him time to evolve as an artist. The things which turned him on at the beginning of his journey didn't give him the same rush anymore. He shuddered when he thought about the first women. As a law student he had been advised to invest in properties, so that they could be used as tax write offs later in life. Geoff bought the property at Breck Road via a limited company. He remortgaged it and sold it on to himself several times, eventually selling into John Ryder's portfolio at a huge profit. The girls in the basement were his teething rings. He dabbled in death and fumbled with their murders. Looking back, he cringed at his unsophisticated methods. He learned a lot from their suffering and blowing the building up had saddened him a little, but he had to slow down the investigation and muddy the waters.

Making his victims suffer became an obsession. Extending their torture was his fascination. Killing the Bissells showed him a new level of terror. It had given him a taste for something that he hadn't experienced before. Their love for each other added an entire new dimension to the horror. Watching each other suffering increased their anguish to levels that he couldn't achieve with a single victim. It had intensified his pleasure. It opened his eyes. He hadn't realised why the Iron Men had fascinated him so much. Yes, he empathised with their loneliness, their desolation and daily entombment by the advancing waves, but what he had missed was their joint anguish. Not only did they suffer individually, they had to watch the suffering of others in the knowledge that what had befallen those further out, was in fact about to befall them too.

It was the same with his new victims. He had to select couples to feel their terror. Watching the fear on the face of a loved one, while he hurt the person closest to them, was priceless. Never had he witnessed such dread as they watched their loved ones suffer, heard them screaming, watched them bleeding and writhing in agony. Never had he seen such desperation in a human's eyes, or heard such sweet pain in their voices as they begged and pleaded for the life of another. It was the sweetest sound ever. And then when he stopped and they realised that it was their turn to experience the pain while their loved one watched the same things happening to them, their fear reached new depths. It took him to a dark place, an evil place. Another Place.

Author Biography

Conrad Jones is a 49-year-old Author, who has 13 novels and has been published by Constable and Robinson, Champagne Books and Thames River Press. The Soft Target Series has six books following an ex-Special Forces operative, who battles crime and the first book, 'Soft Target' is permanently free to download. The Hunting Angels Diaries, A Child for the Devil (Always 77p/99c), Black Angels and Nine Angels is a horror series. The Detective Alec Ramsay Series, including the Best Selling 'The Child Taker' has five novels to date. You can find more about Conrad's novels at.

http://www.fantasticfiction.co.uk/j/conrad-jones/

https://www.facebook.com/conradjonesauthorpage

Made in the USA
San Bernardino, CA
01 April 2015